Almost Paradise

The Broadsword Chronicles: Book One

Steve Ruedlinger

iUniverse LLC
Bloomington

ALMOST PARADISE
THE BROADSWORD CHRONICLES: BOOK ONE

iUniverse books may be ordered through booksellers or by contacting:

iUniverse LLC
1663 Liberty Drive
Bloomington, IN 47403
www.iuniverse.com
1-800-Authors (1-800-288-4677)

ISBN: 978-1-4917-2416-3 (sc)
ISBN: 978-1-4917-2420-0 (hc)
ISBN: 978-1-4917-2417-0 (e)

Library of Congress Control Number: 2014903016

Printed in the United States of America.

iUniverse rev. date: 03/26/2014

DEDICATON

So many people to thank, so little ink. This for Barbara Sue who, so many years ago, believed everything was possible. You live in my heart, mom.

The truth is timely. At the time, this
was the truth.
So forget everything you've ever known.
Except for home . . .

Because I could not stop for death, he kindly stopped for me.–Emily Dickenson

Gulf of Mexico, AD 1739

The ocean can be a fluid hallucination. One minute, a lazy blue sky drifted along; the next minute, the blue gave way and was replaced by dark whites and swirling greys. The heavens cracked loud with rage. The sea became an angry, foreboding stew of churning water and typhoon-like squalls. The skull and crossbones of the Jolly Roger snapped violently in the murderous wind as the sudden storm bore down on the ship like a streaking eagle descending on a helpless rabbit.

Hurricane winds blasted the ship, which bobbed like a cork. Like spiders on ice skates deckhands scattered as cargo and supplies toppled and careened along the deck. At the bow, the hand-painted, bare-breasted figure of the ship's namesake, the hag of Mendoza, slashed through the rain and wind, oblivious to the storm, her scowl forever etched in painted and carved wood.

The *Hag of Mendoza* was an eighty-foot privateer of Portuguese origin. Under the command of Captain Rene Lafleur the Red, the pirate galleon had raided the Gulf of Mexico at will, its twenty-four cannon armament devastating merchant ships of all countries. It was an equal-opportunity pillager. British and French men-of-war dogged the *Hag*, but she had always eluded their heavy guns. Eluding this murderous storm, however, was impossible. It was single-minded and ravenous, pounding the ship from all sides.

Below, in his cramped quarters, Captain Lafleur snored as his hammock swayed. A loud, urgent knock at the door shattered his slumber. The heavy rains lashed at the cabin's lone window; its fury mocked the captain. "Come in!" he yelled over the noise of the squall. The captain was not happy, but then he seldom was.

First Mate Antonio Lempa opened the door just as the ship lurched starboard in the blow. He was flung across the captain's cabin like a rag doll and crashed shoulder-first into the heavy beams of the outer wall. He recovered quickly, stood, grabbed his shoulder in pain, and addressed the captain. His breath came in great bursts.

"Sir, the storm came from nowhere and now is everywhere. The crew is in a panic, and four men have been swept overboard. The men claim El Diablo is in the storm. They pray to the Virgin for deliverance."

"Idiots!" spat the captain. "There isn't a virgin for a thousand miles. And the only El Diablo is in this cabin. So tell those sons of bitches I'll take a hot iron and lash to any man who doesn't do his job. Now get the goddamn sails down, turn her into the wind, and let's ride this bastard out. Move!"

The first mate was fearful of the storm but more fearful of his captain. He saluted and made for the cabin door.

"And Antonio," snapped the captain, "I want a report every ten minutes. If any of our cargo is damaged or any booty lost, it comes out of the crew's end. Understood?"

"Yes, sir."

"Move your ass!"

Antonio would never make his first report. As he headed up the steps toward the deck, the mainsail timber cracked with a noise louder than the thunder of the storm. He reached the deck in time to briefly spy the instrument of his grisly death. When the mainsail snapped its mast, the mast cascaded along the deck toward the stern. The giant timber crushed the first mate's skull as it rolled past the opening to the deck. His head exploded under the mast's immense weight. Six other crewmembers were killed as the timber slid off the deck into the rolling, black sea.

Then an angry ocean threw the huge timber back at the battered ship, which gashed a four-foot hole along the waterline. The sea rushed into this mortal wound, and the ship floundered.

The captain, who had been tossed around his cabin like a kite in a cyclone, feared for his life. He was certain his left leg had been broken, and he was lying in six inches of water. He knew that the *Hag* was going down and that he'd better get topside fast. As he struggled toward the door, he felt a vibration, low and troubling. It built quickly; he was sure his teeth were going to shake loose from his jaws. He grabbed his head in bewilderment. His world went black. A deep, dark fog of unconsciousness enveloped him.

When the captain came to, bright sunshine streaked through the broken glass of his window. Steadying himself, he realized his ship was not moving, but he could hear water lapping at the hull. His left leg throbbed and he could hear men shuffling about topside. He assumed his cabin resembled the rest of the ship, a complete disaster.

Using a broken oar as a crutch, he made his way up to the deck. It was in turmoil. The masts were shredded, the mainsail was gone, and the ship was beached on an endless, white shoreline. Crew members mingled about, dazed, as if recovering from massive hangovers.

"Where in hell is Antonio?" the captain bellowed.

"Dead, sir," cried Silva Jarvis. "The mainsail cracked his skull like an egg." Jarvis was a Spanish naval deserter, a fair shot, and strong as an ox. Lafleur actually liked him; he was not the typical trash that made up most of his crew.

"Silva, you're now first mate. Organize this rabble into work details and report to me with a salvageable inventory in fifteen minutes. Is that clear?"

Stunned, Jarvis said, "Yes, sir." He quickly began grouping the men into repair squads. Teams started removing debris and salvaging what they could. Vast stretches of the beach were littered with pieces of the once-proud *Hag*.

Twenty minutes later, Jarvis reported to the captain, whose leg had been splinted. He was swigging down rum to ease the pain but his mood was still sour. "Well, Jarvis? How bad is the bitch?"

Jarvis hesitated. "Bad, sir. All the sails are destroyed, and the hull has a four-foot gash at the waterline. The mainsail timber is completely gone. Most everything that was topside is gone. The food stores below are contaminated by saltwater, and we have only two barrels of fresh water left. That's the bad news."

"You mean there's good news?" asked an incredulous and pained captain; the rum was having little effect on his leg.

"Some, sir. Most everything is repairable if we can find materials, and the treasure and booty are intact."

That pleased the captain. He gulped heartily on the rum and began to formulate a plan. He wanted to know where they were. Whatever beach they had landed on seemed deserted and was hot. He thought it must be Spanish Florida, but they had been at least three hundred miles away when the storm hit. But the white shell beaches surely meant Florida, and the everglade jungle fifty yards inland seemed right. He decided to see to food and water first, then to repair materials.

"Jarvis, how many men are left?"

"Fifty-two, sir. Eleven of those are injured. We lost nineteen during the storm, dead or overboard."

Lafleur mumbled something Jarvis couldn't hear and did a quick survey of his men. A dozen nationalities milled around him—thieves, cutthroats, murderers, rapists, and deserters all. They constituted a scurrilous gaggle of corsairs, but even they would work hard for riches or to preserve their own hides. He turned to Jarvis. "Arm twenty men and form a foraging detail. They're to take all the containers they can carry, go inland, and search for food and water. There's plenty of daylight left, so get them moving. The rest of the men can pile up the dead bodies down the beach. We'll burn them later." He stared at Jarvis. "Questions?"

"Shelter?"

"We'll sleep onboard the wreck tonight and tomorrow build temporary shelters. Okay, let's move."

The men selected for the foraging detail were the biggest and strongest left. Fruit, vegetables, and water were heavy, and these men had to be prepared to walk miles to find anything. All were armed. Primitive people, alligators, poisonous snakes, and biting insects abounded in this part of Spanish Florida, so the men were prepared. Captain Lafleur watched as his expedition disappeared into the dense jungle. They seemed lethargic and hot as they swatted buzzing insects and melted into the tangle of vines and plants.

Turning his spyglass to the sea, he scanned the long expanse of water. The ocean looked deserted. Two-foot whitecaps bounced along toward shore while the frothy brine lapped at the sand. A cloudless sky showed no pity on the men working to clean up the ship. Shirtless, they cleared timbers and rooted through the mess below decks, scavenging for anything they could use. The cannon were intact, but the powder was wet, and cannonballs were scattered pell-mell throughout the lower level. Muscles strained under the heat and weight of the loose cannonballs.

Thirty minutes after the scavenging party left, the sound of musket shots shattered the placidity of the dense rain forest. Shrieks and screams followed. The men on the *Hag* reacted as one. All eyes focused on the jungle, and everyone went for a weapon. An angry silence lingered. The captain ordered his armed men to the beach. "Shoot anything you don't recognize that comes out of the bramble."

Muskets were loaded, pistols were cocked, and swords were readied. Pulses raced as hearts pounded in heavy chests. The tired, hard men of the *Hag* steeled themselves for battle, but this was nothing new for them. They had matched steel and cannon against many opponents and were still alive to tell tall tales at drunken campfires among fellow freebooters. They watched the undergrowth for movement. No trouble yet.

Trouble did come, preceded by one of their men, a Portuguese named Andreas. Screaming, he staggered onto the beach. His face was contorted in horror. Blood spurted with every heartbeat from a stub where his left arm used to be. It appeared to have been torn off just below the shoulder. His face was white with death as he fell, tried to rise, and fell again. In disjointed Portuguese, he screamed, "Leapers! Leapers! Demons from hell!" The pirates on the beach stood in silent terror. Again, Andreas tried to scream but fell facedown. His shoulder continued to pump blood the hot sand soaked up.

Then the trees and vegetation suddenly came alive. Sharp, high-pitched chortles and barks filled the air. The noise went on for an eternity of nearly two minutes. Mesmerized, the men on the sand could only stare and wait. In groups of twos and threes, the enemy began to emerge from the jungle. Within minutes, hundreds, maybe thousands of these savage forest dwellers appeared. They stared quizzically at the strange buccaneers, who in turn looked on with grim astonishment. The captain stood dumbfounded, unable to find his voice.

A long moment passed; neither group was able to come to terms with what it saw. Bewilderment and nervous apprehension gripped both parties.

The pirates cracked first. The sight of blood-smeared bodies and salivating mouths were too much for some of them. In haste or in madness, a few fired into the mass of probing bodies inching closer. With their backs to the sea and nowhere to run, the pirates unleashed a deadly barrage of ball and shot. But before they could reload, they were attacked from all sides. Death screams soon mixed with the clanging of swords and cutlasses, and the massacre began. Blood ran in rivulets from the white sands to the sea. Death invaded this pristine, once-serene place. The *Hag* and its pirate marauders would pillage and murder no more. Only their mutilated bodies, left on a silent beach to be consumed and scavenged, would give testament to their existence.

With the threat over, the jungle silently took back the pirates' executioners. Like apparitions, they evaporated into the dense undergrowth.

Onboard the *Hag*, on the floor of a ramshackle cabin, the trembling hand of a dying man reached desperately for a puddle of congealing blood. His last living act was to try to leave a warning, using the ink of his own life fluid.

Time for a Cool Change

PART 1

Galveston, Texas, 2002

The Water's Edge marina sits along the Texas coastline a few miles south of Galveston. It is large—over one thousand slips—but quiet. In its moors lay everything from seventeen-foot roundabouts to ninety-foot luxury cabin cruisers. Scarabs, cigarette boats, trawlers, and pontoon day-runners dotted the seascape. All manner of sailing vessels, from Cat 21s to yachts, filled the slips between cruisers. The skyline was laced with fly bridges and great masts. Gulls and other sea birds squawked and drifted lazily along ocean breezes, occasionally diving at the water. The entire marina gently bobbed with the ebbs of the ocean.

The *Monkberry Moon Delight*, a sixty-foot cabin cruiser, made its home in the Water's Edge. Snuggly, the big boat heaved in its space, its twin Detroit diesels quiet but ready to rumble to life with the turn of a key. At nine in the morning, the marina was mostly placid. Joy riders were waiting until later in the day, and fishermen and charters, whose days began at dawn, were long gone.

The *Monkberry* was both pleasure boat and permanent residence. Its owner, John David Stoner, or JD, had been up since six thirty. His day had begun with a four-mile jog followed by the reading of several morning newspapers while enjoying a cheese omelet, wheat toast, hash browns, and iced tea at the Crow's Nest restaurant. Content, refreshed, and with a full stomach, he padded along the wooden docks toward his boat. His right foot ached with the pain of an old injury from a time mostly forgotten.

His business was ferrying ships between Texas and Florida across the cavernous Gulf of Mexico. It was uneventful and steady work that paid well. Not that he needed the money. Endless hours on the open, peaceful ocean were reward enough. That's what he needed as he remembered an old song and silently sang it to himself. "I was born in the sign of water, and it's here that I feel my best. The Albatross and the whale they are my brothers. It's kind of a special feeling when you're out on the sea alone, staring at the full moon like a lover. Time for a cool change."

JD had accepted the job of taking a sixty-foot sloop to St. Petersburg for a wealthy German industrialist. The joy of sailing such a magnificent ship would be boundless. Good weather and strong westerly winds promised smooth sailing. He bounced eagerly from the dock to the back of his boat.

Immediately he knew something was wrong.

He stepped through the open cabin door down into his galley. It was large and spacious and occupied by four men, four men he did not know. The smallest of the four sat in a recliner and promptly stood. He grinned as if they were old school chums and offered his right hand. "My name is Aaron Greenfield," he said sharply.

JD did not take his hand. He walked slowly to the breakfast bar. "My deckhand, Kevin?" he asked without preamble, his emerald eyes were laced with ice.

"Ah, yes," offered Greenfield. "Sleeping in a forward cabin."

"Not like Kev to take a nap this early."

"His sleep was assisted by a blow to the head. He's quite alright, I'm sure. Dreaming peaceably, no doubt."

"No doubt," answered JD. "You should know if he suffers any ill effects I will not be understanding or forgiving. I'll blame people in this room." The words were delivered with the axe of finality. The other four felt the chill. Greenfield pressed on.

"I should like to explain myself. I'm a station chief with Mossad, Israeli intelligence. I have a story to tell you, Mister John David Stoner. It will not take much of your time, I promise."

JD glanced around the room and noticed the other three men had slid into positions bracketing him. They were being very cautious. *Why the muscle?* he wondered. All three had the same look—short-necked, thick-shouldered, broad-chested brawlers itching for a fight. Mossad's henchmen, but why? He looked at Greenfield. "Make it quick. My friend may need an aspirin or a CAT scan."

Greenfield grinned. He was always amazed at Americans' sense of humor. In his country, humor had been lost decades ago, replaced with checkpoints, suicide bombings, interrogations, barbed wire, civilian casualties, and fanatical security. Israeli humor was a thing remembered only in the cobwebs of the past. He realized he missed it.

"Through a reliable source, we learned three days ago that wealthy Saudi businessmen hired an oriental assassin to kill our prime minister. The assassin is being paid ninety million dollars and is on his own time schedule. We also know the assassin is the infamous Glass Tiger. There are no known photographs of him and virtually no information exists about him. He came up through the Chinese military but that is all we know."

Greenfield paused for effect. It had none on JD.

"What's this got to do with me? I ferry boats. Does your prime minister wish to sail the gulf?"

Greenfield was not amused. "Years ago, the Americans created an assassin hunter, code name Nomad. He had only one purpose. One directive. Hunt down and eliminate the world's top assassins. Time and cost were not factors. He hunted Carlos, Longfellow, the Crow, the Diamond Buyer, and others. Even the Glass Tiger. It is rumored he fought the glass Tiger to a draw in Pakistan, or that the Glass Tiger won but spared the life of Nomad. Either way, Nomad can identify the Glass Tiger. He is the only man alive to have seen him. We need the services of Nomad. We are willing to pay one hundred million dollars. What do you say, Mister Stoner?"

JD paused. "I already said it. What's it got to do with me?"

Greenfield was not deterred. "We believe that you, Mister Stoner, are Nomad. We wish to hire you."

JD said nothing, silence. A rather loud silence.

"We've done our homework, Mister Stoner. You are Nomad. We need your help."

"The reliable source you tortured for this information? Where is he now?"

Disappointment showed on Greenfield's face. "Unfortunately, the man's heart gave out under questioning. But we believe the information is accurate. We do not believe he lied."

They probably used a blowtorch on the poor schlep, JD thought. He disliked the Israelis immensely. "If I were Nomad," he said slowly, "why on earth would I help you?"

This seemed to shock Greenfield, but he recovered quickly. His voice was steady and sure. "Stability in the region, sir. We are the only democracy in the area. Your country needs us."

"I don't give a damn about your country. If George W. needs you, go ask his help. He seems ready, willing, and able to kill or bomb anything he doesn't like. Why come to me? Stick your precious prime minister in a bunker and blast hell out of everything non-Israeli. Christ, you do that anyway."

"You mock us, sir. We are at war."

"With yourselves. America needs you like it needs leprosy. But we're stuck with you because twenty years ago, another half-assed president gave you the bomb. And now we're afraid you'll use it. Hell, you will. Before you'd let the Arabs push you into the ocean, you'd nuke Baghdad or the Aswan Dam or Mecca. You'd start World War Three without a thought to anyone else. You tolerate the Americans because we pour money into your little fiefdom. In reality, the Jews have never cared about anyone else. And why should you? Your god says you're the chosen ones. Americans are different. We know we're full of shit, and it pisses us off you won't admit the same about yourselves."

Greenfield stood agape. JD continued, "The Arabs hate us because we support you. If we didn't have to baby sit your temper tantrums we'd be in clover. Terrorists would leave us alone, and George W. could go back to plundering the economy and the environment. Help you? Don't be ridiculous."

This was not what Greenfield and his thugs had expected, but then they knew Nomad had been retired for three years. He was glad most Americans bought into the "We need Israel" spiel from their government. Stoner was right, of course; Israel did not give a tinker's damn about anyone or anything but itself. Jehovah had promised them the land, and that was all they needed to know. Screw the Arabs and other desert niggers! But now they needed Stoner.

"One hundred million, Mister Stoner. What else would you require?"

"A partial lobotomy."

"You're no longer amusing, sir." The words held a veiled threat of implied violence.

"Neither are you, Greenfield. You don't need me, so why don't you and the three stooges here slink back to Tel Aviv. Bulldoze a few Palestinian houses. That always makes you feel better."

"I am losing patience, sir. These men are quite capable, you know."

The threat was no longer implied; it was no longer veiled. JD could sense the tension rising in the three henchmen. He decided to relieve that tension.

"Relax, Mister Greenfield," he said evenly. "You don't need me because I know something you don't."

Greenfield eased slightly. "And what might that be, sir?"

JD strode to a bag of golf clubs leaning against the bulkhead. He stopped when he reached the set of clubs.

"Since you've done your homework, Mister Greenfield, tell me, what else identifies the Glass Tiger? What else do only a handful of people know about him?" JD eyed Greenfield suspiciously.

Greenfield smiled. "The Glass Tiger carries a fourteenth-century samurai sword with a silver inlaid handle."

"Not enough," answered JD. "What else?"

"The weapon has a phrase etched in the blade."

"Yes?"

"It says, 'The sword does not jest', in Mandarin.'"

JD reached into the golf bag and grabbed the topper from one club. But it wasn't a club. He pulled a magnificent sword from the bag and dropped it on a table in front of Greenfield. It was exquisite, a handcrafted piece of art from six hundred years ago. The blade glistened in the low light of the cabin. Greenfield's eyes widened as he looked at the polished steel. There; an inch from the handle in letters a quarter of an inch high, the Mandarin words, "The sword does not jest."

How? Greenfield wondered. *How is it possible?*

JD could see Greenfield's bewilderment. "The Glass Tiger is no more." A certain reverence carried in his speech. "Three years ago, in Kashmir, I took the sword as proof. There was a fight, indeed, but your information is incorrect. There was no draw, only the death of the Glass Tiger. Your prime minister has nothing to fear from the Glass Tiger. Your reliable source lied. You don't need me. You can go now."

Greenfield held the sword. No doubt it was authentic; he somehow instinctually knew that.

"So you are Nomad?" he said, not looking up from the sword.

"I ferry boats across the gulf," replied JD. "And if my friend Kevin doesn't fully recover, you'll hear from me."

A moment of graveyard silence followed. Everyone in the room understood. Greenfield put down the sword and motioned to the others. They began to file out. Greenfield knew he had a labyrinth of lies to unwind, but his mission at the marina was over. He paused at the galley door and looked at JD. "A pleasure, sir."

JD looked away. "Just go," was all he could say. They left, the hard men no doubt disappointed they were not allowed to flex their massive muscles.

JD was relieved he did not have to kill anyone.

A moment after they were gone, Kevin slid open the door to the staterooms and walked into the galley.

"You heard?" JD asked.

"Everything," Kevin replied.

"How's the head?"

"I got a headache that would kill a mere mortal. Other than that, fine."

"They bought it."

"I know. I expect the Chinaman will be happy. He's out now. All the way out."

"Yeah," agreed JD. "All the way. I'm glad to help him." He held the sword and saw his reflection in the blade. "He's probably sitting on a beach somewhere sipping fruity drinks and playing footsies with a babe, counting his money."

Kevin chuckled. "He doesn't drink, but that's what I'd do."

JD thought back two weeks. He had been retired for nearly three years when the Chinese man known as the Glass Tiger came calling. He explained his situation to JD. He wanted out, so he set up the Israeli deal and gave JD his famous sword. He knew the Israelis would approach JD because they needed JD's help to convince them of his death. JD would pass on the information, and everyone would believe him dead. He would disappear and live happily ever after. Simple, if JD went for the deal. And he had. *Why not? I'm out, so why not help the Chinaman? One less assassin makes for a better world. It's good business.* Smiling, JD returned the sword to the golf bag.

Kevin decided to move on. "We're taking the German sloop to St. Pete tomorrow?"

JD looked up. "Yeah. The weather's supposed to be good for a week. It'll be fun."

Kevin knew better than to ask but asked anyway. "Molly going?"

"She loves the water, Kev. It's a two-week turnaround. You know I can't go that long without seeing her goofy grin."

Kevin knew all too well. "I'll make the arrangements. She's a handful."

"I know, but we love her. And I cleared it with the Germans. Their insurance can cover another body onboard. I want to leave by seven."

"Everything'll be ready. You think the Israelis will be back?"

"I hope not. If they do, someone may die."

Kevin said nothing. He picked up the cell phone and punched in a number from memory. Arrangements had to be made for Molly. She was a handful.

Galveston has an old town square dominated by a massive, vintage, stone courthouse. Maple trees planted fifty years earlier lined the square and provided shade for the sidewalks. Tourists and businesspeople strolled the pavements and were cooled by ocean breezes that drifted lazily from the sea some miles away.

That morning, the courthouse buzzed with anticipation. The "twins" were scheduled for their preliminary hearings. These local celebrities would ensure a packed courtroom. Court TV had even set up a live feed. Attorneys were dressed in their best and sported very recent haircuts.

Judge Janice Garcia didn't share the excitement. The last thing she wanted was for her courtroom to be turned into a Barnum & Bailey sideshow. The "twins" were Tim Rothstein and Adam Lyons, both twenty-year-old computer geniuses. Nerds. Instead of slide rules, these boys carried laptops. They were notorious, famous, likable, and a little screwy. No, more than a little, they were downright banana wacky. She had to maintain control of her courtroom, her domain. Justice was needed, but she was not about to allow the hearing to become fodder for late-night comedians. An iron hand was called for. She wished she knew where to find one.

The courtroom was packed by nine thirty. Not an empty seat. The bailiff surveyed the crowd and groaned to himself. His day would get worse, he knew. The district attorney was already seated at his table when the defense attorney, Fredrick Rutburg, ushered his clients to the table across the aisle. Rutburg was forty-five but looked ten years older. He was nearly bald, and he wore glasses that had been in fashion decades ago. Some people referred to them as birth-control glasses; anyone wearing them didn't have a chance in hell of having sex. But Fredrick was frugal; he saw no need to have new glasses and had long ago given up sex with his second wife. She preferred shopping and bridge with her gal pals.

Rutburg was dressed smartly in a thousand-dollar linen suit while the twins looked like refugees from a thrift store; fashion junkies they were not. Their hair was wild, Einstein wild, and their ragged duds looked slept in. Still, the crowd looked at them as though they were rock idols from England.

At 10:01, Judge Garcia entered her bailiwick amidst the silence the bailiff had called for. "Good morning," she said quickly. When she sat, the rest in attendance followed suit. Through wire-rimmed bifocals, she surveyed the crowd. They were packed in as if waiting for a heavyweight title fight. She motioned to her clerk and took a deep breath. The day began.

Though it was only a preliminary hearing, prosecution and defense were ready to slug it out. The prosecution swore the two boys were dangers to national security, while the defense simply called them misguided youngsters. Early on, the judge realized she had to find a compromise between execution and Club Med. The twins, not related at all, sat nervously, as if someone had slipped a couple of trout down their trousers. Like water on a hot skillet, their behinds fidgeted on the stately oak chairs. The state's attorney, a tall, dapper man, near forty, was painstakingly trying to persuade the judge of their villainy. His voice had a barking, seal-like quality, and that was grating on the judge's nerves. She knew what she had to do.

Holding up one hand, she stopped the state's attorney's oratory. "I've heard enough, gentlemen," she stated. "I need to ask these boys some questions." Her gaze bore down on the twins. They felt they were getting the evil eye, a mother's look when you were caught dead to rights in some unpleasantness.

"Boys, I have in front of me a laundry list of things you're being accused of. I won't read them all, but I'll highlight some.

I'd like you to tell me if they're true and accurate. I expect you to be honest."

The twins looked at each other and at the judge. They were master computer nerds, but they were honest. In fact, honesty came easy to the twins, like hacking the mainframe of a major bank or corporation; it was effortless.

Judge Garcia began reading from a stack of papers. "Is it true that back in January, you hacked into the national satellite feed of the president's State of the Union speech and ran an information border along the bottom of the screen during his speech? A few of the phrases that repeated for nearly thirty minutes were 'Mars needs women,' rap sucks,' chicks dig roguish guys,' and 'noise proves nothing.'" She peered at Tim and Adam. There was muffled laughter in her courtroom. The twins continued fidgeting.

Tim spoke. "We didn't know what else to say. It all seemed so bipartisan."

"Yeah, bipartisan," agreed Adam.

"I see," said a skeptical Garcia. "And what about this? You emailed all the United Nations representatives a picture of Vice President Cheney in a pirate's hat, wearing an eye patch, a goatee, and brandishing a sword. Under the picture a caption read, 'Avast, ye scurvy dogs! Prepare to be boarded!'"

Adam spoke. "We figured that at the rate we're conquering countries, we should give them all advance notice."

"Yeah, sort of a courteousy," added Tim.

"Courteousy?" repeated the judge quietly. "Here's a good one. You found out the toilets in the Pentagon building flushed by sensors, broke into the building's maintenance computer, and flushed all six hundred toilets at the same time, causing busted pipes, unexpected bidets, flooding, repairs in excess of eight hundred thousand dollars, and forty-seven Pentagon workers complained of cold enemas."

The courtroom erupted in guffaws as the judge slammed her gavel for quiet.

Adam spoke. "The Pentagon is that five-sided monument to military stupidity. We thought they could use a laugh."

"Higgledy-piggledy," chimed Tim. "It was all higgledy-piggledy."

"Right," added the judge. "Higgledy-piggledy. How about this? You sent Saddam Hussein an email over secured NSA email that read, 'Lunacy recognizes its own.'"

"We were feeling philosophical that day, Judge," Tim said.

"I see. Just one more, boys. Ah, but a goody. You broke into the mainframe White House security computer, hacked the president's private email address, and sent our president an email that read, 'Frat party at Delta House at nine p.m., BYOB.' And then a five-hundred-page advice paper on how to secure world peace and stability."

"It's not what you think, Your Honor. The BYOB meant 'bring your own bombs.'" Adam smiled.

The judge continued. "The paper was entitled, 'Dump Israel, Conquer Canada.'"

"Sure," said Tim. "We had it all figured out, see? We cut Israel loose, let them fend for themselves. What'd they ever do for us but gripe? And then we conquer Canada."

The judge was incredulous. "Conquer Canada? Our neighbor to the north?"

"Yeah. It'd be a cinch," went Adam. "We could take 'em with two aircraft carriers tied behind our backs. No problemo. Then we'd be set."

"Set?" asked the judge.

"Sure," said Adam. "We'd have Alberta's oil, all we'd ever need, and all of British Columbia's timber and natural resources, the diamond mines of the Northwest Territories, which in five years will be the largest on earth, and in Eastern Canada, we'd have, er, well, what?"

"Proximity," whispered Tim.

"Oh yeah, proximity," remembered Adam. "Proximity."

Everyone was confused. "Proximity?" asked Judge Garcia.

"Yeah, to Iceland and Greenland. We could nab them in a heartbeat," went Adam.

The judge shook her head, not understanding, but Tim thought it was obvious. "Then we'd get the Nordic blonde bodybuilder babes. But the paper was much more detailed."

Again, the courtroom burst into noise. Some reporters scurried outside to use cell phones.

"It was no big deal, though, Judge," said Adam. "A few days later, we broke into the army intelligence computer and discovered they already had a plan to conquer Canada. It was way better than ours."

"Yeah," said Tim. "They think they can take Canada in five days. We found out that one of our aircraft carriers weighs more than all the ships in the Canadian Navy put together. And they're not scared of the Mounties."

The judge blanched. She could see the next day's headlines. Her mind's eye knew it would make Republicans furious. A lifelong Democrat herself, she secretly smiled at the prospect. The White House would be pissed. She hoped her courthouse would not be tagged a "clear and present danger" and smart—bombed. Her gavel struck loudly. Quiet was restored; chaos was controlled.

"I've heard enough!" Judge Garcia shouted. "I've decided to rule now."

This stunned the court. A judge ruling at a preliminary was highly irregular at best and possibly illegal at worst. The defense attorney and the state's attorney jumped to their feet with objections. "Sit down, gentlemen," she demanded. "Your objections are noted. Stand, boys."

The twins stood nervously.

"I find you boys guilty. Guilty of computer piracy and computer espionage. You're also guilty of being naïve geniuses. You have tremendous gifts and don't mind wasting them. Guilty idiots. I'm going to give you a choice. You can serve ninety-nine years in the Texas Department of Corrections or sign up for four years with one of our government's military services, the ones you so readily pillage and hack, the ones you make fun of and ridicule, the same services you seem to hold in contempt."

She stopped. She was proud of her Solomonic decision. The courtroom was silent, cemetery silent. All eyes fixed on the twins and what they would say.

"Speak up, boys," urged Judge Garcia. "What will it be? Jail or the military?"

The boys saluted. Tim said, "We're off to be all that we can be, I guess."

The judge didn't return the salute. The crowd murmured. More reporters rushed for the door. Headlines had to be crafted, stories filed, and deadlines met.

"A wise choice, boys. You are hereby released to the bailiff. Mister Amundsen, you are to take these boys directly to the recruitment center of their choice. They're in your custody until they're turned over to a military representative. Is that clear?"

Bailiff Amundsen was as shocked as everyone else. "Yes, Your Honor."

Her attention turned to the boys. "This is your chance, gentlemen. Put that genius to use for your country. Screw up, and I'll bury you in a hold so deep you'll be moles when you get out." She banged her gavel. "We're adjourned. Bailiff, get them out of here!"

Before the twins realized what had happened, the portly Bailiff Amundsen slapped handcuffs on them and escorted them to an exit. The court began filing out, and the hallways filled with cackling debate. The celebrity twins were off to do their duty for their country, in manacles and with an escort just to be sure. Some began to wonder if enslavement was worse than prison. Time would tell.

As the twins were being shuttled from the courthouse, a 1965 black Cadillac pulled into the parking lot of the Water's Edge marina. From the door stepped a bare-chested, potbellied figure of considerable proportions. He yawned, cursed a passing seagull, and made for the slips. The black Caddy rested peacefully in its space but stood out considerably. A replica of an eight-foot tiger shark was bolted firmly to its roof.

Onboard the *Monkberry*, Captain JD Stoner was preparing for his voyage the next morning. He stood on deck, checking all the lines that moored his boat. Everything seemed in order. A piercing sun dominated a cloudless sky. The ocean lapped serenely at the marina.

JD spotted Duke trudging down the dock toward his boat. The hard wood of the dock showed no distress under the weight it had to absorb. Duke, the Wizard of Art, aka Alan Duke Heckle, was a forty-four-year-old retired New York cop, three hundred twenty pounds of articulated Jell-O. Duke always looked the same. He never wore a shirt, and his old-man Bermuda shorts dangled below a beer belly that could hide a keg of beer. The shorts flapped like flags around spindly legs. His body was a deep bronze. Once-powerful shoulders and chest had gone to flab, and his left arm ended in a stub at the wrist. His hand had been shot off in a drug bust gone bad five years earlier in Brooklyn.

Duke had retired on full medical disability and had moved to Texas. He loved the beaches and the tourists. Seven days a week he would set up shop off a boardwalk and paint. Anything a tourist wanted, he would paint. His equipment was simple. Paint, paintbrushes, canvases, easel, and towels. He'd paint portraits of beach scenes, or flowers, or naked women. He didn't care. Pay him and he would paint it. Wheel covers, T-shirts, bodies, cars, houses, boats, anything. Duke was a painting fool. He was a good artist and terrific entertainment. The gender of the company he was in didn't matter; he'd swear like an inmate on death row. His cussing, however, was not malicious; it was good natured and frivolous. Some cringed at his colorful language, but most snickered and took it in stride. Duke was Duke and too old to change, so his "fuck you" attitude was commonly accepted.

JD waved as Duke approached, his belly leading the way. "How's it going, Duke?"

Duke grinned. "Not worth a flying fuck. You look like shit on the street corner eating Fig Newtons, J Douche. You need more fucking beauty sleep, pal."

"Good to see you too, Dukie."

"You're the fucking greatest, J Douche." Laughter came easy around Duke. JD was always glad to see him. It brightened his day, cheered his soul.

"What can I do for you, Duke?" It was always an uneasy question. Duke could easily ask for JD to take off a month and go hunt snow leopards in the mountains of Ceylon.

"I need a goddamned ride, sonny."

"What's wrong with the Dukemobile?"

"That piece of horseshit? It looks good, but it don't run for shit. It won't make it to Dunedin. I need a ride across the gulf. I heard you were sailing a Nazi sloop across for some fucking Kraut."

JD could only laugh. "He's a wealthy German businessman, Duke."

"Fucking Brazil Boy probably. I don't like those SS douchebags. A Kraut is a fucking Kraut." Duke's opinion seemed cemented in stone.

"What's in Dunedin, Duke?" JD knew it was a Greek suburb of Tampa—St. Pete, a wealthy area that was home to Greek nationals and retirees.

"A job! What else, dickwit? Plus I need to collect from that rich son of a bitch Stanopolis. I painted a mural for him at his house. Crazy cocksucker tried to stiff me. It's been two months now. So I called the cunt lapper and said, 'Hey numb nuts! If I thought you was gonna fuck me on the bill, I'd have dropped my drawers, bent over, and come through the door backward. Cough up the moolah, ragpicker!' He starts laughing and says he'll send me a check. I say 'Fuck you! I'll come get it.' Cash, I tell him. I want fucking greenbacks or I'll tell the press about him banging Senator Keatch's daughter at the country club last May. Porked her out behind the dogleg at fourteen. Saw the whole thing. Not much to see, though. He's a dickless douche, and she's uglier than Grandma Moses. A mercy fuck. So I need a ride. It's not like the boat will be crowded unless you already got a fucking floating orgy going."

"No orgy, Duke, just Kev, Molly, and I."

Duke threw JD a pained look, a look he recognized.

"You can come along, Duke. I suppose the 'Kraut' won't mind."

"You're the fucking greatest, J Douche." He hesitated. "Molly's going?"

"Sure, Duke."

"She hates my fucking guts! And she gives me the creeps."

"Sounds coincidental."

"Three months ago, she slapped the immortal shit out of me! Sent me into fucking orbit. Nearly broke my jaw!"

"She was trying awful hard, Duke. She doesn't like all the swearing."

"Fuck," said Duke. "What the fuck is with you two? I tell you, it ain't natural."

"We're good friends, Duke. It's that simple."

"Simple my ass. It's weird. Spooky."

"Just don't cuss around her and it'll be fine. I'll talk to her."

"Fuck me."

"We leave at seven a.m.," JD said. "Be here. Kev and Molly will be back any time. Want to have dinner with us?"

Duke was suddenly in a hurry to leave. He looked around like a burglar casing a job. "I gotta go, J Douche. I'll see you at sun up. And I'm not taking any shit from Molly. She can kiss my rosy red patoot! Say hi to Kev. You're the fucking greatest. See you tomorrow."

JD nodded. Duke headed to his Caddy. The tiger shark glistened in the bright sunlight. It had drawn a crowd.

As the carnival Caddy was leaving the marina, Bailiff Amundsen was quizzing the twins. "Which branch of the service, boys?"

"Horse marines," said Adam.

"That's World War One, sonny, something a little more recent."

"Salvation Army," quipped Tim, his blue eyes flashing hope.

"You're definitely dressed for it," the bailiff shot back. "Look, you computer delinquents; you got your air force, your army, your navy, your marines, or your coast guard. Pick one! One!" He held up his middle finger to emphasis the point.

The boys were in turmoil.

"Maybe the army. Who knows?" said Tim. "Maybe we'll get commissions."

"No way," said Adam. "Straight salary or nothing!"

"Commissions! You idiots! It means officers! God, you boys are dense. Now decide, or I'm taking you to the army. They'll recognize your potential and probably put you in the infantry."

In unison they sang out, "Coast Guard!" It was enough for Amundsen. He headed for the Coast Guard office off Sixth Street. He'd be glad to be rid of these misfits. He worried a bit, though, for the Coast Guard.

JD never worried about much. He was inspecting the German sailboat for last-minute problems. This was an exquisite sloop, sixty feet of maritime elegance. Below decks, everything was lined with fine mahogany. It dark and rich. The boat had three staterooms and every modern convenience—sonar, radar, satellite TV, cellular phone, and twin inboards for cruising with no wind. It would be a joy to sail, a dream. The masts, the rigging, the boom, everything checked out. There was plenty of food in the galley and enough water and fuel. They were ready. With good winds and weather, they'd be in St. Pete in three days.

JD called Kevin. "How's Molly?"

"Temperamental, the usual," answered Kevin.

"Duke stopped by. He needs a ride to St. Pete. I told him okay."

"That'll make Molly happy. She hates that tub of lard. She tried to take his head off a few months back."

"She barely touched him, Kev. Plus, he promised to behave."

"Right. We'll just have to keep them apart. I'm glad it's a big boat. Everything check out?"

"Everything," replied JD. "We leave at seven. Duke will be here."

"I'll be back at the *Monkberry* within the hour. I'd let you talk to Molly, but she's asleep in the back."

"I'll see you, Kev." JD hung up. Next, a short stop at the grocery store and then home.

Home for the twins looked like the office of the U.S. Coast Guard. Framed pictures of sailing vessels lined the room. Polished steel and naugahyde furniture populated the spartan office. It was empty, save the twins, who had been told to sit down, shut up, and wait. They glanced around, trying to appear casual. Then the door burst open, and a large, graying man strode in. With ramrod-erect posture and a blouse full of medals and ribbons, he marched up to the boys and stopped abruptly. He eyed them suspiciously, no doubt expecting something else. "You're late," he barked in a deep voice, a growl, really. "It's a bad start, lads, a bad start!"

The twins looked at him as if he were from another planet. The English accent particularly froze them. "Where in blue blazes is everyone? Damned inefficient, lads, damned inefficient!" He eyeballed the twins. "They said you were new, but damn, boys, a bit casual, don't you think? I realize I'm retired, but goddamn, I'm still an admiral. Goddamned new breed, I guess. You computer technoweenies all look like that?"

Tim answered. "Uh, mostly, sir. We just got here. We're sort of new."

The admiral seemed miffed. "Well, let's go. I told them three p.m. I don't want to be late. It's a bad start, lads. Come along. My car's waiting. Snap to. You'll get proper clothes onboard."

"Onboard, sir?" asked Adam.

"The *Broadsword*, you twits. Bloody hell! Am I the only one around here who knows what's going on?"

Apparently so, thought the twins. They were at a loss. A giant, retired limey admiral was spitting orders at them. Naturally, they went along and soon found themselves careening toward the naval shipyards in the admiral's car, his driver mostly indifferent to the speed limit signs flashing by. As they sped, the admiral talked. "I'm told you lads are the best, so I'll overlook your shameful appearance. It's an honor for me to be taking this tour. I'll have three days to inspect this fancy new tub of yours and report to my old branch, Her Majesty's Royal Navy.

"You boys have to check out all the systems posthaste. A fine-toothed comb is required here, lads. Be thorough. I'm damned glad to have you along." He shook their hands in a vise grip that made the boys wince.

"We'll do our best, Admiral, sir. Count on us," voiced Adam proudly.

"Certainly," agreed Tim.

This made the admiral wince.

Back at the Coast Guard office, Bailiff Amundsen winced and cringed. The twins were gone. He had left them for only ten minutes so he could find someone in charge. When he returned with a Coast Guard recruiter, the office was empty. He should have handcuffed them to a large piece of furniture. Damn! He called the courthouse. By the next morning, a bench warrant would be issued for their arrest.

The naval shipyard security officer spied the distinguished, retired admiral and the two hobos and nearly underwent cardiac arrest.

"Admiral Gerald Fitzgerald," said the admiral, approaching the security post. "Her Majesty's Royal Navy. Retired, of course."

"Yes, sir," saluted the guard. "And, uh, these two?"

"My aides. Fresh from leave. I trust you have proper uniforms aboard?"

"Of course, sir, but we were told your aides had been delayed."

"They're here, obviously, but their bags were delayed. I picked them up a half hour ago from the coast guard office. If there's a problem, I'll be onboard. Anything else?"

The guard shook his head no. He stepped aside as the trio passed and began climbing the gangway to a large ship, the

U.S. Coast Guard cutter *Broadsword.* Commissioned seven years previously, it had been three years being fitted in the navy shipyards at Galveston, 209 feet of shiny, modern, naval warfare. This was no ordinary cutter; it was the first of its class. It was run by a nuclear power plant the size of a family refrigerator and was designed to stay at sea three months at a time. Its sixty-member crew would have every luxury, including a mess hall, an exercise room, a maintenance shop, a theater, a library—books and videos—a computer room, three large holds, and a helipad and chopper. The helicopter was solar powered, and all batteries onboard were solar as well, rechargeable in a mere two hours.

Food, clothing, and other provisions for a crew of sixty were stored in two large storerooms. A Mini Cray III supercomputer hummed quietly in the control room. On deck, water cannon, three .50-caliber guns, and surface-to-air missiles composed the ship's impressive arsenal. She could defend herself and deter most surface vessels. Pirates, smugglers, dopers, and other unfriendlies would think long and hard before taking on the *Broadsword.* She was America's newest weapon in drug enforcement and border patrol. Her task was to keep the Gulf of Mexico safe, to protect America's interests. The ship was the pride of the coast guard.

She was being towed by tugs from Galveston to coast guard headquarters in Key West. After a commissioning ceremony attended by the vice president, she was to do a two-week shakedown run followed by regular service. During its three-day gulf crossing, a skeleton crew would check out all the electronic bugaboos onboard. Computer and electronic specialists would go over all the instruments. The nuclear power plant would operate at full capacity but only a skeleton crew would be aboard on this voyage.

The ship's captain would come aboard in Key West with the rest of the crew. Admiral Fitzgerald had been invited, at the behest of the British Navy, to be a guest for the gulf crossing. He was assigned two computer specialists to accompany him and help him make a report for the English. Britain was deciding if it should purchase two of these ships from the United States, and the admiral's recommendation would go a long way toward convincing the British to buy or not to buy. The admiral was afforded every courtesy.

Onboard, Chief Petty Officer Joseph Hightower saluted and greeted the admiral.

"Hightower, eh?" asked the admiral admiringly. "That's British, chief?"

"No, sir," replied a formal Hightower. "Atlanta, Georgia, sir."

The admiral deflated a bit. "My aides," he said, pointing to the twins, "Tim and Adam. They need clean uniforms, showers, and decent meals. So would I, for that matter."

"Of course, sir. Show you to your quarters immediately. Dinner at eighteen hundred in the mess. The entire crew will be there. Since this is a shuttle, there are only nine of us onboard. It should be very comfortable."

"Excellent, Chief."

Chief Hightower showed the admiral to his quarters first. Leaving a happy Admiral Fitzgerald, he turned to the twins. "I've seen some screw ups in my time, but you fuckups take the cake. You look like survivors of a tornado! I want your names. Full names."

The twins were nearly toppled by the sudden verbal barrage.

"Adam Lyons, sir."

"Tim Rothstein, sir."

"Okay, get this straight. Onboard this ship, I'm god. I don't care if you are the admiral's patsies. Fuck up onboard and I'll personally throw your worthless butts into the drink. Got it?"

"Yes, Chief," came their response.

"Good. Follow me."

They did.

At six in the morning three tugs began pulling the *Broadsword* out to sea. It drew a small crowd of rubberneckers. A few waved good-bye, and the mighty ship eased along leisurely.

Captain JD Stoner, his first mate and pal, Kevin Lohman, Duke, and a restless seagull stood on the back deck of the sixty-foot sailing sloop the *Rhinelander*. Duke was unimpressed.

"If the fucking tub makes it to St. Pete, I'm Jesus H. Methuselah! Nazi piece of shit! And where the fuck is Molly?"

"In the forward cabin asleep, Duke," said JD.

"Asleep already? Goddamn beauty sleep no doubt. She sleeps more than a—"

JD cut him off. "You take the aft cabin. Kev's got the other forward cabin. Stow your gear. We leave in ten minutes."

Duke looked at Kev. "What the fuck you looking at?"

"Always a pleasure, Duke," Kevin said. "I'll just run and grab a wheelbarrow to help you carry that beer gut around. Real svelte, Duke. You lose weight?"

"Yeah, half a fucking pound, asshole! What's it to you? The babes love a little extra."

"Molly will love it."

"Fuck Molly!" Duke blurted out. He looked around quickly to make sure she had not heard.

"I'd hate to be you when she wakes up," said Kevin. "I'd hide in my cabin if I were you."

"No goddamned problem, bucko. I brought a long book to read. I'm steering clear of that bitch!"

JD suddenly appeared topside. "Cast off the lines, guys. We're outta here."

Kev and Duke scrambled to unhook the mooring lines, and JD switched on the twin diesels, which rumbled to a soft idle. He inched the pleasure yacht out of its slip and deftly made his way out of the marina.

Just past the no-wake zone, JD turned off the engines and pushed a button. Like a giant plume, the great mainsail began to unfurl. It was magnificent. Bright blue, yellow, and orange stripes filled the sky. The large sail grabbed the passing wind, and the boat skittered forward, pushed by a steady westerly blow. It knifed along, its bow slashing through two-foot whitecaps. An azure sky and a piercing sun smiled down on the cool water of the gulf.

JD, wearing only shorts and sunglasses, reached for a cap and brought it snuggly down over his head. Kev began lathering on sunblock, and Duke gave the finger to a passing speedboat. Two of the females onboard promptly mooned him with bronzed buns that showed tiny, white Ts that their thongs had covered. Like an adolescent dream, the voyage began.

Onboard the *Broadsword*, the twins had not slept all night. After ravaging their dinners like a couple of homeless alcoholics, they were ushered into the ship's main computer control room. They were astonished.

"A Mini Cray III," whispered Tim in complete reverence. His hand slid along its sleek lines like an altar boy in awe of his first communion.

"It boggles the mind," joined Adam. "You know what this means, don't you?"

"Pillage and plunder?"

"Mostly. We'll probably get in trouble, you know. Thrown in the brig without a blanket or modem."

"Probably. Want to leave?" asked Tim.

"Nah, let's mess around awhile."

Nine hours later, they were still messing around. Codes had been broken, firewalls breached, and secure systems penetrated. They had downloaded an amazing amount of intel onto the Cray's endless storage capacity. The Cray's speed and versatility allowed them to attack numerous systems at once and they tore through vulnerable programs at will, downloading information and storing electronic files. For them, it was like a paid vacation to Disney World. Unbridled enthusiasm and boundless energy kept them going all night. They were kids in a candy store!

Admiral Fitzgerald looked in on them, quite surprised to find them laboring like ancient pyramid builders. "Glad to see you lads getting an early jump. That's a good start. A good start. Carry on now, and call me if I'm needed. I'll be on the bridge. It's a good start, lads."

The twins barely paused. Adam waved aye-aye as the admiral left.

The *Broadsword* plowed through the rolling sea, its new paint gleaming in the bright sunlight. A small flock of gulls tagged along, hovering overhead in search of scraps of food or careless fish. The tugs kept a leisurely distance, escorting the big ship.

Passing ships blasted their horns in playful acknowledgement of the new cutter. From the bridge, Admiral Fitzgerald and Chief Hightower surveyed the deep, dark water with wonderment. Small sailboats skittered along, and powerful speed demons blasted by, skipping like thrown stones, their hulls slapping the waves with loud cracks. Fishermen bobbed lazily, secure in their complacency. It was a glorious day.

Through binocular lens, Chief Hightower spotted a large sailing ship about six miles southwest, its yellow—and orange-striped sail bulging against the blue sky. A carnival scene on the blue water. The sailing yacht rushed along, chastened by the sea but encouraged by the wind. The chief smiled at the thought of owning such a splendid yacht. Such grace and elegance on the water with no worries to dampen such a glorious day meant only the open water and an endless sunshine loomed ahead.

It was three years before the chief planned to retire. He would head for a small cove south of Naples, Florida, to a forty-five-foot, live-aboard sloop he intended tobuy from his brother. Easy payments and an easy life. Sun-drenched days and jewel-drenched widows and divorcees. He hoped to find a wealthy old gal on the rebound and sail off into a secure sunset. *Only three more years* he thought.

Kevin gulped down three more aspirin. He was trying to preempt the headache Duke was giving him. Eleven gin rummy games, eleven straight wins by Duke. Kevin owed him thirty-three dollars.

"I know you're cheating," Kevin said.

"Look, dipshit, I got no shirt on and only one fucking hand. How the fuck could I cheat? Maybe I got an ace up my butt?"

"Maybe," agreed Kevin. "Just deal."

"I am. I only got one hand. You try shuffling one-handed. Can I help it you're a lousy fucking card player?" Duke dealt, Kevin picked up a card, discarded, and Duke yelled "Gin!" as he laid down his hand.

"I quit!" cried an exasperated Kevin.

"Fine. Cough up the dough, pal. Thirty-six fucking big ones! Cash."

"Got change for a hundred?" asked Kevin.

"Fuck no. Do I look like Donald goddamned Trump?"

"You look like a beached whale," Kevin shot back. "You'll get the money when I get change." He stormed off below decks.

"Don't worry," yelled Duke. "I'm making out an IOU. You can sign the fucking thing later."

No answer from Kevin.

Molly had been sunbathing on the forward hull while JD skippered the sloop. The winds were a modest eighteen knots, and the ship responded easily. He had been reading *USA Today* ; its scorching headline read, "White House Considers Conquering Canada." He could only laugh.

From the aft deck, he heard Duke say, "Hey, J Douche. Get a load of that big bastard being escorted." He was pointing northeast at three tugs shadowing a large cutter. JD grabbed his binoculars and scanned the ship for a name. He mouthed the word *Broadsword.*

It looked new. Why was it being escorted? Probably only a skeleton crew, he mused. JD knew better than to try to make sense out of anything military. He merely put down the binoculars and went back to the newspaper. Molly yawned heavily, looked up for a brief second, and went back to the warmth of the morning sun. Her body seemed lethargic in its glow. Stretching hard, she rolled, yawned again, and fell into a catnap. Duke, ever mindful of her presence, cursed under his breath and headed for his cabin.

JD laughed at an article in the newspaper, adjusted the wheel, and looked at Molly. She was sleeping hard; her soft snores filtered back toward him. The sun shone warm, and the wind ruffled her hair. She was more than beautiful. JD thought she was striking. Sleek lines and an elegant, unmistakable grace. Still, she was a handful.

The U.S. military will never be accused of being a paragon of efficiency. And that includes the coast guard. Things do get done, only with the speed of a glacier versus the speed of a cheetah sometimes. The coast guard had discovered its mistake. Admiral Fitzgerald had confused the twins with two other aides who had arrived later. They sat in Galveston while the twins cavorted around the *Broadsword.*

A fair amount of confusion reigned at coast guard headquarters. Captain Thomas was pissed. "There's a chopper onboard, for Christ's sakes. Ferry those idiots back and send out the right ones." His exasperation cracked in his voice.

A yeoman replied. "It's a skeleton crew, sir. There's no pilot onboard. And there's no place to land another chopper if we sent one. The best we can do is rendezvous with the *Ivanhoe* and have them take charge of the imposters."

The captain didn't like it but saw no other choice. He glared at the yeoman. "How soon can they meet?"

"About four hours, sir."

"Do it," he snapped. "And I want those two assholes onboard in a brig ASAP."

"Aye-aye, sir."

The word went out; arrest the twins and haul their sorry butts back to Galveston. Judge Garcia was looking forward to their reunion.

The *Broadsword* lumbered through easy seas, oblivious to the notoriety of its two wayward admiral's aides, the twins having intercepted all communications. Routine stuff for even average electronics wizards, which of course they were not. For an hour, they had been taking a break, touring the ship and meeting the other crew members. There was the ship's cook, Moe "Biggs"

Henry, a fortyish career seaman of African origin. He had a huge smile that outlined piano key teeth. He was affable but ruled the galley like Attila the Hun. The boys had gained his favor when they ordered Adam and Eve on a raft for breakfast—eggs over medium on toast with a slice of cheese. The chief cook hadn't heard that expression in years and immediately thought the boys were okay.

Next, they met the ship's doctor and nurse, Dr. Matilda Moran and Nurse Natalie Armbruster, attractive ladies both. Dr. Moran was a thirty-two-year-old dusty blonde who hid behind severe, black-rimmed glasses. She was fit, close cropped hair, and extremely attractive. A triathlete and former collegiate soccer star. She graduated from Duke medical school and joined the coast guard to help pay off student loans.

Nurse Armbruster was a petite brunette with creamy, satin skin. She had a nervous giggle that was attractive and obliging, piercing blue eyes and a small gecko tattoo on her right calf. She appeared engaging and provocative. Shipmates Arnie Glover and Arvin Billups were less engaging. They just brushed past the twins as if they were mirages on a desert plain.

Chief Billy Johnson was in charge of everything mechanical. He cloistered himself in the engine room or in the ship's elaborate workshop. He was mechanical virtuoso who did not relate well to humans. He liked the boys, though. Apparently, they were somewhat less than human in Billy's mind. Social misfits like him. Reclusive genius recognized its own.

The last of the crew were three female yeoman, Arabella Samuels, Janice Blackstone, and Dawn Frasier. Three Midwestern gals who seemed interchangeable. Buxom farm beauties who loved the sea and the adventure of the coast guard. They loved firearms. All were rated experts in various weapons. They were poster girls for the NRA. They were smart, tough, and formidable, but they looked good, even in uniform. The kind of gals Conan the Barbarian might bring home to meet mom. Warrior babes, lusty and lethal. The twins, who between them had had only one girlfriend, were immediately smitten with junior-high crushes.

Chief Hightower had no time for crushes, however. He cut the twins no slack. Earlier, they had mistakenly called him sarge, and he went off like a roman candle. He threatened to bring back flogging and keelhauling.

Atop the observation deck outside the bridge, the chief studied the horizon. Nervous hairs tickled the back of his neck, and a shiver ran up his spine. A storm was building, seemingly out of nowhere. Clouds began curling and folding in on themselves, creating great towers of spiraling gray and white. Winds were steadily increasing, and the ocean responded with choppy, foaming waves. He could see the tugs climbing and descending waves while the *Broadsword*, heavy and sturdy, simply plowed through.

The mysterious storm continued to grow in intensity. Winds gained speed, and waves grew unpredictable, a surfer's nightmare of waves breaking in odd directions and pummeling each other. The ocean became a cauldron of colliding water. Great sheets of rain began kniving horizontally like slashing shards. The *Broadsword* had battened down and was watertight, but the great ship lurched and fell with every wave. The crew stared in wonderment at the sudden event. Hurricane strength squalls plunged and pounded the ship and its escorts. The tugs struggled mightily between the weight of the *waves* and the force of the gale. The great tug-of-war pitted the power of the tugs against the strength of Mother Nature.

JD, at the bridge of the *Rhinelander*, knew it was no contest; his ship was being hammered. He had managed to get the mainsail rolled up, but the storm did not care. Sail or not, it blasted the *Rhinelander* with equal ferocity.

Molly had gone below, and Kevin and Duke were busy stowing gear and battening down everything that could come loose. The storm was blowing them perilously close to the *Broadsword*. JD could see she was floundering, having distanced herself from her escorts. The tugs had disappeared.

Duke was suddenly at JD's side. "What the fuck?" he managed to say before the ship fell into a large trough, and he was jerked off his feet. JD hauled him up.

"A bit of a blow," he screamed at Duke.

"A bit of a blow's what I get from Mabel! This is a fucking hurricane!"

JD couldn't hear him. The wind had the strength and noise of a locomotive and was getting stronger. He had a grip on the wheel like a vise, but it still fought him. He thought of checking on Molly but knew he couldn't leave the bridge. He saw her come through the cabin door out onto the aft deck. She paced like a frightened child. The storm got stronger, and their situation was becoming desperate.

The *Broadsword* pitched in the ocean. Admiral Fitzgerald was on the phone to the twins in the computer room. "This is bad, lads. We need to get the ship turned around and steer her into the wind. Get up here and help us figure this out."

They were on their way. So was Maintenance Chief Johnson. They met at the bridge. The admiral took charge. Chief Hightower saw the *Rhinelander*. "Christ on rickshaw!" he screamed. Everyone looked. The *Rhinelander* was on a collision course with the *Broadsword*. Neither ship was responding to her controls. Disaster loomed.

JD had left the bridge. The rudder had been sheared off. The *Rhinelander* was helpless. The wind and water tortured the boat at will. Kevin had given everyone life jackets and clung to the hope of rescue. He had relayed their coordinates to the coast guard cutter *Ivanhoe* and felt sure they would be saved. That was before he saw the ominous shape of the *Broadsword* towering dead ahead of them. Impact seemed inescapable. They had to brace for collision and be ready to abandon ship.

Molly was still aft; JD ran to help her. The boat suddenly nosedived into a deep trench and was hit broadside by a huge rogue wave. The impact threw Molly overboard. JD's scream pierced the howl of the wind, and Kevin and Duke craned to see what had happened. Molly was gone. Before either could react, JD plunged into the swirling sea. They ran to the railing; saw him surface and then be swallowed by a wave. Through the diving rain they frantically scanned the breaking swells. No JD. No Molly. Only the frightful water and banshee wind.

The *Rhinelander* struck the *Broadsword*. Not even the rage of the storm could hide the sound of metal and fiberglass interacting in a massive clash. The *Rhinelander* was gored and shoved aside like a toy. On the bridge of the *Broadsword*, the admiral and crew looked on in horror. The large sailboat offered no resistance.

And then a low vibration began, like a vibrating bed in a cheap motel. It grew and grew. It soon felt as if the ship would vibrate to pieces. The glass in the windows shook, coffee cups scampered across tables, and light bulbs popped. It became unbearable. The crew of the *Broadsword* grabbed their heads from the jarring pain pressing on their brains.

Then blackness, sinister and deep. Tombstone silence. Sweet blackness.

The cutter *Ivanhoe* had been racing to the coordinates of the *Broadsword* and *Rhinelander*. Yeoman Terry Barnhart sat at his radar and sonar panels inside the control room and suddenly went white. "Sir," he managed to say to Captain Steve O'Reilly. The captain bobbed his head in the direction of the yeoman.

"What is it, yeoman?"

"Sir, the *Broadsword* and the other vessel we were tracking are gone."

The captain moved rapidly to the console. "What the hell do you mean gone? Gone where?"

"Just gone." The yeoman swallowed hard. "They just disappeared from my screens. Just . . . gone. They were on a collision course, but the smaller ship couldn't have damaged the *Broadsword* enough to sink her. Could it?"

The captain wasn't listening. He stared at the empty console. "You're telling me that our newest, two-billion-dollar, nuclear-powered cutter sank as it was being shuttled across the gulf?" His voice had gotten louder with every word. His decibels and timbre continued to climb. "In a collision with a goddamned pleasure boat? Are you nuts?"

The yeoman fought for an explanation. "Sir, it just disappeared. One minute it was inside a raging storm, the next minute gone. That's all I know. We'll be at its last coordinates in twenty-five minutes." He took a deep breath. "And the storm is gone also. It went from a category—five blow to clear skies in less than five minutes. Freaky."

"That a technical term, yeoman?"

"Ah, no, sir, it's just—"

"Forget it, mister. The damned boat is gone. Call Houston and Galveston for air rescue. Tell them we'll rendezvous at their last coordinates and we'll organize the search. Admiral Sandecker will shit when he hears this. His newest toy at the bottom of the gulf on its first day out. Just great!"

The yeoman could only agree. He tuned in his radio and made the calls. The search for the *Broadsword* and the *Rhinelander* began. It would be one of the largest in naval history.

When Admiral Sandecker heard the news, he was stunned. The dominoes were going to fall all the way to the White House. Twelve onboard missing and presumed dead and a state-of-the-art vessel lost. Five years work and two billion dollars in taxpayers money resting unceremoniously at the bottom of the gulf. Mother Nature at her most brutal.

From behind a massive oak desk, the admiral had been reading reports and fielding phone calls. He chomped nervously on an unlit Cuban cigar and contemplated the inevitable. Soon, one of these calls would be the secretary of defense or worse, the big man himself. He thought of what he might say, what excuse he could proffer beyond the wrath of the sea: *Sorry, sir, the sea just swallowed our best ship* or *Our new ship went down in a storm, sir.*

He realized a catastrophe like this would demand someone's head on the proverbial platter. For reasons he couldn't understand, an old high school football cheer suddenly danced into his mind: "Give 'em the ax, give 'em the ax, give 'em the ax, ax, ax, on the neck, on the neck, on the neck, neck, neck."

His hand instinctively tugged at his collar, and he wondered if his neck would end up a candidate for that chopping block of ultimate responsibility. The ringing phone snapped him back to reality. He slowly picked up the phone and held it to his ear and listened. "Yes, Mister Secretary," he said, beginning what could be a long walk to the gallows.

There must be some way out of here, said the joker to the thief.

PART 2
Somewhere in the Gulf

Onboard the *Broadsword*, they awoke to a soft and creamy souffle day. Gale—force winds and smashing waves had been replaced by gentle breezes and lapping water. The contrast was vivid in everyone's mind.

Admiral Fitzgerald and the crew began shaking off the fuzz, coming out of what seemed to have been a long coma. According to the admiral's Timex, only seven minutes had passed since they had been fearing for their lives in the terrible storm. His gut told him something was wrong, dreadfully wrong. It seemed warmer, more humid. The air was heavier but better somehow; breathing was a bit easier. His confused thoughts were interrupted by voices from below.

"Anybody alive up there?"

All hands dashed to the starboard railing and looked over. A deeply bronzed, one-handed, rotund, foulmouthed man looked up and cursed. "One of you fucking swabbies want to give us a fucking hand?"

Duke was holding an unconscious Kevin while bobbing on a piece of *Rhinelander* debris. Kevin moaned and threw up on Duke's leg. Duke cursed again as a rope ladder was lowered. Chief Hightower and Yeoman Samuels eased down the ladder to help.

On deck, Kevin began to come around. As was the case with the others, he and Duke knew something was wrong. Things looked mostly the same but somehow different, the whole seascape was similar but strange, right but somehow wrong.

The admiral took charge. “You men seem okay. Anyone else on that boat?” Kevin and Duke suddenly realized that they were alone, that the *Rhinelander* was gone. JD and Molly were gone.

Kevin took a swig of bottled water and looked at the admiral. “Our captain, JD Stoner, and his friend Molly. Molly was thrown overboard, and JD went in after her. We saw him surface briefly, and then a wave pulled him under.” Kevin’s voice cracked as he spoke.

Duke only shook his head. The loss was great. What could be said? The admiral understood, but life went on. “Mister Johnson, get me power to those engines. Lads, get on the horn and relay our position. I want a complete damage report in fifteen minutes. Everybody move.”

The crew sprang to life while Kevin and Duke stared at a tranquil sea, the same sea that less than an hour ago had viciously claimed their friends. An unforgiving, unrepentant sea yet a strange sea. They noticed a group of giant somethings or another swim by. Whatever they were swam by at about thirty-five knots.

“What the fuck?” mouthed Duke.

“Whales?” asked Kevin, half-heartedly.

“As big as this fucking boat? No way. To damned big.”

“Okay, genius, what?”

“Fucking Godzilla! How should I know?”

Chief Hightower had seen the same thing. But he also saw something else, something refreshingly familiar. “There,” he said, pointing southeast. “Land. Looks like a small island. About two miles.”

Most of the crew had assembled on the bridge. All heads turned. Mr. Johnson spoke. “The engines are operational, sir. The nuclear power plant is operating at ninety-eight percent. The ship is fully functional. All systems are running.”

“Very good, Chief. Lads?”

"Nothing, sir," Adam said. "It's very peculiar. We've tried every possible way to communicate electronically, but nothing."

Tim added, "We tried radio, all frequencies, email, cellular phones, and even the old Morse code. Nothing! It's like the whole world has been shut off."

"Yeah," said Adam. "All of our systems are working. We just can't connect with anyone."

"Damned odd, lads. Damned odd. Everything works, but all you get is silence?"

"Ditto," said Adam.

"Let's go over it," the admiral said. "We're hit by a category-five storm that nearly sinks us. We collide with and sink a pleasure sloop. We black out and come to some seven minutes later on a peaceful yet odd sea. Our power works, and all our systems are go, yet we find ourselves in a communications blackout. The rest of the world appears silent. Anything else?"

"Yeah," spoke Duke. "Ten minutes ago, a school of bastards the size of subs swam by, and there's an island just over there." He pointed with his left stub. "I say we head over to that island and check out where the fuck we are." His colorful suggestion was readily agreed upon by everyone.

"Ahead one-quarter," said the admiral. The *Broadsword* pushed on through a placid sea toward a small island. A light breeze offered small comfort to those onboard.

A hundred yards from a small beach, the *Broadsword* dropped anchor and gently swayed in an easy sea. Chief Hightower was the first to notice a man on the white sand who was waving. Kevin couldn't believe his eyes. JD was standing there like he was waiting for a cab.

Duke noticed. "Well fuck me running. I don't believe it."

"You know that man?" asked Hightower.

"That's Captain JD Stoner, Chief," said Kevin.

"Yep," added Duke. "J Douche!"

It was a miracle, or at least a minor miracle. JD was alive and grinning like a lottery winner. The admiral wasted no time. "Chief, get the Zodiacs ready. We're going ashore."

"Aye-aye, sir."

Duke looked at Kevin. Great relief rushed over both men. Their friend had survived. If there were tears in Kevin's eyes, the wind swept them away. He sighed heavily. Duke understood. "Let's get to the launch," he said. "And I'm gonna deck that crazy son of a bitch for scaring me out of ten years of my life. Which I can't fucking afford."

Kevin laughed. He felt the same way. Decking JD was probably not a good idea, though.

JD stood at the water's edge and watched the approaching boats. He couldn't believe his eyes. Kevin and Duke were waving frantically. The Zodiacs stopped in the sand. Handshakes and hugs followed. Duke, Kevin, and JD reunited. The admiral and the ship's company looked on with genuine happiness. Three friends back from the brink.

"How—?" was all Kevin could ask.

JD looked like a surf bum in baggy shorts, tennis shoes, and cotton-candy hair posing for *Surf* magazine.

"Yeah," said Duke. "We saw you go under after going in for Molly. What the fuck, Bucko?"

An easy smile stretched across JD's face. "I don't know. I blacked out, and the ocean spit me up on this beach. That's all I know."

"Too fucking weird," shot Duke. "Oh yeah, sorry about Molly." He and Kevin looked down. Molly was the closest thing in JD's life to real family. They knew he would take the loss badly.

Again, JD smiled. "Not to worry, guys. Molly made it. She's off in the jungle scrounging food." Kevin's and Duke's jaws dropped.

The admiral spoke. "Admiral Fitzgerald," he said, introducing himself. "That's the coast guard cutter *Broadsword* out there. It's a miracle, and we're glad you survived, but do you think it's wise to send a lady out into an unknown jungle alone? She could be seriously injured."

Again, a disarming smile from JD. "A pleasure, admiral, but Molly's fine. Before you arrived, I scouted this island. It's about four miles around—an active volcano and rather lush vegetation—a small valley just past the jungle with a freshwater spring."

This impressed everyone and created a short silence.

"Oh, yeah," JD added. "And a large flock of flightless birds. About four feet high and very loud. Pretty fast, too. And agile. Took Molly a while to catch one."

"She caught one?" asked an astonished admiral.

"Sure," answered JD proudly.

"You better tell him," said Kevin.

"Yeah," said Duke. "He and the rest of this outfit are starting to think you belong in a booby hatch."

"They don't know?" JD asked.

Duke and Kevin shook their heads. This time, the smile was more mischievous. JD whistled and clapped his hands twice. A moment later, from the entanglement of creeping vines and swaying vegetation, a large, black—and burnt-orange—striped tiger bounded forward, its powerful muscles dancing with every footfall. The crew of the *Broadsword* looked on with a mixture of surprise and dread. Some readied their weapons, and others began to think of the safety of the Zodiacs.

"This should be good," Kevin said to Duke.

The great cat pounded right up to JD and stopped suddenly. JD bent down, and he and the cat rubbed foreheads. The animal erupted in a great yawn that displayed a fierce set of teeth. JD grabbed the tiger around the neck, and they fell to the sand wrestling. The cat's large forearms and paws grabbed him in a headlock. An astonished crowd looked on.

"This is Molly," said JD. "Sometimes I call her Moose. Right, Moose?"

Molly roared another powerful yawn.

"It's a tiger," said Chief Hightower in bewilderment.

"No shit, Sherlock," said Duke.

"Don't worry, Admiral," assured JD. "She won't hurt anyone."

"She's tame?" asked the admiral. His eyes could not leave the great beast. He was mesmerized.

"Hardly," JD said, "but she has no taste for humans. She prefers real game. She's already eaten a bird." JD grabbed a piece of driftwood and threw it into the surf. Molly leaped and raced into the water, snatching the wood and lumbering back to JD with it. She dropped it at his feet and waited.

"Amazing," proclaimed the admiral. "Truly amazing."

Shipmate Arnie Glover had been watching like everyone else, but he was less impressed. "That's swell," he said sarcastically. "Can she do any other tricks? Can she balance on a beach ball?" A few chuckles filtered through the crowd. *Oh Christ*, thought Kevin. *Not good.*

JD didn't acknowledge Glover. He simply patted Molly's large head, said "Go!" and pointed to the jungle. The cat ran into the undergrowth and melted into the greenery like a phantom. Looking at the admiral but speaking to everyone, JD said. "That cat's very special to me."

The tense moment was broken by Kevin. "We need to find out what happened. This island is on no map I've ever seen for the gulf. And our whole situation seems wrong. All of us blacked out during the storm and now end up on a glassy sea. What the hell happened?"

JD looked out at the *Broadsword*. "Radio Galveston or Houston and find out."

"Already tried," said the admiral. "All our electronic communications go out to silence. We haven't been able to reach anyone. It's like the whole world has gone deaf. I got the twins onboard trying to unscramble the mess. It's strange."

"Tell him about the giant fucking fish," said Duke.

Kevin nodded. "We saw a school of fish nearly as large as the boat swim by earlier, going about thirty-five knots."

"Really?" asked JD. "Earlier, on a rock outcropping on the other side of the island, I saw a school of sharks swim by. They had to be eighty feet long."

"There are no eighty-foot sharks, JD," said Kevin.

"I know, Kev. But I know what I saw."

Everyone knew what he or she had seen; nobody could believe it, however. The ocean had changed. Severely.

"We need to find out where we are," said Chief Hightower. "Assuming the storm blew us southeast, I'd say Florida is due east about a hundred miles."

"But how do we locate our position?" asked ship's mechanic Johnson.

"The old-fashioned way," answered JD. "The stars. We wait until tonight and use the stars to tell us our position."

"Jolly good," said the admiral. "And we can navigate using a sextant. Hell, sailors did it for three thousand years before us. For now, we get back to the ship and wait. If there's a search-and-rescue mission underway, they'll find us. And when night falls, we study the stars."

The admiral motioned to the boats. The others began pushing them to the water's edge. "Captain Stoner," said the admiral, "you and Molly come with us. But the cat is restricted to one of the cargo holds. Understood?"

JD nodded. He whistled for Molly, who sprang from the foliage and met JD at the Zodiacs.

On the *Broadsword*, the twins were exasperated. They had tried every form of communication they knew except for smoke signals; and nothing. Not a peep from the outside world. It was as if an electronic vacuum had swallowed up everything. To the twins, children of the expanding electronic age, it was ludicrous and impossible. They sat, dejected, in the control room, staring at soundless equipment. Their minds raced for explanations and possibilities.

Doc Moran had checked them out, and physically, like everyone else, they were okay. Their blackouts seemed to have had no lasting effects, but a world suddenly devoid of all electronic clutter scared them. They couldn't conceive of such a world. What did it mean? Where was everyone and everything? Only silence echoed at them. A creepy, eerie silence. A churchyard silence.

Admiral Fitzgerald had called a meeting for eleven that night. At that time, the stars would have been analyzed and everyone aboard would get a chance to speak. The outside world was still deathly quiet, and except for the small island, no recognizable landmarks had been seen. Things continued to get stranger.

Around six o'clock, a flock of what appeared to be giant vultures flew overhead at an altitude of a least two thousand feet. The flock was so large and dense that it blotted out the sun. The crews' necks craned, and their eyes strained at the sight. The birds were enormous; their wingspans must have been twenty feet. They cackled and cawed angrily as they swept by the *Broadsword*, not knowing what to make of the glimmering steel of her decks. They seemed on a mission for parts unknown; their brief encounter with the strange ship seemed soon forgotten. Squawking madly, they left the *Broadsword*'s crew with more questions than answers.

The small theater onboard had a seating capacity of twenty. Theater-type connected chairs lined the room in sets of four. High-backed and cushioned, the chairs were the rivals of any cinema on land. JD, Kevin, Duke, and the crew lounged, talking among themselves, as the admiral and the twins made their way forward. The twins were carrying file folders. The admiral carried the look of a condemned man. He wasted no time.

"People," he said, his faced lined with concern, "we have a problem, for lack of a better word, that I don't know how to explain. I mean, I can explain it. I just can't understand it. It's . . . it's . . . incredible." He paused.

JD understood. "The stars have moved," he said evenly. The others looked around in confusion.

"Yes," said the admiral. "They aren't where they're supposed to be. They've changed."

Adam spoke. "Actually, that's wrong, sir. The stars are exactly where they should be. It's us. We've moved. We've changed."

"I don't understand," said Yeoman Frasier. She spoke for everyone.

Adam continued. "We plotted the stars. We noticed they'd moved considerably."

"But stars move," interjected Yeoman Blackstone.

"Right," answered Tim. "But it shouldn't be noticeable in our lifetimes. So we took digital pictures of the night sky and ran them through the computer. The computer tracked the movement, in this case retroactively, and it gave us our answer. We triple-checked. There's no mistake. None."

Confusion still reigned. "What answer?" asked Kevin. "What are you babbling about?" Adam looked at the admiral, who only nodded.

"The night sky above our heads at this moment is from ninety-two million years ago. Approximately." The room fell silent as the information was absorbed; ninety-two million years? Kevin asked the obvious. "You're telling us we've moved back in time ninety-two million years?"

"Approximately," reminded Tim.

"Approx—What the fuck?" Duke chimed in. "You boys doped up or what? That's fucked up."

"But true," said JD. "It also explains a lot. Big fish, giant birds, soupy weather, more oxygen."

"That's right," said Adam. "Back then, the atmosphere was saturated with more oxygen. About two percent more. We should feel better, stronger."

"But how did we get here?" Kevin asked.

"That's the question," said the admiral. "We don't know."

The group began to mutter. Conversation broke out everywhere with the same questions. How did this happen? Was it the storm? How do we get back? What do we do now?

The admiral's voice piped up above everyone else. "Please, people, try to relax. The lads have been working with the computer for some answers. Let's hear from them. So what do you think, lads?"

"We're screwed," said Adam nonchalantly.

"Totally," added Tim.

Duke flipped. "That's just great! Our two wiz kids and their computer tell us we're fucked."

"Screwed," corrected Adam.

"Fuck you," fired Duke.

"Alright, gentlemen, enough," the admiral said. "A dash more scientific, lads, if you will."

Tim took a deep breath. "As to the how, only guesses and speculation. Quantum mechanics. The ideas that alternate universes exist. Black holes. Time continuums. Tears in the fabric of time and space. We were in the same hemisphere as the Bermuda Triangle, where electromagnetic fields fluctuate and things disappear. Take your pick. One explanation is as good as another. We all experienced the same thing, a vibration that got stronger, and then blackout. Surely the storm played a part. As for getting back, unknown. What to do now? Survive. What else?"

Adam took over. "And in this world, survival is no easy matter. We're in the late Cretaceous period, around 92 million BC. A time of giants. We're between now and 65 million BC, when an asteroid hit just off the Yucatan Peninsula in Mexico, causing an extinction-level event and ending the reign of the dinosaurs. This planet has never been inhabited by larger creatures on land or sea.

"On land, we have the sauropod family, what we used to call *Brontosaurus*. These include the *Brachiosaurus*, *Ultrasauros*, and *Seismosaurus*. These animals are as big as houses, thirty to one hundred tons each, as much as a whole herd of elephants.

"Also, according to our paleontologists and archeologists, the *Allosaurus* family is here. That means *T. rex*, *Carnotaurus*, and a host of other predators and scavengers. Some are twenty-five feet tall and forty feet long. Giant herbivores like the duckbilled *Hadrosaurus*, the horned *Triceratops*, and the plated *Stegosaurus*. A smaller carnivore called a *Dilophosaurus*, ten feet tall, one ton, and poisonous. It can spit poison fifty feet, similar to a cobra.

"Then there are smaller predators, such as the *Procompsognathus* or *Compys*. They're the size of chickens and travel in large groups."

Adam looked at the crew. They were glued to ever word. Hypnotized.

Tim went on. "And of course the coup de grâce, the *Velociraptor*. Six foot tall, up to three hundred pounds, the most terrible predator pound-for-pound on the planet. Maybe in the history of the planet."

"Sounds like Jurassic Park," interrupted Chief Hightower.

"Except this is real," said Adam. "That brings us to the seas. In the sea around us, we have tremendous predators. Sharks of all sizes, the biggest and baddest being the *Carcharodon megalodon*, a one-hundred-foot monster that can swim at forty knots. It can tear a chunk the size of a VW bug from a carcass, a truly nasty customer. And killer whales. Not orcas, but sixty—to eighty-foot carnivorous whales, streamlined, fast, and full of razor teeth. Also, the plesiosaur family. Long-necked, small-headed, flipper-finned dinosaurs, the Loch Ness monster variety. But this family has the worst of all predators. The baddest boy ever on the planet. The *Liopleurodon*, one hundred and twenty feet and a hundred and fifty tons. A submarine. This bad boy has something the others don't have. Its flippers are hard and stiff, enabling it to crawl up the shore. It can snatch an animal off the beach.

"Then there are other dangerous marine reptiles. The *Sarcosuchus imperator*, a giant croc forty to sixty feet long and ten to fifteen tons, faster on land than a human being. All of the animals I've mentioned are faster than humans. This is not a world for humans yet. We're still ninety-one point nine million years away from evolving.

"Even the plants are different. Only a few species of plants survived to our time, the most notable being the bonsai tree. Except for the rocks and soil, this earth is as different from ours as is the moon." Adam paused.

"Thanks for the Discovery Channel lesson, boys, but how do we know for sure you're right?" The question came from shipmate Arvin Billups.

"Two ways," said JD. "Like Occam's razor, the simplest explanation is usually the correct one."

"And two, Holmesian philosophy," said Kevin. "When you've eliminated the impossible, whatever remains, however improbable, must be the truth."

"Bullshit!" said Billups. "You're all cracked."

JD regarded Billups as either a fool or an idiot. Maybe both.

"Please give us your explanation, professor," he asked intently.

Billups huffed, folded his arms, and went quiet, like a chastised third grader.

Adam took over. "At this time in geological history, mammals are small, no bigger than dogs. We're probably the biggest mammals on the planet right now, and we're surely the smartest. Our weapons can help equalize our size, but some animals will probably only be irritated by bullets."

"I still say this proves squat!" said Billups. His courage flared up.

"Well, it proves one thing, numbnuts." Duke said. "It proves we're all born in Las Vegas. Life's a crapshoot. A roll of the dice or a flip of a fucking card. We suddenly have the significance of cosmic spittle. How fucking ironic."

Duke's statement drew mild laughter. The twins looked at each other.

"Bridgeport?" Tim asked.

"Camelot, said he," replied Adams with a classic line from Mark Twain's *A Connecticut Yankee in King Arthur's Court*, humor being the last refuge of the doomed.

The admiral realized organization was imperative. "Okay, listen up, people. For the moment, we assume our situation is that we are now ninety-two million years back. Military decorum still exists, which means I'm in charge. All ranks are still in effect. The lads and our guests from the *Rhinelander* are civilians. This is what I want. Chief Hightower, you're in charge overall. Mister Johnson, I want a complete inventory of all parts, tools, and maintenance equipment. Mister Henry, I need a complete inventory of your galley and food projections for two years. Doctor Moran, a complete inventory of our medical supplies. Billups and Glover, inventory the dry goods—uniforms and clothing. Samuel, Blackstone, and Frazier, you ladies inventory the weapons and munitions. Lads, you inventory all our electronic hardware. The three civilians will designate living quarters for everyone. Captain Stoner, you're in charge of your friends and your cat. See to your quarters first, people. I want those inventories by oh eight hundred. We'll meet here again then. Try to get some sleep. It will help us all to be rested."

Rest was a weapon; JD had learned that long ago. He left Kevin and Duke in charge of sleeping arrangements and headed down to the number-two cargo hold. He had much to explain to Molly. She was no longer queen of the jungle, top carnivore. In a heartbeat, she had been reduced to a midlevel predator in a world of rapacious giants. He was sure she would not take the news well.

At eight in the morning, the clamoring in the theater stopped abruptly as admiral Fitzgerald burst into the room. At fifty-nine, he still walked with a ramrod-straight back and broad shoulders. Extremely fit, except for a shock of white hair, he could pass for a man ten years his junior. Dark glasses hid the sunken eyes of someone running on two hours' sleep, and those two hours of sleep had been fitful and broken.

Outside, even a blurry sun could not mask a sizzling day. The sky tried to hide behind a frothy haze, yet the heat penetrated it. It was near ninety degrees, and the humidity hung like molasses. The ship's air-conditioning system hummed along effortlessly, keeping the interior compartments a cool seventy-six.

"We'll start with you, lads," said the admiral.

"All of our electronic gear works perfectly," said Adam. "It's all new. The problem is obvious. We're the only ones on the planet with this stuff. Communication is possible but impossible at the same time. We've no one to communicate with."

"But we did catch a break," said Tim. "Before the storm, Adam and I downloaded a few things onto the computer's hard drive."

"We were basically fooling around," said Adam.

"Yeah," Tim said. "For example, we downloaded the Smithsonian's entire library and archives, all the files from the FBI, NSA, CIA, and NRO. We got all of NASA's files, and, oh yeah, Naval Intelligence and fifty-two different Washington think tanks."

Both boys smiled as if they would be rewarded. The admiral raised a suspicious eyebrow. He realized during the earlier charade that they had boosted those files. Back in 2002, the lads might have been off to the gallows. As it were, he thought, they may have inadvertently boosted the entire crew's chances for survival; they had gone from pirates to saviors in a nanosecond.

"What you lads are saying is that we have most of the world's accumulated knowledge on our computer. Is that it?"

"Correct," answered Adam. "We also have the video library of Blockbuster and the music library of MTV, VET, and the Country Music Channel."

"Cool," said Tim.

"And the Playboy Channel."

"We get the picture lads," the admiral said. "That's a fine job. Any progress on our situation?"

"Marooned," said Adam.

"Quite," replied Adam.

"Fuck," said Duke to everyone's laughter.

"Yes, well let's move on," suggested the admiral. "Mister Henry, our food situation, if you please."

"Biggs" Henry stood. He looked hard at the paper before him. "We're lucky," stated the eighteen-year veteran. "My galley is completely stocked. I have food enough for sixty men for four months. That's two thousand one hundred and sixty meals. At three meals a day and sixteen people, we have a year's worth of grub. If we cut back to two meals a day, I can stretch it to eighteen months.

"Of course, we can supplement our stores with fruits, vegetables, and wild game. Eventually, we'll need to replace staples such as flour and sugar, but with a little innovation, I'm sure we can make out. I've got a lot of storage capacity, frozen and refrigerated, and our equipment is good and durable. We can make out well for two years easy, sir."

That was indeed more good news. The entire crew sighed with relief. At least they would not starve to death right away or miss an episode of *Ozzie*.

The admiral went to Glover and Billups, who looked haggard. "What do our dry goods look like, Arnie?"

Glover and Billups rose. Neither was an imposing figure or gifted speaker. Glover proceeded in a glibless monotone. "We have clothing for sixty men, three sets each, all sizes. Plenty of shoes and underwear, both men's and ladies'. Light jackets and sweaters. Gloves and rain gear, hats and socks. Enough for this crew for years. We have water-survival suits but no extreme wear. Heavy coats and winter gear are not onboard."

"We also have a thousand pounds of dry dog food," added Billups.

The admiral shot him a quizzical look. "Dog food? Why does a naval cutter need dog food?"

"Our captain was going to bring his lab onboard," said Chief Hightower. "I guess dogs haven't evolved yet?"

Most of the crew began to think of past pets, their childhood canines and feline friends now long gone, restricted to memories of a distant but past life. Except for Molly, they would never see a cat of any kind again. Most felt a sad pang as they realized this was only the beginning of things missed and longed for. Gone were automobiles, restaurants, and banks. No more sidewalks, parking lots, or grocery stores. Newspapers and libraries—gone. Phone calls and money—gone; missed but not forgotten. Maybe not even missed. Over time, new things would replace other things, wonderful things not yet realized or dreamed. Life evolves, adapts, and overcomes; it goes on, searching and struggling toward some unseen end.

"Well, we'll just have to find another use for the dog food," said the admiral.

"I ate Gravy Train as a kid," snapped Adam.

"Yeah," said Tim. "My dear, departed, sainted mother said I ate dog biscuits as a kid."

"Your mother's alive in Fort Lauderdale," corrected Adam.

"Well, I still ate dog biscuits."

"We're in a Martin and Lewis movie," smiled Kevin. JD and Duke laughed. The twins were refreshingly sardonic, youthful, optimistic, and delightfully ridiculous. They had taken their places as invaluable geniuses and court jesters, an odd but endearing coupling.

"That's fine, lads," said the admiral, "but let's move on. Mister Johnson, please, give us your report."

Ship's mechanic Billy Johnson tipped a greasy hat back high on his balding head and stood. He was a powerfully built man with wrists the size of pop cans. He glanced around the room and adjusted his belt. "The nuclear reactor is functioning perfectly, and our saline extraction unit is working well, so fresh water is no problem. All of the ship's mechanical systems are operating. My machine shop/tool shop is stocked with everything I need. Short term, we're good. I have replacement parts for everything onboard, but over the long haul, we'll need more parts. Things wear out. That will become a problem. I have no manufacturing capabilities, but our energy is as inexhaustible as we can get. The chopper and Zodiacs are solar battery operated so, again, short term, we're okay. Long term, I just don't know." He shook his head and sat.

"Very well, Chief," the admiral said. "And now the ladies. What is our weapons status?"

The three female yeomen, Arabella Samuels, Janice Blackstone, and Dawn Frasier stood as three peas in a pod. If the lads were the twins, these three were the triplets. All were cut from the same Midwestern mold—ruddy complexions; taut, farmhand bodies; wispy, short hair—one blonde, one brunette, one jet black—and sturdy frames. All three looked as if they could make love or war with equal ability. The twins stirred anxiously as Arabella Samuels delivered their report.

"The armory onboard could invade a small county," she began. "We have fifty ***M16's,*** twenty thousand rounds of ammunition, twenty-two nine-millimeter pistols, assorted grenades—smoke, impact, and conventional—C-four mines, two water cannon, three fifty-caliber machine guns, and forty surface-to-air missiles. Plus some personal weapons and a wide range of knives and underwater demolition equipment."

Arabella blushed. She notice the twins staring at her. They looked like puppies eyeing a soup bone. The triplets sat, and the twins broke into thunderous applause.

"Terrific speech," proclaimed Adam unabashedly. "One of the great speakers of our time." He looked at Tim, who was applauding wildly. "My student council could have used someone like her."

"Mine did," answered Tim. More laughter and whooping.

"Okay, settle down, lads." Admiral Fitzgerald had laughed as well. The lads cracked him up. Duke was coming around to them; even Chief Hightower was. He had been convinced laughter had died when the Three Stooges passed away. In his mind, after the Stooges, comedy had gone the way of the Edsel. Today everything was crude bathroom humor spewed out to the lowest common denominator. The masses today went for farcical championship wrestling and the gutter humor of cookie-cutter comedians. The lads seemed to be a cross between the Marx Brothers and *MASH*.

"On a serious level, people," said the admiral, "from this moment on, it's imperative that we conserve everything. We throw nothing away. What used to be disposable is now critical to our survival. Get the most out of everything. If it can be reused or recycled, do it! And no food is to be wasted. Get used to eating things you normally would not.

"Chief Hightower will assign daily chores to everyone on a rotating schedule. It's important that we not become lazy and complacent. I'll leave the lads in charge of entertainment." He glared at the twins cautiously. "Don't let me down, lads."

"Impossible, General," assured Tim.

"That's 'Admiral,' numbnuts," said Duke.

"You can rely on us, sir," Adam saluted.

The group broke and fell to various jobs. A ship that normally required a crew of fifty was making do with sixteen refugees, displaced travelers in a time that did not welcome them. A prehistoric time that was always hunting season for the many predators that roamed this vast, uncharted land. Large-brained mammals of the human variety were the targets of bigger and faster dinosaurs. A stroll through the forest could put them at risk, and a jog on the beach could turn deadly. Twentieth-century weapons might prove to be small deterrents against such large, determined foes. The top of the food chain was many rungs above humanity's head. A cautious life of adaptation was now the norm. Most of the ragtag crew of the *Broadsword* had not fully comprehended that critical lessons in survival were just beginning.

JD stood at the starboard railing, letting his thoughts drift out among the waves of a languid, blue ocean, an indifferent but peaceful sea. Their situation was beyond understanding, beyond the portals of human rumination. Like the others, he felt vexed trying to comprehend the incomprehensible.

After a few moments, Doc Moran joined him at the railing. She stood silent a short while before speaking. "Last night, at the first meeting, you said you knew the stars had moved."

JD looked at her and nodded.

"How? How did you know that?" Her question implied a need to grasp something tangible, something that made sense of the madness. Her eyes searched his eyes for answers that made sense, but in the hazel reflection of his eyes, she saw a man of riddles, circles within circles, an enigma that was reassuring but frightening. His smile erased some fears.

"It was a feeling as much as anything," he said. "And it somehow made sense. I'm no astronomer. I wish I could tell you more, but I can't."

She understood. She saw in him a simple honesty. She knew he would never lie to her. For a moment, it brought ease into her world of confusion. But then a scream ripped across the mantle of her mind. It burned her like a searing, hot iron. She saw her nurse, Natalie Armbruster, screaming hysterically. She and JD raced to the trembling woman who was shaking like someone with malaria.

JD spun her around. "What?" he yelled through her hysteria. "What is it?"

She pointed to the sea, her hand jittering with every sob.

"Arvin was out near the edge," she managed between snivels. "And then . . . and then . . . a fish leaped out of the water and grabbed him off the deck. It just bit him . . . in half. He didn't even scream. It was so fast. Oh my God!" She broke down crying.

Doc Moran took her hand, looked at JD, and took her below. The others had gathered at the deck, but the ocean showed only one sign of shipmate Arvin Billups—a crimson slick that was fading across the swells.

Arnie Glover spoke. "What kind of fish could do that?" The question was on everyone's mind.

"A big, hungry fucking fish," answered Duke. No one disagreed.

Ninety-two million years ago, the earth was a decidedly different place. There was no Gulf of Mexico. That's because there was no Mexico. It was underwater, under a sea that stretched north through North America and Canada, up to the Artic. There were literally beaches in what is now Colorado. Most of the earth was tropical. Most of the continents had not fully formed. Great storms erupted everywhere. Hurricane-force winds and deluges persisted. Volcanic activity was at an apex, and earthquakes, typhoons, and storms of the century happened yearly. The world was a great, unsettled, and fragile place. Life was hardy and resilient. It has to be.

Even human life adapted, as it had in what ninety-two million years from then would be eastern Montana. It was there that a settlement had taken root and stubbornly held on for fourteen hundred years.

On a natural plateau rising sixty feet above a jungle basin, stretching two miles long and a mile wide, the city of New Romanica sat majestically, surveying everything for miles in every direction. Stone building, houses, and temples peppered the lofty mesa in a distinct Roman style. Temples were fashioned for Jove, and relics of Hercules, Mars, and Venus flourished.

In the great hall of the imperial palace, a forlorn emperor, Anthony V, sat on a jeweled throne and moped. His chief advisor,

Gaius Maximus, and General Derbus Aurelius tried to placate the young, headstrong emperor.

"The games go well, sire," said Gaius. "The people love them, and they adore you for it."

"The games are boring, Gaius," the emperor spat back. "Boring. We need new attractions."

"But the young T. rex killed seven gladiators before falling. It was a great spectacle!"

"The animals have grown tiresome. We need human victims."

"Yes, sire," said Aurelius, "but we have an alliance with the giants in the north, and the Slants and Scales do not venture close enough to capture."

"Your raiders need to go farther, general."

"But, sire," he protested. "The wilderness is a savage place. It takes a man of great courage and ingenuity. Plus it will cost much more."

The emperor sighed. He no longer cared about the danger or the cost. "Organize a raiding party. Fifty men, fully provisioned and armed. They are to sweep all the way to the lands of the Slants and bring back slaves for the games. Men—no women or children. And, of course, any other exotics they can find! I want them to leave within the week. And tell the people they can expect new attractions in the arena. Now go!"

The general bowed deeply and left. A smile slowly drew across the emperor's face. New victims for the games would keep his people happy. It always had, all the way back to his ancestors. Keep the mob happy. Bloodlust always did.

He spoke to Gaius. "Bring in the concubines. I feel much better."

There were no concubines aboard the *Broadsword.* Only the lustful looks of the twins every time one of the triplets was around. As the days passed, life became an uneasy routine. Before leaving the island, the crew had stocked up on coconuts, bananas, island squab, and a fruit the twins labeled "prapples," a cross between an apple and a pear.

The third day on the island produced a bonus. A mostly intact whale carcass washed ashore; this meant gallons of whale oil, which could be used as fuel, lubricants and a host of other things, and hundreds of pounds of whale meat, which, with most of the island squab, were designated for Molly. So far she had shown little liking for the dried dog food onboard. Cats were finicky that way, even tigers.

Since the untimely death of Arvin Billups by fish unknown, no other close encounters with predators had occurred. The island had produced only benign wildlife. Flightless birds, land tortoises, and small lizards were the only creatures procreating on this dot of sand in what later would be the Gulf of Mexico. Predators, insects, and humans had not found their way to this prehistoric paradise. Hundreds of miles of volatile ocean guarded its secrets. But the crew of the *Broadsword* had marked it well; the island refuge might prove handy in the future, they thought. This tiny speck of real estate was the beginning of new charts and maps. Because it had been discovered by the *Broadsword* party, the twins dubbed the island "New Brittany." When asked why, they merely shrugged their bony shoulders and said that it had sounded cool. To them, that was reason enough; it only reinforced the belief in everyone else that the twins were a bit screwy.

Using the stars and dead reckoning, the *Broadsword* set a northeast course for what they hoped would be the shores of the future state of Florida. They had been cruising about three hours when Chief Hightower passed the open bay of cargo hold one. He casually glanced in while strolling by. What he saw stopped him dead in his tracks. There was no mistake about what he saw; it was too large to miss. Without delay, he made his way forward to find the admiral.

The admiral was on the bridge enjoying the company of JD and Kevin and engaging in a rousing, delightful conversation about the historical implications of British colonialism. He had been pleasantly surprised to find Kevin and JD well-mannered and well-read.

On his way to find the admiral, Chief Hightower ran into the twins. Since they were the usual suspects, he wasted no time. "Pardon me, boys," he said as politely as a maître d'. "Are you busy?"

"Well, we're just on our way to the Lido deck for a round of shuffleboard before happy hour," stated Tim. The boys were dressed like tourists on the *Love Boat*—Hawaiian shirts, baggy shorts, sandals, and sunglasses. Each had a golf club slung over a shoulder. Chief Hightower was unimpressed.

"This will just take a moment, boys. I was just past cargo bay one and noticed a turtle in the hold." The boys smiled routinely. "You boys wouldn't happen to know why it's there, would you?"

"Sure," said Adam. "We put him there. It was the only place large enough."

"Him?" asked the chief, knowing he would never understand.

"Norton," said Tim. "We named him Norton. And he's a land tortoise, not a turtle. Turtles live in the water. Norton is a tortoise."

And I'm an idiot for having this conversation, thought the chief. But since he was in this far . . . "The admiral knows about Norton?"

"Of course," said Adam. "He said we could get a pet. Plus, Norton saved our lives."

"Saved your lives?" Naturally, a dumb question.

"Yeah," went Tim. "We were sitting under a coconut tree and a large coconut fell. Norton was behind us and the coconut hit his shell. It might have killed us."

Adam added. "And you know that old Chinese proverb stolen by Gypsies that says, 'If someone saves your life, that someone is able to sponge off you for the rest of your life.'"

The boys smiled as if everything made perfect sense; the chief, however, was getting impatient with these twin sons from different mothers. Going from a calm voice to a building crescendo, he asked, "Does the admiral know that 'tortoise' is as big as a VW Bug? A pet is a goldfish or a gerbil. Norton must weigh a thousand pounds."

"Closer to two thousand," said Tim meekly.

"A goddamned ton! What does he eat?"

"Mostly prapples and palm fronds. But don't worry, Chief. We're going to train him. We're building a litter box tomorrow."

"What?" The chief was in a funk. He threw up his arms and walked off, muttering to himself. The twins, clubs in hand, headed topside.

On the bridge, the admiral and JD were laughing. Kevin had told a joke he'd heard before leaving Galveston. The punch line had all three men chortling. The chief walked in and felt the contagious laughter and chuckled mildly.

"Excuse me, sir," he said.

"What's on your mind, Chief?" asked a still-sniggering admiral.

"It's the twins, sir."

"The lads?"

"Yes, sir. You told them they could have a pet?"

"Yes I did, Chief. Thought it would be good to make them responsible for something. Said to keep it a low-maintenance pet. What'd they get? A lizard? A bird?"

"No, sir. They have a tortoise in cargo bay one. Named him Norton."

"Those boys are cards, I'll tell you. So, what's the flapdoodle, chief?"

"It's a large tortoise, admiral," interjected Kevin.

"It's a two-thousand-pound prehistoric tortoise, Admiral," boomed the chief. "There are smaller automobiles back in 2002. It's nuts, sir. These boys are not normal."

"The lads are a bit unorthodox, I'll admit, chief, but as long as they take care of 'Norton,' let's leave it alone. Sometimes, genius can be eccentric, you know."

"Admiral, *eccentric* is too soft a word. These boys are crackers. Warped. Looney. Nincompoops!"

"I'll speak to them, Chief. Anything else?"

"Yes, sir. Doctor Moran needs to see you as soon as possible."

"Thank you, Chief. I'm coming straightaway. Captain Stoner, you and Kevin have the bridge."

JD nodded. He and Kevin rather enjoyed guiding the big ship through the blue waters of this ancient ocean. Every hour that passed, they saw something new. Sometimes exciting, sometimes frightening. They had seen twenty-foot sharks leap out of the water like dolphins in a marine show. Giant pterosaurs with wingspans of thirty feet drifted by like reapers against a powder-blue sky. Great schools fish had registered on sonar; they must have had hundreds of thousands of fish each. On sonar, they lit up like speeding submarines. And then there were the giants of the deep. Earlier, they had spotted a *Liopleurodon* cruising by without a care. Kevin estimated its size to be at least a hundred and twenty feet. It looked like a submerged aircraft carrier. They had seen large birds venture too close to the surf only to be snatched and gulped down whole by a variety of predatory fish. Sharks were everywhere—large, small, and everything in between. The wide expanse of the ocean yielded every horror man could dream. Patrolling monsters seemed to be everywhere. Ferocious birds and winged dinosaurs cruised the horizons in search of anything traveling too close to the surface.

The *Broadsword*, with its shining metal reflecting like a mirror to the heavens, was not bothered by any of the winged denizens; even the largest of the oceans creatures let it pass without incident. Some sharks and early dolphin cousins swam alongside, but most ignored the ship or viewed it as an awkward inconvenience. This wonderfully strange surface vessel was too large a prey to be reckoned with.

The *Broadsword* skimmed along undisturbed. The sun, high in the azure sky, melted the day; the humans had to get used to days when the temperature nearly always topped ninety-five degrees. The humidity was thick, but westerly ocean breezes kept it bearable. Kevin pointed to his right as a swooping bird dove at the waves. It missed its target and narrowly escaped a large dolphin with jaws of serrated teeth that sprang from the depths in an effort to make lunch of the squawking bird.

The skies were gradually becoming thicker with flying animals, which JD and Kevin took as a sign that land might be near. The island had proven to be a good break, but the sight of real land, a part of a continent, would have a settling effect on everyone. At least that was the hope.

They were sure Florida was not the old Florida of Disney World, Miami Beach, and Jewish retirement communities, but it did offer a bridge to their old world, an identifiable memory in a vast, uncharted frontier. In a world of gloom, hope was necessary.

The nuclear-powered cutter silently whisked along, the foreign world through which it traveled completely uninterested.

Emperor Anthonius V was very interested in seeing off the raiding party. Fifty of the kingdom's hardest men, best trackers, and most-ruthless mercenaries had been summoned. These marauders faced a perilous journey. Predatory dinosaurs lurked around every bend. Bigger, faster, and with better sensory perception, these animals never passed up a chance for a meal. And humans were good eating.

The men would be traveling light, which meant leather armor, short swords, and lances. They would forage and hunt for food, and cages for quarry would be built on-site. Their journey would be a long one. To the edge of the land of the Slants was at least a twenty-day march. The entire trip was expected to take three months, and some of them, they knew, would never see their beloved city of New Romanica again. Predators, accidents, and disease would take their tolls.

The emperor eyed the group with satisfaction. It was commanded by Marcus Sardonius. Like all New Romanicans, he was short, heavily muscled, and had a ruddy complexion. A jigsaw-shaped scar crossed his forehead, a grim appearance that exuded confidence. A veteran of many raiding expeditions and of the Giant Wars, he was one of the emperor's favorites.

The emperor smiled and clutched his wrist and elbow. "You look well, Marcus. I am sorry for the loss of your brother. He was a great Romanican."

Marcus nodded. The memory of his late brother was still fresh. He had been killed by a stegosaurus a month previously. The gentle, plant-eating dinosaur had turned abruptly in fright, and its tail came around and crushed his brother's ribcage. A simple hunting trip had turned deadly. Such was life in this primordial place.

The emperor seemed puzzled. "I thought a giant was going with you."

"Yes, sire, there is. He will join us at the end of the Great Basin. He should prove very useful."

"Very good," said the delighted emperor. "Do not fail me, Marcus. The kingdom needs new foes in the arena. The people demand it, and as their supreme emperor, I am obliged to deliver. See to this, my friend, and you shall be greatly rewarded."

Marcus raised his fist to his chest in proper salute. "Depend on me, sire."

"I am in your capable hands." The emperor bowed.

A surge of pride swelled in Marcus's chest as well as in his men. He had never let the emperor down, and he was not about to now.

"Good journey," said the emperor, waving a dismissing hand. The men saluted and filed out.

The land of the Slants lay to the south. To the Romanicans they were merely filthy, yellow-skinned vermin. Good only for fodder in the arena. They died well. The mob loved a good death.

Death loomed in the sights of everyone onboard the *Broadsword*. After a three-day journey, they had finally come upon land. Anchored some fifty yards offshore in a hundred feet of water, the crew stood transfixed as they spied beaches through binoculars. The beach of fine, white sand looked like a great sugar highway running to each horizon. But what had everyone enamored was the sight of an old wooden galleon aground, weathered and rotting on the otherwise virgin seashore. The old frigate meant humans had been there before. The thought sprang that maybe they were not alone. Maybe others had suffered a similar fate and were waiting to welcome them. It seemed fantastic, yet hopeful.

The faded paint of the ship's moniker was still readable. The Portuguese was strange to everyone but JD. He mouthed the English translation for all to hear. "*Hag of Mendoza*."

"Cool," said the twins in unison.

"Lads, get on your computer and find out about this ship. Everything," the admiral said.

In a flash they were gone.

"What do you think?" Kevin asked JD as they surveyed the old ship.

"The name sounds like pirates. But who knows? One thing for sure, though, we aren't the first humans in this time. If we have survivors, they probably did too. That ship's at least two hundred years old, maybe older."

"Let's go ashore and check it out," Duke said. "There could be tons of gold on that fucked-up tub."

"You volunteering?" asked Kevin.

"You're damned right. I think a sound financial mind should be around. There might be a bonus."

"If there is, where you gonna spend it? Seen any malls or car lots around?"

"Funny, dickweed! I'll just hoard it, and if we ever get out of this queered-up clusterfuck, I'll be rich."

"You're already rich," proclaimed Kevin. "Richly stupid."

"Fuck you."

The argument ended as the twins returned to the deck. They had in tow a computer printout and beamed like stadium lights. They stood there, enjoying their secrets for a moment.

Duke was impatient. Imagine that. "So give, you sawed-off, rummy fucks. What's the dirt on that rotting hulk of shit?"

Tim led off. "The *Hag of Mendoza* was originally a Portuguese frigate. It was commandeered in 1756 by the pirate Rene Lafleur the Red and converted to a privateer. It was said to have twenty-four cannon and to have attacked and plundered over twenty merchant ships. It was last seen in the Gulf of Mexico in 1759. It is presumed to have sunk in a storm, because no record exists of any man-of-war encountering her after that year."

"The ship simply vanished by all accounts," added Adam. "Sound familiar?"

The admiral adjusted his glasses. "You mean—"

"Exactly," said Adam. "The *Hag of Mendoza* probably hit a storm like us and ended up here two hundred and fifty years ago."

"Cool," said Tim.

"Quite," said the admiral. "I'll need a scouting party. Captain Stoner? You, Kevin, Arabella, and Chief Hightower will take a Zodiac to check out the ship. The ship only. We'll stay in touch by radio. Be ready to go in fifteen minutes."

Duke was about to protest, but the admiral cut him off. "If they require a strong financial mind, you'll be the first to go," he said, holding up a hand.

Duke eased back. But the twins wanted to go also. "What about us, admiral?" asked Tim. He was obviously crestfallen.

"Sorry, lads. Until everything is proven safe, the rest of us wait here, you included."

They both made frowny faces. Duke stuck his tongue out at them, and they moped off like kids told to go take baths.

The Zodiac crew of JD, Kevin, Arabella, and Chief Hightower arrived at the ghost ship, the erstwhile *Hag of Mendoza*, and found a gutted, decaying, half-buried and brooding frame of a once-proud pirates' ship. JD and Chief Hightower ventured onto the old ship while Kevin and Arabella waited outside. Kevin shouldered an M16. Arabella, dressed in fatigues with sleeves cut off at the shoulders, sported an M16, six percussion grenades, a Ka-Bar military knife, and a MAC-10 machine pistol. She looked like a female Rambo. Kevin couldn't help think that it was either the best-ever Halloween costume or she was planning an invasion. He thought better not to ask. She stood guard as if expecting the worst. Her finger tensed on the hair trigger of the MAC-10. Kevin wisely positioned himself behind her.

On the *Hag of Mendoza*, JD and the chief tiptoed around broken, three-hundred-year-old planks and timbers. The deck was pitted and pocked like the surface of the moon. Rusted iron and splintered wood were cast about like garbage from many years of uncaring weather. They slowly made their way below decks. It was like skating on Jell-O. Every step was eventful. Half-disintegrated stairs cracked and broke with every movement. Below was a maelstrom of wreckage. Once-fierce cannon lay ravaged by time and rust, monuments to a time of pillage and plunder.

Three complete skeletons were found below. Two were all the way forward, where it appeared they had made a last, desperate stand against some enemy. Ramshackle barricades, brittle with time, had offered little defense for the trapped pirates. The door to the captain's quarters lay open, and across the threshold, the third skeleton sprawled in death. Its shiny white bones stared up from a two-hundred-and-fifty-year nap.

There was nothing to salvage. The ship was dead, a memorial to the ravages of time. JD rummaged around the floor and picked up a piece of plank and turned it over. On the distressed wood was a warning from a dying man, written in blood. In English, it read, "Beware the leapers." The chief and JD looked at each other. "What's a leaper?" asked the chief.

JD shrugged. "No idea. Maybe it's misspelled. Maybe it's 'leper,' as in 'leper colony.'"

But neither he nor the chief believed that. Why would pirates fear lepers? And why would a dying man leave that as his last earthly message? It made no sense. But then, nothing had made sense recently.

As they contemplated the dead pirate's puzzle, Arabella and Kevin shouted from outside. JD and the chief rushed topside to find their friends gesturing toward the dense growth of the jungle that started some fifty yards up the beach. Arabella was pissed. "Goddamn. There's something up there moving around. Watching us. I can feel it. The hairs on the back of my neck are standing like tits in winter."

JD agreed. He too sensed something in the undergrowth, a sinister presence that seemed to be sizing them up. "Let's get back to the ship," said the chief. "No one's going near that jungle until we know what's out there." They all agreed and were soon on the Zodiac, speeding back to the *Broadsword*.

The whole time, Duke and the admiral had watched them through binoculars. "Something's spooked them," said the admiral.

"Scared the shit out of them, I'd say."

"We'll know soon enough, Duke. Damned peculiar, though. Damned peculiar."

In the theater of the *Broadsword*, JD and Chief Hightower made their report. All listened with perked ears. None of it made sense to the crew, just as it had not made sense to the scouting party.

"So you think 'leapers' is really 'lepers'?" asked Adam.

"I don't know," said JD. "It's English, but British English two hundred and fifty years old and written by a dying man. There are probably many possibilities. My guess is that the pirates landed on that beach two hundred and fifty years ago with a crew of fifty or sixty. We found only three skeletons, and the warning implies something fatal happened to the rest of the crew."

"We all felt it," said Arabella. "There's something in that jungle. Something was stalking us. Planning."

"Other humans?" asked Dawn Frasier.

"We couldn't see. But it felt menacing. Evil."

"So what do we do?" asked Adam.

"The chopper," said JD. "We fly over the jungle and check it out. From the air, it shouldn't be a problem." It seemed simple. Spy from the air.

"Just one problem," said the chief. "No one onboard can fly the thing."

JD looked at Kevin. "Kev, any problems flying that chopper?" JD knew there was not. Kevin could fly anything. He was a natural, the best pilot JD had ever seen or known. Kevin had flown everything from a jumbo jet to a one-man prop.

"You're a pilot?" asked the admiral.

Modestly, Kevin nodded yes. "I've looked at the chopper at some length. It's a sophisticated toy, but yes, I can fly it. Probably blindfolded. It's a lightweight recon chopper. Four people only. I'm assuming a rescue chopper was being added in Florida. It has a range of about fifty miles one way. Solar batteries good for eight hours' operation. I can scout the jungle in about two hours, no problem."

The admiral thought a moment. "Kevin, get the chopper ready. Arabella, Dawn, and Arnie will ride shotgun and scout. Arm yourselves for bear. I don't want anybody taking any chances. JD, I'd like to see you and Duke on the bridge in ten minutes. Chief Hightower, supervise the chopper arrangements. Everyone else, return to your duties."

On the bridge, the admiral said, "JD, I'd like you and Duke to stand by with a Zodiac during the chopper flight in case of an emergency. If they should need help for any reason, I want someone ready to go right away."

Both men agreed.

"That pirate ship may have been abandoned or may have met another fate. The skeletons onboard lead me to believe the latter. We're down to fifteen people and can't afford to lose anyone else. We will not be careless. Questions?"

JD said matter-of-factly, "If there's a problem in the jungle, Molly and I will go. I have some experience with that, sir. You'll have to trust me."

The admiral eyed him with suspicion but then shook his head in agreement. Without asking or knowing why, he knew JD spoke the truth. Considering himself an excellent judge of character, the admiral instinctively knew he could trust JD.

"The cat can be controlled and relied on?" the admiral asked. He had no idea his question was unnecessary. Even Duke, who was no fan of Molly's, knew she and JD shared a bond and communication level that was at least different and at most astonishing. Molly was more reliable than most humans Duke had known.

"Let's put it this way," said JD, "I'll not go without her."

The admiral turned to Duke. "Mister Duke, from the moment that chopper leaves this ship, you are to watch that beach. Understood? Your eyes never leave it."

Without cursing, Duke said, "We're family now, Admiral. I'll never let any of you down. My word, sir." There was a certain pride in his confession.

Even JD was moved by Duke's admission. He knew Duke was many things, but he had never known him to lie or to break his word. Despite his bombastic demeanor and his outrageous vocabulary, Duke was a marshmallow at heart, a heart as big as the primeval ocean they floated on.

"Give me a hand," JD said, leaving the bridge.

"Real funny, douchebag. I only got one, you know!"

Then everything was back to normal, as normal as normal gets on the wayward *Broadsword.*

The *Broadsword* chopper was a Bell & Howell four-seater ultralite. Except for the whopping of the rotor blades, it was surprisingly quiet. The solar batteries charged the bird's electrical plant, and everything hummed like an electric toothbrush. Arabella, Dawn, and Arnie had strapped in, and Kevin gave a thumbs-up for liftoff. The admiral, one hand on his hat, signaled back, and the small craft began to rise.

At fifty feet above the *Broadsword*, the chopper dipped forward and began a steep climb. Everyone but Kevin fought to keep down breakfast. Arnie felt eggs rise in his throat. "Sorry, folks," he apologized. "It's been a while."

Dawn Frazier swallowed hard as her fingers dug into the armrest of her seat. A few moments over the ocean, Kevin had the copter performing like he was in an air show. The others found their stomachs and settled down. Kevin gave a quick wave to those on the *Broadsword* as they flew by the ship toward the jungle awning ahead.

As they breached the line of trees, they entered a hostile, ruthless world. Below them lay a dense, tropical universe, and they soon realized the giant conifers that sprouted toward the sky hid everything below. Only a few scattered openings offered a glimpse of the forest floor.

Arabella was the first to speak. "I can't see squat! That tree coverage is denser than bees at a hive."

"I'll make a couple of more passes and then head home. Sing out if you see anything," said Kevin.

They were flying at treetop level. Kevin dared not go any lower. It was frustrating because the jungle ceiling seemed impenetrable. Kevin decided to bank left and take one more swing around when the whirring blades startled a flock of large birds resting in the tops of several great conifers. The frightened bevy of birds took flight as one; the sky was a sudden kaleidoscope of flapping wings and screeching animals. The soaring helicopter found itself awash in terrified birds as the panicked flock flew helter-skelter and ran headlong into the chopper. The great rotor blades slashed and mutilated dozens.

Birds flew beak-first into chopper windows, and several windows cracked from the impact. Kevin fought the stick for control. The small copter zigzagged from the pummeling and then with the suddenness of a pickpocket, the chopper lurched and began spinning out of control. It spun wildly, like a carnival ride, pitching the occupants around like pinballs. Through the whirlwind, Kevin clung desperately to the control stick. Downward went the wounded helicopter, the jungle racing toward it at breakneck speed. Pirouetting out of control, Kevin did the only thing possible: he looked for a soft spot to land, a small clearing. As the main rotor blades narrowly missed several unforgiving trees, the small copter finally thumped to an abrupt landing. Kevin checked to make sure all his teeth were intact. For a moment, the world was still. The four inspected themselves for injuries. Everyone appeared fine. Arabella was pissed. "Goddamned birds," she spat. "They could have killed us."

"They still might," said Kevin. "Let's check out the damage."

The four slowly ventured out as strangers in a strange world. The chopper was dented and marred. Bird parts decorated the outside. Splashes of blood and guts coated window glass and paint. Kevin noticed the real problem—the rear rotor blade had been severely bent, almost at a right angle. It had caused the tail to spin and he knew the small chopper could not take off as it was. He switched on the radio and called the *Broadsword.*

Admiral Fitzgerald and JD listened from the bridge.

"We hit a flock of large birds," Kevin reported. "They bent the rear rotor blade. We landed safely, but we're grounded. The blade has to be replaced or pounded back into shape or I can't take off. It sucks, but that's it." The disappointment was obvious in his voice. It dripped with regret.

"Where are you, Kev?" asked JD.

"About two clicks due east of you. But this jungle is dense. Really dense. Flying over, we couldn't see through the canopy. We'll secure the chopper and head back shortly on foot. We have emergency rations, water, and we're armed. We should be okay. We have no injuries. Two hours, and we should be back."

"Stay in radio communication. We'll meet you guys at the beach. And, Kev," added JD, "Don't fool around. That jungle may be dense, but it's alive. Even if you stumble onto the fountain of youth, get back here pronto."

Kevin suddenly remembered the pirate ship. "We're on our way," he said.

The Romanican raiding party had been on its way for several days. The Romanicans had been moving south along a crest line but needed to turn west in another day. So far, they had been lucky. Skirting the jungle basin and sticking to the rock outcrops, they had avoided major predators. They hadn't seen a single T. rex or any raptors. They had brought down a juvenile sauropod the day before and had feasted on steaks that night. The meat from that single kill would last them for weeks. They had managed to butcher what they needed before any scavengers had arrived to claim the carcass.

In their unsettled world, they had many things to fear besides the animals that wanted to eat them; they faced the possibilities of rock slides, geothermal releases of gases, poisonous hot springs that reached temperatures of 190 degrees, quicksand, and boggy mud that gripped like a fist and could suck a man down. Killer plants with toxic fluids, great thorns and spikes, irritating rashes, and trapping sap dotted the landscape. Plants, like animals, were evolving too. They killed and attacked to survive. Competition for space and the sun's rays was fierce.

Then there were the insects—legions of biting flies and ravenous mosquitoes, and armies of ants and termites, all jumbo-sized compared to their cousins in the twentieth century.

But the raiders had moved easily around these potential pitfalls. At night, they slept on cleared ground warmed by numerous fires. Animals and insects alike steered clear of fire, man's ultimate defense. It would be another four or five days before they could expect to see signs of the Slants. The Slants' great kingdom lay far to the south, but over the years, small settlements had moved increasingly north. Groups of fifty to sixty had ventured out, seeking the refuge of the wilderness. Like the early settlers of North America many years in the future, these settlers braved the elements and a wide assortment of dangers to live free and close to nature.

The leader of the group, Marcus Sardonis, knew each of these colonies held perhaps twenty to thirty able-bodied slaves. Old people and children would be put to the sword immediately; they couldn't travel and were useless in the arena. Women would be used until the men were sated, and then they would be killed. They were distractions and did not travel well, and the kingdom had enough whores and concubines.

The invaders pressed on, hoping they would soon be capturing slaves and raping women. They would be richly rewarded by a generous emperor. The Slants, after all, were good only for slaves; they were well below the station of even the lowest Romanican. Some proved capable swordsmen, but otherwise, they were a race of hideous savages. Even their language was strange—short, broken sounds that only confused the mind. The Romanicans had no use for such primitives except in the arena, the hypnotic spectacle the mob reveled in daily. In a land and time of extreme violence, blood in the white sand of the arena was the only pacifier for the masses. Death in all its grisly forms seemed never to be enough. More was always needed. And it was enjoyed.

The crash survivors were not enjoying themselves. The first thing they were forced to do was douse themselves with insect repellent. Flies and mosquitoes wasted no time zeroing in on the human quarry. Only moments after they secured the chopper, the forest around them came alive. Clicks and chirps began rumbling from the underbrush. Arabella and Dawn leveled their weapons at the curious sounds. There was movement. Shadowy flashes among the trees. More clacks and whistles. Then stirrings from behind trees and undergrowth, the rustling of dead leaves and broken branches. Then more chirps and chortles. It was louder now. Bolder. Closer.

Arnie Glover, pistol in hand, thought he saw a head peer around a tree and capped off a round at the would-be menace. The sound ripped through the fabric of the forest and startled everyone. Dawn jumped for cover, Arabella cursed, and Kevin jerked up and cracked his head on the bent rear prop. "Fuck!" he muttered in pain. "What are you shooting at?"

But Arnie did not have time to respond. A form sprung from the bush, and something slashed him across the back from shoulder to shoulder. He screamed and fell forward, attempting to clutch his back. The gaping wound gushed blood into his hair and down his neck as he fell. Before he could recover, two figures rushed from the entanglement of trees and dragged his flailing body into the undergrowth. Screams pierced everyone's ears. Mind-numbing death wails. They knew he was being ripped apart alive.

Arabella began blasting anything that moved. Another figure raced across the small clearing and rammed Dawn from behind. The blow was sufficient to knock the wind out of her and send her flying. Kevin had fired at two figures and ran to Dawn's aid. Arabella continued to mow down the forest. Splintered branches and leaves filled the air, and in the streaking sunlight, they seemed suspended.

Kevin got Dawn to her feet and was screaming instructions. He fired three more rounds. Arnie's death shrieks had been lost in the gunfire, but everyone knew he was dead. The only sounds from his direction were the ripping of flesh and the cracking of bones.

Pointing behind Arabella, Kevin said, "Get to those rocks over there. Cover us." She did. The forest exploded again as she randomly leveled everything in a killing field of twenty yards. Kevin ran with Dawn, who was vomiting. He could feel the warmth down his leg and socks. Arabella continued to back up and blast away. A moment later, Kevin was helping Dawn sit in a small cave among the rocks. Her breath was coming back in hard puffs, and her head was clearing. Kevin joined Arabella at the perimeter and placed a hand on her shoulder.

"That's enough," he said quietly, "for now. They're gone. Relax."

She looked at Kevin. Her eyes flashed horror; her finger was still on the trigger. "They were as big as us."

"I know. But faster and stronger. Arnie never had a chance." Kevin remembered the terrible screams. "What do we do? It's two clicks to the beach."

Kevin did not answer. He had the radio to his mouth and began talking.

"*Broadsword*?" he said. "This is Scout One. Do you copy?"

"Go ahead, Scout One," responded the admiral; Duke, JD, Moran, and Chief Hightower listened.

"We got trouble with a capital tee. We've been attacked and are under siege. Glover's dead!"

There was a strained silence for a moment. JD asked, "What, Kev? What attacked you?"

"A bunch of animals as big as men but much faster and stronger. Definitely dinosaurs. Muscular hind legs, gripping short arms, rows of razor teeth, feathery coats, and camouflaged. They blend into everything."

JD held his hand over the mike. The twins had joined them. "What do you think?" he asked. But he was afraid he already knew.

Adam said, "It's got to be raptors."

"They're in deep shit," added Duke.

JD took his hand from the mike. "Sounds like raptors, Kev. Is your position secure?"

"Christ, I thought so. Yes, for now we're secure. We took shelter in a cave about fifty yards from the chopper. Dawn was slightly hurt but should be okay. We'll stand by while you guys figure out how to get us the hell out of here."

"I'll call you in fifteen minutes, Kev. Hang tough." JD switched off the mike.

"We form an armed party, go into the jungle, and pull them out," said the admiral. Everyone seemed in agreement. Everyone but JD.

"No," he said flatly. "The risk is too great. We don't know how many raptors are out there or what else might be out there. We could be walking into a buzz saw."

"What do you have in mind?" asked Duke.

JD took a deep breath. "At dusk, Molly and I will go in with parts for the chopper, repair it, and fly them out. Under cover of darkness, we can slip in and get them out."

Everyone looked at JD.

"I'll take a radio and stay in touch. I know how to do this, admiral. I'll get them out."

The admiral believed him. He pointed to the radio. JD explained the plan to Kevin. Kev liked it. He knew JD. He also gave him rough estimates on the size of the damaged rear prop. Mr. Johnson felt he could make something in the next three hours that could get the chopper airborne. A plan in place, all parties began preparations.

Arabella, however, was not keen on the plan. "That's nuts," she told Kevin. "Your friend and his pet tiger are going to sneak in here and help. Right! And the pope's Jewish!"

"You don't know him, Arabella," said Kevin. "He's very resourceful and unique."

"That's great. A carnival act against a jungle of those mindless killers. Jeez, I feel so much better."

"You will tomorrow," Kevin promised. "Let's build a fire. They won't come around it, and it'll help disguise our smell. How you doing, Dawn?"

Dawn smiled. "Much better. I'll help with whatever you need. I'm sorry about Arnie."

They all were. They began to make a fire.

The twins were following JD around like disciples. He was in the armory with Yeoman Blackstone. "Damn," he said in frustration. "If I only had my stuff. Everything was in my golf bag on the *Rhinelander*."

The twins looked at each other. Tim asked, "A golf bag?"

"Yeah," said JD.

"A brown-and-white golf bag?"

"You've seen it?"

"It's in our room," said Adam. "Duke and Kevin had it with them when we rescued them. Sure, we got it."

JD smiled. "Cool!"

"We borrowed a couple of clubs," admitted Tim.

"Get the bag, boys."

Yeoman Blackstone thought she was assisting JD but soon realized he needed her assistance in the armory about as much as he needed bridgework. He had already selected jungle fatigues, boots, Visney Tek night-vision goggles, compass, and a canteen. She was trying to talk him into an M16 when the twins arrived with JD's golf bag. He grabbed the bag, spun it around, and pulled down a side zipper. Reaching in, he withdrew a samurai sword and a pistol case. The twins looked stunned; they hadn't known about the side pocket.

"These are all I'll need, Yeoman," said JD, unsheathing the sword. The blade shone like a mirror. Both twins mouthed *Cool!*

"This is a titanium blade perfectly balanced for me at three hundred and sixty grams. The metal has been folded over two hundred times. It can chop through a cinder block. It was made for me by an old craftsman in Japan."

Yeoman Blackstone lifted the blade; it was light as a feather. She knew weapons. "This is impossible. You need heat of two thousand degrees to forge titanium, and folded over two hundred times? Impossible."

"Yet here it is," said JD. He opened the pistol case and withdrew an odd-looking weapon. It was short barreled with a dull, black finish. It looked more plastic than metal.

"This is a nine-millimeter Anschluss GMBH. It fires a T-round composite of ceramic and Teflon."

The yeoman was dumfounded. She had never seen such a thing. It was a work of art. She held it with reverence, like a precious stone, a priceless painting. In astonishment, she said, "This is graphite. No movable metallic parts, and the rounds would go through an elephant long ways. This too is impossible."

"A prototype," said JD.

The twins and Yeoman Blackstone were looking sideways at JD. "Just who the hell are you?" asked the yeoman. Prototype weapon, experimental rounds, and a sword that rivaled Excalibur meant this was no ordinary ferrier of boats.

"John David Stoner," said Adam. He pronounced each name as if he were filling out a tax return, making sure each name was correct. He looked at both boys; he immediately understood. In a tombstone voice, he said, "It won't help. Not even you geniuses can find out. Leave it alone."

A chill rippled through the twins and the yeoman; ice ran down their spines. Just who the hell was this man? James Bond? 007?

The forest floor was covered in shadows as the sun began to fall. Kevin and Arabella had a blazing fire going. Flames danced and leaped as green wood popped in defiance. The simple ruse had worked. The raptors kept their distance, but they were close—Arabella's neck hairs were sure of that. Even in the heat of the jungle, however, the fire had a soothing effect. Dawn was doing well except for a large bruise across her upper back. Kevin had had the foresight to grab the emergency kit from the chopper; they had food and water in the form of protein bars and bottled Evian, plus a small medical kit. Dawn was doped up on Tylenol for the pain in her back.

The fire helped everything. Insects stayed away, and the smoke helped with mosquitoes and the smell. The jungle had a reptile-house smell, dank and sweaty. The smell of the fire was at least familiar; it reminded them of backyard barbeques or bonfires. But just when the three would find themselves drifting off to other places, a whistle or chortle of an anxious raptor would shatter the silence, shred peaceful moments, and bring them back to a grim reality.

Dawn asked, "Can your friend JD really make it through to help us?"

In the shadows of the evening, Kevin's face told the story. "If anyone can, it's him. But tonight, he's not JD Stoner. Tonight, he's Nomad, and tonight, I would not want to get in his way."

Puzzled looks etched the women's faces; they knew nothing of Nomad.

The sun had now sunk to that line between earth and sky and would soon be gone for many hours. JD and Molly were speeding to shore in the Zodiac as the twins joined the admiral and Duke at the bridge. Doc Moran was there as well.

"JD was right," Tim said. "We couldn't find out anything about him. It's very impressive. We hacked nearly all the government's most secret files, and though his name is there, there's nothing else. The only thing the files say is that he's a 'specialist.'"

"What kind of 'specialist?'" asked the curious admiral.

"No idea," claimed Adam. "Just 'specialist.' It says nothing else."

"A soldier?" asked the doctor.

"A ghost," said Duke softly. "The perfect man for this job. I know these raptors are bad motherstabbers, but they have no idea what's about to enter their world."

"And what's that?" the doctor asked.

Duke stared out at the beach and jungle for a moment. "Death, doctor. Tonight he's the grim fucking reaper."

JD did not believe in the grim reaper. Death was something he had long learned to deal with. It was after all, inevitable. It could be fought and postponed but never defeated. JD simply did not think of it.

He secured the Zodiac on the beach. In the three-quarter light of the prehistoric moon, the beach had a "wish you were here" postcard look. The white sand's reflection of the moonlight challenged the darkness. JD sat next to Molly and checked the transmitter bleeping a signal from the downed chopper. Two miles due east. He whispered in the big cat's ear, "Stay close. No sounds." The tiger yawned.

A moment later, the dark jungle swallowed them. He felt stupid. How could he have made such a mistake? He had not been in the jungle ten minutes before he realized his miscalculation. The raptors were nocturnal. In the dark, their eyes were as good as Molly's, and they were everywhere. Hundreds, maybe more. JD thought the area must be some sort of nest site—a hatchery or breeding spot. There were just too many animals. He thought of his own time when penguins, seals, and walrus converged on the same beach or ice every year to mate and hatch eggs. If dinosaurs really were more like birds, it made sense. Many bird groups congregated annually or semiannually in the same area to breed. But to stumble into a raptor breeding area was the epitome of bad luck. In addition to all their other endearing qualities, they were excited, territorial, and defensive of their young. Mothers would be in a protective state, and males would be in a sexual frenzy. Throw in some hapless human intruders and the mix became an orgy of destruction.

The jungle was very dark; only scattered moonbeams pierced the heavy canopy of trees and spreading vines. JD and Molly eased along like wraiths among the vegetation. They too melted into the background. JD was sure the raptors could smell them, but Molly's odor was new and probably alarming. She outweighed the raptors at least two to one, and they must have sensed danger in approaching her. JD felt he was safe in her presence. At least he hoped so.

Mr. Johnson had fashioned a replacement rear prop from a piece of steel. It was not exact, but it needed to work only long enough to get the chopper back to the *Broadsword*. JD had it strapped to his back, and it was killing him. It weighed near ninety pounds and was very awkward. Sneaking through an unfamiliar jungle at night surrounded by raptors was not his idea of a swell time. He stopped a moment to rest.

The last two times he had stopped, the raptors had probed his position. They were smart and were getting bolder. Molly had killed two in the last twenty minutes. The bravado of the two raptors had proved their demise. With a powerful left paw, she had broken one's neck and slashed the other's abdomen, spilling its guts like a broken garbage bag spills trash. JD had decapitated two others, but the raptors appeared to be learning from their mistakes; they became more wary, more cautious. The devil's games are not restricted to those confined in hell. The raptors were opportunistic and patient.

As JD and Molly forged ahead, the raptors cut off their retreat. JD could swear they were forming strategies. He had been stalked before, but not like this. This was like being tracked by a combination bloodhound and Apache. The weight of the prop dragged on him, but he knew he could not stop again. The raptors would come in numbers next time. He did not like that prospect. They pushed on, JD in the lead and Molly the rear guard. The smell of Kevin's fire told them they were close.

"I hate this," said Arabella to anyone who would listen; in this case, it was Kevin and Dawn. "Waiting is bad for us and good for them."

Kevin understood her uneasiness. He was near cracking himself. He was about to engage Arabella when he heard a familiar whistle, a whistle not native to the ancient forest.

"Hear that?" he said.

"What is it?" went Dawn.

"Well it ain't a blue jay." Kevin returned the whistle. Like apparitions from another dimension, JD and Molly walked into the firelight. Molly brushed against Dawn, nearly toppling her. She stopped, yawned, and lay down. The big cat panted heavily. Without knowing or understanding why, Dawn sat next to her and patted her enormous head.

JD looked at Kevin. "Nice night. Mind if we sit by your fire a while?"

"Help yourself," said Kevin. "Appreciate you taking your sweet time."

"Nice night for a stroll. You in a hurry?"

"And leave this garden spot? You nuts? I got a great moon, a roaring fire, and two gorgeous dames. Why would I want to leave?"

Arabella was ready to leave. "You vaudevillians done?" she asked. She had had enough of the Redford-Newman routine. In her mind, it was time to go; she figured the boys could work on their comedy act later. "Can we go now?" The haste in her voice said it all.

JD was in no hurry though. He had just lugged a ninety-pound prop two clicks through the jungle, but he understood the yeoman's urgency. "Not yet," he said. "We'll leave at daylight."

He was about to explain why when two raptors came screaming from the darkness. In an instant, JD and Molly reacted. JD drew his sword and in two blinding movements killed one raptor. Molly sprang and tackled the other. As they tumbled to the ground, she broke its neck. The flickering fire illuminated the grisly scene. In the background, in the darkness, other raptors chirped and bleated in defiance. The entire event had lasted only twenty seconds.

Kevin had drawn his weapon, but Arabella and Dawn had hardly reacted. Arabella was stunned by two things: the speed of the raptors and the speed of JD. She swore he had moved as fast as the raptors, and he had sliced one raptor nearly in half in a single motion.

JD spoke. "They're getting bolder, Kev. Coming in, we killed four. But there are hundreds out there."

"Hundreds?" Dawn said in disbelief. Whatever hope was left in her eyes began fading.

"That's the bad news. This place is some sort of nest, an aviary or breeding ground. They're everywhere. The good news is that before I arrived here I put on Mister Johnson's prop and in the morning you're out of here."

This made both women perk up, but not Kevin. "What about you and Molly?" he asked with some trepidation.

"You need a diversion, Kev. There are at least a hundred raptors between here and the chopper. Molly and I will make a commotion and take off south. Give us a few minutes and head for the chopper. You should be okay. We'll distract the bad guys long enough."

Kevin looked away. He hated that he understood. "What about you and Molly?" he asked in a whispered voice.

"We'll make our way back to the Zodiac and see you onboard the *Broadsword*."

A long silence fell like night in a graveyard.

"It'll be okay, Kev."

Kevin only nodded. There was nothing to say. Then the words of an old song danced in his mind: "They tell me that a friend is dying, and there's nothing in this world I can do."

An hour before dawn, JD and Molly stood guard like palace sentries. Kevin and Arabella sat at the fire, lost in the magic of the flames.

"I still don't get it," she said.

Kevin broke his trance. "At daylight, JD and Molly will cause a commotion and head out in the opposite direction of the chopper. The raptors are nocturnal. At that hour, they should be settling down, resting, becoming lethargic. JD hopes to startle and confuse them. They should follow him. Then we slip off to the chopper and home."

Arabella thought a moment. "But the shore is the opposite way. How's he going to do all that and get back to the boat?"

In a voice that was difficult to hold, Kevin said, "He won't make it to the boat."

"What?" she said, looking at him and across the fire at JD.

"Arabella, the raptors have the speed of a cheetah. We've seen them bound twelve feet at a time and jump vertically at least ten feet. They're intelligent, and they have a pack mentality. They never pass up a kill. Even if they aren't hungry, they'll kill for sport. My friend over there knows this. He also knows the chopper can't lift us with him and Molly. Molly is over seven hundred pounds. But he won't leave her."

"Jesus, Kev. What can we do?" Reality is a vicious animal, heartless and cruel.

"When we get to the *Broadsword*, I'll drop you and Dawn and head back for him and Molly. It's all I can do."

The fire continued its magic; orange and yellow flames faded into the night sky. Kevin and Arabella were no longer mesmerized, only sad.

JD sat with Molly. The darkness around them came alive with eyes. The great cat growled with contempt at the night figures that crept around the black forest like vultures circling a dying animal. Twice she stood and ran a few steps in mock attack but returned to JD. Daylight was coming, and with it a clearness of purpose. They rested. Rest was a weapon.

The night passed very slowly on the *Broadsword*. Sleep is not a guest when your friends are in peril. Duke and Chief Hightower paced like condemned men. The admiral chewed the soggy end of an old cigar while the twins played poker with Billy Johnson and Moe Henry. Moe was up $48,000, but since there was no money, who cared?

Once again, Adam said, "This plan sucks, Admiral. There's got to be a better way."

For the umpteenth time, Duke said, "Let's hear one, dipshit. My friend and that damn cat could use a better fucking plan, one that doesn't get them killed."

But no one had a plan, and hope was fading with the darkness. Soon, very soon things would get very ugly.

Arabella and Dawn had dozed off. They slept like children who knew their parents were just down the hall. Kevin hated to wake them, but it was time. He gently jostled each girl. "It's time, ladies." They were instantly awake. Dreams forgotten, cobwebs of slumber brushed aside.

When everyone was ready, JD said, "When I throw this log, Molly and I will take off. Wait till things settle down and then get to that chopper. I'll see you on the ship."

The girls were near tears. Kevin felt his rough façade crumbling. JD threw the log. In the first light of the morning, it exploded with sound. Like foxes fleeing hounds, JD and Molly sprang off and were soon devoured by a tangle of leaves and branches.

The raptors reacted, brought to action by the possibility of killing an intruder. They gave chase as if it were a morning exercise. JD and Molly ran for their lives, crashing through the jungle like bowling balls in a glass house.

A few minutes later, Kevin, Arabella, and Dawn sprinted to the chopper. So far so good. They got to the chopper unchallenged. The solar batteries were still charged, and Kevin wasted no time getting all systems online. If the new jury-rigged prop worked, they would be in business.

With the speed of a glacier, the main props began to turn. For Arabella and Dawn, getting the chopper going was like watching grass grow. It could nothappen fast enough.

Before long, the chopper was acting normally. All systems were go, as they say. Holding his breath as if it would make a difference, Kevin pulled back the stick, and the bird began to rise. It finally cleared the treetops. The women hugged and screamed in glee.

Kevin was also happy to be airborne, but he had other worries. The makeshift rear prop was working but not well. The chopper began shaking like a naked man in the snow. He blasted a straight line to the *Broadsword*, desperate to land before something fell off the vibrating rig. He did not relish the idea of going down in the drink. The ocean held worse things than those damned raptors. Being eaten alive by some hundred-foot shark was totally unacceptable. Not to mention ghastly.

He held the stick with both hands. The girls held onto whatever was not shaking and the chopper limped to the landing pad on the *Broadsword*. Twenty feet from the surface, the new prop broke off like a flying boomerang and spun out to the sea. The chopper began spinning but dropped safely onto the deck. Cheers erupted as everyone ran over to the wounded but grounded chopper. It sat on the landing deck, glad to be home.

Home for JD and Molly was up in a conifer. They were trapped. Both bled from various wounds. Molly licked her left paw continuously. JD had checked it a few minutes before; it was broken. In one exchange with the raptors, JD had seen her tumble many times. For over half a mile they fought a running battle with the raptors. Three times they were forced to stop and take a stand. The battles had been ferocious. JD knew he had killed at least a dozen. He was not sure about Molly—maybe the same. Still, the raptors attacked. As smart as they were, when it came to killing, they were mindless. JD had never experienced pursuers like this; they fought like demons spawned from some ancient hell.

Exhausted and half dead, he and Molly had found safety about twenty feet off the ground. The raptors hissed and chortled in frustration. As luck would have it they could not climb. They paced and jumped around the trunk of the tree in anger. The prize was above their heads, just out of reach, but they stayed, laying siege like a conquering army.

Molly sprawled along a thick limb; her left paw drooping from the fracture. JD spent a few moments surveying his wounds. He suffered several gashes. His forehead, shoulder, thigh, and abdomen bled freely. No mortal wounds, but that hardly eased his pain. He lay back along the security of a long branch and closed his eyes. He felt he could sleep for a month. The raptors continued their vigil. JD's blood dropped like rain on and around the rapacious beasts, which only seemed to piss them off more.

Sleep had barely claimed JD when his radio bleeped. Without opening his eyes, he pressed a button. "This better be good."

It was Kevin surrounded by the others on the *Broadsword.* The radio crackled. "How's it going, son?"

"Great. Just lying around, catching a few rays, and chewing a protein snack. I see you made it back okay. Any problems?"

Short silence.

"We got back okay, but the new prop snapped off and took a dive into the ocean. The chopper's grounded. I was going to come get you in it, but now we're going to send a rescue party. I need your location."

"We're up a tree, literally, without a paddle. But hold off on the rescue party. We're about a mile southeast of the beach. We had to stop and rest. You know Molly, she's got no endurance. But don't come in, Kev. There are thousands of these things, and they're single-minded. Even with all your firepower, there would be casualties. These raptors are smart and adaptable. They've set traps for us, doubled back on their own trails, and tried to ambush us, cut us off, and flank us. Thank god *Jurassic Park* was wrong. They can't climb, but these are some bad boys."

Those on the *Broadsword* were listening. Kevin asked, "You got a plan, old son?"

"Sure. We're going to wait until three thirty. It'll be very hot, and hopefully by then, these boys will be bored and tired. Molly and I will slip down and make a break for the beach. Meet us there. If we're not there by four, we're not coming."

Kevin thought. "Sounds kind of iffy. You sure?"

"Positive. I'll call you before we head out. Keep dinner warm. I'm starved."

"Sure thing, son. You guys okay?"

"A bit tired but fine. Time to dance into the fire. I'll look for you. We're out."

"Talk at you later, son. Stay high."

Kevin put down the microphone. No one spoke for a long time. "Can they make it?" asked Arabella.

"No," Kevin said. "It's too far under those conditions. JD was lying. I know him."

"What do you mean?" queried the admiral.

"They're not fine. He and Molly wouldn't need to stop and 'rest.' JD is an incredible athlete. He did the Iron Man in under ten hours and has run a sub-three-hour marathon. And Molly is, well, a tiger. No, they stopped because they're hurt. Tigers don't climb trees unless they fear for their lives."

"And his reference about 'dancing into the fire'?" the admiral asked.

"That's from our days at Sho Lo. It's a tradecraft term. It means when there are no good options, do the least-expected thing. In this case, he's going to attack them at three thirty. If he's in a tree, you can bet twenty raptors are camped out underneath it."

"I saw him, Kevin," said Arabella. "He's an extraordinary man. He's as cold-blooded as the raptors. We have to help him. I'll go myself if necessary." JD had saved her life; she was willing to risk it now for him.

The admiral thought a moment. "At three, Kevin, Duke, Arabella, Janice, and Chief Hightower will go ashore and secure that beach. Take whatever firepower you think necessary. From the ship, Mister Johnson and Mister Henry will train the fifty-calibers on that stretch of sand and cover you. If Captain Stoner gets near the beach, we'll get him and that tiger out. Do I make myself clear?"

There was no disagreement. The twins would help the admiral spot from the bridge. It was eleven thirty. Four more hours, four more long hours.

For two long hours, JD dozed in between being interrupted by cackling raptors, biting insects, and bleeding wounds. Molly slept the sleep of the exhausted and injured, waking periodically to lick her paw. It was swollen and causing her great distress. She growled at JD when he touched it.

The sun was very high in the sky and broiling everything below. The lush branches of the tree shielded them from the heat but not the humidity. JD lay drenched in his fatigues, and Molly panted in great bursts. At this time of day, most creatures took to shade. Even the raptors had quieted down. Some had left, but others were curled up in the shadows. For a short time, it was as if the jungle rested. Insects buzzed, and plants dripped moisture, but otherwise, all was quiet.

From his vantage point, JD looked out at a seemingly peaceful jungle, almost tranquil. The heat of the day had disguised the terror that lurked within. In the jungle, terror had many names. The raptors may have claimed this area as their breeding ground, but other predators had taken no heed.

One such monster was one of the smallest in the jungle, a pygmy among giants, but every animal in the forest gave them wide berth. They feared nothing and ate everything; they destroyed everything in their path and left nothing in their wake. Their single-mindedness and overwhelming numbers made even the mighty T. rex flee in terror. Because they were willing to suffer massive casualties against larger foes, they always persevered. Only three things could stop them: fire, water, or cold. Controlled by a single leader they would willingly sacrifice themselves for the sake of the whole. They were relentless, and they were moving through the jungle. The universe of the forest braced.

Curiosity on the *Broadsword* had reached a fevered pitch; Captain JD Stoner was the subject. The same question bounced between everyone. Just who the hell was he? Since Kevin was back onboard, all eyes looked to him. He decided to tell what he knew. The group had gathered and stood quietly in anticipation. Even Duke kept to himself. He had known JD for two years but realized he knew only the eccentric sailor who had a tiger. They listened to Kevin's tale.

"I met JD fourteen years ago in Sho Lo, Arizona. I was an instructor at a government training facility in the desert south of there. The base trained men in the art of covert military and counter intelligence operations. JD had been recruited by the NRO, the National Reconnaissance Office, a very secret government agency. Turned out he was a natural.

"When we got him, he had already accomplished many things. He had been an Olympic swimming champion and a world-class fencer, and he had a language capacity beyond anyone we'd ever seen. He can become fluent in a new language in a matter of days. It's uncanny. And his reflexes are incredible. He tested higher on our machines than any drag racer ever did.

"And at age twenty-four, he had already become a master of Shaolin kung fu. Not just one discipline; he mastered all of them. He was and is a prodigy."

Kevin stopped and gulped some water. The crew hung on every word.

"The government created Nomad, a man whose job it was to track and eliminate hostile assassins. An assassin hunter. A long dog, to use their terminology. And for six years he did." Kevin paused.

"Did what?" asked Moran.

"Hunted assassins."

"You mean kill them," said Arabella. "He hunted the hunters."

"Yes."

"Jesus," said Dawn. "It sounds like a Ludlum novel, Jason Bourne and all that."

"But it's true," Kevin said. "He quit two and a half years ago. He called me, and we set up our ferrying business. We were doing well until the storm."

"But what's the deal with Molly?" asked Adam.

"I'm not sure. He doesn't talk about it. But he and Molly share a remarkable bond. It has something to do with his childhood and the loss of his parents then, but I don't really know. I just know he'd die for that cat."

"And the government has his files buried," stated Tim. "We couldn't dig up jack on him. In the computer files, he's like a ghost. He's there but without substance. It's spooky."

"It explains his weapons," offered Janice. "I'd never seen such exotic stuff. It was like Q Department in a James Bond film."

Kevin chuckled and smiled but turned grim. "These raptors are the worst. If he makes it to that beach, I'll do whatever I can to get him out. He's the closest friend I've ever had. I'm even fond of that cat."

"I know," said Duke. "I'd give anything to see that goddamned cat again. And JD's bony ass too."

They all felt the same. If JD and Molly got to the beach, they would make it. Arabella drove home a clip in her M16. It made a hard, metallic sound. "I want another go at those bastards," she said. "We owe them, Kev."

Kevin agreed. The terrible screams of Arnie Glover still echoed in his mind. They began preparations for JD's and Molly's extraction. The white beach leading to the raptor-filled jungle was about to become a killing field.

The first to arrive were the scouts, the advance guard of an immense army. JD noticed a handful scurrying about the branches of the tree, zigzagging their way forward. He had seen soldier ants and fire ants before, but nothing like this. These early relatives dwarfed their twentieth-century descendants. These ants were a good three inches long and could bite like a mouse, JD had found out. So far, it had been easy to kill or knock away the intruders, but like an inching glacier, their numbers were increasing.

It had been an hour since he had seen the first ones, but peering through his binoculars, he saw the full force approaching. Just south of his position, an enormous column was laying waste to everything in its path. A moving black sea of certain death twenty feet wide and stretching behind to oblivion, a mass of moving legs and bodies, was trudging forward. It was a bizarre sight, millions of army ants advancing as one. Scouts, workers, and soldiers pressed ahead, searching for anything edible.

JD realized they were in the path of an insatiable juggernaut. Staying in the tree meant a torturous death of being eaten alive. No thanks. Even the raptors that had laid siege had retreated. JD glanced at his watch: 1:30. Damn! He had to move. He'd call Kevin and tell him they were leaving early. That is if he could find the damned radio.

He realized it was not on him. Impossible! He searched the tree limb and Molly. Nothing. He glanced below and spied the radio, smashed on the ground. It must have fallen while he slept, and the raptors had either stepped on it or tried to chew it because it was definitely broken. What now? Send up the bat signal. He could fire his pistol, but as powerful as it was, it was also very quiet. They would never hear it on the *Broadsword*. He and Molly would have to go now, while the raptors retreated from the ants.

He looked at Molly. "Don't stop. Stay close. I'll deal with the raptors. If we stop, we die. When we get to the beach, go for the water. It will equalize their speed and strength. If I go down, go on without me."

The cat growled her disapproval, but she was ready to go. They were both ready to go.

No one on the *Broadsword* was ready to go when the twins called the admiral to the bridge. Kevin and Duke came along. Adam handed the admiral binoculars and pointed. "There, on the beach," he said.

The admiral peered through tired eyes. There, on the pristine shore, were a dozen long objects that appeared to be sunbathing.

Duke said, "What the fuck are those?"

"*Sarcosuchus imperator*," replied Tim. "That's Latin for giant crocs. Those are forty—to sixty-foot saltwater crocodiles. Bad boys. Ten to fifteen tons each."

"Christ on a seesaw," spit the admiral. "What next?"

Tim said, "There are more cruising the surf. Getting to shore will be tricky."

"Tricky?" chided Duke. "We'll have to blast our way in. Maybe use the .50 calibers from the deck. That's just fucking great. Those bastards are half as big as this boat, three times the size of the Zodiacs."

Frustration set in like a bad cold.

"How long will they stay?" asked Kevin.

"Who knows?" said Adam. "Through the heat of the day probably, at least five or six more hours."

"If JD gets to the beach, he'll be trapped," Duke said. "Raptors and giant crocs. What a goddamned pickle this is. What the fuck do we do?"

"We'll go in at two thirty," answered Kevin. "If the crocs are still there, we'll pick them off one at a time. Let's call JD and let him know."

The radio produced only static. The silence could mean only two things: his radio was out, or he was unable to answer, probably dead or dying. Kevin refused to believe the latter. They would go with the plan. JD would be there. Kevin believed it.

JD believed in Molly and his sword. As they limped through the jungle, two vagabonds in a lost world, the raptors challenged them at every turn. JD's sword had chopped and hacked until it became lead in his hands. Molly stayed close, limping badly from her shattered paw. Even though she was wounded, the raptors still feared her as she growled and snarled her hatred for them.

As they closed to the freedom of the shore, away from the horror of the moment, drained and injured, they collapsed for a moment. The raptors were right behind them but stopped short, sensing the crocs. Even an adult male raptor would not venture too close to a tanning croc. Nothing would.

Leaning on his sword, JD looked up at the crashing surf and saw the crocs. They lay there like luggage. Dormant but forever vigil, crocs were faster than humans on land. He looked to Molly. She had collapsed in the sand. Her broken paw useless, her breathing labored. She looked bad, really bad.

The whole situation looked bad and the bastard raptors had begun to inch forward. JD realized even if he could get by the crocs to the Zodiac, he could not carry Molly. He could not even drag her. They would have to make a stand. He looked at the panting tiger. "We'll take turns fighting. One fights while the other rests. I'll go first. You don't look so good, Moose. You rest first."

The tiger tried to stand but fell back on the sand. JD turned to face the raptors. He raised his sword and set himself. He would exact a terrible toll before he fell. The raptors approached him cautiously. They feared the shiny weapon he wielded with such grace and skill. Many in the jungle were dead because of that terrible instrument of war, but millions of years of predatory instinct forced them on. They would kill or be killed. It is all they knew.

On the *Broadsword*, everyone knew everything was screwed up, or fucked up, as Duke would say. A jungle full of deadly raptors, the beach patrolled by giant crocs, JD not answering his radio; what next?

Next was Adam screaming at everyone and pointing to the shore. Fifty yards away stood a man with a sword, a tiger lying helplessly on the ground, both surrounded by manic raptors. The eyes on the *Broadsword then* witnessed a battle of titans. The raptors, their bravado strengthened by their sense that the victims were near death, attacked from all sides. The flash of metal and screams of dying and injured raptors echoed for miles. JD was like a whirling dervish in a dance of death. Raptors advanced but were cut down. Limbs and heads flew, and blood covered everything. It was a carousal of death, JD's sword the instrument.

A large croc suddenly advanced from the rear. The raptors fell back as the monster reptile scampered forward. JD turned to see the croc. It had sensed the carnage and came to scavenge the dead raptors. Molly lay helpless, exhausted and wounded many times; the large feline had given up moving. She was prepared to meet whatever lay in store.

But JD was not. With newfound energy, he rushed the croc, which seemed startled by the smaller animal's courage. As it hesitated, JD drove the sword through the croc's enormous skull. It immediately went into a death roll, which attracted the attention of the other crocs. The dying croc looked good to the others, an easy meal that would not fight back. The other crocs began migrating toward their fallen brother. This made the raptors retreat.

But Molly was still in jeopardy. JD stood over her, ready to challenge any threat. The dying croc had stopped flailing and had settled at the water's edge, its great carcass about to be sustenance for the others. They began ripping huge chunks from the dead croc; it was a tug-of-war between mighty beasts. The fallen croc, still warm in death, was being shredded by other crocs, busy gulping down monstrous pieces whole. It was a savage sight.

While the giant crocs turned their attention to their next meal, the raptors began circling JD and Molly again. JD hovered over the cat and looked to the next battle. The raptors seemed endless; each one was a photocopy of the other vicious, snarling, kill-driven beasts. He steadied himself and raised the sword.

And then the familiar rat-a-tat-tat of an M16 filled the air. The spitting bullets began to pulverize the defenseless raptors. Arabella and Dawn sprayed the crowd at will. Raptor parts flew in all directions. More gore and blood. The crocs were kept at bay by Kevin and Chief Hightower with their own M16s and most raced back to the ocean now for cover.

The raptors retreated to the jungle. Arabella was relentless. She continued to blast anything that moved. The beach was now a raptor graveyard; bleached bones would be their tombstones.

Kevin rushed to JD. He stood covered in blood, his own and raptor, and gasped like a sprinter after a race. Kevin smiled broadly.

"If I had known you were going to stroll," said Kevin.

"And if I had known you were going to swim," replied JD as he collapse into his friend.

Duke was there. "Goddamn, JD. You look like, well, er, well you look like shit."

"Hey, Duke," said JD, weak as a kitten.

"Yeah, pal."

"Fuck off!"

Everyone laughed. JD passed out.

The Romanican raiding party passed the rock formation known as Caesar's Tower, named for Antonius, a young Caesar who, three hundred years previously, had climbed the steep peak and fasted at the top for two days. He sought wisdom and to be nearer the gods and his ancestors. The tower was very sheer and quite dangerous. As far as the Romanicans knew, no one else had attempted the climb.

Marcus Sardonis glanced along the trail that was well used by humans and animals. Creeping vines and weeds continually threatened the path, but Marcus knew the way. He knew they had to be very cautious the next two days. They were in the land of the T. rex and his smaller cousin, the dilophosaur, a ten-foot-tall, one-ton carnivore that had several unique qualities: it was a chameleon, and it was poisonous. It could spit poison fifty feet accurately. The venom could blind if not kill a man; the venom went straight to the central nervous system and paralyzed its prey. Slow suffocation resulted. It could also blend into almost any environment; it was a great ambush hunter. Most men walked right up to it before they realized their mistake. By then it was too late. These mini, camouflaged T. rexes could bite a man in half.

The raiding party crept along, avoiding possible ambush sites and sticking to the trail. Marcus and his men were feeling especially fortunate. So far, neither predator nor nature had claimed any of his men, and they were in their second week of traveling. The gods of rare fortune must have been smiling down on them.

But like most good fortune, it did not last. The raiders had no way of knowing a mother T. rex and her juvenile sons had stampeded a herd of brachiosaurs about a half-mile north of their position. The brachiosaurs had been grazing on treetops when the younger T. rexes attacked. Their plan was to scatter the herd and isolate a juvenile, but the brachiosaurs stuck together and ran as a herd. Adults, juveniles, and babies, over one hundred, broke in a southerly direction together. The stampede was on.

The first indication Marcus and his men had of any danger was when the ground beneath their feet began to shake. An adult

Brachiosaurus weighed up to fifty tons. When the herd moved as one, the ground became a victim.

The T. rexes, joined by momma, gave pursuit. They hoped to pick off a struggling baby or youngster, but the herd stayed tight, the adults on the outside, flanking the smaller ones and the tyrannosaurs could not break the massive barrier of pounding flesh. They ran alongside, waiting. They knew from experience the herd would get tired and slow down, and then they would get their chance at a sick or exhausted member. Sometimes patience was better than ambush or strategy.

The men in the raiding party knew only that they were in a prolonged earthquake or in the path of a major stampede. Either one was bad, especially when you are standing in a small clearing without cover. They did not have trees to climb or rocks for shelter. They ran. They ran for their lives. A stand of tall trees and smaller rock formations were directly ahead, about half a mile. They ran like rats from the light.

The brachiosaurs ran also. Some took strides of ten yards or more at a time. When faced with certain death, these goliaths could run very fast. They thundered along at forty miles per hour, flattening small trees and all shrubbery. The dust they raised blotted out any view behind them.

The men scrambled, but not nearly as fast as the beasts. A deadly race was on; the men ran for the safety of the trees while the imposing herd bore down on them. To the brachiosaurs, the humans were no more than large insects; they paid them no heed whatever.

About fifty yards from the trees, the brachiosaurs caught up with the humans as a tidal wave sweeps over calm beaches. Some humans were crushed under gigantic feet; the immense weight and pressure exploded the human bodies. Flattened bodies that oozed gore and puddles of warm blood littered the clearing, but somehow, most of the men made it safely to the rocks and trees.

The mighty herd passed, but the tyrannosaurs stayed. They were great scavengers as well as hunters. They tore apart the trampled bodies. The men who made it to safety had no desire to interfere with the rexes. After all, there would be no need for burial. They knew that when the rexes left, they would be followed by smaller and more-efficient scavengers. Nothing would go to waste. By morning, only drying bones would remain.

The raiders regrouped and took stock of their injuries and casualties. Seven dead, two slightly injured, and one fatally injured. The mortally wounded man had been stepped on by a brachiosaur but had been dragged to the trees by two comrades. He would be dead in minutes, however. His abdomen had been crushed; there was no hope.

Marcus surveyed the survivors, forty-two. They waited until their dying comrade passed before starting west, picking up the old trail. They left their fallen friend for the T. rexes and other scavengers. His body had been sacrificed so the others could journey without being hunted. No one thought the dead man would mind.

Marcus calculated they were still three days' march to the great sea. At the sea, they would turn south and begin their sweep for Slants. Their villages were easy to spot; their fires were easy to smell. With forty-two men, Marcus felt he would have no problem capturing as many slaves as he could manage, but he could not afford to lose any more men. They would stay sharp and be cautious. In this land, it was all they could do. They pressed on westward. The great sea awaited them.

On the third day after the battle with the raptors on the beach, JD clung to life in the ship's infirmary. Shortly after coming aboard, an infection and fever set in. For two days, a temperature of a hundred and four ravaged his wounded body. He tossed in delirium constantly. At one point, Doc Moran had to restrain him, afraid he would injure himself further with the flailing. The fever preyed on his body, its attack fierce and unrelenting. Spasms came in great waves, and he babbled nonsensically off and on. It was as if he were being tortured by an unseen demon.

Intravenous fluids and the doctor's care sustained him. Moran thought his battle with this fever was as remarkable as his battle with the raptors had been. JD's dogged determination, his will to live and fight, were very strong. The injuries he sustained should have killed him. It had taken her over two hundred stitches to close four horrible wounds. She wondered what kind of man this was. The other scars on his body proved he was no stranger to pain. She kept a steady vigil as JD fought an unseen foe. She prayed it was not a deathwatch.

The admiral decided to take Horace Greeley's advice of ninety-two million years in the future and head west. In the Smithsonian computer files, the twins had found a map of what cartographers guessed the area looked like ninety million years ago. They used it to chart a course around the horn of Texas and then north, up the inland sea, to Montana. The hope was that the weather would become milder as they moved north. They hoped to explore and perhaps find an island to settle on. They would stock provisions at islands along the way. Hopscotching their way north, they would chart the vast ocean and any land mass they found. They felt like Lewis and Clark setting out to explore unmapped territories.

Before they left Florida, they crowned it Raptorland and decided to never go back. Future generations would be warned to stay away. The raptors were better left to their own devices.

The *Broadsword* ventured west, its crew happily settling into a routine while Captain JD Stoner fought for his life.

The morning was percolating, hot and steamy. A fine yellow haze veiled the sky. Duke had started calling this a nitroglycerin morning because, to use his terminology, it looked ready to fucking explode.

Chief Hightower whisked along on his morning routine of inspecting the deck when he passed cargo hold one and spotted the twins' pet tortoise. Someone had painted an enormous peace symbol on its shell in bright yellow. As he was contemplating the cosmic symbolism of such an act, the twins joined him.

"Cool, huh?" asked Tim. "Duke painted it for us."

"Just fine, boys. But why? See any hippies around here?"

Adam said, "It's a symbol of our non hostile, nonaggressive, and totally peaceable intentions. It's way cool."

"Way," agreed Tim.

"And just who's going to see it?" challenged the chief.

"Anyone who flies over, of course," said Adam.

"Right. Have a nice day, boys. Stay out of the sun. It's frying your brains." The chief walked off. The twins looked down at Norton, who was happily crunching prapples.

"Cool," said Adam.

"Way," said Tim.

The triplets, as they had become known, Arabella, Dawn, and Janice, were on the forward deck with Duke. They were all still chattering on about the fight with the raptors.

"I know," agreed Duke. "It was un-fucking-believable. I'll bet he killed twenty of those bastards."

"At least," said Arabella, "Maybe more. It was like something out of a chop-socky movie. The man was a machine."

"A very attractive machine, too," Janice said, flicking her eyebrows. "You could bounce a dime off those abs."

"And those arms," swooned Dawn. "Like pythons."

Duke realized it was time to go. If these bubblegummers were going to prattle on about JD as if he were some movie star, he was out of there. "I'll catch you girls later. I'm going to check on our pretty boy. See if he's ready to do a few hundred pushups. Tootles." The girls went back to chattering. The last thing Duke heard as he walked off was something about "and a great butt." He looked back at his own. Great!

Kevin sat in the infirmary with Doc as JD tossed fitfully in fevered sleep. His brow dripped sweat despite the damp cloth across it. Every few minutes, the doctor would wipe his forehead and check his pulse.

"Your friend is amazing," said Doc Moran. "With this fever and those wounds, he should probably be dead, but he hangs on. He's a tough bird."

Kevin shook his head in agreement. "He has a higher pain threshold than most. He pushes it further than anyone I've ever known. But why the fever, doctor? His wounds are bad, but not that bad."

"It's an infection. The raptors' mouths and claws probably carry a multitude of germs, like komodo dragons from our age. They scavenge almost anything—rotten meat, diseased meat, anything. Their own systems can handle it, but it has a slow effect on their victims. JD's immune system is fighting back, but these are new germs, prehistoric germs. They shock our system. We all have to be careful. This world has many things ours didn't, bad and good. The dinosaurs may carry germs that are lethal to humans. Even the plants could be toxic to us."

Kevin was impressed. He had not thought of this world in terms of germs or viruses. The doctor was right. There was probably more to worry about in this world besides land and sea predators; invisible germs and poisons could be just as deadly.

"So tell me about JD," the doctor said simply and directly. Kevin realized the answer might not be as simple or as direct. He looked at the doctor and at JD, who was enjoying a brief respite from the fever. He seemed to be resting peacefully. Like a child taking a nap.

"He's a solitary man, Doc. Few friends and no enemies worthy of him. Sometimes I think he's from another race entirely. Stronger, healthier, better color, and boundless energy. His movements create a kinetic sculpture in space. I know it sounds crazy."

The doctor thought crazy was relative. She looked at the prone JD and saw an enigma, a twentieth-century riddle that was incomprehensible but attractive. A killer of men and beasts with a soft heart. An affection for Molly and his friends, and a willingness to sacrifice for them. A paradox. Certainly not what she had expected. She found herself inexplicably drawn to him, like a moth to a flame. The danger, the excitement of liking something mysterious and forbidden stirred in her heart. "Was he married?" she asked, surprised at her boldness.

"No," said Kevin. "The odd girlfriend, but nothing serious. Sometimes I think he loves that cat more than people. He probably thinks that given his past, it would be hard on a relationship."

"How so?"

Kevin smiled. "How would you explain a past like that to a mate? Hi, honey. I used to hunt and kill people. What's for dinner?"

"Love is understanding," said the doctor.

"That looks good on a Hallmark card, Doc, but in the real world, it's a bit more complicated."

JD was snoring. It surprised both Kevin and the doctor.

"It's a good sign," said Moran. She put the back of her hand to his forehead. She grinned. "His fever has broken. He should sleep easy now."

"How long?" asked Kevin.

"Not for long unless you two quit yakking," said JD in a shallow voice. "How about a little quiet for the near dead?"

Kevin fought back tears. "It's good to see you, son. You've been gone awhile."

"How long?"

"Three days," said the doctor. "You've had a fever for three days. Infection from the wounds. The raptors are filthy animals. You're immune system took a while to overcome the new threat."

JD's eyes fluttered. "Molly?"

"She's in the cargo hold. Alive. Her immune system apparently is tougher than yours. And we fixed her up a splint for the broken paw. She's recovering nicely. She misses you."

"Yeah," agreed Kevin. "Every day, Duke and I would carry you down there and sit with her. She'd lick your face and growl at Duke."

A smile grew across JD's face. But even smiling took energy. He still had only the strength of a newborn. "I'll see her after I take a little nap." He faded off.

In the cargo hold, Molly yawned and put her head down. Soon she too was asleep.

The *Broadsword* was a dream to operate. Mr. Johnson kept the engines running, and the twins saw to the computerized controls. To them it was like learning a video game.

It had been three days since JD's fever had broken, and he was strolling the ship. He was weak, and his wounds were sore, but it felt good to be moving around. He'd spent many hours sitting with Molly. Her splinted paw looked exceedingly ridiculous but was healing. The diet of island squab and whale meat was working also. The great cat had regained her strength and was anxious to test her repaired paw. It was too early for that, so JD restricted her to short walks only. But they napped together often, and that seemed to placate the feline.

Life became established on the *Broadsword*. Everyone seemed to produce a normal routine, as normal as you could get on a floating refugee circus.

The twins continued to amaze everyone. One morning, they stopped JD on deck. They were duded up in dress uniforms and carried notebooks and pencils. JD thought; this ought to be good.

"Morning, boys," he said.

"Good morning, sir," said Adam with the formality of a G-man.

"We're census takers," said Tim proudly.

"Congratulations. Do we need to take a census? If my memory serves me right, there are only fourteen of us onboard. We need a census for that?"

"Sure," quipped Tim. "We need to chart trends, create demographic charts, and predict changes in population. Vital stuff."

"Then, ten years from now, we can look back and see how things changed," Adam said.

JD shot them a Benny Hill look.

"Come on, JD," whined Adam. "Please."

JD took a deep breath and reluctantly said yes.

"Cool," said Tim. "Now just answer these few questions. Ready?"

"Sure."

Adam said, "We got your name already. So, age?"

"Thirty-six."

"Address?"

"Here! The floating zoo!"

"Right, the *Broadsword*," said Tim. "Political affiliation?"

"What?"

"Are you married or happy?"

"What?"

"Organ donor? Aisle or window seat?"

"Are you nuts?"

"Sugar or Sweet'n Low?"

"What?"

"Where were you born?"

"Lake Winnipasaki," JD said, deciding to play along.

"Spell that, sir."

"D-R-O-P D-E-A-D!"

"Oh, hostile, eh? We're just doing our job, sir. No need for rudeness," Adam said.

"Thank you, boys, but I'm late for a squash game. Call me in ten years."

"Come on, JD. This is important," said Tim.

"So get someone else. How about Duke?"

"We got Duke already," answered Adam.

"You did?"

"Sure. He answered all the questions the same, though."

"Really?" asked JD. "What'd he say?"

Adam began shuffling around through some papers. "It's here somewhere," he said. "Tim, I think you have it."

"Oh yeah," said Tim. "Here it is."

"Well, what'd he say?"

"Ah, let's see. Oh yeah. He replied 'Fuck you' to every question."

"Sounds like Duke."

"Besides," said Tim, "in ten years, you can look back and know you added substantially to the population boom."

"What population boom?" JD was curious.

"The one we're gonna have," said Adam. "We expect you and Doc Moran to have five by then."

JD's eyes bugged wide. "What? Me and the doc? Five kids?"

"Cut it out," said Tim. "We see the way you two eyeball each other. Like a couple of schoolyarders."

"Yeah," said Adam. "Odds are you two will be doing the horizontal hula in less than a month."

"What odds?"

"We got a pool going," answered Tim. "Duke picked the lowest time frame. Forty-eight hours. The admiral said thirty days. He called you guys old-fashioned."

"The admiral's in on it?" JD was boggled.

"Sure," said Adam. "But you and Doc can't be in the pool for obvious reasons. Know what I mean?"

"This is nuts, you know."

"Listen, JD, we'd really appreciate it if you let us know when you and the doc, you know . . ." Adam pumped his fist forward.

JD understood. "I got to go." He walked away in utter bewilderment, laughing but bewildered.

Tim pointed across the way at Chief Hightower and back at Adam. "A customer," he said gleefully.

"Yeah," said Adam. "Let's go."

The chief had no idea he was about to have his census taken. Officially, of course.

Later that day, JD walked into the weight room onboard and ran into Moran. She was at one end of the room doing a series of kata. JD was stunned. She looked amazingly different. It turns out that under that medical frock she was muscled up like a gazelle, and without the horn-rimmed black glasses, she had the face of a cherub. The sweaty T-shirt she wore only added to her beauty. Some women had to smile to be beautiful. Not Dr. Matilda Moran. Soft, brown eyes and porcelain cheeks tanned by the prehistoric sun created a beauty he had rarely seen. There was a quiet elegance about her. JD couldn't believe he had not noticed her like that before. He suddenly felt old.

He walked toward the bench press. They nodded casual greetings to each other. "That's one of the Heian series of kata, isn't it?" he asked, trying to make his question sound unpremeditated.

She smiled, her face sweaty and perfect. "Yes," she said. She was completely amazed by this. "It's Shotokan."

"The original school of Japanese karate," JD responded.

"Right again. I have a brown belt. I've been working at it for five years."

"You're very good," said JD. There was no patronizing her. She really was very good.

"That's high praise. I talked to Kevin while you were in sick bay. You're a Shaolin master. Not many occidentals have achieved such status."

JD looked embarrassed. "Kevin talks too much, and you can't believe everything you hear."

"You forget I saw you on the beach with the raptors." She suddenly grew apprehensive. "It was horrible. Such death and destruction. Savage animals."

JD wondered if he was included as a savage animal.

"You were magnificent," she said. "I expect you have few equals."

He did not answer at first. He sat at the bench press. "Thank you for saving my life. I'm in your debt."

She was taken aback by his comment, but she recovered. "I'm not sure I had much to do with it. Your body fought the infection."

"Still, I'm grateful. For Molly, too."

She thought a moment. "The relationship you and Molly enjoy is, well, fascinating. How long has she been your pet?"

That struck a nerve. "She's not my pet, Doctor," he said. "She's . . . we're friends."

The doctor was intrigued. The cat was his friend. He did not regard her as a pet. "I see."

"No you don't, Doctor," he chided. "But then, it would be very difficult to explain it to you. Perhaps when we have more time." He grabbed the bar and began to bench the weights.

The doctor, however, was not about to let him off the hook. "Okay, when? I appear to be free all decade. How about tonight? We'll grab our meals and sit down in the cargo hold with Molly.

You can tell me all about you and her." She began toweling the sweat from her face and neck. She was preparing to leave.

"Uh, sure," JD stammered. "I'll see you in the mess hall later."

"Good," she said, heading for the door. "Just don't think this means Duke's going to win the pool." JD nearly dropped the weights on himself.

"You know about the pool?"

"Sure. I may be a doctor, but I'm not completely dim, you know. I'm inclined to go with the admiral. I'm a bit old-fashioned, and combined with your cowardice, it just may be a month or more. See you later." She breezed out the door, leaving JD to pick up his jaw from the floor.

The twins timed it so that they would run into the triplets on the way to chow that evening. It created the perfect bottleneck in the narrow passageway of the ship.

"Hello, ladies," said Tim. He and Adam had on their best *Revenge of the Nerds* outfits.

"Hi, guys," said Arabella. "Lost?"

They laughed. Adam said, "We're babeaholics, you know. Hopelessly addicted." It was a subtle yet endearing approach.

"And what's that got to do with us?" asked Janice.

Tim said, "We thought maybe after dinner you'd like to slide over to our pad for a little hooch-ee-skoo-ka-doo." He winked mightily while hinting the obvious.

"What?" asked Arabella. "You two and us three?" She calculated the possibilities.

"Sure," said Adam. "A late happy hour. A few cocktails and then a game of naked Twister. What do you say, dolls?"

Arabella went first. "Drop dead, sharkface."

Dawn followed her. "No dice, dudes!"

Janice waited until last. "I'll come under three conditions. One, cook me a meal. Two, donate all your money to charity. Three, get a partial lobotomy."

The twins stared at her. "No way!" said Tim. "We can't cook!" No way they could get around that one.

"Tough tootles, boys," she said. The trio inched by the duo and made for the sanctuary of the galley.

The twins, forever optimistic, thought their first procreative encounter with the triplets had gone well. At least they did not get jap-slapped or punched in the eye. That was a good sign. They immediately began to formulate their next move. Maybe nude bungee jumping into giant vats of Malt-O-Meal? That would be cool. Way cool!

For JD, cargo bay two was way cool. He sat with Dr. Moran and Molly, enjoying his dinner. Molly lounged like a lazy cat, indifferent to the world. Mr. Henry's specialty that night was tuna casserole. At least everyone thought it was tuna. Kevin had caught the fish the previous day. It surely did not look like any twentieth-century tuna, but since it smelled like tuna, everyone called it tuna, and it was good. Molly happily finished what JD and the doctor could not.

Stomachs full and bodies content, they lay back against Molly and stared at the deep-black sky peppered with tiny lights. They saw a meteor. Both pointed at it. Quiet contentment evolved.

Dr.Moran said, "So tell me about Molly."

"She's an Indian tiger, seven hundred and twenty pounds, the largest land carnivore in our time. She's four years old and has been with me since she was one week old. I bottle-fed her for nearly a year."

"I don't mean vital statistics. I mean the relationship. You promised." She made a pouty face.

JD had promised. "I felt a kinship toward her. It goes back to when I was a child. I've never explained it to anyone before, but I'll try. When I was four, my father was a diplomat stationed in India. My mom and I flew with him one day from Calcutta to Kashmir. The plane crashed in northern India, in a remote jungle area. My parents and the pilot died right away, but I lived. At age four, I didn't know what to do. I stayed at the crash site for two days. I finally got hungry enough and wandered off." He paused.

"That's awful. How did you survive? Four years old?"

"After walking about two hours, I heard some kittens in the bush. I went over and found three cubs. But I was tired, so I lay down with them and fell asleep. When I woke up, a mother tiger was lying next to us. I wasn't afraid. It was weird. The tiger just licked me like she licked her cubs. She knew I wasn't a threat. So I just hung out with the tigers.

"I had no concept of time, but when missionary people found me, it was five years later. Apparently, searchers thought I had drifted away from the plane, got lost, and died. But here I was, five years later. I had forgotten how to speak, but I had the gift of mimicry. I picked up English again in about a week."

The doctor was awestruck. "You survived five years in the Indian jungle? That's incredible."

"That's what everyone thought. The tigers raised me. Looked out for me. I did everything they did. I learned to swim and love the water. My reflexes developed so I could grab a fish or swat away a snake. My hearing and sense of smell developed. I can hear a hawk in the sky. I can smell another human fifty yards away, and I can run for hours. I can pick out the injured and sick from the rest of the herd. I can track anything. I'm a product of my environment. It's really very simple.

"I got Molly because I missed the relationship. Their life is simple, uncomplicated. They rest, hunt, and eat, and they mate when they can. They live a solitary existence. I admire their clarity."

"Kevin said you were a solitary man. Few friends, and no enemies worthy of you. Sound familiar?"

"If you mean I'm like a tiger, I'll take that as a compliment. I know how they think, so I can communicate with them. All cats tend to view humans in two ways. They either feel that they need to mother you or that you're completely inept and not worth their trouble. They communicate with mannerisms, expressions, and levels of noise. If they attack a human, it's to kill, not eat. They don't like human meat. They prefer buffalo or deer. Yes, I suppose I am solitary. I just never looked at it as a bad thing.

"What about you, Doc? Most doctors I know live solitary lives as well. Doesn't seem very conducive to relationships."

She smiled. "It's not. You're always working or studying or worrying about working or studying. It's very satisfying but, yes, lonely. Men are usually intimidated by smart, successful women."

Molly yawned and rolled over; her splinted paw stood straight up. She looked silly, not exactly dignified for such a royal beast.

They sat quietly a while before resuming their discussion. Their feelings for each other were strong and strange. Like primitive art. They were drawn to each other without knowing why.

"So you worked for the government," she said. Her brown eyes reflected the starlight. He realized she was quite beautiful. They inched close to each other, deft movements in the dark.

"Yes, I was Nomad. Assassin hunter. Long dog for the good old USA."

"You sound less than passionate. What happened?"

"Many things. I was supposed to hunt just foreign assassins, but things were changing two and half years ago. A new administration. The fraternity White House. Their answer to everything was to attack it. I told Cheney and the other henchmen to bugger off. Their leadership would only create hard feelings and lasting enemies. The frat-boy mentality. Do it my way or I'll ruin you. So I left."

"They just let you leave? It doesn't sound like the George W., I know."

"They let me leave because I knew secrets. I can stir up trouble."

"They could have killed you," she said quietly. She touched his arm. They moved closer.

"I wasn't a threat. Plus, they had bigger problems to worry about. Environments to spoil, countries to bomb, and elections to win. Hell, I'm of no consequence when you've got to stir up patriotism and go to war. I'm glad I'm not there to see it. If I were Canada or Mexico, I'd be shaking in my boots."

The doc laughed. JD went on. "We have so much magic back in the twentieth century. Our world has everything. Nuclear power, fiber optics, medicine, computers, and smart people. It was all magic, but children died every day from malnutrition, the old suffered, and the poor languished. Men killed for what they couldn't gain by their own labor. How to share the magic has been our problem throughout history. The rich are jealous of their wealth, and greed leads to crime and injustice. Even without all the magic, here in this primitive time, we still seek what all men have searched for through the ages."

"And what is that, oh grand swami?" Her gentle tease made him grin.

"We want justice, we want comfort, and we want love."

He had said more than he had planned, but she was special. He could feel it, but he wondered what she saw in him.

She looked into his green eyes and saw a hard, complicated man, a man she wanted to know better. "You're right," she said, taking his hand. "But I want one other thing as well. I want you to kiss me. Right now. Don't think about it. Just do it."

She decided wait for him. She took his face in her hands and gently kissed his lips, a warm, probing kiss. He reacted in kind. The kiss lingered a while as their minds computed the possible meaning.

As if on cue, light background music came over the intercom., soft Frank Sinatra. The kiss broke up into laughter. Goofy laughter.

"I'm gonna kill those boys," promised JD.

The doc could not stop laughing. "They mean well. They're trying to hedge their bets."

"They probably have the whole place wired," said JD. "Come on. I'll walk you home." He took her hand.

"Why, thank you, gallant sir," she said, bowing. "But stay with Molly. I'll see myself home. Tomorrow you can tell me all about Shaolin kung fu."

They kissed again, and the doc left. Molly stood, walked to JD, and rubbed his head with her forehead. She sat and put her head in his lap. He massaged her scalp. "I like that one a lot," he said. The tiger purred and put her paw on his shoulder. He lay back, and Molly plopped to the floor. She settled in for the night, and JD laid his head on her chest and shoulder. He stared at the sky a long time before finally falling asleep. Both were soon snoring, content in the security of soft slumber.

There was nothing soft about the freebooter, Constantine Orlov. He was a third-generation pirate whose grandfather had been transported back ninety-two million years in time sixty-five years previously. His grandparents had taken a ship from St. Petersburg through the Gulf of Finland, where it disappeared during a storm.

Grandfather Orlov took up piracy immediately. He soon realized this time was ripe with refugees from the twentieth century and it was not long before he had a crew of merciless marauders and began attacking any other humans he came in contact with. In the north, he avoided the land of the giants and the militaristic Romanicans. He raided Slant villages on the frontier but stayed away from the main city in the south. Everything else was fair game. He wasted no time with new arrivals. Anything of use or value was plundered. Children were killed, and women taken as slaves and concubines.

Great-grandson Constantine Orlov had followed his father and grandfather's large footsteps. He was king of the buccaneers who scavenged this world. Near forty and heavily muscled, Constantine was a formidable force. He boasted that he had killed over twenty men in combat. He ruled his ship and men with an unforgiving fist. It was said that he threw a man overboard once for looking at him wrong.

He sailed a 1915 schooner dragooned with six whaling harpoon cannon looted from various plundered craft. A crew of thirty manned her decks. Earlier in the week, they had boarded and pillaged a small pleasure craft. Under torture and before dying, its crew of four told of seeing a great metal ship heading west without the use of sails. They said it was powered by unseen forces and moved at twenty knots or more.

The information seemed reliable. After all, what man would lie while slowly being skinned alive? So Orlov and his men headed west. The lookouts' eyes squinted across the horizon, scanning for a large metal ship. So far, nothing but a sapphire-blue ocean lay in their path, but they had time and the wind at their backs, so they skimmed along in search of a great prize.

On one fine day, it irritated Constantine that he had to discipline two men for fighting. It is not that he minded the fighting, but the damned fools had accused each other of stealing. On a ship full of thieves, he could not abide a thief among them. His action that morning had to be swift and decisive.

The two men stood on deck, glaring at each other. Constantine looked at both as if he were measuring them for coffins. "Both of you stand accused of stealing from fellow shipmates. Though the charges have not been proven, I will assume there's some truth in them. There can be only one punishment."

He turned his back on the men as if to walk away but with the speed of a mongoose, he drew his cutlass, turned, and in one clean sweep chopped off the head of the taller man. Blood sprayed the other man, who began screaming. The others on deck watched in bated amusement.

Constantine pointed to the trembling man covered in blood. "You! Clean up this mess and get back to work. Keep your hands in your own pockets or your head and blood will grace this deck as well."

The poor bastard nodded and began mopping blood and gore from the deck. A disgusting job, but one he had to be alive to do. He had no complaints.

Constantine walked away, pleased with his Solomonic judgment. The men went back to their duties as the body and head were thrown overboard, food for monsters of the deep. On mild winds, they sailed in search of a ship of steel.

An island intersected the path of the *Broadsword* on the morning of the sixteenth day after they had left Raptorland. The island, maybe six miles around, was a welcome sight in spite of its small size. JD, Kevin, and Molly explored for one day and reported it was a good place to stop for a while to rest.

A small herd of hornless Zuniceratops roamed the island, feasting on its lush vegetation, but JD and the others had seen no other signs of life. Pristine beaches gave way to a forest and an inland lake fed by a towering, thirty-foot waterfall. It was a Club Med poster in the making, another oasis in this great desert of an ocean.

The other *Broadsword* voyagers disembarked and had a leisurely time of surf, sun, and slackitude. Again, they had been lucky. The island provided a wide assortment of fruits and edibles. More prapples, bananas, coconuts and some berries that resembled gooseberries but tasted like boysenberries. They promptly became known as "goosenboys." Fresh water that tumbled from a small rock formation created a spectacular cascade. The water, warm and clean, made a great natural shower.

The Zuniceratops were small, about the size of goats. Molly began stalking the small herd as soon as she came ashore. Her left paw was still tender; she favored it slightly. But the Zunis, having no island enemies, did not even attempt to escape from her. To Molly, the island became a large banquet, and she feasted.

Everyone feasted. Oversized coconuts produced nearly a gallon of sweet milk, and the prapples and bananas made this small pebble of a place a veritable Shangri-La. The twins flitted around as if they were on an extended Love Boat holiday. The sun shone brightly from a clear sky; the afternoon heat scorched the little island, but life was carefree and easy. The raptors, dead pirates, and monster fish were soon forgotten as thoughts turned to soft beaches, warm surf, and blazing sunsets. It became a time of happy contentment, a time of healing and reflecting. JD healed, and the twins reflected about their sprouting love life.

Even Norton came ashore and rambled the island. Molly had no idea what to make of the elephantine tortoise. At one point, she jumped on the great shell and sat content, like a queen on a throne. Norton could not have cared less. He made for the prapple trees and munched eagerly. Norton moved with the grace of the wind and the speed of growing grass.

Stubbornly, the twins tried to teach him tricks.

"He'll never jump through that hula hoop," said Tim with great authority.

"Oh ye of little faith," said Adam.

"He's got no knees. He can't jump."

"Quit bugging him. Give him a chance. Come on, Norton old pal," said Adam.

"Maybe if you set him on fire," suggested Tim.

Adam frowned as Duke walked up on the surreal scene.

"Just what are you two ass wipes doing?"

"Adam's trying to teach Norton to jump through a hula hoop. But he's got no knees."

"He's deaf as a stone, too," added Adam.

"Why can't he hear?" asked Duke.

"He's got no ears—stone deaf. But we're gonna teach him to read lips."

"Yeah," said Tim.

Duke looked away; his face was plaintive; his expression was one of mystification. "You boys got brains like Napoleon," he said, walking away.

The twins thought briefly. Adam yelled, "But Napoleon's dead."

"I fucking know it," answered Duke, leaving the twins to assimilate the vast implications of his words, but they looked only dazed. They resumed turtle tricks with Norton.

"No way," said Tim. "You'll never get him to play the accordion."

"How about the piccolo?"

"Nope. He's got no lips."

For the next hour, Norton's physical dexterity was tested every which way. The twins came to a resounding conclusion. The tortoise could not do squat. He was about as athletic as a house, had the flexibility of a piece of steel, and he slept like a hibernating bear. Definitely not trick material.

The twins, dejected and bummed, left Norton to the prapple trees and headed in search of bikini-clad babes. They hoped to catch the triplets sunning in the nude. Or at least get them to say hi. The twins were easy; near nudity or simple civility would be a step in the right direction.

The dreaded pirate Constantine Orlov had been pushing his men and ship for two days. Little sleep and a boiling sun kept his men on edge. His lash had reminded any loafers of his determination to press on. But he knew he could not keep up this pace. The men needed rest. He called his first mate to his side. He had a chart open in front of him. "We'll make for this island, here," he said, pointing to a dot on the map. "We'll rest two days and gather provisions. Spread the word to the men."

This pleased the first mate. The men would be happy as well. He remembered the small island well from previous stops. A gentle waterfall, a small herd of Zuniceratops, and plenty of fruit. It would make for two days of relaxation. He hurried to tell the men. They needed some good news.

The sun stuck its head out; the morning erupted. The sky was blue emptiness with a fiery globe of orange. The water's reflection of the sun nearly blinded everyone. Trial and error had taught the crew of the *Broadsword* that the morning sun was best for sunbathing—hot but not too hot, whereas the afternoon sun could burn the meat right off their bones. Around eight that morning, the triplets headed up the beach to a private lagoon, far from the prying eyes of their schoolboy admirers. Arabella toted an M16 and promised she would shoot any uninvited trespassers. They spread blankets, peeled off their clothes, and stretched out to soak up the rays, bottled water and sunglasses their only protection.

What they had forgotten to take into consideration was the ingenuity and resourcefulness of the twins, not to mention the raging hormones of sexually repressed twenty-year-old lads. While the lovely trio lounged, the twins were on the upper deck of the *Broadsword* with a telescope. They brought iced tea and sandwiches and decided to make a morning of it.

A game was devised so sharing the telescope did not create friction that could possibly result in a nerd fight. A word was decided on, and each boy got a turn at the telescope until the other used the word in a phrase. They would alternate until one lost. The loser would have to sit out a ten-minute penalty.

The telescope zeroed in on the tanning, buff trio, and since they were all facedown, the first word was *moon*. Tim looked first, his eye as wide as a saucer.

"Moon over Miami," said Adam.

"Carolina Moon," said Tim, grabbing the next look.

"Moon Mullins," answered Adam.

"What's that?"

"An old comic strip."

"Okay, 'Moon River.'"

"Good one. 'Blue Moon Tonight.'"

"*Moonraker*."

"Cool," said Adam. "Double-o-seven. Moon walk."

"Damn, I was gonna say that! Uh, the cow jumped over the moon."

"No fair!" blasted Adam. "That's from "Hey Diddle Diddle." I win. I get a whole, sweet ten minutes."

"Rats," said a pissed Tim.

What neither lad realized was that Chief Hightower had been standing behind them for the previous five minutes. He had not yet figured out their game but was sure it was nefarious at best.

"Damn," said Adam. "They turned over."

"Ha! That means a new game," demanded Tim. "What's the new word?"

"What else, pal? *Bush!*"

"Cool," said Tim. "I'm first. Busch Beer."

"Spelled wrong," said Adam.

"Close enough."

"Okay. Busch Series, auto racing."

"Good one. Ah, George Bush."

"Ha, George W. Bush," snapped Adam.

"Bush's Baked Beans. I know that's plural, but there are three girls."

"Okay," agreed Adam. "Busch Bavarian Beer."

Tim winced. He was going to use that. Snaked again.

The chief had heard enough. "Just what in sweet Jesus is going on here?" he bellowed. A surprised Tim nearly toppled into the water. Adam grabbed his chest. "Jeez, Chief, you scared the horse hockey out of us," he claimed.

"Just what in hell are you numbskulls looking at?" He put his eye to the telescope; it immediately snapped wide. "Moons and bushes, eh, boys? Real cute."

"Cute doesn't cover it," said Tim. "They're gorgeous, tremendous."

They had the chief there. He had to admit the sight was spectacular, and boys would be boys, even these idiots. "You forgot one, boys," he said. They both looked at him puzzled.

"Moon pie. I always loved those things. Will probably miss them a lot, too. You boys carry on. If anyone asks, I'll say you're stargazing. Just remember, if Arabella finds out you've been spying on her, she'll have your balls roasting over an open pit, and I'll be happy to hold you down while she snips them. Have a nice morning, you peeping perverts." The chief was off, whistling a happy tune. The girls on the beach flipped again, and the game continued. The new word was *jugs*.

The pirates aboard Orlov's ship were carrying jugs topside. The island they were coming up on had a freshwater spring, and they needed to replenish their supply. Darkness was drawing over the sky, and they wanted to make shore before complete blackness came on. Men grunted and backs strained as fifty—and hundred-gallon jugs, kegs, and urns were toted up to the main deck. Constantine observed with a watchful eye. The men were tired and bored. Resting on the island for a few days made sense. The men would be good for two more weeks of searching after this break. If that steel ship existed, Constantine was going to find it. Find it, capture it, and keep it. That ship would make him lord of the seas. He could go anywhere and plunder anything; nothing would be able to stop him. He had to have that ship, but he needed his men healthy and rested, so the island stop was crucial. They should be there with in an hour or so. The rest would be *good for everyone.*

On the west side of the small isle, the *Broadsword* group had a raging bonfire going. Everyone had come ashore for an impromptu luau, everyone except Mr. Henry, the cook, and Mr. Johnson, the ship's mechanic, who stayed aboard. Mr. Henry was giving the galley and mess a good cleaning, and Mr. Johnson was tinkering with the engines. It seemed he was rarely satisfied with the ships mechanics.

The others went ashore to enjoy an evening of camaraderie and fraternity. The fire roared and crackledas smoke drifted into the cloudless evening sky. A westerly breeze cooled the skin and made blankets, sweatshirts, and long sleeves welcome friends. An informal circle formed around the fire.

JD and Dr. Moran huddled close while Kevin and Arabella chatted away about mostly nothing. The twins positioned themselves near the two remaining triplets, Dawn and Janice, and Nurse Armbruster made conversation with the admiral, Duke, and Chief Hightower. They had been engaged in various conversations for about fifteen minutes when Kevin announced he had a theory about their sojourn into this time.

"I think we could be the original Atlanteans," he announced rather easily. This tweaked everyone's attention. The twins moved strategically closer to Dawn and Janice. Warning looks, like daggers, flew from the woman's eyes, but the twins had seen them naked and were guided by youth and hormones, a deadly combination. Dawn came to the realization that before the night was through, they would probably have to physically rebuff the hopeful pair.

"Think about it," Kevin said. "The stories and myths about Atlantis have startling similarities with us."

"How so?" asked a skeptical admiral.

"Well, the Atlanteans were supposed to have been a race of very intelligent humans, as advanced as our society. They had roads and machines, and they could fly, and they had lasers or powerful weapons. We can do all those things now. In this world, our ship has unlimited nuclear power."

"But ninety-two million years, Kevin," challenged Chief Hightower. "Could legends and myths survive that long?"

Kevin shrugged.

"It does make some sense," said Adam. "We know that in twenty-eight million years, an asteroid will hit the earth near Mexico and cause an extinction-level event. Only a few small mammals and insects will survive. Eventually, humans will evolve. Most Atlantis myths say the island kingdom was destroyed by some natural disaster."

"Like an asteroid or some other natural event," added Tim. "Like a volcanic explosion, earthquake, or tidal wave. This is an unstable time in geological history. We have all those events occurring rather frequently. An island or settlement could be wiped out in a human heartbeat."

"An island," said Doc Moran. "It would have to be an island. If we set up a permanent town, it would have to be an island. We'd have to have a place free of predators, with food and water. A volcanic island would be such a place. Freshwater springs, fertile earth, and small animals. We could be wiped out almost instantly by an eruption despite our technology. Look at Pompeii. The whole city was covered in ash and lava in a few hours when Vesuvius erupted. It does make sense."

JD sat like a proud father, captivated and impressed by the doc's insight.

"There has never been any direct evidence found to support the existence of Atlantis," offered Tim.

"After ninety-two million years, I suspect everything's biodegradable," JD said. "Even steel."

Duke wasn't buying it. "Come on, people. We're talking ninety-two million fucking years. A thousand civilizations could have come and gone. If we're the Atlanteans of mythology, I'm Bo Damn Diddly!"

"Nice to meet ya, Bo," said Adam. "But I think it's entirely possible."

Kevin said, "Look, Duke, I'm just saying there are some parallels here."

"It's an interesting notion," said JD. "If we truly are the real Atlanteans, it's a big burden. We have a lot to live up to. Though it's unproven, the Atlantean myth pervades our old society. Atlantis was looked up to and respected. We can't let them down."

The group grew quiet as minds raced to embrace the idea that they could possibly be the Atlanteans of legend. A feeling of pride surged through everyone. Maybe they would found the great island of Atlantis. Maybe ninety-two million years later, people of the twentieth century would be thinking about them, about a civilization of intelligent people who lived in safety and peace in a world of untold and unimagined dangers. A civilization that ended as fast as it had sprung up. Maybe . . .

Thoughts came back to the present. Dawn said, "Okay, you guys. I know a joke. What kinds of bees give milk?" Her face was a large innocent grin.

"Boobies," exclaimed Duke. And everyone broke into laughter. It was silly but funny, just right for the moment.

The dancing fire cast uneven shadows over everything. Arabella was sleeping on Kevin's shoulder, snoring softly. Dawn and Janice had curled up in blankets and were letting sleep come. The twins lounged close, hoping against hope. Duke and Natalie were drawing pictures in the sand while the chief and the admiral had walked to the water's edge and were engaged in a hardy conversation about naval tactics during the Revolutionary War. The admiral naturally held the view that British tactics were far superior to those of the woefully inept colonialists. The chief was not backing down, though; he continually reminded the admiral of John Paul Jones.

JD and the doc grabbed blankets and headed for the spring and waterfall; Molly followed them. The doc was not exactly

Jungle Jane, so she was happy for Molly's company. She had a certain feeling of safety knowing a seven-hundred-pound tiger was her friend and was walking beside her.

The doc held onto JD's arm, and they walked slowly in the moonlight. As they approached the small spring, the moon was high above the waterfall. It was a Kodak moment, the perfect setting on a perfect island with the perfect person. The waterfall tumbled down in gentle, crashing sheets, while above, stars spun webs of spidery luminescence.

Molly wasted no time in diving into the shadowy water. Leaping and bounding like a preschooler, she raced through the shallows, splashing and pouncing and shaking her giant head. She slung water pell-mell across the little spring. The night erupted as satin rivulets bounced off the surface of the pool.

Impulsively, the doctor began stripping off her clothes. JD was momentarily dazed, but he soon found himself taking off his shirt. The doc was down to her panties and running for the warm water.

"You going in topless?" called JD.

"Why not? You are. Besides, no one's around."

"Just me and Molly."

JD was nearing the water. The doc dunked her head briefly and came up shaking her hair. "Yeah, but you both love me."

JD came up near her, and they embraced. They kissed long and hard. Lips and tongues explored their opposites. Their skin was wet and they hard pressed against each other. They were in their own universe and maddened by tenderness.

They moved quickly to the softness of the blankets. Their passion was white hot. They sought the limit, but there was none. No boundary. Like teenagers, they believed that no one else had ever done these things before. Like youths, they thought they were the first and only. They surrendered to mindless, tingling frenzy. The world was forgotten. God was a memory, but in a place outside the world. Faith was reborn.

On the east side of the island, two longboats packing twelve pirates each were rowing to shore. Orlov's ship sat anchored in dark water, resting peacefully on easy waves. Illuminated by torches and lanterns, the landing party made for the white beaches of the slumbering island. The plan was to make camp and form details to gather water, fruit, and any other supplies they could find. The men would come ashore in groups, leaving only a few onboard.

Constantine came ashore with the first group. His feet were always glad to touch dry land. The dank jungle filled his nostrils with wonderful odors. There were so many things he missed while at sea including the smell of green plants and the aroma of fertile earth, bananas and other fruit trees. That first step from the boat to solid ground. The blast of new sensations, and the almost immediate memory of the salt and wind of the ocean; a great combination.

The pirates got organized. Eight grabbed containers and headed for the spring. Another eight made for coconut and banana trees. The last group of eight began setting up a makeshift camp. Constantine stayed with the last group, who were cutting palm fronds for bedding and shelter and starting an enormous fire. He had promised the men a feast that night, but some preparation was the first order. All would enjoy grilled fish, fresh fruit, and plenty of wine.

The eight men assigned to fetch water from the fresh spring made enough noise moving through the jungle to wake the dead. Molly was the first to hear the advance of the pirates and came quickly to attention; JD followed a few seconds later. The sounds were heavy and loud, without concern, the noise of people unafraid and confident. The sounds of hard men.

With a delicate touch, JD woke the doc. He whispered, "No sound," as he put a finger to his lips. Panic flashed in her brown eyes. "We have company. Unwelcome company. Molly and I will take care of it. Stay here and be quiet." His voice was barely audible.

"Don't leave me," she begged.

His hand touched her leg. "I'll be close. Don't worry."

It calmed her, but she was still afraid. "What's out there?" she whispered.

"Pirates. Now don't move."

JD moved to a position where he and Molly flanked the eight men. They had moved to the water to start filling their containers. JD motioned to Molly, who let out a low, rumbling roar. It froze the men like statues. They began looking around at the dense vegetation. Molly growled low and deep again. The sound pierced the men's souls. They drew swords in anticipation. Muscles bulged as hands gripped steel.

JD stood and walked out of the shadows. He had his sword drawn and stared at the eight baffled pirates. To them he must have seemed like an apparition, a smoky figure from the night. They all tensed.

One pirate found his voice. "Who are you?" he asked in a language that was a hybrid of Russian, English, and Italian, but JD understood him. He did not respond. Off to the left of the men, Molly again roared, this time loud and angry. It forced the attention of the men to that direction. Like a night reaper, JD attacked the men. It was over very quickly.

From her vantage point, Doc Moran could hear Molly and a lone voice in a language she did not understand. She heard the striking of steel and the muffled sounds of men dying or in great pain. Then silence.

Out of the darkness, JD appeared at her side. She instinctively grabbed him and held on tight. "I heard a voice and then swords. Are you okay?" Her grip didn't let up.

"I'm fine. But we have to go. The others at the fire may need our help."

Terror again. "But won't those men follow us?"

"There were eight men. They won't follow us." His voice was as cold as arctic ice. It made her shudder.

"They're all dead?"

He took her arm. "We have to go. There will be other pirates. Stay close and no sounds. If we get separated and you need help, click this." He handed her a small metal cricket, the kind kids love to play with.

"Click this, and either Molly or I will soon be there."

She shook her head in understanding, but her mind drifted in thought. Pirates? JD had just told her he had killed them all. In cold blood. She was a doctor and sworn to help the sick and injured, but JD left no injured. Only dead. What kind of man did that?

Two hours earlier, they had made love like college kids, the intensity of which she had never known before. Now this tender, loving man had brutally killed eight men. Confusion reigned in her mind, but there was little time to think as they raced to the campfire. She was amazed how silently JD moved; he was catlike. She shivered in the warm evening air. He and Molly moved through the jungle as if they owned it. It was scary.

They could see the beach fire just ahead; its flames were still leaping, the wood still crackling. JD stopped. Doc crouched next to him. She heard what he had already heard. Voices. Mostly Russian. Her stomach knotted as she realized the pirates held their friends. The fire had been spotted easily by the second group of eight pirates who had pushed into the jungle. They had been startled by the presence of ten people slumbering cozily around a fire on the beach. It had been easy to approach the snoozing group, and they were very happy to find four pretty females among them.

Their captives spoke a language they could not understand, so ordering them around became confusing. They were eager to take the men as captives for sale to the Romanicans and equally eager to have their way with the women.

Arabella had already demonstrated her hostility and had been brutally slapped for it. Duke and Kevin had suffered head wounds from trying to intervene on her behalf. Brutality was a way of life for these men. It came easy, and it came first.

The captives were herded into a group. Dawn and Natalie tried to help the injured. A great welt had risen on Arabella's right cheek, threatening to close her right eye. Duke and Kevin sat, their heads pounding from the vicious strikes they had endured. The pirates eyed the group with malicious intent, their filthy faces highlighted by rotting teeth and leering looks. Their bulging eyes saw only helpless victims; their bulging crotches knew only demonical lust. The pirates paced around, deciding what to do. JD knew he had to act fast.

One pirate said, "We bind the men and then take turns with the women. After that, we take them all back to Constantine." He pointed at Dawn. "I'd love to make that one scream." This drew laughter from other pirates, who all had the same evil thoughts.

JD turned to Matilda. "Stay here. No matter what, stay here. I'll take care of this." He looked to Molly and pointed at the doc. "Stay." Molly understood. Doc Moran was now her charge. She would see to her safety.

JD stood and walked toward the pirates. They noticed him as he came into the light of the fire. He carried a long sword that flashed in the flickering flames of the bonfire. He made no sound. The pirates moved toward him with fascination and fear. The talkative pirate said, "Who the hell are you?"

"I am Nomad. These are my friends. Leave now and live."

This drew mild laughter from the pack. Their superior numbers fortified their bravado.

The garrulous brigand spoke again. "I think we'll kill you, rape these harlots, and take the others back to sell as slaves. What do you think of that? I'll be poking that one while your blood is still warm." He pointed at Dawn. She cringed. She didn't understand the language but understood its meaning.

"Just don't expect help from the other eight at the spring," said JD. He still had not moved.

The pirates widened their eyes. What did this man mean? Were the others dead? Had he killed eight of their comrades? Impossible!

"Time to die," said the bold pirate. The others began advancing, trying to circle the solitary JD. He did not move. Doc watched from the underbrush, and the other *Broadsword* survivors watched in shocked dread as the group of cutthroats surrounded its prey. But this was no ordinary prey. This was Nomad.

The first pirate died from a twenty-inch slash across his abdomen that spilled his intestines. The next thirty seconds went by in a blur of splashing steel. Seven pirates lay dead or dying.

The mouthy one had retreated to the captives. He grabbed Dawn by the hair and held a sword to her throat. "Come near me and I'll kill her," he screamed in the desperation of a man with few options. Dawn struggled, but he twisted her hair even tighter. Gasping whimpers followed. "I'm leaving here with her," announced the pirate.

"No you're not," stated JD in a voice as black as death.

"What?"

"Go ahead, kill her," said JD.

"What?" The pirate was puzzled.

"Go ahead, kill her. After you kill her, I'm going to kill you."

The pirate was sure he faced a lunatic. What sane man would risk a captive's life? He panicked. He shoved Dawn down and ran for the jungle. As he approached the trees, a great orange-and-black blur sprang from the depths of the forest and tackled him. They tumbled briefly as Molly pinned the terrorized pirate. Her great paws had slashed his face and sword arm. Blood pooled around his shaking body. She stood over him, her teeth inches from his bloody face.

"No!" JD screamed as he ran to her. "We need him alive." Molly grabbed his ankle in her mouth and severed his Achilles tendon. The pirate, permanently disabled, howled in pain. Molly sat next to him, eyeing his every move and ready to end his agony if asked.

Doc Moran came rushing from her position just as the others ran to JD. He had suffered no injuries. She jumped at him and clung to his neck. Bloodied pirates littered the ground. Death had descended on all. The others stared in grisly fascination. Morbid curiosity had grown from their terror and fear. Their bedraggled captors now lay dead, killed by a single man. That same man gave them orders. "We have to get back to the ship. There will be others looking for these. Probably a ship on the other side of the island. We need to move."

No one disagreed. They gathered their belongings and made for the Zodiacs.

"What about him?" the doc asked JD. The wounded pirate was writhing on the ground, still being guarded by Molly.

"I'll take care of him, Doc."

She cut him a hard look.

"No, I won't kill him. I'm just going to give him a message. I don't want the others following us."

Relief flooded over her. No more killing.

JD walked to the wounded man and spoke in his language. "Tell your leader what happened here. If he pursues us, I will kill all of you. This cat and I protect these people and the great steel ship out there. You live only to deliver this message. Do you understand?"

The pirate nodded. JD motioned to Molly. The two began to leave. They were met at the beach by the twins and Doc Moran.

"What did you say to him?" asked Adam.

JD faced the twins. "You don't want to know." The boys took the hint and wandered off.

"I want to know," said a defiant Moran.

JD took a large breath. He'd never lie to her.

"I told him to tell his boss to leave us alone."

"And if they don't?" she asked, fearing she already knew the answer.

"I told him if they followed us or attacked us, I'd kill them all."

She took a step back. She knew he meant it as sure as she knew ice flowed in his veins. It scared her.

He sensed her fear. "I'm sorry, Doc. We're outnumbered. I'll do what I have to to protect you and my friends. It's what I know."

"I hate that about you," she said. It came out harder than she meant. "Killing is so easy to you."

That dented the armor. "I'm sorry you think that, Doc. Despite what you may think, killing is never easy. Never." His voice trailed off.

She knew her words had hurt. Regret came in a flood. In a low voice, she said, "I didn't mean to . . . I mean . . . I didn't . . ."

"I know. We need to go."

Fifteen minutes later, the vagabond crew of the *Broadsword* weighed anchor and began a westward trek out into the bright night atop a dark ocean.

Constantine Orlov had been raging like a wild man for five minutes. He had smashed containers and thrown bottles at will. His meaty fist pounded the table in front of him.

"Tell me again!" he bellowed at the wreck of a man across from him.

The injured pirate recited the story once again. Through surging bouts of pain, the hurt and bloodied man told the tale. Constantine and the rest of his men sat spellbound. Near the end, the injured pirate's voice began to fade. He was ghostly white; the pain and loss of blood had exacted a toll.

Constantine shook his large head. "Fifteen men. You're telling me he killed fifteen of my men? By himself? Impossible!"

But the mangled pirate could only tell the truth. "Yes. He killed everyone. He had a great, fur-covered beast with orange and black stripes. It walked on all fours and growled like a demon. Great fangs and claws, weighed the same as three men. He called it a cat. The steel ship is twice the size of ours. With small boats that don't need oars or sails. He carried a sword, like the Slants do, but never have I seen such skill. Never. He said that he was called Nomad and that anyone following them would be killed. He's a demon, I tell you. A demon!" The man choked on blood and coughed hard.

Constantine had heard enough. The only demon on this island was himself. He would find this steel ship. This Nomad. He would take the ship and dip his finger in the blood of this man. That he promised.

He stood so fast that it startled everyone. "We leave tomorrow," he announced. "Gather all the food and water. We will find this steel ship and make her our own. There will be loot and women for all. Get to work."

The men let out a rousing cheer and began to move away. The wounded pirate looked up in terror. “I need help,” he said weakly. “Please help me. I beg you.”

“And I shall help you, my friend,” said a benevolent Constantine. He drew his sword and cleaved the helpless man from shoulder blade to sternum. Blood spurted as the dying man fell over. The blade of the sword had stuck in the man’s collarbone. Constantine put his foot on the man’s head and tore the sword loose. A gurgling sound accompanied the blade. The sound made another pirate wince. Constantine laughed. “Get rid of this garbage!” he shouted at two other pirates who had witnessed the horrific act. They scrambled to pull away the hacked body. Blood formed a river as the body was dragged.

Constantine sat and fumed. Nomad’s warning served only as a catalyst to drive him on. He had to have the steel ship. He must have vengeance on the man called Nomad. He must look into his eyes at the moment of death and see his fear. Hatred drove him.

I never dreamed home would find me, where I don't belong.

PART 3

Around the Horn of Texas, 92 Million MYA

The days moved on. The air was dead. No wind. Not the slightest of breezes. The sun was a blistering ball of red and orange and very cruel. For two weeks, the crew of the *Broadsword* had been island-hopping around the Horn of Texas. Some islands were lifeless chunks of sand in blue water while others spilled over with life. Some were gardens of fruits and vegetables; others were barren, bleak, rock gardens.

Their food stores were sufficient; even Norton and Molly enjoyed an abundance grub. Naturally, the twins were up to something. For weeks, they had hoarded fruit, mostly prapples, in their quarters and refused to reveal the reason why. An emphatic sign on their door warned trespassers, "Disturb us and you will be dipped in Alpo and thrown to a pack of rabid French poodles. We swear!"

With such a warning, everyone left them aloneas they tinkered away day and night in their mad-scientist laboratory of a room. Conjecture ran wild among the crew. What evil experiments were the boys up to? Were they cross-cloning some terrible beast? Were they building a ten-foot-tall Frankenstein monster? God only knew, and he was suspiciously quiet.

Besides, there was no god yet. In 92 million BC, God had not decided to show up. He was waiting for humans to evolve more than ninety one million years in the future. A time cannot have a god without the mindless worship and adoration of human beings. Before they do anything else, humans make gods. The revolving door of deities throughout human history has proven the power of fantasy over reason. Humans died by untold millions in the names of various gods. It was easy to be right with God on your side, and it was just as easy to kill and damn in the name of that same god.

The *Broadsword* travelers were lucky. They could make up new gods if they wanted. There were no challengers. Duke could be god if they wanted; that would make cussing not just acceptable but encouraged. The first swearing god in history. Why not? Why does God have to be a pious Goody Two-shoes? Maybe God should be fun. That would be a change.

The twins continued their nefarious, closed-door hooliganism, laboring nonstop in total secrecy. Speculation and imagination whetted the crews' curiosity. Duke was most succinct about the boy's clandestine activities. "I don't give a tinker's douche about what those two loony sons of bitches are doing. Those boys are off their fucking noodles!"

Days passed as the *Broadsword* meandered along, hugging the coastline. The crew was treated to many spectacles, some captivating and wonderful, others gruesome and ultraviolent.

One afternoon, they spotted three adolescent T. rexes scavenging a carcass on the shoreline. The three predators took turns tearing huge chunks from a dead whale and snapping at each other. The beached whale had enough meat for ten T. rexes, but as is the case with predatory scavengers, greed played a pivotal role in their lives. They gorged as if it were their last meal.

For one T. rex, it was his last meal. The water's edge can be a dangerous place in this prehistoric world. Larger carnivores always seem to be lurking. The rapacious T. rex was lost in the frenzy of shredding the giant whale when a massive liopleurodon hit the beach and in one deft move grabbed the startled T. rex. The liopleurodon, a hundred feet long and as many tons, crushed the struggling T. rex with viselike jaws. The dying T. rex was dragged underwater. It was a ghastly sight, a struggle of life and death in an unforgiving time. The sheer helplessness of the mighty T. rex was nerve shattering. The great beast had had no chance against the liopleurodon. The other T. rexes continued to eat, but they did so more warily. The drama ended. For a time.

On another day, a great herd of pterodactyls soared overhead, gliding effortlessly among the powdery clouds. The incredible sight drew the entire crew out to the deck. This herd of winged dinosaurs had to be a thousand or more strong. They cruised the heavens leisurely, occasionally flapping their enormous wings while floating on the humid air. It was a spectacular prehistoric pageant. The crews' necks craned as their eyes beheld this flapping phenomenon in the morning sky. They noticed the water directly beneath the great flock was being pelted. Pterodactyl poop. Everyone scurried for cover. Some were faster than others.

Duke, however, had not looked away from the sky and hence did not noticed the others diving for shelter. Like a tree, his good hand holding binoculars to his moving eyes, he was unmoving and stoic. It was them a huge glob of pterodactyl shit drenched him. From the top of his head to his bulging beer belly, he was swamped in grayish-green shit. He stood, frozen in time, an overweight statue of human body and dinosaur dung. The sight was supremely ridiculous. Duke scooped a handful of glob from his face and slung it overboard. The others burst out in laughter. Duke went into a colorful yet entertaining explosion of verbiage.

"What the fuck! Goddamned dinosaur dildos! I'm covered in this slimy shit! Jesus, Mary and Houdini, I'm fucked!"

Resounding laughter continued unabated. So did Duke.

"Fuck me running! Cocksucking, prehistoric shit. What the fuck do I do now?"

"Don't move," shouted Kevin. A moment later, a bucket brigade was formed; the crew began dousing Duke with buckets of saltwater. No one wanted to get very close, so most threw the water at him from five feet away.

Arabella threw her bucket while Duke was in mid curse, and he swallowed a half gallon of saltwater. Gagging and choking, he yelled, "Take it easy, you pricks! You're fucking drowning me!"

No one heard his pleas. He was ripe, and they wanted that smell off the ship. It was another ten full buckets before they let up. Duke looked like a large drowned rat. A freshly pissed-off drowned rat.

After a moment's reflection, he looked up with a face full of smiles and began laughing. He had been pooped on by dinosaurs. Even he found humor in that. From that moment, Duke began carrying an umbrella everywhere; "personal protection," he called it. "Like a fucking condom."

Dinner on the *Broadsword* was a community event. At six in the evening, everyone would gather in the mess for a delicious meal, current events, gossip, and other small talk. Mr. Henry would prepare a meal, and all would attend. It became a time of social interaction for the drifting folks of the *Broadsword*.

As Duke's rotund figure passed through the entrance to the mess hall, he noticed the twins sitting dejectedly alone. He and JD ventured over to the forlorn pair. Duke spoke first. "What's the matter with you two jerkoffs? You look like goddamn death on the street corner eating fucking Fig Newtons!"

JD, just like the twins, had no idea what Duke's comment was about. The twins looked up with expressions of gloom, as if their computer had died.

Tim said, "We programmed the computer right. Everything was correct, and we get this." He handed JD a printed page.

JD glanced at the paper and read it aloud. "Oodles of green noodles make blue poodles jump der schtroodle." He looked at the boys.

"We asked the computer the ultimate question," explained Adam. "What's the nature of God? And this is what it said. We're severely bummed."

"Severely," repeated Tim.

JD and Duke glanced at each other. The boys sat, shoulders slumped; they were like kids who had just learned there was no Santa Claus.

Duke could hardly resist. "What would you two fuckups charge to haunt a house?"

"How many rooms?" asked Tim.

"Fuck off," replied Duke.

"Boys," said JD. "This just means that the computer doesn't have a definitive answer. It's a subjective answer, that's all. It cannot define the indefinable."

The boys looked up with new expressions. "We know," said Adam. "But it was a shock. The computer has all the accumulated wisdom of our time, and it's still dumbfounded. It's scary. So we naturally spiraled down into a murky state of utter depression."

"Utter," said Tim.

"Utter this," said Duke, grabbing his crotch.

JD changed the subject. "So how goes the sinister experiments in your quarters?"

This perked the boys right up. "Swell," replied Adam. "Four more days and we'll reveal to the world our latest creation."

"Yeah," said Tim. "It will knock your knickers off."

Duke grunted and walked off. There was food to be eaten. Maintaining his bowling-ball figure required calories. Massive numbers of calories.

JD saw the doc sitting with Nurse Natalie and the admiral. She had not spoken to him since the incident on the island with the pirates. He realized that side of him made her uneasy. He understood. He sat with Kevin and Arabella and ate quietly.

Kevin and Arabella had become an item. He was fourteen years her senior, but they carried on like school kids with funny faces and nonsensical humor. They appeared to thrive on each other. Kevin, easy going and humble, and Arabella, leather-tough and brazen. They worked well together, and the crew enjoyed their adolescent horseplay. It was fun to see love blossom, even in a prehistoric daydream.

Dinner was a sensation. Mr. Henry had ground Zuniceratops into delicious hamburger steaks and garnished them with fresh fruits and vegetables. The meal seemed to bring the twins out of their blue funk so much so that Tim, feeling his bravado swell with his stomach, approached Dawn as she was leaving. He sauntered over to her like a lounge singer in a Holiday Inn bar. "Hi ya, toots," he drooled. She only nodded hello. "I was wondering if you'd like to go to the Halloween party with me." He batted his eyes.

"Halloween? It's July."

"I know. I figured I'd ask you early."

"Are you daft?"

"No, I can hear fine. How's about it? Me, you, a full moon? It will be spookily romantic. What do you say, doll face?"

"I say get bent!"

"Oh, I know. You're worried about costumes. No problem. I got it all figured out. You dress up like a brick, and I'll dress in boots and overalls and carry a trowel."

"So what's that make you?"

"A bricklayer, of course!" He burst into laughter at his own joke.

Dawn grinned her complete disgust. "I got a better idea," she said. "You dress like an old-fashioned drug store clerk, and later that night you can jerk yourself a soda or anything that comes up!"

She strode off, enjoying her metaphor, as Tim melted off to find Adam. He secretly felt he was wearing Dawn down with his charm. Any day she would be putty in his geeky hands. He smiled to himself at the prospect.

The prospect of catching the *Broadsword* looked grim. Constantine and his crew of murdering corsairs had been laboring day and night in search of the great steel cruiser but had nothing to show for it. His crew was growing bitter and impatient, and they were sixteen men lighter after the island fiasco. Constantine knew the men were apprehensive. A single man had killed fifteen of their comrades. He must find this man and destroy him or the man's legend would continue to grow, and before long, the men would be giving this "Nomad" superhuman qualities.

He pressed the men, but more subtly. And he encountered bad luck. For three days, they had had no wind. His ship had drifted aimlessly in search of good air but had found none. He knew the steel ship did not depend on wind, so that put him at least three more days behind in his search.

He cursed the wind, but the wind could care less. It had its own schedule regardless of how the pirate bellowed. He vowed he would catch up to that ship within a week. Then, death to Nomad and his people. A long hard death.

Death had already visited the Slant village before Marcus and his raiders arrived. It had come in the form of an invisible assassin. Disease. A fever and loss of bodily functions had ravaged the small hamlet, killing everyone.

The Romanican party had come upon the village early morning and found only skeletal remains. Even the animals had left the bodies alone, probably recognizing the signs of disease.

"Burn it! Burn everything!" commanded Marcus. He could ill afford to lose any of his men to an unseen killer. They were two weeks behind schedule, and he had sent a runner back to the emperor to explain.

Finding the Slant village, however, was a good sign. It was bad luck that everyone was dead, but it meant they were in Slant country, at least its outer reaches. It would not be long before they would encounter more villages. Then slaves could be taken and women used. He knew his men longed for the release that could come only from being with a woman, even a filthy Slant woman.

Bad news came in the form of a sixty-foot reticulated python. One of his men at the eastern edge of the village had stumbled upon the great snake. Before he knew what had happened, the snake had coiled around him, crushing his ribcage like an egg. He was dead by the time others had chopped the snake to pieces to release him. Blood poured from his mouth, nose, and ears; the snake's constrictions had popped his eyes from their sockets. His friends blanched at the sight of his broken, twisted body but the great serpent had proved no match for their steel. It lay in writhing pieces; it was dead, but its muscles had not become aware of that fact yet.

Marcus was now down to thirty-eight men, still enough for the job, but at that rate of attrition, he needed to find some live Slants fast. They would continue south a few more miles and camp. Snake steaks would make for a fine meal. They had plenty.

JD had made sure Molly had plenty to eat. The triceratops meat and island squab kept her full and happy. She and JD had been wrestling when Doc Moran came by the cargo hold. She stood in the doorway, arms crossed, watching JD and the massive tiger romp.

When JD noticed her, he looked up and took Molly's paw across the jaw. He declared Molly the winner of the play fight, and nursing his jaw, he walked over to the doc. "Lose your way?" he asked.

She smiled. "I've missed you, but I'm a doctor, and that trouble on the island made me think."

"I'm too dangerous for you," he said in a quiet voice.

"No, but you're an enigma, a paradox that's hard to justify. But you saved my life. All of our lives. For that I'm grateful. You're a hard man to reconcile, but I love being with you. And I'm probably falling in love with you. So I'm here because I'm miserable without you."

There, she had said it, a cathartic confession. The excitement of the flesh had finally yielded to the heart's resolve.

"I love you." The words were spoken in a scarcely heard voice in a private place, which added intimacy. He moved to her, and they held each other. A long moment passed before lips found lips. They were hungry for each other. It was beyond understanding, beyond human perception, but neither cared. Even Molly recognized the rapture and moved to the two tightly wrapped bodies. She brushed up against both, and the melded lovers briefly looked down. "Jealous?" asked the doc.

Molly only yawned and rubbed her head against their legs.

"She approves," said JD.

"Thank God. I think she could take me in a fight, you know," joked Doc.

"It'd be close."

Duke and Kevin stuck their heads over the edge up top. Duke said, "If you two lovebirds can quit humping for five seconds, you need to come topside and take a look-see."

"What's up?" asked JD.

"Probably you," Duke laughed. "But we're coming up on an island."

Doc whispered, "He's right, you know." Her pelvis was still mashed against his straining erection.

"Later," he whispered. He yelled, "What's so special about another island?"

"Someone appears to be cooking on it," said Kevin. "Campfires."

JD and Doc looked at each other. More people? The world was becoming more populated every day.

"We're on our way," shouted JD. They made their way up and found the others surveying the island with binoculars. It was true. Smoke floated lazily skyward and carried the unmistakable scent of cooking meat and vegetables. All minds wondered. What kind of people inhabited this place? More pirates? Head-hunting cannibals? Poisonous pygmies?

It was decided the *Broadsword* would circle the island and try to establish the intent of its residents before the crew risked going ashore. This time, everyone going ashore would be armed.

Reverend William Wainwright, his wife, Maggie, and eighteen faithful followers had been living on the island for just over four years. Life was simple and God-fearing. Reverend Wainwright made sure of that.

The reverend and his wife had founded The Resurrection Church of San Bernardino, California, eleven years previously. It had started in a basement of an old middle school with a broken-down organ and twenty-two members. Within five years, it had grown into a congregation of three thousand at a six-acre site, complete with worship cathedral, Sunday school, and parking garage.

For an hour every day, Reverend Wainwright and his wife hosted a television program, *The Blessed Savior*, on the popular, *Inspirational* cable network. It was an instant success. Money poured in, and religious trinkets poured out. Prayer towels, inspirational tapes and books, cathedral replicas, and miracles. Every day, someone somewhere in the viewing audience was healed of some ambiguous disease or malady. Of course, the good reverend and his wife became rich. Rolex watches, thousand-dollar suits, fancy automobiles, chartered flights and fine dining. They became celebrities and lead a blessed life. God was alive and rich in San Bernardino.

Then church planned a retreat for major contributors. A luxury yacht was rented for an eight-day cruise and revival, a floating prayer meeting. That was four years earlier. The yacht had vanished in a terrific storm, and everyone was presumed to be walking the golden streets in heaven and conversing with the saints. The official record said they had been lost at sea.

Unofficially, questions of tax fraud and misappropriation of church funds led to speculation that the good reverend and friends were living the high life on some exotic island. That speculation, as it turns out, was partially correct. They were on an island and were alive, but they had slipped back in time some ninety-two million years. As for their god? Conveniently, he could not be located in this timeline. Some have suggested the Christian god moves in mysterious ways. Surely, this was one of his more-mysterious.

When the marooned islanders spotted the U.S. Coast Guard cutter *Broadsword*, they thought they were rescued, their beachcombing days finally at an end. When the *Broadsword* voyagers spotted the wayward islanders, they thought they had found friends, other stranded but sane people. The islanders and the *Broadsword* folks would soon realize they were both wrong.

"Look at that," said Chief Hightower. "They're sending a raft to meet us. Under a white flag. Incredible."

"Only two on the raft," confirmed Kevin through binoculars.

Arabella and Dawn had already leveled fully loaded M16s at the approaching raft; they were taking no chances. One wrong move and they would send these peaceniks to a watery grave.

As the small raft neared, two male figures became obvious. The taller man was in his fifties. He had a bald spot surrounded by grayish white hair, dark and leathery skin, and a trim body. The shorter man was younger, broad shouldered, and barrel chested. Same leathery skin but long, black hair. They waved furiously at the *Broadsword* spectators.

"Ahoy on the ship," yelled the taller man.

The admiral replied, "We're armed and want no trouble. Put your hands in the air and we'll bring your craft closer so you can board. Understand?" The two men nodded yes.

Five minutes later, they stood before the *Broadsword*'s crew. Introductions and pleasantries were exchanged. Each group relayed the saga of its particular journey. The islanders were stunned. They had no idea about the time change. They had assumed they were marooned on a deserted, uncharted island. Like Gilligan.

"I remember you," said Duke in his usual way. "You're that fucking TV preacher that fucked over his flock. Where are all your miracles now?"

The taller man, Reverend Wainwright, said, "I'll thank you not to use that language in my presence, sir."

"And I'll thank you to double up and fuck yourself, holy man," replied the Duke.

The admiral interceded. "Reverend, we are perfectly capable of helping you and your comrades and offer you the hospitality of our ship."

"Thank you, sir. But please be our guests tonight on the island. Over a good meal, you can explain to the rest of our company what has happened to us."

The admiral agreed. "Excellent idea, Reverend, but the *Broadsword* will be on full alert and armed. Experience has taught us to be vigilant."

Terms accepted, everyone prepared for an interesting evening.

Kevin turned to JD. "This should be a real hoot."

"Yeah," said JD. "I wonder how they're going to take to Molly."

Duke had overheard them. "I hope she has a taste for fundamental meat. There's going to be a shitload on that island. Fucking holy men. Never trust a man in a dress is what I always say."

"I've never heard you say that," challenged Kevin. "Besides, they're not catholic, genious." JD began laughing.

"Hey Kev, eat shit, okay?"

JD realized only the best people would attend dinner. He hoped a knock-down, drag-out brawl could be avoided. Why was civility always a casualty of religious conversation? God only knew. But then the reverend had a pipeline directly to the big man, so maybe he could answer a few nagging questions. Surely, a fun time would be had by all.

The meal went well. The hosts were generous and obliging, and the guests were courteous and grateful. Fresh fruit and vegetables were served along with fried clams and boiled lobsters, the biggest lobsters the *Broadsword* group had ever seen. One lobster fed five people, but Duke finished his without assistance. The *Broadsword* supplied a dessert of baked prapple pie. Mr. Henry had whipped up the pies, and everyone agreed they were delicious. Coffee was served courtesy of the *Broadsword*. It was a sumptuous feast.

After dinner, around a blustering fire, both groups settled down to quiet conversation. The islanders had many questions. Most were still trying to assimilate the news of being back in time ninety-two million years. Sure, they had seen strange things in four years on this island—giant fish, bizarre birds, and other strange flying animals—but none ever considered being back in time. The twins offered the usual explanations. Time rifts, quantum mechanics, space-time continuums, and of course the various, strange "triangles" around the world in which ships and planes were always getting lost.

These were of little comfort to the stranded islanders. Their strong faith and deep commitment to God was being tested. Where was God in this primeval world? How could Jesus come again if he had not come yet? They lived for the rapture of the second coming but had suddenly and curiously been pushed back to a time; they realized the rapture would not happen for much longer than they had originally anticipated. No saints had ever lived or died. No Mary and Joseph. No Bethlehem. No Pontius Pilate, just a handful of people, alone and isolated, in a brutal world.

Most of the islanders' questions, however, were not theological. Who won the World Series? Who was president? What happened on New Year's 2000? How many billions is Bill Gates worth now?

Current events were related. George W. had stolen an election in 2000. The Diamondbacks were best in baseball. Hillary Clinton was a senator from New York. Terrorists had flown planes into the twin towers of the World Trade Center. Regis Philbin was no longer hot, and Rush Limbaugh could hear again.

Since most of the islanders were fundamentalist wingnuts to the right of the ayatollah and most surviving Hilter youth, the news was met with quiet enthusiasm. Given the mixture of the group digesting dinner around the fire, sparks would soon be flying, and not from the campfire.

Reverend Wainwright was a gracious host but a forceful man. He was blunt and outspoken, a natural sermonizer and a gifted orator. He was the Lord's servant and did not care who knew it. So the ensuing storm began not with thunder but with a gentle inquiry.

The reverend sat on a chair made of ship wreckage and twine, hands laced across a full stomach, the picture of contentment. "So tell me, admiral, who attends to the spiritual needs of your crew? You have no chaplain."

The admiral was a veteran of nearly thirty-five years in Her Majesty's Royal Navy. He chose his words carefully. "No, sir, we have no chaplain. Frankly, our journey so far has been fraught with danger at every turn. There hasn't been much time for Sunday school."

Reverend Wainwright laughed softly. "Ah yes, the raptors and the pirates. Terrible ordeals indeed. It proves Satan is alive and well in this world also. Our journey has been quite different, of course. Our boat limped to this shore and was destroyed by another storm. Yet by the grace of our Lord Jesus Christ, we have survived very well. He has supplied us with all we need, fresh water, food, a temperate climate, and the fellowship of good Christians. Even as we are marooned in this time, he has supplied all our needs." His voice trailed off.

Adam spoke up. "Maybe you could help us, Reverend. Tim and I programmed our computer with all the information and wisdom of our time and asked it, 'What is the nature of God?'"

"And what did your computer say?"

Tim handed the reverend the Cray III's reply. The reverend studied it a few seconds and looked up. He read the reply out loud. "Oodles of green noodles make blue poodles jump der schtroodle? I don't understand. What does it mean?"

The boys shrugged. "Beats me," said Tim. "We were hoping you'd know. I mean, since you talk to God all the time."

"The nature of God? Ah, yes. The nature of God," he repeated. "He is a merciful, loving father. An omniscient, omnipotent, and compassionate being. One who is involved in our daily lives. God is everywhere, and God is love."

The reverend was content with his answer, as were his followers. But not everyone at this shindig had been convinced. Some remained skeptical. Some had no problem being as vocal as the reverend.

"I'd applaud," said Duke, "but I only have one hand. An important preacher is asked what the nature of God is, and he throws out every cliché known to man. Why is it so important to know what God is?"

The reverend's back stiffened. His chest puffed as he prepared for holy battle. "Without God, we are lost. Only in him can we find salvation and peace. Open your heart to the Lord and let him in, brother. It is the only way."

"Bullshit," said Duke to the islanders chagrin but not the crews' surprise. "That's your way! If God stood next to you right now, you wouldn't know him because it's not a him. God is an it. I hate the way you always describe God in human terms. What a disservice. That must really piss God off."

"So you're an agnostic," shot the reverend. "Interesting. I always thought an agnostic was an atheist without the courage of his convictions."

"And I say an agnostic is a deeply religious person with at least a small knowledge of human fallibility. I call myself an agnostic because there isn't compelling evidence that God exists, at least your kind of God. And since more than half of the earth's population is not Christian, Jew, or Muslim, I'd say there are no compelling arguments for your kind of God.

"If your God wanted to convince us of his existence, he could do a much better job of it. Why so vague and ambiguous? Why be wrapped up in two thousand years of Hebrew ceremony? A few things have happened since then. The Renaissance, the Enlightenment, the Industrial Revolution, and now the Computer Age. Yet you cling to a two-thousand-year-old idea that cannot be proven or verified."

"It's called faith, sir," said the reverend, dismissing Duke's statements with three words. "We have faith."

"Faith, that vague and nebulous catchall word you use to describe belief in something unseen or unproven. How convenient for you. How lucky you are to have a fallback position in the face of reality. Your God has given you five senses and a brain, but these days, you can't use them to prove his existence. Instead, you use purposely vague words such as *faith*, *revelation*, or *inspiration*, intangibles that cannot be tested or verified, only debated. How amazingly curious."

"Not to us, sir," protested the reverend. "The Bible makes things extremely clear."

"Why is that? Why is God so clear in the Bible and so obscure in the real world?"

"He is not obscure at all. He is all around us. Our prayers are answered. Millions of people have been born again and have witnessed God's grace. The Bible speaks to us as clearly today as it did in the time of Moses and Jesus."

"Except there wasn't a Bible back then, as I recall. A bunch of eighth-century monks put it together. Let's get real. Where are the burning bushes, the pillars of fire, the great voice that says 'I am that I am' booming from the sky? Why does your God manifest himself in such subtle and debatable ways? Surely he could make his presence unambiguous? I mean, if your God two thousand years ago wanted to leave a record for future generations, it would be easy, trivial. After all, he's supposed to be omnipotent and omniscient. A few simple phrases would do."

"Such as?" challenged the reverend rather irreverently. He was growing more agitated by the moment. The last thing he expected from a cretin like Duke was an astute and razor-sharp tongue.

"Such as, 'The world is round,' or 'E equals e=mc2,' or 'You cannot travel faster than light.' Anything they could not have possibly known three thousand years ago."

"Any others?" chirped the sarcastic reverend.

"Sure. How about, 'There are no privileged frames of references' or 'A body in motion tends to remain in motion.' Your trouble, Reverend, is a failure of the imagination. Anything you don't understand you attribute to God. You sweep away all the mysteries of the world under a God rug, all the challenges to your intelligence. You simply turn your mind off and say God did it or it's God's will. How simple. How easy. How cowardly."

The reverend rose, his face red and ready to burst in reply when JD said calmly, "Perhaps we're all just wayfarers on the way to the truth."

This seemed to take the edge off the building bitterness. The reverend's attention turned to JD. "You're a Christian?"

"I'm a Christian and a Buddhist."

"How can you be both? You either believe in Jesus or Buddha."

JD said, "I'm a Christian because I believe Jesus Christ lived and died. He was an admirable historical figure. I do not believe he was God or the Son of God or even the great-grandnephew of God. Buddha was a philosopher, not a God. Buddhism, like most Eastern philosophies, is just that—a philosophy. You strive to follow a path." It was JD's turn to wax philosophical and demonstrate his eloquence. Doc Moran sat mesmerized by the conversation.

"And what path is that?" the reverend asked.

"To be worthy every day. To be an individual among millions and still have the chance to make a difference."

"In a world without God?" questioned Reverend Wainwright. "I would find such a world completely offensive."

"I know," agreed JD. "That's why you wrap yourself in some fifth-century religious mania. And you tend to talk only to others like yourself. I resent that this is some sort of faith contest and you're the hands-down winner. Why must Christians always be fighting something?"

"We fight for God against evil and the devil. Science and philosophy will not get you into heaven. You question everything, or try to. Truth to you means empirical, sensory data, things you can see and touch. There's no room for inspiration or revelation in your world. You rule out of court almost everything religion is about. I mistrust scientists and philosophers because they mistrust everything."

JD was impressed. He thought the reverend had stated his case very succinctly.

"Don't judge everyone else by your own limited experience," said the reverend. "Just because you reject the Lord does not prevent other folks from acknowledging his glory. Our faith preserves us."

"Really?" asked Duke, jumping back into the conversation with both feet. "And my faith preserves me too. With my senses and my brain. Go down to the beach tomorrow at high tide. I'll mark the highest tide level and let myself be buried up to my neck in sand one inch beyond the mark and feel perfectly safe. I know the water won't go any farther than that mark. Science and my brain tell me that, and I've tested my faith."

"So what's your point?" asked an incredulous Reverend Wainwright.

"My point, sir, is this. Would you be willing to test your faith in a similar fashion? Would you agree to be buried up to your neck a foot in front of the same mark and pray to your God to shorten the tide?"

All eyes looked to the reverend. Duke had thrown down a gauntlet. Face—saving rescue was needed, and the admiral quickly supplied it.

"Been a lovely evening," he stated in typically understated British parlance. "Good food, lively conversation, and wonderful hosts, but there are things on our ship that need tending to. I'm sure you folks have much to discuss about your situation. As I've said before, we're heading north and have plenty of room to accommodate you. We are happy to take along anyone who wants to go. We'll come ashore in the morning and talk to you about it. Thank you for your hospitality, but we should go."

He motioned to the other *Broadsword* members, who began shuffling for the Zodiacs. The admiral and the reverend shook hands as if they had just signed a peace treaty. Smiles hid distrust and skepticism. Nothing like a frank exchange of views to help the digestive system along.

As night deepened, the islanders and the *Broadsword* crew looked forward to a new day. Things were always clearer in the sun's light, and everyone had faith the sun would rise.

Four hundred miles north, the sun had risen and had begun torturing the day. The cloudless sky predicted unrelenting heat and humidity. Marcus and his band of roving raiders from Romanica wormed their way along a riverbed, quietly looking for signs of a Slant village. They had still not come across any signs when they realized they were being followed.

For the previous five minutes, Marcus was sure something was stalking his men. But what? It was subtle and careful but very deliberate. A subdued chortle broke the noiseless air, and he knew. No they were not being stalked; they were being herded. He drew his sword and pointed to the trees.

"Everyone up! Now!" he shouted. "Raptors! Get up in the trees!"

Horror swept the men. It was their worst nightmare. Raptors. They scrambled for footholds and began climbing trees. Maddened by fear, they ascended to the only safe places around. They knew raptors were indiscriminate killers that never passed up an opportunity to butcher their prey. They could think of few deaths worse than being ripped apart and devoured by such merciless beasts.

Just as Marcus had thought, the raptors broke their cover and appeared from all sides. They had set a trap for his men and had been preparing to ambush them but alertly now his men sat safely up in the branches, safe for the moment.

The raptors began grouping under the trees. They squawked in protest and snapped viciously at each other. They were not climbers. They would have to settle in for a long siege or move on to easier prey.

Hunger and a lack of patience prevailed; the group of famished predators slowly drifted off. There would be other days and other humans. They had become one of the raptors' favorite meals. Today they passed and moved on to something else, hopefully another victim of opportunity would present itself.

The Romanicans had been lucky. Marcus knew they could have all been killed. He had hoped to find the Slants before he ran across any raptors. He knew the Slants took precautions and built fortifications against predators, but unlike the grounded raptors, he and his men could climb. For the time being, they would wait in the trees. Then they would find some Slants and head home.

The morning cracked like a howitzer shot overhead. Lightning flashed, and great sheets of rain were blown horizontally by the wind. The *Broadsword* rocked and pitched in the violent ocean. The admiral, JD, Chief Hightower, and Kevin had come ashore. They could easily accommodate the reverend's group and were anxious to get underway.

"I'm sorry, gentlemen," said the reverend in a regretful but direct tone. "We voted last night and have elected to stay on this island. We have all we need."

All four members of the *Broadsword* were mortified. "We have plenty of room," implored the admiral, "and this is a dangerous world. You have no idea what's out there."

"Sure we do. And it's out there. Here, we are safe and have every comfort. For us, this is paradise."

Chief Hightower shook his head in disbelief.

JD said, "Sir, we were attacked by pirates, which proves there are other humans here. They could be following us. Our ship is a great prize. If they stop here, only the lucky ones would be killed. The others would be taken for slaves and concubines. I beg you to reconsider."

The reverend's eyes narrowed at JD. "What did you do in the real world?"

"I worked for the government. I fixed things." JD's answer was slow and calculated.

"Sort of a problem solver," quipped the reverend.

"More like a problem eliminator," suggested Kevin. JD gave him a hard look.

"Well, Captain Stoner, I appreciate your concern, but I'm afraid our minds are quite made up."

"We'll leave you some weapons, sir," said Chief Hightower. "A few M16s should deter any problems."

The reverend shook his head. "No weapons. They would lead only to violence and unrest among the people here. We will be fine. The Lord will sustain us."

"If we come back this direction, we'll stop in on you. We'll not divulge your whereabouts to anyone," said Admiral Fitzgerald.

"Take care of these people, sir. They depend on you. That's easy to see."

Everyone shook hands whether they wanted to or not. Walking to the Zodiac in the driving rain, Kevin asked JD, "What do you think?"

"I think he's an egotistical fundamentalist, and if we ever get back here, we'll find only bleached bones or graves. They're lost, Kev, and this is their sanctuary. One way or the other, they'll die here."

Kevin agreed. He put his hand over his eyes to shield the rain.

As the Zodiac pulled away from the island, its occupants wondered if they would ever see Reverend Wainwright and company again. The pelting rain prevented them from waving.

The twins had become the unofficial entertainment directors of the *Broadsword*. Every Friday night, they showed a double feature in the video room. That night was dubbed "Monster Chiller Horror Theater Night," and the double feature tonight included *The Birds* and *Psycho*, two Hitchcock classics.

Attendance was usually considerable. Going to the movies was a link to their former lives, a bridge to the past. The twins stood at the door like ushers. Each one had a flashlight and wore an admiral's hat.

Kevin and Arabella arrived arm in arm, like teenagers off on a dreamy date. They approached the twins.

"Smooching or non smooching?" asked a well-mannered Tim.

"Smooching," replied Arabella rather formally.

"Right this way, folks," said Tim, leading them to the back row. "Enjoy the movie."

When Admiral Fitzgerald arrived, Adam said, "One for the VIP section," and led the admiral to a center aisle seat.

Duke arrived next. "Ticket, sir?" asked Tim.

"Fuck off, dipshit."

"One for the XL section. Right this way, sir."

JD and Doc Moran eased up to the door, and Adam greeted them.

"Groping or non groping?" he inquired.

They looked at each other. "Groping," said the doc in a bourbon-and-buttermilk voice.

"Two more for lovers' lane," he announced. "Follow me, folks." He seated them in the back row with Kevin and Arabella.

Adam said, "I feel like I've been here before. What do you call that?"

"Déjà voodoo," answered Tim. "No, wait . . . Voodoo tata."

"Déjà vu," corrected Duke from across the room. "Who are these douche bags?" he asked no one in particular.

At last, everyone was seated, and the first movie rolled. Both were classics in black and white. At the end, the lights went up to thunderous applause and a few catcalls.

"What did you think?" Tim asked Dawn and Janice. He and Adam had sat behind the girls during the movies.

"They were good," said Dawn. "Even when you two idiots were screaming 'More skin! More skin!' during the shower scene in *Psycho*."

The boys tried their best to look innocent. They were not very good at it, but they had a surprise they were about to spring on everyone and they quickly turned their attention to it. Adam had slipped out of the room earlier and came back pushing a cart. On the cart were two ten-gallon plastic water coolers and two stacks of Styrofoam cups.

"And now, ladies and gentlemen," announced Tim. "For your edification, the piece de resistance, the coup de gracie! May we present our newest and boldest concoction to date? Tim and Adam's *Prapple Tonic*. It's good for what ails you and will clean anything from clothes to a barbeque grill. Step right up and taste this marvelous elixir."

Adam said, "One at a time now. No pushing or shoving. There's plenty for everyone."

Slowly, cautiously the group made their way to the cart. The boys were filling cups and handing them to everyone. JD, Doc Moran, Chief Hightower, Admiral Fitzgerald, Kevin, and Arabella stood in a circle, examining the strange brew. As if on cue, all took a taste. Reactions varied. Doc Moran and Arabella began choking. JD acted like his mouth was on fire. The chief and admiral continued to sip theirs cautiously. Kevin downed his in one gulp.

"What is it?" asked a stunned Chief Hightower.

"I know what it isn't," stated the admiral. "It's not Napoleon brandy."

"Why it's, it's shattering," said a recovering JD. His mouth felt like the inside of a volcano.

Kevin held up his glass. "I don't know. I rather like it. I think I'll have another one." He walked to the coolers.

The twins were circulating through the crowd and made their way to the admiral's group. "How do you like it, sir?" asked a partially bombed Tim.

"It's really quite different," the admiral managed to say as he eyed the queer drink.

"Did I mention not to smoke around it, sir?" slurred Adam. "No smoking."

"So this is what you boys have been brewing for the last two weeks in that cellar you call home." said Chief Hightower.

"Yeah," said Tim. "We got the recipe out of the computer. Tasty, eh?"

"And highly flammable," warned Adam. "We gave some to Norton and he did a backflip."

The boys had been nipping the velvet liquid a bit more heavily than the others and were well on their way to being boiled, but their efforts to engineer a good party had worked. The room was alive with laughter and camaraderie. Though few realized it at the time, all were on their way to historic hangovers. A few would have knee-crawling, commode-hugging blackouts. No one would forget Tim and Adams *Prapple Tonic.* So far, it the hit of the social season.

"How do you feel, lightweight?" asked Doc Moran through parched lips.

JD did not want to open his eyes until the world quit spinning. He touched his head. "God, even my hair hurts, and little tiny men with ice picks are dancing on my brain. Are we dead?"

"No, and we're not in Kansas either, Toto."

JD and Doc had left the party and gone to see Molly, where they both had promptly passed out. They both nursed enormous prapple hangovers.

"The entire German North Africa Corp has walked through my mouth," said JD. "How could I get so drunk? They were such small cups."

"Yeah, but you had twenty-nine of them. I had to drag you out of there. You and the admiral kept screaming something about war monkeys!"

JD laughed, which hurt his head. "That's war mongers!" he corrected.

"Whatever. The point is everyone on the ship was soused. For all I know, Norton's driving the boat!"

JD looked at Doc. Even through bloodshot eyes she looked terrific. He had become very close to her. They worked well together. Aggravations were laughed away, and arguments were diffused with funny faces and giggly kisses. He noticed she was scratching her chest.

"Problems?" he said softly.

"Yeah, we've been sunbathing topless out on deck these last few days, and it itches. If there's anything I hate, it's peeling boobs."

Hung over and more dead than alive, their minds reached the same conclusion—the world's best hangover cure. Doc asked, "Right here? You think Molly will mind?"

JD only smiled. They were hungry for each other. A breeze blowing over the open cargo hold, undisturbed by their lovemaking, was cooling their skin. Molly snored her approval. The great cat was content for their happiness.

After the lovemaking, Doc said, "Fan-fucking-tastic! How do you do that?" She was just finally catching her breath.

"I was a butterflyer in college. I swam the two hundred fly. Flyers do it better."

"Really? Why's that?"

"You have to learn a two-beat dolphin kick, and you have to have strength and endurance. It's a deadly combination."

"I'll say," agreed Doc. "I'm glad you still remember it."

"You never forget it." He kissed her very softly on the cheek. "I'm a lot of things, Doc, some good, many bad, but I promise you I'll love you for the rest of my life."

She was struck by his honesty and was near tears when he said, "No matter what happens in this world, if we are ever separated, stay alive. No matter what, stay alive. I'll find you. No matter how long it takes, I'll find you."

"I know," she said, pulling close. "I'll never let you go, JD Stoner. I've never been happier. I love you too. I've never been closer to anyone."

They kissed again, long and slowly. There was no need to rush. They had a shared lifetime to explore the limits of their love. The wind cooled their skin, and Molly snored.

The twins were making every effort to appear not hung over.

"You boys look chipper this morning," said a sober Mr. Henry. He noticed they had both passed on breakfast in lieu of black coffee.

Duke noticed too. "Got fucked up last night, eh?"

There was no denying it.

"Smashed," said Adam.

"Bombed," agreed Tim. "Boiled, blotto, zonked, slobber-knockered, blasted, and tore up from the floor up!"

"Yep. Wasted," Adam said. "We bit the bullet. Toked the unit. Embalmed we were."

"Okay, I get it," said Duke. "That was some good shit, though. And a hell of a party. How'd you do with Dawn and Janice?"

"Not so good," admitted Tim. "I threw up on Dawn's shoes."

"And I hit Janice with a bowling ball," said Adam. "Accidentally, of course."

"A bowling ball? How the fuck?"

"Don't ask," begged Adam. "I was so hung over this morning I put Preparation H on my toothbrush."

Duke laughed. "That will fuck up your morning, eh boys? You boys have a good day, now. I'll stop by later with a nice lard sandwich smothered in garlic." He grinned. The twins grabbed their mouths and ran for the nearest toilet.

"What's the matter with them?" asked Kevin as the twins rushed past.

"Weak constitution," said Duke. "They can't hold their fucking liquor."

"Morning," said the admiral. "What's with the lads? They looked a bit peaked."

"Pantywaists," said Duke, just as the ship was jolted as if struck by a massive force. The blow sent people and objects flying. The intercom crackled. "This is Arabella on the bridge. I'm gonna need some help."

Reverend Wainwright and his fellow islanders were in desperate need of help. As they slept snug in their beds, Constantine and his pirates had slipped onto the island. When the sun came up, the islanders found themselves captives of a vengeful, merciless scoundrel.

Interrogating the islanders created pandemonium. The pirates had trouble understanding their captives' language, so what good was torture? No matter what the victim said or screamed, it meant nothing to the pirates.

Not that the good reverend did not try to communicate. He readily told everything he knew. He just could not get anyone to understand him.

The pirates did the expedient thing. They stripped the islanders of anything useful. They pilfered stores of food and water and killed all the men. Reverend Wainwright was the last to die. The pirates thought him pathetic. He sniveled and cried like a girl before Constantine slit his throat. As he fell to the ground, trying to hold his gushing throat, Constantine spit on him and cursed him for his cowardice.

The reverend and the other men had been lucky. Death had come in a gruesome fashion but had come quickly. The female islanders were not as fortunate. The next forty-eight hours were some of the worst of their lives. They were all repeatedly raped and abused. The pirates spared them no humiliation. They were allowed no clothing, and any man could use any woman at will. Refusal led to brutal beatings.

Hell had descended on this Christian island. As the blood of Reverend Wainwright cooled in death, his once-lovely wife became a concubine of the feared Constantine. Alone and forced into deprivations she could never have imagined, she silently prayed. She needed her God now. Would faith be enough to sustain her?

She closed her eyes as Constantine, raging drunk and demonical, pried her legs apart and began grunting like a crazed animal. There was no fight left in her, only the nothingness of submission. Tears stained her face as the mad pirate thrust into her savagely. She thought, *Where have all the good men gone? And where are all the gods?*

The *Broadsword* had been jolted by a hundred-and-fifty-ton *Liopleurodon* that had been escorting her calf when the curious youngster swam over to investigate the shiny metal ship. The youngster became frightened and veered away, which alarmed momma. She swam directly at the *Broadsword* and rammed it broadside. Her huge body bobbled the ship, and in the process, she was momentarily stunned.

Topside, the crew watched as the mother *Liopleurodon* floated, unconscious. Her baby nudged her to wake up. It was a tender sight—mother and child. But like most things in this world, matters turned brutally savage.

"Oh my God," exclaimed Arabella as she pointed to approaching fins. They were unmistakable. *Carcharodon megalodon*, a hundred feet and thirty tons of carnivorous shark. A whole school of them. The stunned *Liopleurodon* was recovering when the first shark hit her. She could have killed one shark easily, but this was twelve on one, and she was still dazed. The sharks were savage, relentless, powerful killers with massive jaws.

The baby *Liopleurodon* was ravaged by four sharks. They ripped the youngster to pieces, devouring everything. The mother had been set upon by at least eight sharks, and mercifully, death came fast. As the great marine reptile floated helplessly, the sharks took turns tearing off chunks of meat the size of automobiles.

The crew watched in horror. The frenzied spectacle was cold and unnerving, grisly, and sickening—a sight that would be forever imprinted on their minds. The *Broadsword* steamed away, leaving the sadistic sharks to their loathsome task. They were efficient predators. Nothing would be wasted. It was nature at its worst. Death for some meant life for others. It was a simple equation, one that would continue for at least another ninety-two million years.

JD and Doc Moran stood at the stern, watching the dark-blue water slide by the moving ship. A stiff breeze buffed them from behind, but it allowed them to tolerate the high humidity. It had been two days since they had spotted any land. Behind, the ocean was a vast universe of endless water, cool liquid under the blazing sun.

"You're in deep thought," said Doc, taking his arm in hers.

He was in a pensive mood. "I was thinking about the Reverend Wainwright and his followers. We should have made them come with us."

"You know you couldn't do that," she said. "They're adults. They make their own decisions."

"But I don't think they did. I think the good reverend decided for them. I don't think he had that right. This is a bad world, Doc. There are many others here, vagabonds like us. Probably not many, but enough. Roving bands of marauders preying on everything. It's the way of this time. I fear for those decent people who won't be able to defend themselves against any real threat."

"Reverend Wainwright believes God will guide them, protect them, and provide for them," the doc said.

"But he won't," answered JD. "I listened to the reverend, and I thought his god was too small. One paltry planet, a few thousand years, hardly worth the attention of a minor deity, much less the creator of the universe."

"He thinks if there's no God, we wouldn't know what to do or how to behave. He's worried about being lost, I guess," said Doc.

"He's not worried about being lost. He's worried about not being central. There's plenty of order in the universe. Gravitation, electromagnetism, quantum mechanics and super unification. He wants people to believe in God so they'll obey the law. The only means that occur to him is a strict, secular police force and the threat of punishment by an all-seeing God for whatever the police miss. He sells human beings short, and he sells nature short." JD took a breath, slowed down.

The doc smiled and teased. "I just love it when you get all philosophical." She kissed the side of his mouth.

"I just don't understand people sometimes," he said as he tossed a rock out into the ocean. "We all have a thirst for wonder. It's probably a truly human quality. I'm just saying that you don't have to make up stories, you don't have to exaggerate. There's wonder enough in the real world. Nature is much better at inventing wonders than we are."

Doc stared off. "The first things men do is make gods. I heard that somewhere. I guess it's true."

Kevin and Duke walked over to them. No one spoke for quite a while. Thoughts drifted with the passing water.

"Did you see this?" asked Kevin finally. He handed JD a sheet of paper. It brought a smile that lit up his face.

"Those boys just won't quit," JD laughed.

"What is it?" asked Doc.

"The boys are starting a fraternity," said Kevin. "This is announcing that next week is pledge week. Everyone onboard, male of course, can pledge."

"Fraternity?" asked an incredulous Doc. It was weird even for them.

"They think Dawn and Janice will like them if they're in a frat," Kevin said. "They think frat brothers get all the babes." He shrugged.

"They been snorting that prapple tonic shit," said Duke. "Their brains have gone soft. The only fraternity those two could get into is the 'I douche a dork' frat."

They all laughed.

"Next thing you know, they'll be taking out classified ads," laughed the doc.

"They already are," said Kevin, "Check out the bottom of the page."

JD's and Doc's eyes scanned to the bottom of the page. It read, "Small-nosed sorority girls wanted for manhandling and light housecleaning. Fabulously attractive twins seek tomatoes for a little koo-koo-chee-koo!"

"Like I said, they just won't quit. You have to admire that," said JD.

Molly came topside and slid in next to JD and Doc. She growled at Duke, who took a step back. The breeze felt good along her thick fur, and she yawned deeply. JD rubbed her head.

Chief Hightower appeared above them on the aft section of the bridge. "Land," he cried. "To the starboard, land!"

They all saw it. Land! And not just any land. What they saw would be the future United States of America. They stared at what would become the western coast of Texas. Instead of a vast desert, Texas was a tropical rain forest, a dense jungle complete with a wide variety of carnivores. Large carnivores.

They recognized immediately their old friends, the *Sarcosuchus imperator*, the great crocs. They spotted dozens sunning on the shore; massive, sixty-foot reptiles that could outfit a dozen families with luggage and shoes. Above the jungle canopy, great birds and winged dinosaurs soared, held aloft by unseen breezes as they spied the jungle for prey.

The sight of the land produced feelings of apprehension and joy; apprehension because the memory of the raptor encounter was still fresh, and joy because humans love the stability of solid ground.

"That ain't Sam Houston's or Jim Bowie's Texas," said Chief Hightower. "It's more like the everglades in Florida."

"This whole world is a bubbling bowl of chicken noodle soup," claimed Kevin. "A percolating place of placid prehistoric paranoia."

"Say that three times," challenged the doc.

"We going ashore?" asked Duke.

"Not here," said the chief. "Too many bad guys. Those crocs look lazy, but they're always hungry."

As the *Broadsword* drew closer to land, the air buzzed with pursuit and escape. Birds the size of eagles chased mosquitoes the size of dragon flies. Great aerial dogfights played out in front of everyone. Mosquitoes were chased and eaten by dragonflies that were chased and eaten by birds that were chased and eaten by flying dinosaurs, which ruled the roost. For the human observers, it was a great display of aeronautics.

What happened next scared everyone aboard right down to his or her toe nails. A forty-foot T. rex burst from the tree line, stumbled briefly, and straightened. The colossal dinosaur roared and swung back at the trees. It was wounded but defiant. A jagged gash across its left haunch bled freely. The tyrannosaur bellowed in anger again, its mighty head swinging from side to side.

A few seconds later, the tyrannosaur's nemesis appeared. It crashed through the tree line, splintering branches and throwing limbs everywhere. Three great horns protruded from a huge head backed by a giant armor plate. A full-grown triceratops. Blood dripped from its eight-foot horns. It shook its stout head and pawed the ground. The earth trembled as the thirty-ton beast moved forward. The injured T. rex retreated slightly and roared again. The triceratops was built like a tank, low to the ground, with powerful legs. It charged the T. rex with surprising speed, the great horns projecting like advancing pikes. The T. rex wanted no more of the triceratops. It backed away, bloodied but alive. Backing away proved a terrible mistake.

The sunning crocs smelled blood, and before the T. rex could react, a large croc attacked. The speed of the croc startled the T. rex, but it avoided it and snapped at it in frustration. The crocs were experienced hunters however; avoiding one was not enough.

Two others advanced and lunged at the T. rex. One missed, but one grabbed a leg and began to roll. The weight of the fifty-foot rolling croc twisted the T. rex's leg out of its socket, sending it to the ground. The remaining crocs sprang to the struggling, helpless T. rex, inflicting massive, tearing wounds. The T. rex gurgled as it tried to roar. Finally, its great head lay down in defeat. The crocs feasted. The triumphant triceratops withdrew to the trees. The mother had defended her young and slipped back into the jungle to secure them. The battle of titans had ended. The predator had become the prey. Tomorrow? Who knew?

The *Broadsword* crew had witnessed another example of the ferocity of the times—giant beasts in an eternal struggle for supremacy. The sheer savagery of death and destruction in the world was a continuous circle. On the bright side, civilization and its improvements were only ninety-two million years away. And time marches on.

Marcus and his Romanican henchmen marched through the countryside, looking for signs of Slant life. So far, nothing. That was curious. The Slants were being more cautious, or they had not ventured that far north, or something had prevented them from settling there. Probably a combination of all three, thought Marcus.

In a small clearing, they came across a herd of hadrosaurs browsing the foliage. These great, duckbilled dinosaurs were herbivores, but at nearly thirty feet tall, they were formidable just the same. They grazed easily among the tall conifers, oaks, and smaller trees, giving the intruding humans scarcely a second thought. One would occasionally glance at the parading humans and promptly go back to chewing food with the same nonchalance as a cow in a pasture. These odd-looking bipedal beasts were about the business of eating; nothing else seemed to matter. The passing men watched in wonder as the gentle giants fed on the herbage, carefree and easy going. One would occasionally emit a loud trumpet sound, and the others would stop, pop their queer heads up, and listen. The bobbing heads were quite funny to the men.

At the far end of the clearing, a great trumpet blast rang out. All heads and ears turned in that direction. Nothing happened. No rampaging T. rex appeared; no roving band of raptors eased into view. This greatly relieved the anxious humans.

Then a curious thing happened. A hadrosaur at the end of the meadow began running, creating sort of a general-direction stampede. Trumpeting became loud, and it was coming from numerous beasts. Marcus's men crouched, waiting to see what had frightened the large plant eaters.

Then it became clear. A giant, black, buzzing cloud materialized out of the trees. The men recognized the whirring sound. Bees. A large swarm of prehistoric killer bees. A hadrosaur had probably disturbed a hive, and the solider bees had grouped to attack. These bees were the size of oranges, and they had a powerful, debilitating sting. Multiple stings were usually fatal. The bees, like their ant relatives, feared only three things—water, smoke, and fire, but none of those elements were around. The bees also hated noise, and the trumpeting, escaping hadrosaur had made enough to wake the dead.

The men froze. The dark cloud of annoyed bees flew forward, and the men ran. Forty raiders and a giant crashed through the forest in a mad dash for a pond they had passed a quarter-mile back with the angry insects in hot pursuit. Fatigue was not a consideration. To stop meant a painful, gruesome death. They ran for the safety of the water. Random chance played a hand in their desperate plight. Two of the fleeing humans had run wide of the others. The pond was boggy mud and quicksand, and the two raiders found themselves mired in knee-deep mud. They freed themselves only to run into a large bed of quicksand. They were stuck, partially buried up to their waists. They cried out, which was a dreadful mistake. The noise of their pleas drew the maddened bees' attention.

What happened next no one would forget. The struggling men were swarmed by the killer bees. Like lunatics, they fought the bees, swinging, swatting, and screaming. Their upper bodies and faces were completely covered with frenzied, stinging bees. Guttural moans soon replaced the screaming.

The bees were pitiless. Each man sustained hundreds of agonizing stings. Half-inch barbs repeatedly stabbed their skin, injecting a painful toxin. Their comrades had found safety in the water but were powerless to help their friends.

The bees, satisfied with their retribution, buzzed off in the direction of the hive, leaving the swollen, distorted bodies to the gulping quicksand. The bodies, bloated and purple, sank quickly into semiliquid graves.

Marcus cursed fate. Two more dead, and they still had not seen one Slant! Soaked and tired from the panicked run, his men emerged from the pond. Bedraggled and weary, they assembled around their leader. Marcus was about to give the men a rousing speech when his nostrils caught the unmistakable scent of a cooking fire. The men also understood the smell. Someone was cooking not far away. Slants! It had to be!

After a month on the trail, they were finally about to make contact. They would track the fire to the village and recon the area. They would formulate a plan and take action. Slaves and women at last! His men would soon be catching slaves and raping women. Everyone's spirit was raised at the thought. They marched in two columns toward the smoke, content in the knowledge that conquest and pillage would soon follow.

"Okay, lads, so what have you got?" asked Admiral Fitzgerald. He had joined the twins, JD, Kevin, and Chief Hightower on the bridge.

Adam, hunched over the radar screen, said, "There, just at the edge of the radar screen." He pointed at an object that lasted a second or two and then was gone. "There's something out there, Admiral. Just at the limit of our radar. It comes and goes."

"A ship?" asked Chief Hightower.

"From the signature, yes," answered Tim. "A ship, but it hovers at the edge of our radar. Strange."

Kevin, JD, and the admiral looked at each other.

"What about sonar? Any noise?" asked Kevin.

"No noise."

"No screws," JD said. "It's a sailboat. It fades in and out because of the wind. It gains on us with good wind and loses ground when the wind dies."

"But who?" asked the admiral.

"Pirates," said JD. He looked at Kevin. "I should have taken care of the rest back on that island. They want this boat. They'll dog us till they get a chance to attack us. We'll have to fight them eventually."

"Let's wait on them and confront them," said the chief. "We display our superior firepower and they leave. Easy."

But JD was not sure it would be so easy. He knew what needed to be done. No one else would say it. "We have to eliminate them, sir," he told the admiral. "There's no other way."

"You got a lot of hard bark on you, mister," the admiral said. "You'd kill them just like that."

JD was not fazed. "They'd kill *us* just like that. With this ship, Admiral, the bad guys could do anything they wanted. This is not a civilized world. There's no high tea and crumpets."

"So we sink to their level?" asked the admiral.

"We defend ourselves and survive. Sometimes we preempt an enemy. You're in charge, sir. What do you want to do?"

The admiral stood, arms behind his back in a pose of deep thought. He neither blinked nor breathed. "I assume you have a plan. Perhaps we should discuss it."

They all nodded. Kevin knew JD probably had a dozen plans. He was sure they all ended the same—with the bodies of dead pirates.

Two hours later, a compromised plan was reluctantly agreed upon. They would backtrack and intercept the trailing pirate ship.

JD didn't like it. "Let me take a Zodiac," he implored. "I'll be back in two days. I guarantee we'll have no more pirate trouble. Better to risk one than the whole ship."

The admiral looked at him. JD was a brave man but not a sacrificial lamb.

"Captain Stoner," he said, "look around you. This ship is a family now. We'll help and support each other. Friends help friends. You'll do your part, and we'll do ours. We may not be international assassins or kung fu experts, but we will contribute. Now, Mister Hightower, your estimation on our rendezvous with these pirates?"

"Uh, well, sometime tomorrow, depending on their speed, sir."

"Good. Let's prepare ourselves, gentlemen. Step lightly now, lads. I'll have no lollygaggers on this ship."

Adam turned to Tim. "I haven't lolled a single gag all day," he whispered.

The admiral shot them stern looks. They saluted and bugged out. He turned to JD. "You sure you want to do this?"

"Is there a choice?"

"But to attack them? They'll have no fear of us. And you'll be alone. Much could go wrong."

"It always does, Admiral. I'll be fine."

The admiral persisted. "But you'll be in the open sea for a while. That alone is dangerous. Once you leave the ship—"

"I'm on my own, I know. I'll keep you informed on the radio, and if I can't handle it, you hit them with the fifties. The Chief and Kevin will turn their boat into Swiss cheese."

"Why take the fight to them? We could just stand off two hundred yards and blast them." The admiral had a valid point.

"Three reasons," said JD. "One, we need information. What do they know? Who have they talked to? Two, because they won't expect it. Three, because I can."

The admiral saw the coldness in his eyes, the dead eyes of a ghost. The crew of the pirate ship would think hell itself had come aboard. He was glad Nomad was on their side. They began preparing.

An alliance with the devil is justified as long as it's temporary, so thought Constantine Orlov. For ten days, he had pursued an empty ocean, but there was no sign of the great steel vessel he prized above all else. He had learned much; the woman called Maggie Wainwright had been very helpful. He was learning her language, and she was proving a capable cook and mistress.

She had told him all she knew of the steel ship called *Broadsword* and its crew, but she did not know anyone called Nomad. She had never heard that name. To make sure she was not lying, he had burned her thigh with a white-hot metal. The singed flesh would heal, and she had learned the penalty for lying.

Taking the great ship would not be easy, he knew. His pirates were not experienced fighters, but if he could just get close, he felt he could rule the ocean unchallenged. Even the Slants and Romanicans would stand aside. Forget being emperor of a tiny plateau or city. He would be emperor of the world! All would bow and cringe in his presence, and he would be ruthless. He closed his eyes, enjoying the possibilities.

Maggie Wainwright broke his daydream as she entered the small quarters. She carried a tray with fruit and bread and a jug of wine. He leered his approval as she set down the tray and began serving him. He knew later he would force her again into unspeakable sexual acts and displays. His member grew hard at the thought but now he needed to learn and understand. He looked at the shattered soul of a woman and said, "Teach me more of your English, and tell me again of the great steel ship."

She bowed slightly. Her eyes never met his as she sat. He swilled wine and bit huge chunks of fruit. He ate like a barbarian. His unshaven, scarred face was a testament to his savagery. She folded her hands and was about to tell her tale once more when he abruptly cut her off with a wave of his fruit-smeared hand.

"I've changed my mind, wench. I wish to hear you scream with pleasure first! Strip off those clothes and assume the position, dog! My sword grows hot and hard for the holes of that body. First, I pleasure you, and then you tell me of the *Broadsword*."

Again she bowed and began removing the rags he called clothes. She knew what was expected and offered no resistance, only cowling submission. Her world was a jumble of surreal events and humiliation. She wished she had the courage to kill herself.

She wondered how suicide under her conditions could be a mortal sin. Surely, God could understand and let her into heaven. Or maybe this was her hell. Forever relegated to this misery for eternity. She cried silently as the pirate violated her. She needed a savior, and not necessarily a god.

Doc Moran burst into cargo hold two like a hurricane named Matilda. Her body language left little doubt that she was pissed. JD and Molly instinctively tensed. "What the hell is the matter with you?" she demanded. "What? Are you the only hero left on this godforsaken planet? Why you? You want to die? You selfish son of a bitch!"

He moved to her, but she recoiled. "No, damn it! Tell me why you have to go."

In a soft voice, he said, "Because I can. It's what I'm good at, Doc. No one else can do this."

"You're going to just slip aboard that ship? There are probably thirty men on it. Then what?"

In a voice as cold as Siberia, he said, "I'm going to kill them. Kill them all."

She looked at him. She was shaken by the lack of anything in his voice. "That's crazy! No one, not even you, could do such a thing." Her voice trembled. "Goddamn you, JD. I love you. Do not do this. There's so much I've learned to live without, but not you! Please. Let's just go. Outrun them. Lose ourselves forever. Please."

She was near tears when he held her. They held each other as close as two human beings can.

"I love you, Doc. But there's no future with this kind of threat. Never will I let anything or anyone hurt you. Never. I do this because it's necessary. I'll come back. I promise."

"And no Spartan bullshit. None of this 'with my shield or on it' nonsense. You come back to me, JD Stoner. You hear?" Tears streaked her face. He kissed each eyelid softly. They fluttered like butterfly wings.

"I'll be back, Doc. I'll be back."

They held each other. Molly came close, yawned, and laid her head across JD's feet. As he held Doc close, he looked into the eyes of the great cat, and Molly understood.

The lookout recognized what he saw and sounded the signal alarm. Captain Constantine Orlov and men raced to the deck, eyes scanning the azure-blue ocean in the direction of the lookout's outstretched arm. There, like a floating steel beast, was the *Broadsword*. The pirates stood in awe of the mighty ship.

The lookout called down to Constantine. "We no longer have to chase, Captain. The great ship comes to us."

"What? You're sure?" Constantine bellowed.

"Yes, sir. She sails toward us."

Concern etched the pirate's ruddy face. Why was the *Broadsword* coming at them? He had been prepared to attack her but was not ready to be attacked. The pirate thought quickly. "Turn her into the wind!" he yelled at his helmsman. "We'll wait here for that great steel bitch. Prepare yourselves!"

The men scrambled to their battle stations. Harpoon cannon were primed, and swords and cutlasses were readied. Constantine's schooner floated gently in a calm sea, awaiting the *Broadsword*. To him the steel ship was magical . . . a dream, something too unreal to be real, but real nonetheless. He prayed the one called Nomad was aboard and vowed to avenge the death of his men on the island. To kill Nomad and take this ship would be a great victory, the kind that produced legends, myths—immortality.

He slid the blade of his cutlass along the deck railing. The sword was razor sharp and had tasted the flesh of many men. Soon, he thought, he would have everything he wanted, including the head of Nomad.

JD sat with Arabella and Kevin in the armory, going over last-minute details. He would travel light for this operation. He would have to swim at least five hundred yards, so equipment had to be kept to a minimum. He would take his sword, the 9 mm Anchluss, a radio, and some C-4 explosives. Arabella had checked everything a dozen times, including the radio. No one wanted any problems.

JD took swim fins and hand paddles. The sea was calm at the moment, but if the waves and chop picked up, they would come in handy. He could push twice as much water with them, and it would be easier to plane over the surface. An old swimmer's training technique.

Arabella handed JD a detonator. "Stick this in the plastic," she said. She handed him a small transmitter. "Press this button and boom! It has a range of a hundred yards."

JD nodded. Kevin handed him a small, watertight pouch to carry everything. He said, "All we need is some darkness."

The plan was simple. The *Broadsword* would confront the pirates but come no closer than five hundred yards. As the pirates waited in confusion about what the *Broadsword* might do, JD would swim across to their vessel under cover of darkness, plant the C-4 on the hull under the waterline, board the ship, and learn what he could. Before leaving, he'd call the *Broadsword*, kill as many pirates as possible, and blow a hole in the hull. The sea would claim any surviving pirates. Kevin and Arabella would pick JD up in a Zodiac. Simple. That's if you were James Bond or Nomad.

JD watched Kevin. "Doc's pissed," he said. Kevin and Arabella looked at him.

"She doesn't want to see you hurt, or worse," said a stoic Arabella. "She loves you. Just like I've come to love this big ape here." She poked Kevin in the ribs. "If he were going, I'd be pissed too. I'd probably break one of his arms so he couldn't go."

JD handed Kevin a note. "Later, when I'm gone, give this to Doc. And if anything happens—"

"I know," said Kevin, cutting him off. "If anything happens, I'll take care of both of them. My word."

JD smiled. He knew Kevin would see to Molly and Doc. He trusted him completely.

It would not be dark for another four hours, so JD headed to see Molly.

What in hell are they doing? thought Constantine. The steel ship had been circling his ship at a distance of over five hundred yards for over an hour, and nothing. No sound, no demands, no communication whatsoever. What were they up to? He hated the waiting. Waiting was always bad for you and good for the opponents.

Constantine knew he had to get close to the *Broadsword.* His harpoon cannon would have little effect on her steel body, so he had to find a way to board in large numbers and kill the crew without destroying any of the ship. He needed the cover of night. Under the night sky, he would send twenty-five men to infiltrate the *Broadsword* and capture it. They would take longboats and silently slip up next to her, scale the hull, and kill everyone onboard. It seemed a sound and efficient plan. He had the men prepare. All he needed was darkness.

Admiral Fitzgerald stood on the bridge of the *Broadsword,* studying the pirate ship through practiced binoculars. He turned to Chief Hightower. "Your report, Chief."

The chief set down his binoculars and began scribbling on a pad. He looked up and focused on the admiral. "They have four old, spring-loaded harpoon cannon on deck. Range about a thousand yards. They can't hurt us with those. I count thirty-plus men. No firearms or other advanced technology, only swords and cutlasses. They'll have to storm us and take the ship hand-to-hand."

The chief paused. "Unless of course they have something we're not seeing."

The admiral peered again through his binoculars. JD and Kevin stepped on the bridge.

"They'll come after dark," the admiral stated. "Quietly, by small boats. The timing on this will have to be on the money. Captain Stoner, you sure about this swim? These waters aren't exactly the pool at Annapolis."

"I'll make it, Admiral. As soon as I'm in the water, you back off another thousand yards and hit your searchlights. The pirates in the small boats will be caught at sea. I'll be on and off that tub before they know what's happening. By the time the others get back, there'll be a five-foot hole in the hull."

"We'll have the Zodiac standing by," Kevin said. "When we get your signal, we'll be there in three minutes. I'll drive, and Arabella will cover. She's the best shot onboard. We'll have enough firepower to take down a herd of brachiosaurs."

"If you're late," joked JD.

"If we're late, we're dead. Then you'll have a fun swim." He grinned at JD.

"Just tell Arabella to keep that M16 pointed away from me. That gal is dangerous. She mowed down half the jungle when we tangled with the raptors."

Proud as a peacock, Kevin said, "Yeah, she's a real doll."

"I've got to check in with Molly," said JD. "I'll be ready when the time comes." He headed for the cargo hold and Molly.

The admiral pivoted to Kevin. "This is dicey, even for him," he said. "Between the monsters in these waters and the pirates on that ship, he's gonna have a tough time. Even in the Zodiac, it'll take you five minutes or more to get to him if he needs help. Those are not good odds, my friend."

Kevin wore an anxious look. He too was concerned for JD. He had seen his friend accomplish many remarkable things and survive encounters with less than a 20% chance of surviving. But that was in the old real world. In this prehistoric world, random chance could play a much greater and more deadly role. A human life could be in jeopardy just by being out in the open. Opportunistic predators lurked everywhere. To many, human prey was a delicacy. Kevin worried but prepared for his role. He and Arabella would be there to pick up JD on schedule. Nothing would go wrong on his end.

JD sat with Molly in the cargo hold. Two anxious warriors, but only one was going this time. The other would endure the terrible agony of waiting for its friend to return safely. The big cat leaned against JD as he rubbed her head. She yawned in approval.

JD began speaking to her as if she were human and could understand him. Doc appeared in the doorway. Neither JD nor Molly noticed her. She listened.

"Don't be mad at me, Moose," JD said. The cat seemed to enjoy the nickname. "The swim is too far for you, and there are many bad things in this ocean. I have to do this alone."

Molly growled her disapproval.

"If something happened to me, I know you'll sense it first. Then it'll be your job to look after Doc. Humans need help in times of loss. She'll need you. Protect her from the bad guys. If I'm gone, they'll be here. Doc doesn't know the really bad side of humans, so you protect her. I love that woman. As long as she lives, she'll never know how much. I'm sorry she sees this terrible side of me, but sometimes, survival isn't pretty. Down the road, maybe, she could forgive the man called Nomad. I don't know. I just know I have to do this.

"The men on that boat would kill us all in a heartbeat. But as long as I'm capable of stopping it, I will. So stay strong, Moose. I'll be back later."

Molly pushed him over and began rubbing her head on him. They wrestled a short while. Doc had decided not to disturb them. She had heard everything and slipped back out of sight.

Damn him, she thought. Just when she had convinced herself he was a miserable son of a bitch, she overheard that. Yes, she loved him, and yes, she would forgive the man called Nomad when he returned. First, he had to return.

The sun was dropping from the sky. The gray of dusk fell over the ocean as the ship's shadow began stretching across the deep water. A sliver of a moon was appearing high in the blue vault of the heavens but splashed little light over the darkening earth. Constantine's pirates had been preparing for hours. Two longboats with twelve men each would sneak out in the black night and slip quietly over to the *Broadsword*. They would take grappling hooks, swords, and daggers. When they had secured the ship, they would signal Constantine by lighting a fire on the forward deck.

Constantine and his twelve remaining pirates would then sail to the *Broadsword* and take command. Instructions were explicit. All men but Nomad would be put to the sword. He was to be taken alive so Constantine could kill him personally. Women who resisted were to be killed. The others could be used at will by any of the men.

The twenty-four men chosen to board the *Broadsword* stood at attention on the deck before their feared leader. The hardened men were veterans of murder, rape, and plunder. Most had killed or maimed numerous men, women, and children and would have little compassion for the *Broadsword* crew. Much like the raptors of old Florida, these men killed for the pleasure of killing. It was sport, an enjoyment of the macabre. They were soulless men who went through life stealing others' souls. Constantine smiled at the lot; they would help him in his quest for immortality.

"I want the one called Nomad alive," he shouted. "Any man who kills him better have a damned good reason. Take the women if you want, but keep Nomad for me. Questions?"

Not a single man spoke.

"You'll leave in thirty minutes, and I shall await your signal fire. That is all." He dismissed the men. He stared at the *Broadsword* through his looking glass. "Soon," he said softly, "soon you will be mine."

"How soon?" Doc Moran asked Kevin and Duke, who stood on the bridge spying the water. "How soon until he leaves?"

"He left five minutes ago, Doc," said Kevin. "He's in the water on the way over." Kevin brought out a folded paper from his pocket and handed it to her. With a trembling hand, she took it. "He said to give you this after he left."

She peered around the bridge. Kevin, Duke, Chief Hightower, and the admiral had the same grave look. "Please let me know when you hear anything," she said. "I'll be in the cargo hold with Molly." She left the bridge.

Molly walked over to meet her as she entered the bay. Doc sat, and Molly gently sat alongside her. Doc began reading. It was not a letter, only a poem. She read it over and over, each time tears filling her eyes.

Cobblestones and schoolyard poems, forgotten streets and names.
Isn't it sometimes beautiful?
And isn't it all insane?
And don't we two fit together somehow?
Or is it only just me?
Is anyone home, or
Am I swimming alone, in this
Dark, troubled part of the sea?
Stay with Moose. I'll see you soon.—JD

Molly brushed against Doc's arm, and Doc hugged the cat's large head. She purred softly, and Doc looked into her eyes. "I don't know how or why, but I think you understand. I love him too. I'll be glad when this night is over." In a voice as soft as cotton, she said, "You're not alone, JD. The two of us will always be with you. Always."

But JD was alone, at least in the physical sense. The ocean was a black as indian ink. Just as well. As he free-styled across the top, he was glad he could not see what lurked below the surface—all manner of deadly fish, marine reptiles, and mammals. He hoped his black wetsuit gave him the necessary camouflage to make the swim safely.

The five-hundred-yard swim would have been nothing in college. Hell, he used warmed up with more yardage than that. But now, it seemed he was swimming the English Channel. He breathed every stroke to try to relax as much as possible and he kept up a two-beat crossover kick to conserve energy. The hand paddles enabled him to pull the water efficiently but conservatively. About every ten meters, he would stick his head up to get his bearings. He and the pirate ship moved with the currents, so he had to constantly adjust his course. His equipment weighed on him, but he was up to the challenge.

Like a stealth warrior, he skimmed across the shadowy ocean toward the pirate ship, the dim lights of its lanterns his only landmark. Yard by yard, he inched closer until he could hear the water lapping against the old schooner's hull, its dark form framed by a starlit night. He could not see them, but in the distance, to the north, he could hear the oars of the longboats as they glided over velvet water. So far, the timing was good.

Constantine's men had been rowing quietly when they realized the *Broadsword* had moved a thousand yards from its previous position. The pirates were confused but continued to row. Then suddenly bright, piercing lights erupted from the big steel ship; the great beams reached into the darkness in all directions. The hapless pirates had never seen such a thing. These lights shattered the darkness and frightened them. They knew they would be seen if they tried to get close to the *Broadsword* so they stopped. What should they do? They had not considered such a possibility. Should they go back or continue? To continue meant being discovered, and being discovered could mean being killed by the crew of the *Broadsword*. Confusion caused them to reevaluate their situation.

Their confusion also gave JD the time he needed to get to the pirate ship undetected. As he reached the ship, JD realized something was wrong. From outside the hull, his keen ears picked up the voices of pirates but also female voices. He thought he recognized one. Like a specter, he hooked his legs around the anchor line, and hand over hand, pulled himself up to the deck. With a silence that defied logic, he eased aboard.

He moved wraithlike around the ship. The first pirate to die had been leaning against the starboard railing half-asleep. With a deft move, JD slit his throat and pushed his body overboard. The ocean swallowed him.

The next pirate came walking by, whistling an unfamiliar tune. As he passed, JD clamped a hand over his mouth from behind and drove his sword through the man's back, into his heart. He died gasping as blood filled his throat. Once again, the ocean proved an effective grave.

A third pirate sat on a stool smoking a rolled cigarette. As before, an iron grip clamped the surprise pirate's mouth, but this time, JD spoke in a whisper. "How many more onboard?" JD's hand eased.

"Eleven," the pirate said.

"And women?"

"Five."

"From the island?"

"Yes."

"And the men on the island?"

"Dead."

"All of them?"

"Yes, all of them."

The pirate lurched forward as JD's sword ran him through. His death cries were muffled by JD's grip. For the third time, the ocean became a watery grave.

JD returned to the forward deck. He clicked his radio three times, the signal to the *Broadsword* to listen but not reply. "A new development. Five women from the Wainwright island are aboard. Will need both Zodiacs for pickup. Have eliminated three bad guys. Nine to go. Will secure women and call back with rendezvous information. Nomad out."

Everyone on the bridge of the *Broadsword* reacted the same. The Wainwright women? It could only mean the pirates had visited the island and the Wainwright group had succumbed to bad times.

"Damn!" said Duke. "Those fucking pilgrims never had a Chinaman's chance in hell. The fools."

"Those poor women," lamented Arabella.

Kevin said, "Duke, you and the Chief will take the second Zodiac. We'll get those women off and back here."

The admiral nodded his agreement. "Lads," he said. "you, Janice, and Dawn prepare quarters for our guests. These ladies will be traumatized, so take it easy with them. Tell Doc Moran each one will need a complete physical and have Mister Henry prepare a solid meal. They'll need clothes, so pull out the necessary items. Look sharp now, lads, these women need our help."

The twins scurried off. Duke and the chief headed for the armory.

JD headed below decks. He could hear hushed cries coming from a cabin in the forward end. He crept to the door and with absolute quiet cracked it a few inches; he wished he had not seen what he saw.

Three women slumped against the wall, crying softly. Two pirates stood next to them laughing. A fourth woman was bent over a bench with one pirate taking her violently from behind while another pirate gyrated in her mouth. The woman cried as she was repeatedly slapped.

One of the laughing pirates said, "Which one of you bitches will be next?" The women continued to sob. The vocal pirate grabbed one by the hair and punched her in the stomach. She collapsed to the floor in agony.

It was then JD drew his word and stepped into the small room. The women noticed first. Their eyes locked in astonishment; the two laughing pirates froze for a second. JD kicked the pirate who was behind the hunched woman, sending him across the room and hard into the wall. With a left-handed backhand, JD cut the pirate in front from left shoulder to navel. As he fell from the woman, his intestines spilled onto the floor. He died seconds later.

The two laughing pirates went for their weapons but were much too late. In one move, JD's sword flashed high and slit both men's throats at the same time. They drowned in their own blood. The kicked pirate lay dead with an oddly bent neck, his eyes open in a death gape.

All four women went into shock. Blood covered the small room. Four freshly dead bodies littered the floor. Blood and gore collected in pools on the wooden surface. Two of the ladies began to vomit.

JD put a finger to his mouth and whispered, "Shhh." In a calm voice, he asked, "Where is the other woman?"

One woman found her voice. "She's in the captain's cabin, in the aft end."

"You ladies stay in this room until I return. Keep quiet. I'll get your friend and be back for you."

"Be careful," said a second woman. "That captain Constantine is a real monster."

"Don't worry. So am I."

He left, gently closing the door. The frightened ladies looked around the blood-splattered room at their dead tormentors. "God forgive me," said the raped woman. She kicked one dead pirate and spat on the other. Her three friends felt the same way. Sympathy for these dregs had died long ago. They huddled, waiting for JD. Waiting for salvation.

Constantine had gone topside to wait for the signal fire. He and three of his men faced the *Broadsword*, which was lit up like a carnival boardwalk. He knew this was not good. He hoped his men were already boarding the steel craft and putting its crew to the sword.

JD crept toward the aft cabin. A guard was posted at the door. He slouched against the wall in total boredom.

Sometimes, the best way is the most direct. When in doubt, act like you own the place, someone had told him, probably Kevin. JD walked up to the dozing pirate and hit him across the face with the end of his sword. He heard the pirate's cheekbone break. The unsuspecting brigand fell to the floor. JD kicked open the door and dragged the man inside.

Maggie Wainwright looked stunned. There stood JD Stoner. He carried a sword and was dragging an unconscious pirate.

"Ma'am, I'm here to help you. Are you alright?"

The words were fresh air to her. For the first time in weeks, a smile hinted at her face. "I'm . . . I'm okay," she muttered. "And the others?"

"They're fine. You're all coming with me. Are you ready?"

She nodded. He took her hand.

"Go ahead of me," he said. "I'm taking this one along." He grabbed the drowsy pirate and pulled him to his feet. "Let's go," he commanded and pushed the man forward. They stopped at the steps leading to the main deck.

"Madam," he said, "go to the forward cabin. Your friends are there. Take this radio and call Admiral Fitzgerald. Tell him to send the cavalry now. Then, you and the ladies go to the forward deck. I'll meet you there."

"What are you going to do?"

"I have to see this Constantine about funeral arrangements. Go."

She went to find the others, clutching the radio as if it were a priceless artifact. JD tuned to the recovering pirate.

"Go and tell Constantine and the others to prepare themselves. Tell them Nomad comes for them. Tonight, you will all sleep for the last time. Go!" He shoved the man hard toward the steps. Like a threatened child, he stumbled up the stairs to the deck. He turned to look for Constantine and touched his broken cheek. It was swollen and hurt like hell, but he hurried forward in search of help.

Constantine saw him. "What in hell happened to you?"

The injured man came up to the big pirate, his face a swollen mess. "The one called Nomad is below. He killed the others and hit me. He said to prepare yourselves because he's coming for you."

Constantine looked to the others. He could smell their fear. "What of the women?" he asked.

"They're with me," came a voice from the darkness. Then JD, the one called Nomad, stepped into the light. His sword flashed in the lantern glow. Constantine stepped forward.

"So you are Nomad. The killer of my men. You don't look like much to me."

JD didn't move. "Opinions vary."

"As we speak, my men are taking your ship."

"I hope they're better than the others. You have to answer for the women."

"And you have to answer for my men. I will enjoy watching you breathe your last." He motioned to his four men. "Take this dog. His head will grace the bow for all to see." They began to circle JD, who still had not moved. There was a scream as the women came through the gangway. The pirates attacked.

The pirates in the longboats were caught in no man's land. They could not advance on the *Broadsword*, so they sat, stymied. At last, they decided to go back to their ship. Constantine would be upset, but better he was upset and they were alive than to go forward into a trap and be killed.

As the pirates paddled back, the two Zodiacs raced to the buccaneer ship. They skimmed over the waves like rocks over a smooth pond. Arabella and Chief Hightower manned M16s and prepared for the worst. As they approached the ship, they saw five people waving from the forward deck. They were five women, but where was JD?

Before Constantine could blink twice, it was over. His four men lay in various poses of death. Two had been gutted like fish, one had been beheaded, and the other had died from several injuries, including a severed right hand. The deck was awash in crimson, clotting blood. Constantine stood alone against his avowed enemy.

JD looked like a ghoul. He was covered in blood. The whites of his eyes glowed in the darkness. For the first time, Constantine felt fear, genuine fear.

"Only in the Romanican arena have I seen such skill with a sword. You are very good, my friend," complimented the pirate.

"We are not friends, Constantine," said JD with ice in his voice.

"So be it," answered the pirate. He readied his sword and moved forward.

Kevin had thrown a rope ladder to the ladies and had begun climbing up. Once on deck, he saw that the women looked horrible. Their clothes were mostly rags, and all were covered in blood. He felt like the Americans in World War II who liberated the death camps. Such utter misery was humbling.

"Is everyone alright?" he asked. They nodded. "Where's Captain Stoner?" No one had to answer. He turned around in the direction of clanging swords.

Maggie Wainwright said, "He went to kill Constantine." She pointed toward the other end of the ship. The din of the swords went on. The clangor of steel was the only sound that pricked the night.

Kevin turned to the ladies. "Very carefully now, start down the ladder, one at a time." Arabella had come topside. "Stay with the ladies," said Kevin. "I'm going to get JD." He leaned over and kissed Arabella on the cheek. He went aft for JD.

JD and Constantine had fought a titanic battle all over the aft deck and the mighty pirate was suffering from numerous minor wounds. He had no idea JD was only toying with him. He was exhausted; the sword was lead in his hands.

JD could see his opponent laboring and decided to end it. With a mighty blow, his titanium sword broke the pirate's sword. Constantine looked at the shattered stub of his sword, astonished. The other piece made a loud splash as it hit the ocean. He looked at JD with eyes on fire. "You are a devil," he said.

"Only a man," answered Nomad. "But you're about to meet the devil. Say hello for me."

With blinding speed, JD made two cuts. From each shoulder to each hip, red lines crossed the pirate's abdomen in an X. For an icebound second, the dread pirate stared in horror as gravity pulled his insides out. Internal organs burst onto the deck. The pirate's body fell, his fiery eyes cooled by death.

Kevin had come alongside JD. He studied JD and turned his eyes to the dead pirate. "Jesus," he said mildly.

"We have to go. The others will be back soon," JD calmly remarked.

Kevin could not agree more. "The women are okay and onboard the Zodiacs. Let's blow this tub and go home." He took JD by the shoulder and guided him. "It's over. Let's go."

JD said nothing, but he moved with Kevin. A few minutes later, they were on a Zodiac, moving away from the pirate ship.

The two pirate longboats were in view, and Arabella and Chief Hightower were raking them with M16 fire. It was now JD reached into his pocket and withdrew a transmitter. Before boarding the pirate ship he had attached a demolition charge on the outside of the ship along the water line. Without looking back, he pushed the button. The booming explosion startled everyone. The hull of the pirate ship burst into orange and yellow flames; wood splinters flew across a gentle ocean. Soon the old schooner began nosing into a watery tomb. The longboats also began to sink, leaving helpless pirates to an unforgiving sea. Distance soon quieted their pleas for help.

The Zodiacs sped back to the *Broadsword*. Its crew was about to grow by five.

That which is past cannot be recalled.

PART 4

SLANT TERRITORY, 92 MILLION BC

"I give up," said a confused Chief Hightower. He and Duke stood above cargo hold one, watching the twins. They were skipping around the cargo hold, one playing a wooden flute. Norton was in his usual posture, dead weight. The shrill tune emanating from the homemade flute was a kaleidoscope of disjointed noise.

"Just what are you boys doing?" asked the chief.

They looked up, happy to see Duke and the chief.

"Go ahead, tell 'em," Adam said to Tim.

"Yeah, please tell, you madcap fucking lunatics," said Duke. He knew this would be good.

"Well," started Tim. "You remember the Pie-Eyed Piper of Hamlin?"

"What? Who? Pie-Eyed?" asked the chief.

"Yeah, that's him," said Adam.

"Anyway," continued Tim, "we figured if he could pipe rats pie-eyed, we could pipe turtles sober. Simple, huh?"

"Yeah, like fucking brain surgery," lamented Duke. "I thought you douchebags told me turtles don't have ears. How's that beast gonna hear that flute?"

The twins looked at each other in dismay.

"I forgot," said Tim. "Norton's got no ears."

"No wonder he just sits here," lamented Adam.

"If you boys had a sliver of a brain, you'd be in politics," laughed the chief. He and Duke waved good-bye and went to the galley for coffee. The twins decided to go back to the computer room. Their latest project was downloading all the Pamela Anderson pictures they could find in the Cray III's computer files. This new file was codenamed, "The Can-Clanging Queen of the Curb." Their work was never done.

By ten in the morning, the day was already withering; heat and humidity choked everything. This world, however, was good for humans. The oxygen level was as much as 3 percent higher than back in the twentieth century, which helped humans considerably; it punched up their cardiovascular systems. On average, they were fitter and healthier as a result.

It had been four days since the confrontation with the pirates. JD and Doc had found renewed passion for each other. The five women seemed to be adjusting well. Maggie Wainwright was helping Mr. Henry in the galley. She said it was good to be busy, and no one could disagree. The other ladies sought refuge in rest. They ate, read, and relaxed. Recovery was slow but steady.

On the bridge, JD and Doc took their turn studying the progress of the *Broadsword*. The ocean lay in front of them like a great, indigo-blue carpet. It rose and fell in gentle waves. A keen sun floated in a sky, uninhibited by a few lazy clouds. JD's and Doc's thoughts drifted with the summer weather.

JD found himself studying Doc. At thirty-two, she looked good for her age, but then, she made her age look good. Her skin was a tanned chestnut brown, her sun-streaked hair a golden yellow. She looked at him and smiled.

"What?" Doc asked as if they were on a middle-school playground between kickball games.

"You really are beautiful."

She smiled. "I never thanked you for the poem. It was very nice. Thank you."

"You bring out my best," he said unabashedly.

"You're an amazingly complicated man. An all-American swimmer, world-class fencer, advanced degrees in history and philosophy. Marital artist, linguistic wiz, and international assassin. Have I left out anything?"

"I flunked my first swim lessons at the YMCA as a kid."

She laughed. "And let me guess. Years later, you went back and broke all the pool records, right?"

He shrugged. "Maybe."

"Do you always win? Are you always better than everyone?" Her tone had a more serious timbre.

"It's not about winning," JD said. "It's about being prepared. If you're prepared for trouble, you can usually deal with it. Most of those who look for trouble aren't prepared for it when they find it."

Doc was about to challenge his premise when something caught her eye. "Look at that!"

JD turned to the open sea. "What?" he asked.

"There!" She pointed northwest. "You see it?"

He saw it. A large pterodactyl, wingspan of thirty feet or more, was flying about ten feet off the water, carrying a struggling human. Its great clawed feet gripped the man like robotic pincers. He fought the giant winged dinosaur, but the beast paid little attention to his efforts.

Both JD and Doc sat mesmerized. Thoughts of what to do raced through their minds but were quickly forgotten. As the pterodactyl soared above the waves, a thirty-foot shark burst from the water and latched onto the helpless man. A brief tug-of-war ensued between two prehistoric giants; it was decided when the man's puny body ripped in half. The shark fell back to sea with the man's lower torso, while the pterodactyl flew off with what was left, blood dripped from the dangling corpse as the huge pterodactyl winged away. The gruesome sight made them both think the same thing. *A man? Where did he come from?*

"He looked oriental," said JD.

"From where?" was all Doc could say.

The twins spilled onto the bridge with a start.

"Did you see that?" asked Tim.

"It looked like a Chinaman," added Adam.

"This world just keeps getting stranger," Tim said.

Tim, Adam, and JD had the same thought simultaneously.

JD said, "Can you boys track and correlate missing ships and boats for the last two thousand years on your computer?"

"If there's a record of a ship missing or presumed lost, we can," said Adam.

"Give us an hour," Tim said.

"Good," said JD. "Maybe we can start to figure out who else might be in this world. We know we're not the only ones. It might help us predict future encounters."

"Can't hurt," Doc added. "Maybe a much larger group had made the transfer, enough for a town or small city. There could be descendants and cultures going, maybe civilized people like us. Houses, farms, roads. Who knows?"

"Lions, and tigers, and bears, oh my!" chimed Tim.

"Let's go," insisted Adam.

JD turned to Doc. "It's good to have hope and I hope you're right. So far, it's been a world of carnivorous beasts and murderous humans. It's starting to remind me of home."

"That's because you're a mook, JD Stoner."

"A what?"

"A mook!"

"Should I be offended?"

"You should be many things, but I'll settle for your presence in my quarters in thirty minutes."

"Really? And what should I wear?"

"As little as possible, you big stud. Be there or lose me!" Her voice had the gravel of a country road.

"We're on a ship. How could I lose you?"

"Don't show up and find out."

"See you in thirty minutes," he said. "I'll bring the gorilla suit."

"Don't forget the midget," she said, walking out the door. She waved good-bye like a stripper leaving the stage.

The twins, who had witnessed the dueling lovebirds, looked at JD. They were more than confused.

"Midget?" asked Tim.

"Gorilla suit?" asked Adam.

JD walked off, whistling. Neither boy could make out the tune.

There was nothing unique or fascinating about the ceiling in Doc Moran's quarters. Steel painted gray hardly got more boring. Yet both JD and Doc stared up at the ceiling as if some great cosmic truth were being revealed or as if it were a Michelangelo mural.

"You take my breath away," she said in a whisper.

Round one of an afternoon sexual marathon was over. Both participants glowed in the fatigue of aftershocks. The ceiling had become the refuge of the exhausted.

"What do you think love is?" the doc asked. "Ever thought about it?"

The ceiling blurred a bit. JD turned his head toward her. They lay side by side in a recovery mode. "Sure, I've thought about it," he said. "I have a degree in philosophy, you know."

"I know, so?"

He hesitated. "Love is a religion of two. A paired world. Something steady and lasting. Forgiving. Sharing. Belonging to each other. Something lasting."

Silence followed for a few moments.

"That a philosophical answer?" she asked with a lilt in her voice. Whatever it was, she liked it.

"The only one I know. What about you? What's love to you?"

"Fruit Loops," she answered without hesitation.

"Fruit Loops. That a medical answer?"

"Nope. Practical. When I'm around Fruit Loops, I can't get enough of them. I am insatiable for them. I have to have them. They drive me stupid. For me, it's Fruit Loops."

"Makes perfect sense."

"That's you, mister. You're my Fruit Loops. I love you. There's no doubt in my medical mind."

He kissed her, and passionate wrestling began anew. Round two was officially underway. There would be only winners.

Later, in the conference room, JD, Doc, Kevin, the admiral, Duke, Chief Hightower, and Arabella assembled to listen to the twins' report. It began in a manner they had become accustomed to.

"Hey Chief, ask me what my watch says," Tim said.

The chief, always the sucker, asked, "Okay. Hey Tim, what does your watch say?"

"It don't say anything. You gotta look at it!"

The group broke up. It was an old one, but still funny.

"Fucking genius idiots," quipped Duke but then he had laughed as hardy as anyone. His big belly shook like Jell-O.

"If we could get serious, lads," said the admiral. "What have you found?"

Adam glanced at a paper he held. "We pulled records of ships and boats reported lost at sea under mysterious circumstances and concentrated on only large groups, initially ten or more. We thought a group that size had a reasonable chance of survival."

"But the list was huge," said Tim. "Over four hundred incidents, so we narrowed the parameters to groups of over fifty. We felt groups that size could not only survive but also endure. Maybe even prosper."

Adam continued. "That brought our list down to just six incidents, but they're doozies."

The boy stopped and spied the audience for a moment.

"So give," said Arabella, her impatience obvious. "What are they?"

"I'll go in descending order," said Adam. "The largest group first. In AD 1292, over a thousand Chinese-Mongolian ships vanished in a storm in the Sea of Japan. It was an invasion force. Estimates are that as many as fifty thousand men, horses, and supplies were lost. The rest of the fleet took the disappearance as a bad omen and returned to China."

"Christ on a unicycle," said the admiral. "That's eight hundred years ago. There could be a whole population of Chinese-Mongolians here. Amazing."

"We estimate that without birth control, a population like that, unchecked, could be around half a million by now, maybe more," said Tim.

"Jesus H. Methuselah," barked Duke. "Once again, the world's full of Chinamen."

Adam went on. "Next, we have the disappearance of a Roman legion on its way to Sardinia in the Tyrrhenian Sea. A legion averaged around six thousand men, but wives, children, and slaves usually went along. This group could have been as large as ten thousand. It went down or vanished around AD 212."

"This is too weird," the chief said.

"It gets weirder, Chief," conceded Adam. "Our next group is a batch of seven merchant ships in 1492. Seven British merchants. They vanished in a storm off the Spanish coast near Gibraltar. Approximately two hundred and twenty men."

"Finally some civilized wayfarers," boasted the admiral. "Nothing like English blood to raise the level of humanity."

"Quite," said an unconvinced Kevin. "Go on, boys."

"The fourth is an obscure ocean liner named the *Queen Mother* in 1931. The reports are vague, as if someone or something was trying to cover it up. It apparently went down in the North Sea on its way to Lillesand, Norway, from Great Britain. Again, over two hundred Englishmen were lost or vanished in a storm."

The admiral smiled at the prospect of more countrymen on this wild planet.

"The fifth entry is the most uncertain and less detailed. In 97 BC, an Egyptian fleet disappeared in the Mediterranean. These were sail—and oar-powered boats full of soldiers and slaves. Five ships were lost, but no figures on people. We pulled up information on vessels of the time and estimate between three hundred and five hundred men, a mixture of slaves and soldiers.

This group, we think, would have the lowest chance of survival because of the primitive gear they would have had. But of course, anything's possible."

"And the sixth?" asked the chief.

Tim said, "The last is a group of about seventy who vanished in a storm off the Great Barrier Reef in Australia in 1959. They were part of a sailboat armada that hit a sudden storm. They were never seen again. There are others, but these are the biggest and best documented. It could mean this world is not as devoid of humans as we might have thought."

Agreement was unanimous.

Adam said, "Of course, it doesn't mean all these groups found their way to this time. There are probably other time rifts besides this one, and there are probably other incidents we don't know about, but it does add to the possibilities. I think it's reasonable and likely other humans have survived and are living on this planet now besides those we've run across. I'd guess there are two or more large settlements."

"But from a technology standpoint," Tim added, "we're the most advanced. Even groups that may have modern weapons wouldn't have been able to sustain their use without spare parts or manufacturing capabilities. Again, it's reasonable to hypothesize that the level of weaponry is at the bow-and-sword stage, maybe gunpowder, if the Chinese are here in large numbers. But projectile weapons or firearms? Probably not although the pirate had harpoon cannon. And water transportation is most likely limited to sail or oar. Anyone with diesel power would have simply run out of fuel."

The boys had done a thorough job, despite their juvenile shenanigans, and everyone was visibly impressed.

"That's fine work, lads," said a pleased admiral.

"Yeah, you boys did good," remarked Duke. "Take a dollar out of fucking petty cash."

The lads beamed in humility and gratitude.

"Now all we have to do is find these other people," suggested Arabella, as if that would be easy.

"A needle in a goddamned haystack," said Duke.

"Maybe," said Kevin, "but that man today looked oriental. It makes a strong case for the Chinese-Mongolian possibility. Plus, it may prove there's a settlement or at least others close. The pterodactyl probably picked him up around here."

"We should be looking for signs of human life," said Doc. "Man-made structures, campfires, footprints, that sort of thing."

"Animal traps," added Chief Hightower.

"And defensible areas," said JD. "For humans to survive, they would have to build in trees or on plateaus or mesas, dig moats, or build walls. The animals on the planet are just too big and too strong."

"And too fucking hungry," reminded Duke. "Islands would be perfect locales. Water, vegetation, and manageable animal life. Plus the whole fucking ocean around them. No worries."

"Except for pirates, storms, heat, and other marauding maniacs," reminded Doc. "Let's face it. This is a hostile planet for humans. We have no idea about disease or toxins or other poisons that may pose threats to humans. Our immune systems may not be very good in this time."

"Agreed," said the admiral, "so our best course of action is to be skeptical and cautious about everything. This boat is our safe haven and must be protected. I want everyone to understand that. We protect the ship. Without it, we're at the mercy of a malevolent time."

The admiral turned to Doc Moran. "And how are our guests doing? I see Maggie Wainwright in the galley, but the others are less visible. How is their progress?"

"I'm happy to report all five ladies are recovering," said Doc. "Physically, they're fine, considering their ordeal. All were beaten and raped repeatedly. Their wounds will heal, but psychologically, I don't know. It'll be a slow process, but over time, I expect them to recover. Maggie is bouncing back faster, though. She'll be a good addition to our crew. The others, too, in time."

"That's splendid," said the admiral. "If there's nothing else, I suggest we get back to the business of survival. Lads, I expect you to keep working on these disappearances." The twins said they would. The meeting broke.

The *Broadsword* crew was nineteen strong, nineteen mortals in a world of giant, prehistoric beasts. It hardly seemed fair, but this was a time of cruelty and mayhem. It was not the time of humans.

After two murderous weeks of tracking, Marcus Sardonis and his Romanican raiders were closing in on a Slant village. Quietly and at a great distance, they had been following a Slant hunting party. Once they had spotted their campfires; Marcus decided to follow them to their village. He had no idea how far they had ranged from their village, but the time they spent following them would be well worth it if they led the Romanicans to a large encampment. It would mean many slaves and prisoners; it would also mean promotion and riches for Marcus. The emperor would be very generous.

The Slant hunting party had been very successful—many animals captured, and much fruit harvested. The fifteen Slants were moving silently and efficiently along the trails and through the dense forests. Marcus had to admire their resourcefulness. These Slants were neither stupid nor unskilled. He was certain they would be great entertainment for the arena.

The southward trek behind the Slants had been adventurous. He had lost no men; they had been fortunate. They had escaped a rockslide, poisonous gas, and a deadly tar field. They had maneuvered around raptors, avoided a dozen compy flocks, and survived a rampaging herd of ultrasaurs. And they had not been spotted by the Slant trackers. A miracle? Maybe. But in this wilderness, Marcus welcomed miracles as much as he did fresh water. They would soon come upon the Slant village, probably a bustling outpost in this unsettled region. That is what he hoped.

He knew his forty men could take twice that number in captives. They just had to find the village and not get killed in the process. The journey had been long and arduous, but in the end, it would be worth every pain endured.

They tracked the Slants as cheetahs track gazelles, quietly and deliberately, patiently waiting for the moment to strike, coolly waiting for the moment of death.

"It's called geometric thinking," said Kevin. "Or nonlinear thinking." He and Doc Moran were sitting on the aft deck, watching the sunset. They had been talking about Doc's favorite subject, Captain JD Stoner. Kevin was a wealth of information. "It's a tradecraft term," he told her.

"A what?"

"Tradecraft. Tradecraft is the language of the intelligence community back in our time. We recognized it in JD back in Arizona. It's the ability to think in different directions at the same time, to think around problems and obstacles, to think in terms of contingencies."

She looked at him, face scrunched in confusion. He could tell she did not understand.

"You see, most people think in a linear fashion. They connect the dots with straight lines, the shortest distance and all that. And they get lost or confused when an obstacle gets in the way of their straight-line reasoning. But JD doesn't contemplate things that way. His reasoning goes around or under or over, or slantways or sideways, or whatever. His mind solves things geometrically. He sees curves and trapezoids and circles instead of lines. It's very advantageous for someone in his line of work."

"I thought he ferried boats," joked Doc.

Kevin grinned. "He used to. Now, like the rest of us, he's just a refugee. He's also in love, Doc. I've known him as long as anyone, and it's amazing to see him so goo-goo stupid in love."

Doc shrugged. "Surely he's had other girls. He's a handsome man, Kev."

"Oh sure, he's had a few girlfriends, as I had mentioned, but most were scared off by Molly, me, or some of his lesser-endearing qualities."

"You mean like his ability to be a coldhearted son of a bitch almost at will?"

"That would be one, yes," said a thoughtful Kevin. "I'm sure it takes a unique person to understand and tolerate his many flaws." He looked straight into Doc's brown eyes.

"Or a complete idiot," she suggested. "I took an oath, Kev. I heal people. Cure the sick. Help the injured and infirmed. And he . . . he kills people with the same zealousness. It's scary."

Kevin stared out into the vastness of the passing water and the gentle wake behind the *Broadsword*. "He knows he can't justify his actions to you, Doc. He only wants your slightest acknowledgement that his actions are sometimes needed. That's all. He lives with himself. In the end, that's all any of us can do."

The ocean behind the ship rippled toward the horizon as an orange sun slowly sank. Like all sunsets, it was spectacular. Above them, in the distance, a flock of birds squawked.

Doc rose from her chair and kissed Kevin on the forehead. "You're a good friend, Kev. He's lucky to have such an advocate. I'm lucky too. Thank you."

Kevin nodded. Doc left. The ocean continued to glide by, smooth water filtering out all confusion. The sun slid beyond a linear horizon and quietly blinked out.

Paulinus Messala was the Romanican aedile, the political official in charge of the games. He stood in the cavernous hall of the emperor's palace. In front of him, on a throne of marble and gold, sat a bored Antonious V surrounded by servants who accommodated his every wish. A few other officials, lackeys of an arrogant leader, stood around sharing the emporers' boredom.

On a plateau that soared eighty feet about the surrounding basin, the city of Romanica stayed cool year 'round. Predators were frustrated by the sheer cliffs, so the Romanican people lived in relative safety while the great city provided all their needs. A library was built for the accumulation of knowledge. Houses, taverns, schools, and markets stretched from one end to the other. The emperor's palace, the great temple, and of course the coliseum and arena stood as well. All of these were connected by roads. It was a grand city.

Paulinius had been called before the emperor to explain the status of the games. He was nervous; he spoke in an irritating, high-pitched voice. The emperor found it difficult to take the squeaky man seriously.

"My dear Paulinius, Marcus and his raiding party are delayed. Another month before their return. They should have fifty or more slaves for the games when they return. I need to know from you what we do in the meantime. What have you planned?"

Paulinius swallowed hard. He knew disappointment was not taken well by this emperor. He chose his words carefully then proceeded with caution. Like a barefoot man walking on glass, he began. "Sire, between now and Marcus's return, we can do many things. Raptor pit fights are very popular, and we can continue those."

The emperor's eyes lit up. "Yes, those are great spectacles. But must I always free a slave if he defeats a raptor?"

"It is tradition, sire," offered Paulinius softly.

"Damn!" said the vexed emperor. "What else, Paulinius?"

"Something new, sire. We call them gladiatrixes, women gladiators battling each other. It should prove very entertaining. They will be naked except for minimal armor. The crowd will love it, sire."

The emperor looked pleased. "Female gladiators huh? I wish to meet some of them, Paulinius. The prettiest ones, of course. Arrange it. Tonight!"

Paulinius understood the demand. He bowed and started to leave. The emperor stopped him. "And Paulinius," he said casually. "Make sure these gladiatrixes have bathed. It will not be necessary for them to be clothed, but they have to have bathed. Am I understood?"

"Yes, sire, completely." Paulinius bowed again and left.

The emperor called for his physician and retired to his quarters. He had to rest if he was going to be up to servicing the gladiatrixes that night. Ah, the demands of royalty.

The twins had taken a bartender's course they found in a computer file and invited everyone to the video room for their first frat party. A bar was set up in the corner for this gala, and they had arranged for the movies *Animal House* and *Revenge of the Nerds* to he played continuously on the big screen.

The boys boasted they could mix any drink anyone asked for, no matter how obscure or weird. The first to mosey up to the bar were Kevin and Arabella. "What can I get you kids?" asked Adam.

"I'll have a dry martini," Kevin said. "There should be dust on the olive, and the lady will have a sloe gin fizz."

"Coming right up," said Tim.

Adam handed each a glass of prapple wine. Kevin and Arabella took sips.

"How are they?" asked Adam.

"Smooth," coughed Kevin, "Real smooth."

Duke was next.

"Yes, sir?" asked Adam.

"Can you do a bare-breasted Japanese servant girl?"

"Sure," said Tim.

"Bring one over," added Adam

The boys laughed heartily.

"Jerkoffs!" said Duke. "How about a herring fannybanger?"

"Sorry, we hardly know you," said Adam.

Tim handed Duke a glass of prapple. He went off grumbling something about "the same old shit."

Dawn and Janice arrived. They looked like centerfold material. They made their way to the bar, where the fawning twins stood like groupies.

"Gee, I don't know what we want," Dawn said.

"How about a shingled roof?" Tim suggested.

"A shingled roof? What's that?" asked Janice.

"You know, on the house!" said Adam. The boys laughed at their own joke.

Like everyone else, the girls settled for glasses of prapple wine. Even Maggie Wainwright enjoyed a glass or four.

Three hours later, everyone onboard was once again tanked. Maggie danced on a table with Duke, stripped to her underwear. It was a bizarre sight.

Dawn puked on Adam. Janice punched Tim in the eye. She objected to the way he played "radio."

Chief Hightower and the admiral argued over Patton and Monty while Nurse Natalie and Mr. Henry snuck off to the galley for "more fun with food."

Doc and JD carried each other home, singing "Waltzing Matilda" to anyone who would listen.

Molly and Norton were the only sober biological organisms onboard. The rest of the crew floated in the feral arms of fermented prehistoric fruit, hammered out of their skulls!

During the following twenty-four hours, the *Broadsword* cruised on through hangovers while near-unconsciousness gripped the crew. The dreaded prapple stupor had infected them like malaria. Some shook like *Titanic* survivors while others moped around like zombies, alive but dead.

The twins looked for a new hobby, their wine-making days over. And only two hundred cases of prapple tonic left.

The village was inland, about two kilometers from the sea. The site had been chosen carefully; it had been made defensible and was well fortified. A six-foot wooden fence encircled the compound, and outside the fence, a moat had been dug around the fence. The moat was twelve feet across and deep. Manned lookout posts were every thirty feet, and sentries guarded the gate. Small domesticated mammals roamed freely, barking at anything suspicious. Outside the moat, the ground had been leveled of trees for twenty yards.

The village was an island in a clearing. *The Slants have done well*, thought Marcus. He and his men had been studying the compound for over three hours. They had counted at least forty adults and maybe twenty children. It would be a good capture.

They made camp about a mile northeast, behind a small hill and planned to probe the village for weakness the next few days and formulate a plan for attack. They would also rest. The return to Romanica would be long and difficult, especially with a party of slaves in tow. His men rested and made ready for the assault.

Marcus was not worried. He had chosen his men well. All were strong, capable veterans, expert swordsmen and trackers. The village would fall, slaves would be collected, and soon they would be heading home.

A few mornings and many aspirins after the frat party, most on the *Broadsword* had recovered enough to function normally. Normal, of course, depended on the person. Doc and JD were working out in the exercise room; which had become one of their daily routines. They liked watching each other sweat. The primitive sexual energy proved very exciting.

JD was showing Doc some of the Shaolin kata movements, specifically, the praying mantis. He was very patient, and she was very impressed.

"I'm told it can take a lifetime to master one of the Shaolin disciplines," she said between deep breaths. "There are six, right? The praying mantis, the tiger, the snake, the monkey, the dragon, and the crane."

"Very good, Grasshopper," answered JD. "And yes, it can take a lifetime to master one."

She looked at him in wonderment. His movements were as graceful as a prima ballerina, as forceful as a steel bar. He exuded an impossible confidence.

"And you've mastered all six," she said, not skipping a breath.

His movements continued. "Yes."

She began imitating the dialogue of the old *Kung Fu* television series. "It is said a Shaolin priest can walk through walls. Looked for, he cannot be seen. Listened for, he cannot be heard. He can walk across rice paper without leaving a mark."

He laughed. "Would you like me to snatch the pebble from your hand, Grasshopper?"

It was her turn to laugh. Their kata routine fell apart. They tumbled to the ground in a free fall of giddiness. Enjoying the foolishness was fun.

Then, a couple of marketing executives, the twins, strolled into the exercise room. They looked as if they had come straight from some Wall Street office. Their slicked-back hair and pressed clothes completed a polished presence.

JD could only laugh. "Whatever it is, we're not buying, boys."

"Let me guess," said Doc. "Snake oil? Or maybe five-acre lots back in Raptorland?"

Tim and Adam remained unruffled, detached, all business.

"Very funny, madam," replied Tim, "but we are here on legitimate business."

"That's right," said Adam. "We thought it would be a good idea if we collected sayings and witticisms from all the crew to be sealed and handed down to future generations, like passing along wisdom and advice to others down the line. So, you see, this is not a frivolous undertaking."

"We are quite cereal," said Tim.

"Serious," corrected Adam swiftly.

Doc rolled her pretty brown eyes in a gesture of skepticism.

"And what wisdom have you collected so far?" asked JD.

"Finally, an earnest question," stated Adam.

"Well, for example," said Tim, "Admiral Fitzgerald gave us, 'A man travels the world over in search of what he needs and returns home to find it.'"

"I like that," said Doc. "What else?"

"Kevin said, 'Sanity is madness put to good uses,'" said Adam. "And Arabella said, 'When in doubt, shoot!'"

"Very poetic," swooned Tim.

"What did Duke say?" JD asked. He thought it might be colorful.

Adam thumbed through papers like an accountant. "Let's see. Duke's quote was, 'Fuck me running!'"

He has a way with words, thought JD.

"Pure metrical composition." Doc waxed poetic. "Genius."

"So would either of you like to offer some universal truth or cosmic realities to future generations?" asked Tim. He grinned like a used-car salesman. When he smiled, he flashed his bright white, perfectly symmetrical teeth.

"I would," piped Doc. "Take this down, boys."

Adam readied a pencil.

"The opinions of future generations will be worth no more than the opinions of the past and current ones."

"Excellent!" said an impressed Adam.

Doc smiled. "What about you, JD?"

"Yeah, give us something," begged Tim. His teeth flashed again with the piano mouth.

JD thought. "Okay, try this. The music of a brook silences all critics."

"Cool," said a happy Adam. He scribbled the words on a pad.

"What about you boys?" JD asked. "What have you put down?"

Adam said, "Mine is, 'Video killed the radio star.'"

"And mine is, 'Groupies welcome!'" said Tim.

JD and Doc exchanged quizzical looks.

"By the way," said Doc. "I'm curious. What did Maggie Wainwright say?"

The boys grew solemn. "We were going to mention it to you, Doc. It's a little screwy," said Tim.

"It's goofy," said Adam. "She said, and I quote, 'I can't see how the human race is going to survive now that the cost of living has gone up two dollars a six-pack!'"

JD turned to Doc. "Interesting," he managed.

"It's crackers, Doc," said Adam. "I think she's gone nutso."

"That your medical opinion, Doctor Adam?" asked Doc with great indignation. "Maybe she was trying to be funny or whimsical."

"Whimsical?" asked JD.

"Oh shut up! I don't know. The woman's been through a terrible ordeal. Cut her some slack, you jackals! She's entitled."

The twins knew when to leave. It was time. They slipped out, papers in hand, off to the next victim. Chief Hightower.

JD said, "The boys were joking, Doc. They meant no harm. They're concerned, too."

"I know," she said, walking up to him and hugging him hard. "It just scares me that this world is so unforgiving, so gruesome. What happened to Maggie could happen to anyone."

He stroked her hair and kissed her forehead. "Don't worry, Doc," he said gently. "We'll be okay."

She believed him because she knew he could be as unforgiving and as gruesome as anything on this planet. She loved him, but that scared her. They held each other close a long time.

Doc pushed away abruptly and said, "Now, show me how to walk through a wall, oh wise one." She bowed slightly. He returned the bow.

"As you wish, Grasshopper."

"Get me the giant," yelled Marcus.

A man at the campfire said, "The giant is on patrol, sir. Won't be back for an hour or more."

Marcus was furious. "What idiot authorized that? A ten-foot monster stomping around the forest. Think anyone will notice? By the gods! If the Slants spot him, we're finished. Do I have to think for everyone? Idiots!" He spit on the fire in disgust. "You!" Marcus pointed to a man on his left. "Get out there and bring that titan back. We haven't come this far to blow it now. And tell him to report to me immediately. Damn fool!" The man took off in a flash.

Marcus was right. The giant could be spotted a mile away even in a jungle. He stuck out like an oak tree in a desert. He was along because his size and strength were intimidating and he struck fear into anyone he came in contact with. At nine feet ten inches and four hundred and eighty pounds, he was a massive figure. All the giants were. The lived far north of Romanica in what would be the future Northwest Territories of Canada.

Heavily built and covered in coarse hair, these giants preferred the cooler forests of their homeland. The tropical jungles farther south proved too uncomfortable, too humid, too hot, but in recent years, the giants had formed an alliance with the militaristic Romanicans. On occasion, some giants would visit the great plateau city and observe the games in the arena. Before the alliance, Romanicans had forced captured giants into the deadly games. They became crowd favorites quickly, dispatching men and beasts and displaying great skill and courage. Even raptors feared the giants. The giants had become adept at grabbing the fierce creatures and twisting their necks in a single motion.

The giant traveling with Marcus was named Egnid Troose; he was a veteran of the war with Romanica and a veteran of the games. He had killed over forty men in single combat. A great jagged scar crossed his forehead; it was a raptor souvenir from his pit-fighting days in the arena. His age was unknown, but he appeared to be in the prime of life. He wore his black hair long and shaggy, and unlike his Romanican counterparts, he did not shave his face. Some suspected he did not bathe either; a pungent order followed him everywhere.

When the giant returned to camp, he reported to Marcus at once. He stood before the smaller Romanican and brushed his hair back from his eyes. "You wanted to see me?" he said in a tangled Latin. He towered over Marcus like a tree.

"Until our attack on the Slant village you are to remain in camp," Marcus ordered without preamble. "The risk of them spotting you is too great. And when we do attack, you are ordered to take no women until I give you the word. I don't want you permanently damaging any women before I can decide if they are going back with us. Do you understand?"

The giant grunted displeasure and understanding at the same time. He loved abusing the tiny Slant women but would obey Marcus's order. He knew he would eventually get to use the women, and he would make sure some would never breathe again. The sadistic giant looked forward to his prize.

Chief Hightower and Duke were looking forward to a quiet afternoon of fishing and relaxation. They had taken up positions in chairs on the aft deck. A cooler of prapple wine at their feet and fishing poles in their hands, they were ready to catch a big one, whether fish or hangover. By the end of the day, they intended to have one or the other. Maybe both.

Their goal was to catch another tuna-type fish so Mr. Henry could whip up another tasty tuna-type casserole. They fought the afternoon sun with sunglasses, hats, and sunblock. Still, it was stifling. Cold prapple wine offered some relief. Their fishing lines drifted in the wake behind the boat. So far, nothing. Their efforts had produced diddly squat not even a nibble.

"Could be the bait," suggested the chief. "What are you using?"

Duke chugged a large mouthful of prapple and let out a loud *ahhh* sound. "Same shit as the other day."

"Dog food?"

"Sure. Why not? It's not like anyone's gonna eat that shit. Seen any dogs around?"

"Why would fish eat dog food?" the chief wondered out loud.

"Fish are fucking stupid. They'll eat anything!" Duke said, like a marine expert. "What the fuck are you using?"

"I am using an age-old, proven bait." He opened the bucket and showed Duke. "Worms," he said.

Duke looked into the bucket. "Worms? Christ, those are the size of small snakes. Small moray eels! Where the hell did you get those?"

"Dug 'em up on that last island."

"Fuck me. You'll probably catch a goddamned whale with those. Maybe one of those *Carcharodon megalodouches*."

The chief muttered something and settled in for a lazy afternoon. Like a couple Florida retirees they were enjoying the day until the twins suddenly materialized.

"Go away, boys," said the chief. "You're liable to get hooked and baited."

"We're putting the band back together," Adam said in a deadpanned Blues Brothers imitation.

Duke bit. "What fucking band?"

"Our band," answered Tim. "Adam plays the tuba, and I play the accordion."

"Tuba and accordion," laughed Duke. "What do you play? Patriotic polka? Fuck off!"

"And what do you call your band?" asked the chief.

Tim answered, "Crosby, Stills, Nash, Lyons, and Rothstein."

Duke spit prapple as he broke into laughter. "I can't wait to hear the harmonies with a tuba background. You realize, of course, you boys are totally fucking nuts!"

"We're going to charge four hundred dollars an hour to play," said Adam.

"Four hundred dollars an hour?" asked the chief.

"How much *not* to play, you yakoffs?" Duke asked.

"Oh, you couldn't afford that," said Tim.

Duke had had enough. "Listen, boys, do me a fucking favor. Get the douche away from me before I pitch you overboard, okay?"

"Our agent will contact you with dates we are available," Tim said.

"Yeah, and you pay only three hundred and fifty an hour," Adam said, "'cause you're a pal."

The chief took a coin from his pocket. He turned to Duke, "Heads you kill 'em, tails I kill 'em." The boys ran like actors from a soap opera.

"Crazy, mixed-up kids," said the chief after the boys were gone.

"Yeah," agreed Duke. "But they crack me the fuck up."

The chief nodded and pulled his hat low over his eyes. Still no bites. But they had time.

A few minutes later, Duke noticed the chief was snoring. He quietly reached for the bucket of snake-like worms.

Major Tom Crowley of the U.S. Air Force shook his head vigorously as he returned from the blackness of unconsciousness. He quickly glanced at his watch. Thirty seconds had expired. It had seemed infinitely longer—hours, or even days. He scanned the HUD, the heads-up display on his F-16F Fighting Falcon. Everything was normal. All systems were operational and functioning.

He checked the sky; powder-blue had replaced the fury of the squall that had sent him into a blackout. No booming thunder, no spiraling clouds, and no torrential rain. But no squadron. The sky was blue but empty. He tried his radio. Nothing. Silence. Panic gripped him. Where was he? And where was everyone else?

He punched buttons on his computer and swiftly brought up a return flight plan. It would he simple; retrace his flight to his squadron or to his base. He banked hard right. No afterburners; he would conserve fuel. In seconds, the F-16F was cruising back. Back home.

The twins were trying to convince everyone they knew the way home.

"Okay, lads," said the admiral. "One more time in English, please." The lad's initial explanation had been mired in quantum mechanics and scientific gobbledygook.

Adam said, "I'm sure we entered a naked singularity. Did anyone have any sense of causality inversion?" All shook their heads. No one knew what he were talking about.

"What's a causality inversion?" asked Arabella, asking for everyone.

"Anything bizarre, really crazy," said Tim.

"You mean beyond waking up ninety-two million years back in time?" cracked Duke. "I'd say that's pretty fucking bizarre."

"No," said Adam. "Tim means during the event. During the blackout. Maybe about how you were thinking. Like a broken glass window reassembling itself. Clocks running backward or doing everything in reverse."

Again, they all shook their heads no.

"So how does this help getting home?" questioned Kevin.

"A naked singularity is like a black hole," answered Adam. "It grabs everything it comes in contact with. Nothing escapes. And we know there is at least one and probably more around the planet. All we have to do is find one."

The boys smiled in unison. They had read and studied everything the computer had on black holes and quantum mechanics. All of Hawking's and Sagan's theories as well as a dozen others. As far as rational explanations went, this made the most sense to the genious twins.

"How do we know a singularity is naked?" giggled Dawn. "I mean, we can't see it, right?"

"Right," said Tim. "Apparently, we can feel only its vibrations, but we cannot see one."

"So how do we find one?" asked Kevin.

Adam shrugged. "We don't know. Not yet. But I think the vibration we felt before blackout was the event horizon."

"The what?" asked Chief Hightower.

"The event horizon," said Tim. "Once you're inside, there's no way to escape the singularity."

"So we just float around, hoping to run into one?" asked Duke. "That could take another ninety-two million years. We're fucked!"

"Maybe," said Adam. "It's in the physics and mathematics. Tim and I are working on a computer program that might help, but it'll take another two or three months to work out. We just thought everyone should know."

"That's good work, lads," said the admiral. "Anything constructive helps. We're grateful."

The boys were about to delve into further explanations and theories when the radar screen on the bridge console lit up and pinged.

"Jesus, Mary, and Aristotle," exclaimed Admiral Fitzgerald. The boys rushed to the screen. Everyone else followed.

"I don't believe it," said Adam incredulously. "It's a bogey!"

Tim said, "About two hundred miles north bearing, six two seven at around four hundred miles per hour."

"It's a jet fighter," said JD. Everyone let out a breath. Relief filled the air.

"How do we contact it?" asked Tim.

"We have to assume it's a new fighter," JD said. "If it is, it's hooked up to SAT COM, a radio data-link network that sends coded information to a time-sharing relay satellite for rebroadcast to Earth stations. It's high speed and secure."

"But there are no satellites to relay information," said Tim. "How do we communicate with him?"

"Goddamned smoke signals!" offered an irritated Duke.

"No," said JD. He looked at Adam. "Go to GUARD. They're the internationally recognized emergency radio frequencies, VHF Guard is 121.5 and UHF Guard is 243.0."

Everyone looked at JD, stunned he would know such a thing. Adam began turning dials to the proper frequencies.

"The pilot will realize his regular communication channels are closed and will try to monitor the emergency channels. It makes sense," said Adam.

The crew tensed. Collective breaths were held. The admiral took the microphone.

During his thirteen years in the air force, Major Tom Crowley had never experienced anything like this. He was flying in a silent sky. The world had gone eerily quiet, and he recognized nothing. Below, the land formations were different, and the water and coastline were out of whack. Nothing made sense.

The F-16F was handling fine; he could detect no malfunctions. The lightweight, single-engine, single-pilot, counter-air and attack fighter built by General Dynamics was in perfect working order. It carried a wide variety of weapons and was designed for high maneuverability and flexibility, and everything worked. But it seemed to be the only thing in Major Crowley's world that did.

An Air Force Academy grad from La Crosse, Wisconsin, the major could not understand what had happened. Flying deaf in a world of electronic clutter made no sense. What did make sense was his fuel gauge. It continued to drop. He would have to land soon.

Not only could he not communicate with the outside world; that world was weird. Jungle canopies covered everything. Endless ocean to the west, no sign of civilization—no roads, no buildings, no nothing! Where had his world gone? The glass bubble of his cockpit had become a porthole to a strange, seemingly unexplored planet. He suddenly felt more like an astronaut than a pilot.

He knew the protocol; he scanned the VHF and UHF bands. After a few seconds, his radio locked on to VHF 121.5, and he heard an astonishing thing. A static crackled voice in proper British English.

"This is the United States Coast Guard cutter *Broadsword* to the unidentified aircraft one hundred sixty miles northwest. Come in, unidentified aircraft." He repeated the message twice.

Major Crowley took his mike. "This is Major Tom Crowley of the United States Air Force to the cutter *Broadsword*. Nice to hear a friendly voice. I'd appreciate it if you could tell me what the deuce is going on. Over." The major heard joyous exuberance over his radio.

On the *Broadsword*, the crew went into a frenzy of catcalls and high fives. A link to their past had been realized, an American pilot in a modern jet fighter. It was beyond their wildest hopes, a fellow wayfarer from their own time.

The admiral spoke, "This is retired Admiral Gerald Fitzgerald of the marooned cutter *Broadsword*. Welcome to the late Cretaceous period, Major. you traveled back in time ninety-two million years. Over."

"Say again, *Broadsword*," came the reply over static.

"You heard correct, Major. How do you feel?"

Short silence. "Like my world is topsy-turvy. I expect you can explain all of this to me, Admiral, but I have a more immediate problem, sir. I'm about to run out of JP-4. Any service stations around?"

"Negative, Major. Can you find a place to put that bird down? We can retrieve you once you're on the ground."

"Affirmative, sir. From my position five clicks inland, there's a narrow strip of earth about a quarter-mile long. I can land there. But I have to land within ten minutes or I'll have to ditch. How soon on retrieval?"

The admiral looked at Chief Hightower, who was bent over another console. The chief said, "At full speed to his coordinates, about eight hours. Then five clicks into the jungle, another two, ten hours, sir."

"About ten hours, Major. And we'll need a landmark where you entered the jungle from the sea. Is there anything distinguishable?"

Static. "Sure. You can't miss this. About a hundred and fifty miles north, you'll see an enormous walled enclosure made out of timbers. About forty feet high and two hundred yards long. You literally cannot miss it. I'm going to land about five miles east of that enclosure, and I'll stay put, admiral. But you should know there's a small village about two miles inland from the enclosure. Just a heads up, sir."

"People?" queried the admiral.

"Don't know. The jungle canopy is dense, and I saw no movement. But I'll wait on your rescue team. I'll call you from the ground. Crowley out."

The admiral set down the mike. "Okay, let's go get him, people."

Marcus and his men had been reeling from the sight and sound. A giant, steel bird had streaked across the sky. A white plume of smoke trailed behind, etching a line through the blue. Surely a god, thought Marcus. What else could do such a thing? His mind raced, begged for a metaphor, a lifeline to a more familiar experience. He found none.

His men stood in awe, slack jawed and humbled. Even the giant looked on in wonderment. The sight was beyond their understanding. Only the gods of their religion could provide sanctuary for their thoughts. It had to be a god.

It was a good omen, Marcus decided. They would attack the Slant village that night; he was sure the gods were with them. Blades were sharpened and manacles checked. The plan was straightforward. Under a starlit sky, they would traverse the clearing leading to the compound, ford the moat, and attack the main gate. They would overpower the guards, crush all resistance, and capture the able-bodied men. The children would be killed, and the women would be used for whatever the men wanted. Later, most of the women would be killed and the village burned to the ground.

Then the trek back to Romanica. Slaves in hand, they would return as conquering heroes to a grateful emperor. Fortune and fame awaited. The gods were with them. The proof was in the sky.

Major Crowley's F-16F was hurtling toward the narrow clearing he thought he could land on. He had quit looking at his fuel gauge; it had been on empty for some time. Empty meant land fast or be forced to land hard, maybe crash.

The landing site he had been forced to choose appeared long enough. It was the best of bad choices. Rocky outcrops lined the eastern edge, and tall, narrow trees picketed the western side. It should be easy, he thought. All he had to do was land in between those unforgiving obstacles, miss any holes, rocks, or boulders along the forest runway, not blow any tires, and softly brake to an easy stop. Easy, like calculus or Hebrew.

He looked to his heads-up display, a large piece of glass mounted atop the instrument panel. It reflected projected information in the pilot's line of sight so he did not have to look down.

The fighter suddenly began to cough and sputter. He had control of the plane, and his altitude was dropping at a manageable rate. That was the good news. The bad news was he could not reverse the engine to slow his speed. He would have to brake the fighter to a stop, which meant he needed a longer runway. His runway was fixed. It was what it was, not Andrews Air Force Base, so he would have to make it work.

Gently, like a young boy on his first bicycle ride, he started to ease toward the landing site. Inching closer, he dropped the flaps a hair, decreasing his speed. The hard firmament was rising up at him like a great beast. With a softness he did not think possible, his jet touched the earth. But this was not a smooth runway at an airport. Almost immediately, the jagged surface began to rebel against the jets tires. Rocks, plants, small trees, and other parts of nature made Major Crowley feel as if he were landing on the moon. The fragile jet bucked and tossed; it had not been designed for this type landing. Crowley fought the stick for control. He was slowing, but not as fast as he hoped.

Then the jet's front tire blew. It could have been a jagged rock or a stump or a broken tree limb. Crowley recognized the sound but did not panic. He held on as the deflated front tire dug in and grabbed the earth. The rear of the jet was now moving faster than the front, forcing the nose toward the ground. Crowley knew he had only one choice. He blew the cockpit canopy and pushed the ejector button. He was launched a second before the jet nosedived into the earth and flipped. The plane tumbled. The wings broke off and most of the body was ripped apart. There was no explosion; the highly flammable fuel was gone. Still, a hundred yards of wreckage graced the landscape. The jet no longer resembled an aircraft; it was bits of crumpled metal and broken composites.

Major Crowley resembled a circus performer shot from a cannon. His cockpit seat peeled away as the parachute opened automatically. He had been shot over the forest and watched as huge conifers rose up from the forest floor toward him. Because he had gained little altitude, he dropped like a stone. The sword-like limbs of the trees rushed at him. He was an intruder in their ordered world.

He tried desperately to maneuver his decent, but the trees were unavoidable. Like a missile he dove into the dense cover of hardwoods. Limbs, branches, and boughs took turns ripping and pounding him as he fell. He was the ball in a deadly pinball game. As he crashed topsy-turvy, his helmet saved his life more than once. Mercifully, after endless tumbling, his chute caught a large branch and held. The whiplash nearly broke his neck, but he stopped and hung, suspended, swinging wildly.

That is when he struck a redwood four feet in diameter. Like an out-of-control pendulum, he hit the tree, bouncing only slightly. His fragile body had the wind knocked out of it, and despite his helmet, the blow drove him into the blackness of unconsciousness. He continued to swing like a hanged man. His form was flaccid, as limp as a rag.

In his comatose state, Major Crowley had no idea his ordeal had drawn the attention of living things far and wide. The jungle was suddenly alive with malevolent curiosity.

Doc Moran knew he would go. Nothing she could say would persuade him otherwise. It hardly mattered that he was the only one capable of such a rescue. JD was hooked on danger. Risk sweetened everything in his world. She sat quietly as JD laid out his plan to rescue Major Crowley. The admiral, Chief Hightower, Kevin, and Arabella listened to JD's plan. He had drawn a crude map based on Major Crowley's information and was pointing to spots on it as he spoke.

"We anchor offshore here," he said. "Molly and I will take a Zodiac into shore. From there, we'll zero in on the major's signal and track him to the plane. Once secured, we'll head back to the *Broadsword*. Molly and I will recon the village, and we can decide what to do from there."

The plan was simple and straightforward. It appealed to everyone, everyone but Doc. She hated it because it involved JD. Over the last months, she had grown to love him, to cherish their time together. She had become greedy when it came to him. Like all lovers from the beginning of time, the rest of the world was secondary to her; JD was her focus. To lose him meant she would lose part of her soul. Melded by love, she was part of him, and being part of him, she understood his need to go. Love was understanding, she knew that, but understanding did not exclude a person from worry or fear. Everything in this world could be dangerous. A person did not have to look very far; it lurked around every corner. She sat, listened, and worried for her love, who looked about as worried as a man on vacation, sunning on a beach.

After the others left, JD said, "I won't take any unnecessary chances, Doc. I promise." He could feel her concern.

She smiled an uneasy smile. "I know," she said. "I had a long talk with Molly. She promised to keep you in line."

They laughed gently.

"There's been no further word from the pilot. Do you think he's landed okay?"

"I don't know. There's only one way to find out."

"Yeah," she said, understanding. Someone had to go out and look for him, find evidence of what had happened. And JD, her lover, was the best one for the job.

"I know you'll be careful. Just come back. Just come back."

Major Crowley was slowly coming back from the land of blackness. His eyes fluttered open as the fog of unconsciousness began to disappear. He was suspended in midair, held by parachute lines tangled above him. He looked down through a maze of branches to the forest floor some forty feet below.

A quick physical inventory told him his body was battered but whole. Scratches, a few punctures, and a billion bruises and contusions dotted his frame. His flight suit was a shredded mess. But smashed and discolored was always better than dead. He took off his helmet and let it fall. It careened off branches and bounced to the ground. The wilderness around him was alive; he heard chortles, squawks, and yips all around, unfamiliar jungle chatter to his military ears. He felt for his pistol. He had no intention of becoming something's lunch.

An eerie feeling teased his spine. The feeling was broken by a gentle poke in the ribs. His body recoiled from the light touch. He turned quickly in the direction of the jab. To his right, about six feet away, sat two figures. Men. They crouched on a thick limb and stared at him in wonder. He could tell they were short even though they were crouching. Maybe five-five to five-eight. Dark skinned with black hair. Their faces and exposed limbs were covered with black stripes, but he could make out oriental features. They looked Chinese.

They prodded him again with a stick. He realized they were offering it to him as a way to pull him over to them. They nodded and smiled and spoke to him in a language he did not understand, but it was clear they were offering help. He grabbed their lifeline, and they pulled him over. With great care, they held him as he freed himself from the entangled harness. They gestured for him to follow them.

The forty-foot descent was agonizing to his bruised body, but once down, he was glad to feel firm earth. With manic waves, his rescuers beckoned him. It was apparent they were in a hurry to leave; they feared something in the forest. Since they had showed him nothing but kindness, he was inclined to believe them; their motives seemed genuine.

They moved fast and quietly. His body throbbed in pain, but he pressed on. He collapsed to his knees after about a mile. His chest heaved. His legs were concrete. His small deliverers picked him up and began helping him along.

Soon they entered a clearing that surrounded a walled village. They raced, dragging him across a bridged moat and through the front gate. Then they dropped the major and dropped to their knees, exhausted themselves. It was then he noticed a large group of two-legged, human-sized dinosaurs at the far end of the clearing. They snapped and chortled in anger, outraged their prey had escaped.

The major knew his new small friends had saved his life. He gave them a thumbs-up, to which they showed only bewilderment, but he knew from their smiling faces that they accepted his gratitude.

A crowd had gathered. Short of stature and oriental, they all had curious smiles. He suddenly felt like Alice discovering she was in Wonderland. He remembered he had to contact the *Broadsword*. His stomach knotted as he realized his radio was forty feet up in a redwood a mile and a half away. Exasperation filled him as he lay on the ground. His brain tumbled like dice; exhaustion gripped him. He was soon fast asleep.

The *Broadsword* was fast and had made good time. They dropped anchor about five hundred meters offshore, adjacent to a gigantic, timbered wall. An old wall. The *Broadsword* crew looked on in fascination.

"What the bloody hell," said Admiral Fitzgerald. The aged, time-weathered barrier stood at least forty feet tall, and it was at least a quarter-mile long. On each end, it curled out into the ocean about twenty yards, where it was anchored to enormous timbers four times the diameter of the others. Waves pounded against the ends, creating great splashes. In the middle of the wall was a gate about thirty feet tall. Crude, lashed hinges looked to still be operational. Parapets were strategically placed. Everyone had the same thought. The movie *King Kong*.

"Cool," Tim said.

"What do you suppose they were trying to keep out?" asked Arabella.

"What else?" barked Duke. "A big fucking monkey! Fay Wray is probably on the other side, tied to a tree, waiting for King Kong and his big schlong!"

Arabella made a face at Duke. He made a face back. *Kids,* Duke thought.

"Whatever the original intention," said Kevin, "it's abandoned now. And it serves as a great landmark. A blind man could see that thing."

The admiral swiveled to JD. "Still no word from Major Crowley. Can you find him in that clutter of jungle?" It was a good question, but JD was confident. "I'll find him, Admiral. If he's alive, I'll bring him back." The admiral signaled his assurance.

Kevin, Duke, and Doc would accompany JD to the shore. He and Molly would head into the jungle while the others waited with the Zodiac. They would leave at any sign of trouble. Doc had insisted on going; Major Crowley might need medical attention. Reluctantly, JD caved. With no word from the major, it was possible, indeed likely, that he was injured or incapacitated.

Those left onshore would be covered by the *Broadsword*'s fifty calibers. Arabella and the chief would handle that duty. Finally, everything was readied, and the rescue team departed.

As they neared the shore, Molly bounded into the surf. The big cat loved the water. The Zodiac was secured and it was time for JD and Molly to go.

"I'll find him," said JD as he moved to Doc. They hugged. JD looked to Kevin, who shook his head in acknowledgement.

They were dwarfed by the immense wooden structure. It really did resemble the wall in the King Kong movie. Kevin said, "This thing is hundreds of years old. It means people have been here a while. But it's a puzzle, alright. I'm not sure it's to keep something out."

"What do you mean?" asked Doc.

"It could have been a trap or a corral," said JD. "Designed to keep something in once it got here. It's puzzling."

Kevin shook his head in agreement. "Time to go, old son," he said. "I'll throw a few shrimp on the barbie and wait for you. Don't dally, okay?" He wore his concern like a mask.

"No worries, mate," said JD. He turned to Duke, who had been strangely quiet. "You okay, Dukie?"

Duke walked up to JD and hugged him hard. "Get going, you fucking douchebag. We ain't got all fucking day!"

JD smiled. He whistled, and Molly came running, her surf antics over for thr time being. She shook her great body furiously, soaking Kevin, Doc, and Duke.

"Goddamned cat!" shouted Duke in disgust. Molly growled low and deep, and Duke retreated to JD.

"Come on, Moose," yelled JD. They ran toward the great door of the walled enclosure. JD's sword, slung across his back, flashed in the afternoon sun.

They were soon through the opening and fading into the dense forest. They faced a five-mile jog to the makeshift landing site. Dappled sunlight streaked through the tree ceiling of the forest, but at ground level, it was cool and damp. They slid like specters through the trees and coverage, disturbing hardly a leaf. They owned the rain forest in their old world, but this was a prehistoric forest. The melodies of this jungle included the fluted sounds of predation. Though they moved silently, they could not overcome one huge problem.

In this jungle, they were like perfumed whores in a slaughterhouse; they reeked of the unfamiliar. Every predator downwind would pick up their scent. They moved fast and cautiously, scented intruders in a savage netherworld.

The air was clammy. JD's fatigues were stained with sweat. The damp forest floor sprouted toadstools, enormous ferns, and crawling vines in an entanglement of greens and browns. A riot of colors sprang from certain patches of earth. Massive redwoods stretched skyward, reaching for the endless blue above. Beyond the forest canopy, birds and winged dinosaurs squawked and blared and circled endlessly, on the hunt for prey. JD and Molly moved through dappled sunlight that dotted the forest floor.

After two hours, they stood by the wreckage of Major Crowley's jet. The amazing sight was surreal, set against the backdrop of the prehistoric landscape. The jet had been reduced to biodegradable rubble. Within a year, the creeping jungle would swallow it.

The pilot's seat was gone, which was good news. It meant Major Crowley had ejected. But the plane was so mangled and demolished that there was no way to tell which direction the major had gone. It was pick-a-direction time.

JD looked to Molly. "We'll start southeast and make a circular probe at about two hundred yards from the crash site." Molly yawned. "Stay within ear shot, and no noise unless you spot something."

The big cat disappeared into the jungle. JD followed behind about thirty yards. The major could be anywhere, and JD knew they had to find him before something else did. Something that was big and hungry.

Marcus and his men were hungry for action. They would attack the Slant village that night and at last satisfy their aggression. Slaves, women, plunder, and wealth would be theirs. Marcus stood next to the giant and asked, "The traps are set?"

The giant nodded. "Yes. The woods in front of the compound are now filled with man traps. Any escaping Slants will be caught like animals before they go twenty yards. Snares, pits, and nets are laced throughout the underbrush. We'll grab any who escape the village."

"That's good," exclaimed a happy Marcus. "We need as many as possible for the trip home. An hour before dusk, take six men and check all the traps. A few may need to be reset if any animals have gotten snared. Tonight we feast in the Slant village."

The giant gripped the handle of his sword and smiled, a menacing smile that made even Marcus wince. Then he gave a rakish bow and swaggered off. Marcus was glad the giant was on his side. The thought of facing this maniacal monster in combat was the thing nightmares were made of. He hoped the giant would stay in line; it would be a waste to kill such a fearsome creature. This raiding party's purpose was to capture Slants for the games, not kill and maim indiscriminately. If the giant's bloodlust became too uncontrollable, Marcus would have to deal with him harshly, probably fatally. This was business, and Marcus was accountable only to the emperor, so he would wait to see how the giant acted. Just three hours until they attacked. Three long hours.

Molly stood guard at the foot of a giant redwood. Forty feet up, JD was busy collecting an empty parachute harness that hung precariously from shorn straps. It was definitely Major Crowley's chute, but where was he? His radio and emergency pack were not with him; JD was holding them as he tried to figure out what had happened. Why would Crowley take off on foot without these lifelines? It made no sense, but little in this world did.

With mild frustration, he took his radio and called the admiral. "Nomad to *Broadsword*," he said over crackling interference.

"This is *Broadsword*, Nomad," came an equally crackling response. It was Admiral Fitzgerald. "How goes the search?"

"I've located the wreckage of Major Crowley's jet, but he's gone. Ejected. I found his harness and emergency equipment but not him. He appears to have survived the crash and his ejection. I'm going to continue the search and check the village a few clicks from here."

Kevin and Doc had been monitoring the radio exchange from shore. Kevin asked, "Any hostiles, son?"

"Nothing yet. Our old friends, the raptors, are about, though. There's fresh raptor dung everywhere, so you guys stay put. Don't come into these woods. I'll call again from the village. Nomad out."

He clicked off the radio. Molly made a low, guttural sound. She darted into the dense ground cover. JD slowed his breathing and became part of the tree. A minute later, a party of men passed beneath the tree. They were moving fast and quiet. A patrol, men with a purpose. None looked up as they passed and they soon faded into the jungle.

JD continued to sit in his perch. He thought he had just seen a Roman patrol walk by. Short, muscular, and definitely Italian. This world seemed to get stranger, he thought. Romans? What would he see next? Zulus and Vikings?

Molly reappeared below, telling JD it was safe to come down. On the ground, he turned to the cat. "They're tracking something, Moose. I suppose we ought to follow. Major Crowley will probably need help. And it was nice of them to leave us this swell trail. Stay close."

JD looked at the ground. The clumsy Romans had left a trail a child could have followed. They had no fear of being tracked, he concluded. That meant they were experienced or arrogant or both. He also concluded that these were not careless pirates. They carried Roman short swords and pila, Roman military javelins. And if he remembered his history, Roman foot soldiers were rigorously trained and capable fighting men. JD followed at a safe distance.

"So where's the pilot?" bellowed Duke at Kevin and Doc.

"A little louder," joked Kevin. "I'm a trifle deaf in this ear." He pointed to his right ear, which Duke had just blasted. "How do I know? For all we know, he's stumbling around the jungle injured. JD will find him. Relax, big guy."

But Duke could not relax. He was pacing and waving frantically. "It's gonna be dark soon. What then?"

Kevin said, "We wait. JD will contact us one way or the other. We wait."

"I hate fucking waiting!"

"I noticed. What do you want to do? Play pinochle?"

"Fuck you, Kev. I'm worried, alright. I like that scrawny son of a bitch."

"So do we," said Doc. "I love that scrawny son of a bitch. He'll be okay." Her voice had been soft as a rose petal and reassuring. Then in the voice of a wild angel, she said, "Now quit moping around like some flaming douchebag and buck up or I'll kick your scrawny ass all over this beach! Get me?"

That created a look of mystification on Kevin. Duke broke into a large grin. "I just love a gal that talks dirty," he said, showing his pleasure.

"Good!" roared Doc. "Now shut the fuck up! I'm worried enough. I don't need you reminding me." Like Duke, she hated waiting, but there was nothing else to do. JD would contact them. She looked out at the rolling sea and wished that scrawny son of a bitch would hurry.

JD and Molly were in no hurry. They had been following the Romans for half an hour on a trail that had more twists and turns than the Gordian knot. Something was wrong. JD could feel it. Molly had paced ahead a few yards when without warning a trap sprung, a net shot upward, grabbing the huge cat and catapulting her off the ground. She roared in defiance as she hung suspended, tangled in the net.

JD drew his sword and moved toward her. He heard the shaft slicing through the damp forest air but much too late. The arrow tore a path across his left shoulder before striking a tree in front of him. He swung around as two more arrows blitzed from the jungle. One he deflected, but the other struck him mid thigh. Without thinking, he broke the protruding shaft from his thigh and pushed the arrowhead end through the meaty part of his leg. He dove for cover, tumbling hard into a large conifer as he tried to avoid future arrows.

His shoulder seared in pain as he hit the tree. His thigh was pumping blood from entry and exit wounds. He could hear the sounds of men around him. Escape and elude, then come back for Molly.

He struggled to his feet and began pushing through the forest. Dogged pursuit followed. He ran but was unfamiliar with the area and soon found himself at an outcropping some thirty feet above a shallow basin. He would need to climb down or be trapped. The climb would be difficult with his injuries, but he had no choice. Fatigue and pain robbed him of his keen senses. As he was contemplating the descent, he was struck from behind. His head exploded in shooting stars and fireworks. The blow sent him over the edge. He hit the ground in a tumbling fall and sprawled on the ground, unconscious.

Above, two figures looked on. “I’ll go down and make sure he’s dead,” said the smaller man, though he was sure no one could survive such a fall.

“No,” said the giant. “We go back for the orange and black animal. This one dead. No one can survive a blow from this.” The giant held up his enormous hand, the size of a shovel.

The smaller man nodded. He decided not to argue with the giant. He took a last look at the strange man below. Indeed, he looked very dead.

Looking dead and being dead are hardly the same. Six hours after JD had tumbled from the cliff, he woke with a start. It was the smell. The jungle was rich with the scent of smoke. It had dragged JD back from the darkness of unconsciousness. His injuries racked him with pain. A quick glance at his watch told him how long he had been out. Not good. His pursuers had abandoned him, probably in favor of returning to Molly and completing her capture. He had to get up and check things out, but when he tried, his body rebelled. His head felt like he had been hit with an anvil. His shoulder screamed, and his leg throbbed. When he was finally able to stand his head swirled like a cloud in a storm. He shook his head to clear it, which made it hurt more. He staggered to a rock and leaned against it for support. He wondered, comically, how it was that in a prehistoric forest he had been hit by a train.

His sword was intact, but his radio looked like a bunch of broken components. Damn, he could not keep a radio safe to save his life. He also realized he had lost Major Crowley's radio as well. Another smoke-filled breath reminded him to get moving. The reek of dried wood told him the village was probably the source. Slowly, on rubbery legs, he ventured off in the direction of the smoky order. A mild zephyr blew cool and damp through the forest. He followed the heavy, smoke-choked air toward its source.

After a mile stumble, JD downed half the water he had left. A tempest still raged in his head. The water helped. With labored steps, he trudged toward the odor. A night as black as silt had grown over the jungle. The only source of light was a half moon. Shredded beams pierced the canopy and cast dancing shadows everywhere.

In the distance, the orange and yellow of numerous flickering fires invaded the darkness. JD stepped from the trees to the clearing surrounding the village compound. The village was ablaze. Fires raged from one end of the structure to the other. Great columns of billowing smoke created paths to the heavens. The fires had kept the scavengers at bay, but soon, the smell of charred flesh would be more than most of them could endure. They would invade the smoldering ruins and feast on freshly cooked meat. JD knew if he was to find survivors he would have to go now and look; later would be too late.

Crossing the open field, he could feel the eyes, hidden in the jungle, of nature's cleanup crew. Raptors, T. rexes, even compys would soon feed on the dead. The bridge over the moat had been destroyed after the fact. JD eased into the black, cool water. At first he shivered from the cold, but the water soon felt good on his tattered body.

He cleared the moat and entered the compound and walked directly into a massacre. Bodies in all poses of death littered the ground, mostly women and children. Nearly all had been cleaved or butchered. It was a sight out of anyone's version of hell. JD shuffled through the burned-out wreckage and carnage and felt close to tears. These people had not been killed by prehistoric beasts but by other humans. Who could abide such slaughter? All the bodies had an oriental appearance. From the looks of the wounds, he knew all had been killed by Roman short swords and pikes. A truely horrific way to die.

He found only three males among the dead. This told him there had not been much of a fight. The village had probably surrendered, and the women and children had been executed. It was dreadful. The weak had been massacred; the strong and able had been marched off to lives most likely of slavery and misery. No sign of Molly.

His head and body forced him to sit. Despite the horror around him, his own body was near failure. During his period of unconsciousness, he had lost blood, and his thirst was raging.

He sat, a near corpse among many real corpses. Molly captured, Major Crowley missing, and a once-thriving village destroyed. And now his own body nearly defeated. He had to get back to the *Broadsword*, recover, and track the mercenaries who had perpetrated this horror. Heavily lidded eyes told him to sleep first. Rest a while. Rest was a weapon. He slumped to the ground, the sandman in complete control.

"You can't reach anyone?" the admiral asked the twins. It had been over eight hours since the *Broadsword* had heard from JD or Kevin and the others. Adam tried the radio again. Only static. It was after midnight, and everyone was alarmed. Silence could spell only trouble.

Chief Hightower said, "Arabella and I will take the other Zodiac to shore and check things out. We'll radio from there."

Everyone looked at each other. Four of their friends gone, a dark, hostile landscape their last known whereabouts.

"Meet me at the Zodiac, Chief," said Arabella. "I'll grab some equipment. Let's go find our friends."

Adam tried the proper radio frequencies, but again nothing only dead air and agonizing silence. Arabella and the chief went off. The admiral turned to the twins. "It's a bad start, lads, a bad start."

JD woke with a start. In his exhausted sleep, he thought he had heard a childlike, angelic voice calling to him. It had brought him back from the blackness. Now he was awake, and the voice continued. His sleeve was being tugged. He looked into the eyes of a soot-covered face. Behind the dirty face was a child, four or five years old. She spoke to him in commingled Mandarin and Cantonese. It took a moment for him to assimilate the words, but he understood.

"Hey mister," she repeated. "Can you help my mom? I can't get her to wake up. She has slept a long time." The little girl spoke with the innocence of a cherub. Her voice was curious and pure.

"Where is your mom, wee one?" JD said as he stood.

"She's over there." She pointed. "You don't look so good, mister. And you talk funny."

JD smiled. "I'm not from around here. Let's go see your mom, okay?"

"I'll help you 'cause you're hurt," she said and took his hand. *The irony*, JD thought. In the middle of all this destruction and bloodshed, a child demonstrates the best of humanity with a small, unselfish gesture.

She led him to a patch of open ground near a burned hut and pointed to a woman lying lifeless on the cold earth. "Can you wake her up, mister? I'm scared without my mom." Small hope filled her eyes that were trained on JD. He knelt beside the dead woman. Her throat had been slit, and she had been viciously raped. It was a scene straight from a Clive Barker horror novel.

JD sat. In a gentle voice, he said, "Your mom has gone to heaven, wee one. But I was a good friend of your mom's, and I promised her I'd take care of you. Do you understand?"

Her eyes filled with tears. Her tiny head shook its understanding. She grabbed JD around the neck and cried hard. Her small frame trembled with every sob. JD found himself fighting tears. He hated the brutal unfairness. Why should one so small and tender have to deal with such grief?

Through teardrops, she said, "I promise I'll be good, mister. You won't hurt me like those bad men, will you?"

"My name is JD. And no, I'll never hurt you. What is your name, wee one?"

"My name is Keiko, Mister JD." She looked at the destruction of the village. "What do we do now?"

JD sighed. "We go home, wee one. We go home."

There was no time to bury Keiko's mother. JD placed her body in a smoldering hut. The planet would take back her remains via the many scavengers that would soon appear.

He checked his compass, and calling on strength he was sure he did not have, he set off with Keiko to find the *Broadsword*. He thought the smell of dead and burned flesh would keep the raptors and others occupied for the rest of the night. He needed to make it just the two miles to the beach. Help waited there. He was so tired. Every step was agony. The little orphan gripped his hand; she was afraid to let go in the dark. She had stopped crying soon after they had left the village. He realized she was a tough kid; he was determined to be tough enough too. He was not about to add his and her demises to that grisly total.

Like a marathon runner who is hurting but determined to finish, he pushed on to the giant walled enclosure at the beach.

Luck or perhaps fate was with them. They faced no challenges from predators and made it through the cruel jungle without incident. Keiko was quiet the whole way. She was not surprised or frightened by the great beamed wall; JD realized she must have been there before.

Hobbling painfully and racked with exhaustion, he entered the walled site with Keiko in tow. He could see lights at the far end, near the water, and he called out and waved. The lights began moving in their direction.

He said to Keiko, "Don't be afraid. These are my friends." He could feel her smile in the darkness. Her tiny hand held on tight. But his head was beginning to feel light. Pain, blood loss, and oxygen deficiency combined to sap his strength and reserves. Keiko felt his hand give way as he blacked out and fell hard to the sand. She stared at her fallen hero as the advancing lights reached them. She heard voices speaking a strange language.

"Call the *Broadsword* and get help. He's near dead." It was a woman's voice, strong and in control. It changed to a voice as soft and became easy as summer rain. "Hi, there, short stuff. Don't be afraid. We're going to help you." Keiko found herself in the strange woman's arms and heading for a strange boat. A few moments later, exhaustion claimed her also. She was fast asleep when they reached the *Broadsword*.

They were moving slower than a glacier. At this rate, it would take three weeks to reach Romanica. That displeased Marcus greatly. He longed to be home and to be over with this arduous mission. The good news was that they had more than fifty physically fit slaves. The emperor would be very happy, very grateful.

The capture had gone well with a few unexpected bonuses thrown in. Even the sadistic giant had behaved reasonably well and they had lost only one man in their encounter with the Slants.

They had marched the entire night; by midmorning, everyone, captive and captor, was tired. Marcus held up his hand and motioned the group to stop. He turned to his men. "We make camp here and rest. Secure the slaves in an area over there." He pointed to a small clearing. "Feed them, and post guards. We rest until tomorrow morning." His words brought relief to his dog-tired men. They began to make camp. It was already another hot day.

The giant appeared at Marcus's side. "I want the woman," he stated in a cold voice. Marcus could see the evil desire behind cool, black eyes.

"She's a fine specimen," said Marcus. "I told you, the emperor may want her. I don't want her damaged before he sees her. Besides, you had plenty of women at the village. If the emperor says no to her, she is yours. Not before."

The giant's face grew into a menacing scowl. Marcus, however, could care less. He could read the giant's thoughts. He put his hand to the handle of his sword and in an acid-laced voice said, "You know me, giant. Challenge me and I'll kill you."

The giant stared long and hard. His black eyes probed Marcus. He had seen Marcus kill many men in the arena. He had seen him kill raptors and even giants. The giant considered Marcus the finest swordsman in all of Romanica. To challenge him would be suicide. Discretion over folly, decided the giant. Life over death. He grumbled and stormed off angry and headed to the slaves' holding area.

The captives sat on the ground, hands bound and hopes forgotten. Egnid grabbed one of the male slaves, and as if tossing a ball, he threw the startled man against a tree ten feet away. The hapless man crumpled into unconsciousness. Marcus was furious.

"If he's permanently damaged, giant, you'll pay!"

But the giant also could not have cared less. He strode off in silence, his anger temporarily abated. Marcus sheathed his sword and took a deep breath in relief. The men went back to making camp, and the new slaves sunk into desperate imaginings.

The day grew hot and Marcus sat in the shade of a towering conifer. A breeze drifted by but was not enough to cool his sweat-covered skin. He leaned back, closed his eyes, and sank into a light nap. He was soon dreaming of home.

JD faded in and out of dream-filled sleep like a bird passing through clouds. One second, everything was clear as the open sky; the next second, he was enveloped by a hazy, soft whiteness that blurred everything. When he woke, he found Nurse Natalie perched over him like a doting grandmother.

"Good morning," she said softly. "How are you feeling?"

JD took inventory. His head ached, his shoulder burned, and his thigh throbbed. Oh, yeah; his mouth was as dry as a salt flat. "Not bad." He looked around the small room. "What? Doc out making a house call?" He smiled, but Natalie went ghostly-white and fled the room. He wondered what had upset her.

A few moments later, the admiral, Chief Hightower, and Arabella filed into the small room. They wore masks of gloom and despair. JD wasted no time. "Spit it out," he said, rising on an elbow. "This looks like the night of the living dead!"

The admirals' face was painted in distress. "We're glad you're okay, son, and the little girl, Keiko, is fine also."

"But?" said JD.

"But there's no good way to tell you. Doc, Kevin, and Duke are gone. Disappeared. The chief and Arabella found you and Keiko when they went to investigate the others. I'm sorry, son. There's no trace of them."

Arabella started to break. She couldn't stop her tears. Kevin was gone. She feared the worst.

JD took the news like a rock. "I know who took them," he said in a steady but icy voice. "How long have I been here?"

"Two days, son. Natalie stitched up your leg and shoulder, but you suffered a hell of a concussion. And we can't understand the little girl. Some sort of Chinese, right?"

"A mixture of Mandarin and Cantonese. Her family's dead, their village destroyed. Molly was captured, and they left me for dead."

"Who?" asked the chief.

"A raiding party. Slavers. They looked like Roman military."

"Roman?"

"I think the twins were right. A large population of Roman descendants are in this area as well as a contingent of Mongolian-Chinese and probably some Japanese."

"That's what Keiko is," realized the admiral. "She's a descendant. That means both groups have survived here for hundreds of years. The Roman raiders must have stumbled onto Kevin, Doc, and Duke and overpowered them. Took them for slaves."

"Right," said JD. "That's the bad news. The good news is that they're probably still alive. The other good news is that I can track them."

"But they have a two-day lead, JD," Arabella said. "And frankly, I don't think you could drive a wheelchair let alone track slavers through a prehistoric jungle in your condition. You should see yourself, pal. I've seen healthier cadavers."

JD rose to a sitting position. He head went into a spinning maelstrom. He fought for balance as his equilibrium spun wildly.

"You see? You're a wreck," Arabella said.

"Maybe," he said. "But I'll get better, and we have to find them before they get to their destination."

"Why's that?" asked the chief.

"Because it was a raiding party. They were interested only in strong, able-bodied people."

"They want good slaves," remarked the admiral.

"They want good victims, Admiral. I'd bet my last dollar they're going to some games."

"What games?" asked Arabella.

"Oh my god," said the chief, his eyes widening. "They want them for gladiatorial games!"

"Right," answered a foggy JD. "But they have a large group to move, so they'll be slow. Plus, we have a couple of advantages."

"Such as?" asked Arabella.

"They're arrogant, so they won't expect anyone to follow. And they think I'm dead."

"And we have better weapons," added an enlightened Arabella. "I'll start packing our gear. We'll leave in three hours."

Three sets of stunned eyes looked at her. Was she nuts?

"What do you mean 'our' gear, lady? You sure as hell aren't going." JD spoke emphatically. The others nodded in absolute agreement.

"Now listen up, hotshot," she boomed. "I'm going, and I don't care who doesn't like it! It makes sense. I'm the fittest onboard, the best shot, and I'm motivated. You lead, and I'll carry the gear until you've recovered enough to pull your own weight. I'll be your rear guard and your pack mule. Get your broken self together while I get organized. You got three hours!" She bolted, leaving the three men silenced by her brisk retort.

A recovering Admiral Fitzgerald said, "She has a point, son. I don't think we could keep her from going if she really wants to, and she really wants to. You sure you can find them?"

JD was sure he could. And he knew Arabella was right. He was a walking intensive care unit at the moment. "Yes, Admiral, I can find them. And I'll accept Arabella's help. To use your terminology, she has a lot of hard bark on her. She's gonna need it, too. That raiding party isn't going to turn over our friends just because we want them to. We're going to have to take them, and it's going to be messy and nasty. Help me get up. And tell Mister Henry I'll need that special recipe I told him about. He'll know."

The chief and the admiral helped a limping JD down the corridor toward the armory, where a busy Arabella was collecting gear.

"You're as pale as milk," she said. She threw a tube of C-4 explosives at him; he caught them with a little trepidation. "Good. Your reflexes are still decent. Tell me what else we're gonna need."

A painful grin appeared on his face. *Arabella will be okay*, he thought.

Images of Doc flooded his mind. Was she alive? Was she suffering? What had they done to her? He remembered telling her once that if they were ever separated, he would find her. No matter how long it took, he would find her. It was a promise he meant to keep.

As for her Roman captors? They were on his better-off-dead list. He owed them a debt in blood and he was prepared to start wearing out equipment in the pursuit of that debt. Nomad was on his way.

Doc, Kevin, and Duke sat with the other prisoners on the damp ground, hands bound. The leather binding that the Romanicans used as manacles were terrible. They had been lashed on wet; as they dried, they became tighter. Some of the prisoners' hands were turning black or blue, but their captors were blissfully unconcerned. Molly had given up struggling and lay with her paws tied to a large tree. She panted heavily in the midday heat.

There had not been much conversation for two days. Duke and Kevin had sustained multiple bruises and contusions in their struggles on the beach with their captors. They were just starting to get over those injuries. Doc was the only woman in the group, and Duke and Kevin always stayed close. The others were all oriental men, and their captors appeared to be Romans—short, muscular, Mediterranean types.

Kevin leaned to Doc. "JD will come," he said. "We just have to hang on. No matter what, we have to stay alive."

Doc looked at Kevin. "You mean Nomad will come."

"I guess so. Yes."

"Kev, there are over thirty of these Roman monsters. And that horrible giant! He loves hurting people. How can JD or Nomad help us against them?"

"He needs an edge, Doc. And that edge is you. For you, Doc, he'd face the devil in hell. These poor bastards have no idea what's coming their way. He won't be forgiving, and he won't be understanding. He'll be a killing machine. They'll think their gods have abandoned them and that the world's on fire. Just hold on, Doc. Hold on."

"He's gonna fuck up their world, Doc. Big time!" Duke said.

For the first time that day, Major Crowley spoke. He had been captured at the Slant village with the other men and had spent the last two days in a state of continued disbelief. The *Broadsword* captives had explained the circumstances of the "new" time to him, but it had taken him a while to absorb the information and adjust to its implications.

"Who's this Nomad?"

"A friend," Kevin said. "If he's alive, he'll come for us."

"One man," said a bewildered Crowley. "Look around, my friend. Our captors are seasoned mercenaries. Your man is either hopelessly insane or a bastard with a death wish."

"The gods love a bastard," quipped Duke. "And no offense, Major, but what do you care what kind of man our friend is? He's coming to help us. He'll risk his life for us, for you, someone he doesn't even know. So do me a favor and shut the fuck up!"

Crowley was about to respond when Doc interrupted. "Relax, boys. Our captors shouldn't see us fighting. Both of you put it back in your pants."

Duke and Crowley returned to silence. Kevin shrugged at Doc. Her brown eyes reflected her concern. Like Kevin, she wasn't sure JD was still alive. The capture of Molly was a bad sign. They knew JD would never have left her unless he had had no choice. And no choice meant he was incapacitated, badly injured, or worse. In the silence of her mind's eye, she cried. She desperately clung to the thought of JD's survival and their deliverance. "Stay alive," he had told her. No matter what, she vowed to stay alive.

Those on the *Broadsword* knew JD was alive. He and Arabella had left thirty minutes previously. JD was moving like a ninety-year-old, his body proud but battered, while a grimly determined Arabella carried their equipment.

Chief Hightower, the admiral, and the twins watched them disappear through the large hinged entrance of the giant wooded Kong enclosure. From the bridge, the four men looked on with troubled expressions.

"JD doesn't look too good, Admiral," said Tim with palpable concern in his voice. "He may not make it a mile."

"The man is a different breed, lad," said the admiral. "And Yeoman Arabella is cut from the same mold. They're warriors. They'll do what's necessary. There's no other way to explain it."

"Romans and Mongols," ventured Chief Hightower. "The irony is extremely bizarre."

"What do you mean, Chief?" asked Adam.

"In human history, the Romans were regarded as the finest foot soldiers ever and the Mongolian horsemen the finest mounted cavalry ever. But they missed each other by six hundred years. Here, in this prehistoric backwater, they're contemporaries. They represent the two greatest empires in human existence. It must be an amazing clash of cultures. And it must make for a brutal coexistence. Both civilizations dealt harshly with enemies. They were not known for their mercy."

The others stood in quiet agreement. Their planet was a quagmire of violence and predation. Not only was it populated by the largest and most vicious land and sea predators in the earth's history, but also, the small human population consisted of some of the harshest, most-brutal inhabitants to have ever graced the planet.

Adam laughed softly. "You know, except for a few hundred minor inconveniences, this time would almost be paradise. I mean, if we didn't have to worry about being eaten or poisoned or captured, this would be cool."

"Almost paradise," echoed Tim.

Then, as if to remind everyone that paradise was relative, a screaming, terrified, juvenile brachiosaur plodded through the same gate Arabella and JD had used. It raced into the open corral only to abruptly stop at the water's edge. The frightened brachiosaur turned in confusion in time to see a large male spinosaur slip through the same gate. The spinosaur was nearly thirty feet tall and weighed fifteen tons. A giant meat eater with a curved fin cresting its back from neck to tail. Except for the great protruding tail, it looked remarkably like a T. rex. Its great head was a bit flatter, its mouth a bit narrower, and its grasping forearms a bit longer than a rex but remarkably similar.

It roared in delight at the trapped brachiosaur, which immediately made for the water, confusing water for safety. The maddened spinosaur strode after it as it waded farther into the pushing waves. The brachiosaur walked tentatively along the bottom, its huge feet stabilizing it against the waves. It had no idea a forty-foot trough was directly offshore. As the huge, teenaged brachiosaur moved forward to escape the deadly spinosaur, it inadvertently stepped into the trough, plunging into the sea. It recovered quickly and began dogpaddling up the beach, away from the frustrated spinosaur.

Knee-deep in the surf, the incensed spinosaur bellowed. It had no desire to follow the foolish brachiosaur and was angry at missing an easy meal.

However, one predator's missed opportunity was another ones good fortune. The brachiosaur, pleased to have escaped the ferocious spinosaur, had no idea it was being stalked by an even more malevolent creature.

The twins were the first to spot the harbinger of death. Fins. Giant fins. Meglodon fins. The brachiosaur was a good swimmer despite its giant size. Each of its huge feet pushed a ton of water through the ocean. It was slow but efficient, but this was the domain great carnivorous fish and reptiles. The gigantic sharks struck the plodding brachiosaur and in seconds the ocean turned red as the sharks took turns ripping gaping holes in the doomed creature. It was over very fast.

The floating brachiosaur carcass drew a large crowd of marauding sharks. The disappointed spinosaur roared its displeasure from the safety of the shore. It had been smart enough not to follow the brachiosaur into the deadly waters, but its hunger still burned, so grudgingly it trotted back to the jungle. There would be other prey, other chances.

On the *Broadsword*'s bridge, four friends watched the ordeal with troubled fascination. The pissed-off spinosaur had just retreated to the jungle where JD and Arabella had strolled not an hour before.

"I thought spinosaurs was indignant to the Egyptian mainland," mentioned a puzzled Tim.

"Obviously not," countered Adam.

"This is not a good start, lads," said the admiral. "Not a good start."

"Not to worry, Admiral," the chief said. "Arabella took enough firepower to knock down a building, and Captain Stoner's the toughest son of a bitch I know. They'll get through okay. And they'll get the others back safely."

The beach and the deadly surf were now strangely quiet. The lapping water had washed away the carnage. A lone gull walked the shoreline, snatching up insects. The scene was *almost paradise.*

With injuries that should have required a week's bed rest, JD prowled through the dense jungle. Like every other day in this world, the weather was predictable. A high of ninety-five, 95% humidity, and a 50% chance of a thunder storm was inevitable. The withering heat sapped JD's and Arabella's strength. As if JD needed any more sapping. Nonetheless, he pressed on like a driven madman. Arabella was forced to keep up or get left behind.

They had picked up the Romanican's trail easily enough. The destruction at the village had appalled Arabella. The burned dwellings and the decaying, preyed-upon bodies of women and children were horrifying sights. JD had been right. The Romanicans had left a trail a blind man could have followed. With captives, the party was nearly a hundred strong, and they were foraging the entire way. Their camps were easy to find; smoldering fires and human waste made tracking even easier.

The first day, they went fifteen hours before camping. Arabella thought the only reason JD had stopped was because he was dead. They spent the night twenty feet up in a redwood to escape raptors. JD fell into sleep almost immediately. Lying on the broad limb with his sunken eyes and pale skin, he looked like a dead man. Arabella noticed he had tied himself to the branch. She did the same.

It took her longer to fall asleep. The night sounds of the dark forest kept her tense and alert. She cradled her M16 like a newborn. Finally, sleep came, complete with rolling dreams and fantasy flights. Her body rested as her mind drifted. A yellow moon looked on from a brooding sky at two bone-weary travelers. It was their only friend that night.

The jungle came alive in the morning. Many of its residents required the heat of the sun to get their reptilian bodies going, but birds and insects hit the dawn running. Arabella was awakened by a three-inch, furry, tree spider that was trying to nestle into her right boot. Gripped by near hysteria, she used the muzzle of her M16 to flick it away. It creeped her out.

JD was awake. "How'd you sleep?" he asked. He stretched hard, forcing his aching body to come to life. He calmly grabbed a four-foot constrictor coiled next to him and threw it to the ground.

"Jesus!" piped Arabella. She scanned her area for snakes and breathed deeply when she found none. "I slept like I was in a tree scared out of my wits all night. How do you think?"

"Get used to it, sweets. It'll get worse." He slugged down half a bottle of water and took a package from her backpack. He unwrapped it carefully and tossed her a piece of what looked like shoe leather. She gave him a quizzical look. "It's pemmican," he said, biting off a piece and chewing vigorously. "I had Mister Henry make some up weeks ago."

Arabella smelled it carefully, like a child inspecting spinach for the first time.

"It's strips of beef, dried and pounded with berries, fruits, and nuts. It has everything a person needs to survive. Vitamins, proteins, and minerals. No better survival food. Native Americans invented the best traveling edibles ever. I always liked it." He chewed like a happy camper. She bit off a chunk and crunched curiously. It was good, a beef jerky salad.

In the morning light, JD looked a hundred times better. His skin had color, and he had bags only under the bags under his eyes. Definitely signs of recovery.

"You look better today," she said as she crunched the pemmican.

"Thank you, but I'll feel better when we catch the Romans."

"I presume you have a plan?"

He looked at her through worn-out eyes. "It's going to be bad when we confront them. They're disciplined veterans of a militaristic lifestyle. Don't expect them to surrender. We'll have to take the prisoners. Those Romans will resist, and we'll have to kill them."

"That's what I thought." Her apprehension and concern showed. "Back on Raptorland, I killed raptors, but it happened so fast. There was no time to think, just react. But this is different. I've had lots of time to think about this. I'm scared to death. I don't want to let you down. I hope I can find the courage."

"I'm not worried, Arabella. You're a woman. You possess courage I'll never have."

"What? What do you mean?"

"Men have tremendous courage. It takes great courage to march off to war. But it takes even greater courage to be the mother of a son marching off to war. The female's most basic instinct is to protect her young. Females in every species do it. Every mother would gladly die for her children. But it takes a special courage, the highest courage, to watch your child go off to war and stand by unwavering, to not cry out, 'Spare my child!' for the greater good. A woman's courage is always superior to a man's, Arabella. I'm not worried about you at all."

Chewing the last of the pemmican, she contemplated his words. She had seen JD's courage in the battle with the raptors, and she wished for only a fraction of it when they came upon the Romans.

She took a breath and changed the subject slightly. "Why the sword? Why become a master of a weapon rarely used in the other world?"

He did not hesitate. "Thermopylae. Do you know about it?"

She racked her brain and nodded. "A mountain pass in Greece. There was a battle there."

"Correct," said JD. "In 480 BC, the great Persian army under King Xerxes advanced on Greece, and the Greek nation states were not prepared for war. A group of three hundred Spartans plus three thousand allies met the Persian army at a narrow mountain pass at Thermopylae. The vast Persian army was made up of two million men, warriors and veterans all. The Spartans held the pass for six days against the Persians. Because the pass was so narrow, the Persians couldn't use archers or cavalry, so it was swords and pikes. Six days the Spartans held. Of course, they all died. Completely wiped out. But they inflicted over twenty thousand casualties on the Persians and bought Greece enough time to build an army.

"They saved democracy as we know it. The free Greek nation states, including Sparta, were the first democracies on this planet. These brave men sacrificed themselves for a much grander purpose. And they did it with swords against impossible odds.

"As a boy, I studied this battle and was overcome by the heroics of these defenders. I wanted to know, as they did, the power of the sword. So I began studying fencing."

"But you use a samurai sword," said Arabella. She had sat in wonder as JD spoke.

"Yes. It's my weapon of choice. The Spartan short sword, like the Roman short sword, was designed for close-in regimental fighting. A single warrior is more effective with a longer sword.

"We should be going."

She agreed.

Five minutes later, they were trotting through lush vegetation. JD followed the trail like an experienced bloodhound. Arabella was continuously amazed at how he read signs and tracked. His sight and smell missed nothing. His ears heard things days before hers did. It was maddening. Refreshing but maddening. Just once, she wanted to see or hear something before he did.

Despite the rigors of the journey, JD's strength was returning. The thigh injury still hobbled him a bit, but his gait was getting longer and faster every hour. Arabella pressed herself hard to keep up. She realized that even at full strength she could become a burden and he might leave her like a speedboat leaves a rowboat.

They moved cautiously and swiftly across the jungle floor, avoiding dangling vines, gnarled branches, and fallen trees. They had to be careful. Many plants had thorn defenses and poisonous leaves, and drugstores were still many millions of years in the future.

The scenery was incredible. They passed lazy herds of brachiosaurs and hadrosaurs happily munching foliage, carefree and uninterested in the passing humans. Spectacular outcroppings and jagged rock formations punched holes in the earth as if they were struggling for the sky. Frequent ponds and watersheds dotted the terrain.

The heat and the insects were the worst. At most watering holes, they would stop and smear new mud over their exposed skin. Biting flies, mosquitoes, gnats, and ornery bees and wasps filled the air with constant buzzing. The thin-skinned humans had to be careful. Mud was the only solution. Arabella yearned for the *Broadsword* and a hot shower.

The two searchers' days were long and the nights short, but JD knew they were gaining ground on their quarry every day. They were closing in, and he was feeling stronger. That spelled trouble for the unsuspecting Romanicans.

Keiko had no trouble being adopted into the *Broadsword* family. Maggie Wainwright and her lady friends readily took to the orphaned child. The language barrier was bridged by facial expressions and hand signs. The little girl was smothered with motherly love and genuine affection. She had won the hearts of the male crew as well.

The twins showed her games on the computer and pulled up children's books, vast collections stored in the hard drive. Her tiny, contagious, jack-o'-lantern smile brightened everyone's day. One of the rescued ladies made clothes for her, and she was quite a sight in a baseball cap. Everyone felt she would make a complete recovery and adjustment to her new lifestyle. At four years old, time was on her side.

The admiral and the chief kept in radio contact with JD and Arabella every six hours. It had been five days since they had left. The worried crew could tell from JD's dispatches that they were getting close to the raiding party. Soon, an armed conflict would be inevitable; JD and Arabella against God only knew how many ruthless slavers. As each hour ticked by, the mood on the *Broadsword* grew more solemn. More taciturn.

Keiko, blissfully unaware, scampered around the ship with boundless, joyful energy. The innocence of the playful enthusiasm helped keep the crew upbeat and hopeful. She proved a wonderful addition.

"Don't move!" said JD in a firm but quiet voice.

Arabella stopped dead. She was behind JD about six feet and could see him slow his breathing and relax. In slow motion he pointed. "Look to your left."

Arabella's eyes turned. Dense vegetated underbrush and trees. Whatever it was, she did not see it. "What?" she whispered.

"There, about thirty feet. In front of the vegetation. Look close. See the outline?" She peered harder, focusing. She saw it. A ten-foot-tall dilophosaur. A one-ton chameleon predator dinosaur perfectly blended into the environment. It stood silent and still as a marble statue, waiting.

"I see it," she said, trying to conceal her terror. "Why isn't it moving?"

"It's an ambush hunter. Another ten feet and it would have attacked us."

Summoning her courage, she said, "No problem. I can blast it from here." She started to raise the M16 to obliterate the artful carnivore but JD stopped her.

"No, Arabella. The unnatural sound of your rifle will carry for miles. It'll attract predators and alert our quarry. We have to do this quietly."

"Do what? I'm sure as hell not going to wrestle it! And it's probably much faster than us."

"Much."

"So?"

"Do you trust me?"

She hesitated. "Why? Sure. I mean I guess so. Why?"

"There are two of them. I can't spot the other one. But it's here. I can feel it."

Arabella shivered. Christ, another one. Now what? "You got a plan?"

"I'm going to walk over to this one. When it attacks me, I'll kill it. That will draw the other one out. If it gets the drop on me, shoot it, but only if I can't handle it. Understand?"

"Sure. Are you fucking nuts?"

"Probably. Get ready."

JD drew his sword and walked toward the immobile dinosaur. He was impressed that the silent beast patiently held its position. With only ten feet separating them, the cloaked killer made its move. The mongoose-like speed surprised JD. It pounced at him, snapping its impressive jaws while its clawed hands reached for him.

JD was equally fast. He dove, tumbling past and behind the charging beast, and sprung up as the outmaneuvered foe turned. His sword severed a forearm. A backhanded slash to the right gashed a mortal blow to the beast's throat. It staggered back in a death dance and fell in a thumping heap.

But there was no time to enjoy the victory. Its partner in crime emerged from the scenery about twenty feet away. Maddened by the death of its mate, the beast raced at JD. Arabella took aim, but JD motioned no and stood his ground.

The second dilophosaur charged recklessly, incensed by the earlier slaughter and JD took advantage of its mistake. Instead of moving or diving, he turned his back to the beast, and as it closed on him, he made an inverted stabbing motion that caught the animal in its chest. His blade sunk nine or ten inches. The wounded animal bellowed in pain and surprise.

JD ripped the sword free and came down overhand with the blade, nearly severing its left leg. Its roar of pain echoed across the jungle like a thunderclap. Wounded and frustrated, the defeated beast limped into the underbrush, leaving a trail of blood in its wake.

Arabella lowered her weapon and rushed to JD. He was wiping his bloodied blade clean and catching his breath. He sheathed his sword.

"That was incredible. Are you okay?"

"Yes, and thank you for not shooting."

"Sure," she said, still stunned by the spectacle.

"Let's move. This body will attract scavengers soon, and I want to keep going. We're getting close."

Her interest was piqued. "How close?"

"Another day, not much more," he said, already running in front of her.

She took in behind him at a brisk pace. She could sense his urgency, feel his commitment. She thought of Kevin, the gentle, older man she had fallen in love with. He needed her, and she would be there for him. Determination gripped her like an invisible hand. She began to run harder.

Discouragement began to overwhelm Major Crowley. For six days, he had endured all manner of humiliation and degradation. His captors were harsh and severe. Food and water was plentiful, though. At first, he thought this strange. Then he understood. Near-dead slaves were worthless. He was kept alive and in decent condition because they needed him for something. Probably something far worse, probably something deadly. He despaired at the thought. Like most of the captives, he resigned himself to the hopelessness of his situation. It perplexed him that the *Broadsword* people maintained such upbeat attitudes.

It was obvious that whoever their friend was, he was not coming. For six days, they had spoken of this savior who had not shown up yet. He was sick of hearing about JD or Nomad or whoever the hell he was. They were obviously deluded. Hopeful but deluded.

He sat, dejected and downtrodden, waiting for salvation that he feared would never come. He took a shallow breath and looked at the misery around him and at the surrounding savage jungle. What hell, what unholy place was this that he had tumbled into like a drunk through an open manhole? He kept hoping to wake from this nightmare of despair, but it went on and on, pulling him deeper into its labyrinth of dread and aversion. He was slipping, sinking into a black well of self-pity and resignation. Soon, he would no longer care if he lived or died. He just wanted the suffering to end.

Kevin and Doc could see Major Crowley slowly giving up. Each day, he withdrew more and more. He never spoke; he only stared vacantly through sunken eyes. Many of the oriental prisoners were the same way, hopeless and zombie-like. The three *Broadsword* captives kept each other up. They talked of anything and everything to keep their spirits alive with the possibility of rescue and escape. Help was coming, and to be rescued, you had to be alive, not just in body but also in mind and soul. When JD arrived, they needed to be ready to assist his efforts, ready to think fast and react fast. They kept a glimmer of hope alive. It was all they had.

JD and Arabella had stopped for the night. Like cat feet, twilight crept over the jungle. Experience had taught them safety was in the trees so they kept a cold camp to keep concealed. At night, in this jungle, it was not good to draw attention. On this sixth day of their pursuit, they hunkered down twenty feet up a tree. Arabella realized there was no way to get comfortable sleeping on a tree limb no matter how hard she tried. Her back was in a constant state of discomfort. She would never again complain about the firmness of a mattress after sleeping on hard bark and she marveled at how JD would settle in and sleep soundly, cradling himself among branches like a man in a backyard hammock. Water, pemmican, and protein bars had made up their sixth straight dinner. Arabella's thoughts were wandering when JD spoke.

"We'll catch up with them tomorrow."

His nonchalant delivery took her by surprise. "How do you know?"

He gave her a sideways glance. "I know, Arabella. Tomorrow in the afternoon. From their tracks and their campsites, I estimate their force to be about forty, their captives near fifty."

"Forty," she mouthed in dismay. "So many."

"I'll recon their position tomorrow night. We'll take them later that night."

She was amazed. He spoke as if he were making plans for a casual dinner outing. She realized he had truly achieved what all warriors, all heroes, never seek but indeed find, a contempt for death that allowed him to transcend himself and touch the sublime. That is why he never spoke of battles except to those who had been there with him. The truth is too holy, too sacred for words.

When a man battles not for himself but for his brothers, when his most passionately sought goal is neither glory or his life's preservation but to give his all for his comrades and not abandon them, his heart is pure, and he has truly achieved contempt for death.

She looked across the tree at JD and understood. He was the ultimate foe because he cared more for his friends than himself. To be worthy of that friendship was everything to him. It was an invisible wall his enemies would never breach. Thermopylae indeed. Like the hopelessly outnumbered Spartans who had defended their country without question or reward, JD was about to wade into the din of battle, knowing the noblest thing he could do, despite the odds, was to try. The failure to try was worse than death to him.

When slumber finally overtook Arabella, she slept well, dreaming of the fields of winter wheat back in Iowa, billowing waves of green under a soft winter sun rustled by gentle northern breezes. It was peaceful and soft.

There was nothing soft about Kevin's head. The giant Egnid had cuffed him hard an hour earlier, but miraculously, he was still conscious. The giant had become enraged when Kevin came between him and Doc. The great denison might have killed him had not Marcus stepped in and reined in the brute. Kevin could see the cruel intent in the giant's eyes toward Doc. Those black pools of stone could not hide the criminal design behind them. The giant oozed sadism when around her. Kevin and Duke took turns coming to her defense.

Every time the group would stop to rest or to make camp, the giant would eventually get around to harassing Doc. The pigeon Latin all the captors spoke was incomprehensible to the *Broadsword* group, so the giant would become angry with Doc when she refused his overtures. She would simply shrug and try to walk away.

Marcus, too, was tiring of the giant's antics. He was sure the emperor would have a keen interest in this fair-skinned slave, but not if the giant had had his way with her first. They still had a two-week journey to Romanica, and the bothersome giant had worn out Marcus's patience. He was not about to let this colossus kill or damage his prize for the emperor. The giant was brooding. Marcus decided to leave him alone for the time being.

Marcus had one of his men tend to Kevin, he needed every slave sound of body for the arena. A great purplish bruise was rising on the side of Kevin's head, but he was otherwise okay. Doc understood just how close he had come to death. She took over nursing his wound.

"How many fingers on this hand?" she asked, holding up two.

Kevin studied the fingers. "What hand?" he replied, smiling.

"Oh, a funny man with a cracked skull," lamented Duke. "Just what we need, a brain-damaged comedian." Kevin peered at Duke through half-glazed eyes. "Thanks, Duke. I knew you cared all along." His eyes drifted in the direction of the giant and back to Duke. With a subtle nod, Duke signaled his understanding. The next time the giant got close, they would try to tag team the monster. It was a long shot because they were bound but if they got lucky, maybe they could injure him, or worse. A silent pact was agreed upon. The giant would die. At the earliest opportunity, they would make their move.

Arabella moved. JD had poked her with the end of his sheathed sword.

"What?" she mouthed, annoyed at being jarred from slumber.

In a barely audible whisper, JD said, "Below. A pride of raptors."

A chill eased down her spine. Damn raptors, these devils where everywhere. The planet apparently teemed with these human-sized monsters and a gaggle was camped out like a scout troop under their tree.

In unison, like a group of prairie dogs, the raptors jerked west and were motionless. Their long narrow shadows streaked south in the moonlight. For a long moment, the raptors stood like Greek statues. Still. Silent. Then, like rats fleeing a sinking ship, they bolted helter-skelter through the jungle.

JD knew something was wrong. The raptors were fleeing. If something had scared them, chances are it was something large, terrible. He glanced at Arabella. She caught his eye.

"Up. Start climbing. We need to get another twenty feet up. Move!"

Like monkeys, they began scrambling up the tree. At a safe point, they stopped. Arabella was trying to catch her breath. It came in quick bursts. "What . . . What is it?"

JD motioned her to be quiet. All sound had left the jungle. A graveyard eeriness swept the area. Then like a cat burglar, a night stalker appeared in the form of a twenty foot tall, fifteen ton, full-grown spinosaur. It deftly picked its way through the foliage like a gangster through shadowed streets. Its massive feet slipped through the trees and ferns in near silence. Like an expert hunter, it moved slowly but deliberately. Its night vision was acute. Every ten feet or so, it would stop, listen, and sniff the air for the smell of prey. It stopped under JD and Arabella, tilted its huge head skyward, and snorted loudly. It seemed to be peering through the tangled branches, trying to spy whatever was up there.

Arabella held her breath. JD merely lay back, hands locked behind his head. He closed his eyes. "It can't climb, Arabella. Unless you're going down there, I'd get some sleep."

"You're a horse's ass, you know that?"

"Yep, I know it. There'll be plenty of bogeymen tomorrow. Right now, they're sleeping peacefully, so I suggest you do the same. Sleep is a weapon."

The spinosaur snorted again before creeping into the black of the jungle. Arabella closed her eyes but sleep did not come for some time.

When soft snoring finally overtook her, JD opened his eyes. The next day, he would face the enemy who had taken a part of his soul. The most important things in his life struggled in bondage less than a day away. He would become a hound of war, a dog from hell. His opponents would not have to venture to hell to find him because he lived there. Nomad was kin to the reaper. Closing his eyes, JD hoped the woman he loved would understand. He was going to march into hell, and despite the elysian cause, he would probably be tainted by it again.

A few moments later, JD joined Arabella in a chorus of gentle snoring. He would not dream that night.

Dawn spilled over the mountain plateau of Romanica in streaks of yellow and orange. The eastern windows of the emperor's bedchamber suddenly flooded the room in light. The emperor and six gladiatrixes, clad only in the cool morning air, rustled lazily at the break of day.

So taken was the emperor with these women warriors that he had refused to let them fight in the arena. Instead, he had made twelve his personal escorts. They accompanied him everywhere, dressed in leather armor and little else.

Raptor pit fighting had temporarily quelled the mob's taste for death and gore, and though overdue, Marcus and his raiders would surely be retuning soon. The games would have new blood to be spilled, and perhaps then he let the gladiatrixes he had grown weary of put on a show in the arena. A fight to the death between naked warrior women would surely prove a favorite with the mob.

His bedchamber was decorated with the supple, muscular bodies of six female fighters. Before exhaustion had overtaken him the night before, he had taken two of the brutish beauties and had enjoyed watching the others frolic in amatory pleasure. With the sun's light came renewed vigor, and the amorous emperor began playing with the sleepy blonde next to him. His manhood stirred as he traced the outline of her back and buttocks. The royal member soon stood like a flagless pole. Royal relief surrounded him in the form of naked gladiatrixes who would not fight to the death for the enjoyment of the mob; they would bring enjoyment only to the emperor. Soon enough, the slaves of Marcus's raiding party would join the dance floor of death in the arena. Until then, the gladiatrixes would service the emperor, a personal harem of buxom warrior babes at his beck and call.

An hour into the morning, the emperor was interrupted from his salacious exercises by a royal steward. A runner had arrived from the raiding party bearing news the emperor would want to hear. The report was simple and of good tone. "Very successful hunt. Will return within two weeks. Have in hand over fifty prime slaves and one extraordinary woman. Have also captured a black-and-orange, fur-covered beast. It will be a great addition to the games. Your faithful servant. Marcus."

The emperor looked up from the parchment. It was very good news indeed. He summoned his chef and told him to make preparations for a great banquet upon Marcus's return. The whole town would celebrate. His great plateau city would buzz with anticipation. Two more weeks of pit-fighting raptors and then new blood for the arena. Like the rest of the city, the emperor salivated at the prospect. Blood on the dance floor. The mob loved it.

The raptors and the spinosaur were long gone. So were JD and Arabella. They plowed on at a brisk pace through the damp morning air. Around noon, they stood next to a small brook, taking a short break. Arabella took a pistol from a leather holster and held the weapon aloft, looking up the sight.

"What have you got there?" asked JD.

She handed him the weapon butt first. "It's a baby Glock, model twenty-six with a modified New York trigger," she said proudly.

"Nice and light," offered JD. "Short sight radius, though." He handed it to her.

"I was taught Kentucky windage."

"What's that?" he asked.

"You get close enough to not worry about windage or elevation. You just blast away." Her face lit up like a hundred-watt bulb. Turning serious, she asked, "How much longer?"

He finished gulping down half a bottle of water.

"Between two and three hours. I need you to do me a favor. Take that popgun of yours and fire off three rounds into the air. Nice and slow."

"Any particular reason? The other day, you wouldn't let me shoot that dilophosaur because it would make too much noise. Now you want me to just fire three rounds randomly?"

"Right. Look, the Romans won't know what to make of the noise. To them, it will seem odd and out of place, but that's all. We'll take our chances with any animals around here."

"So why do it?"

"Because, my dear, Kevin will know the sound and realize we're close. He'll also figure we'll move at night, so it'll give him time to get ready for our play. So fire the shots, okay?"

She fired three times in two-second intervals. The shots echoed through the jungle for miles. Birds took flight. Herbivores looked up from their foraging. Predators stopped dead in their tracks. For a brief moment, the jungle fell quiet.

"That should do it," said JD. "We should be going." He started out. "Kentucky windage." He chuckled. "I like that."

She took up her backpack and fell in behind. His pace was more deliberate, more determined now. Off to their right, a small herd of compys, maybe twenty, nosed around a small clearing.

Compys were roughly the size of ducks but with larger necks. Their small heads jerked up and down like chickens pecking in a barnyard, but they were dangerous. Their bite inflicted a slow-acting poison that could kill or cripple. They were miserable little scavengers that would pester larger animals. Curious, tiny bastards that provoked anger and frustration from everything but they let Arabella and JD pass without incident. The fast-moving humans were not worth their trouble. They hopped off in search of slower victims to aggravate.

The sky bristled with screeching birds and darting, flying dinosaurs, a vast aerodynamic spectacle. It was hot. The jungle dripped with humidity. JD and Arabella wore water-soaked headbands under their caps and bandanas around their necks. The insects seemed less bothersome, but the two kept a constant vigil for any predators.

They passed a bubbling, hot spring that stunk of sulfur and looked like a witches' brew. *Double trouble, cauldron bubble* thought Arabella as they eased by, careful of poisonous gases. At the water's edge, a half dozen ten-foot crocs sunned effortlessly. Motionless, like future suitcases, they lounged in silence. Across the small expanse of steamy water, giant ferns with leaves the size of truck tires sprouted everywhere. In all directions, an entanglement of vines, plants, and trees competed for space and a chance to find the streaking sunshine. It was the Amazon rain forest times ten. Small, furry mammals scurried around in frantic activity, careful to avoid dinosaurs and reptiles. The age of the mammal was still forty million years distant; these were no bigger than large dogs, tasty snacks for most predators on the prowl but nothing more. Woolly mammoths, saber-toothed cats, and giant sloths were yet to be evolved by Mother Nature.

Through this maze of verdure, JD and Arabella tracked the Romanicans and their captives, the distance between them closing every mile. The chase would soon be over and then the real work would begin—extricating the captives and eliminating the Romanicans. Nomad was about to send a message that would reach all the way to the halls of the emperor's palace. It would be delivered under the cloak of darkness that night and it would be lethal and exacting. The myth of Nomad would be introduced to the Romanican culture like Hiroshima had been introduced to the atom bomb, with shock and with the finality of an executioners ax.

The three successive gunshots shocked everyone in the Romanican traveling party. The Romanicans reacted with defensive curiosity, afraid and anxious about the foreign sounds. The *Broadsword* trio and Major Crowley knew exactly what the noise was, however.

"Son of a bitch," whispered Kevin. "JD's behind us, close. That's a signal. I expect he'll come tonight. We need to be ready to move anytime."

Doc smiled with obvious relief. Even the zombie-like Crowley felt hopeful. Duke was the most animated. In a booming voice, he shouted for all to hear, "Cinch up your balls, you Roman assfuckers! The prince of fucking darkness comes tonight! Bend over and lather up. You're about to get fucked!"

The Romanicans had no idea what the one-handed, rotund, slimeball was shouting about. It was foreign gibberish to them. They blew it off as the rantings of a crazed prisoner.

Doc leaned to Duke. "Aren't you glad they don't understand English?"

"Fuck yeah," confided Duke. He yelled again. "And your mothers are all pink-faced, whore, bitch dogs!"

"Enough," warned Kevin. "From now on, no provocations. We wait for JD."

"I'm gonna piss on their corpses, Kev. That okay with you?"

"Fine. But for now keep your foul mouth shut!"

"Yes, ma'am," he mouthed silently to Kevin.

It was about seven hours to dusk. They walked on knowing salvation would come with the night sky. Doc's heart pounded. There had been times over the last days that she thought she would never see JD again. To be so close was nerve racking. She looked around, wondering if he was stalking them, close. An expression from Kevin told her to keep her eyes down, to draw no attention to herself, to just walk. Like millions of nights before, this one would surely come.

Duke began whistling, and Molly rose in her wooden cage. The great cat roared long and deep. She too sensed the gathering storm, not a storm of rain and thunder but one of impending doom for her Romanican captors. She growled again in morbid anticipation. She hoped to be part of that storm. Her tormentors had been vicious. Confined in a cage so small she could not turn around with little food and water. And endless teasing by the Romanicans, who prodded her with sticks and swords. The great cat longed to demonstrate her prowess to these fools. Panting heavily, she lay down. Rest was a weapon.

JD stopped, surprising Arabella, who was a few paces behind.

"What?" she asked. "Raptors?" She brought the M16 level with the surrounding jungle.

"No. Molly. I just heard Molly growl. She's alive."

"What does that mean?"

"It means, dear Arabella, that tonight just got easier." She could feel JD's spirits rise. He loved that cat. And he was right. A 720-pound Indian tiger would come in handy.

JD moved on. Arabella was sure his step was lighter, his demeanor more robust. Her thoughts turned to Doc, Duke, and Kevin. Their hardships would soon be over, and she and Kevin would be chasing each other around the *Broadsword* like schoolyard sweethearts again. She slung the M16 and moved on behind JD. The heat of the day mugged their lungs, but that was no concern to them. Catching the raiding party was all that mattered.

"What matters most," Tim said to Dawn, "is that Adam and I graduated with the highest temperatures in our class. Ask anyone." His goofy grin reached ear to ear.

"Is that right?" she asked with a curious lilt.

"Correct."

"Good. Then you should know the definition of a simp."

Tim thought quickly, but he was blank. Dawn helped him.

"A simp, my seriously unbalanced suitor, is someone who deprives you of solitude without providing you with company. Get lost before I demonstrate the optional use of a baseball bat."

"Such as?"

"Such as caving in your skull."

As Tim was preparing a delightfully witty retort, Admiral Fitzgerald rescued him from a sure beating. "Follow me, lad," he said, shuffling Tim off toward the bridge while saving his life.

"I think she's warming up to me, Admiral. What do you think?"

"I think you should consider cybersex. That woman hates your guts."

"Nah, she likes me. She just can't admit it. So, what's up, Admiral?"

"JD and Arabella have caught up with the Roman raiding party. Tonight, they make contact. I want you and Adam minding the radio twenty-four seven. I want to know everything as soon as you do. You can take shifts, but someone's always on that radio. No flapdoodles."

"Flap what?"

"No screwups! Got me, mister?"

Tim saluted smartly. "Aye-aye, General," he snapped.

The admiral shook his head in dismay. The twins were exasperating, well intentioned, Eskimo pie-brains, but he wondered what he would do without them. Resigned, the admiral said, "Adam will be along shortly. When you hear something, one of you find me." He left as Adam was walking onto the bridge.

"What's with the colonel?" asked Adam.

"He said no flapdoodles. I mean flopdangles. No . . . er . . . uh . . ."

"Screwups?" suggested Adam.

"Yeah, no screwups. That's it."

"So how'd it go with Dawn? She proposed yet?"

"Hardly. She threatened to hit me with a baseball bat. You know, a normal person would take that as a negative reaction."

"That's a break for you, then. You're abby-normal. Try the Tarzan routine next time. It always works. 'Bwana make juju?'"

"Yeah, she'll melt like Jell-O. Guaran-damn-teed! Dames love the ape man."

"Cool."

The boys turned serious. "You think JD and Arabella can get Doc and them back?" asked Tim.

"If anyone can, they can," answered a solemn Adam. "You take the first watch. I'll give you a break in three hours."

Tim picked up the telephone from the control panel and put it to his ear. Adam looked confused. That phone had not worked since they traveled back in time.

"What are you doing? There's nobody on that line."

"I know," said Tim. "But I'm expecting a call."

Adam rolled his eyes. "Put it down!"

Arabella put down her M16 on a forked branch. She and JD were forty feet up in a great redwood. Exhausted from the climb, she took out her water bottle and slammed down a few mouthfuls. The cool water felt good going down her parched throat.

She had no idea why they were in the tree. JD had just said they had needed to go up, and she had followed. Aloft in the redwood, she looked around but saw nothing. "What is it?" she pressed. "Another humpbacked T. rex cousin?" referring to their old pal, the spinosaur.

JD signaled no. "We're gonna wait here a while. Be very quiet."

She did not understand, but she needed the rest. Her head moved back to the thick branch and then closed her eyes. She slowed her breathing and began to relax. It felt wonderful.

Ten minutes into her short snooze, JD tapped her. She saw him with his finger to his lips. He pointed down. She focused her eyes below, but her ears noticed first. She heard voices, an unfamiliar language, but definitely human voices. And the voices were coming toward them. Then her eyes saw what her ears had heard. Humans.

Passing below were short, broad-chested men carrying bows and swords. They were thrashing through the forest, heading north. They really did look like Romans. There was no mistake about it. She spotted Doc, Duke, and Kevin. Their hands were bound, and they were tied one to the other by ropes. A tall air force officer walked alongside them. The other captives, over forty, all looked oriental, like Keiko. They were being herded like cattle.

Arabella focused on Kevin. He looked uninjured, but like the other prisoners, he looked bedraggled and bone-tired, dead on his feet. But he was alive. They all were alive. Even Molly, who was caged in a wood-slatted pen carried by six laboring captives, appeared to be in good condition. She sat in silence as the group filed by, oblivious to the tree-topped spies above.

Then Arabella spied the giant. She shuddered in disbelief. He was a massive brute at least ten feet tall, muscular and heavy, perhaps five hundred pounds. She had never seen anything like this man. He towered over the others like a tree dwarfing shrubs. He was beyond scary. He was menacing, terrifying.

The group passed by and disappeared into the vast jungle. It was five minutes before JD spoke.

"We'll take them tonight. There were thirty-nine Romans, including the giant, and fifty-four captives, including our people. Molly looked to be okay."

"The giant," said Arabella. "Did you see the giant?" Fear gripped her voice.

"I saw him, but he's just a man, Arabella, just a tall man. That's all."

"Jesus, he was ten feet tall! And the others looked like seasoned warriors. Jesus H. Christ!"

"Relax," JD said calmly. "I doubt any of them can dodge a bullet. Listen to me. Here's what we're going to do." He laid out his plan.

"The plan is simple," said Marcus to one of his men. "I will take six men and double back a few miles. Something didn't feel right today. I got the feeling we were being watched and followed. It could be Slants tracking us or even raptors. We'll slip back and check things out. You make camp. We'll stay here tonight. Our scouting party will be back by dusk. Feed the slaves and the animal. Post guards and stay sharp."

The man hesitated. "What about the giant?"

"Don't worry about him. I'll be back by dark. If there's trouble, send a runner south. We'll intercept him. Make camp."

The man saluted, fist to chest, and walked off.

All day long, Marcus had felt something was wrong. The hairs on the back of his neck reminded him of his days in the gladiatorial arena. They always twitched before combat. He could be overreacting; it may just be the giant and his nasty disposition, but he was a cautious and superstitious man. It would not hurt to check things out. He gathered six experienced men, left the camp, and doubled back on their trail. The hot forest soon enveloped them.

JD and Arabella had moved northwest about a mile from the encamping Romanicans. They were busy double-checking their equipment.

"Why didn't you tell me we had moved ahead of them?" she asked while oiling her pistol.

"No need. And it was the best way to get a firsthand view."

"You weren't afraid we'd be seen?"

"People never look up. It's an old thief's saying. If you want to hide something, hide it high."

She thought a moment. It made as much sense as anything. "So what's our plan?"

"We hang here until dusk. Then we slip into the camp and recon the area. I'll eliminate the guards. You lead everyone out."

"And what will you do?"

In a voice that held no emotion, he said, "I'll deal with the Romans."

"All of them? Thirty-nine and the giant? Christ, that's crazy, even for you!"

"Your job is to get everyone back to the *Broadsword*."

"But how? I don't know the trail. What'd you leave, some bread crumbs?"

"Molly will lead the way. I'll catch up later. Just keep moving. Kevin is good in the woods. Rely on him and Molly. Rest at first light. And keep your wits about you. Raptors and other predators won't give you a free pass."

"You can't take on all the Romans. That's nuts. This isn't Thermopylae, and you're not a Spartan."

He looked at her pleading eyes, soft blue and full of concern. "If I don't, they'll follow us. Hunt us down. More gentle, innocent people will get hurt or worse. I need to leave them a message. One they'll understand and not forget." He took her hand. It trembled. "I'll be okay. And I'll join you later. Finish checking your gear."

"You're one cold bastard, JD Stoner," Arabella said, gazing into his azure eyes. "I'll do my part. Don't worry. Just make sure you get back so I don't have to explain this conversation to Doc, okay?"

JD looked away. "I love that lady. No matter what happens, tell her that."

Arabella felt the same about Kevin.

"What the hell's wrong with him, Doc?" asked Kevin. Major Crowley was prone on the ground, shaking and sweating like a shanghaied man on a Japanese junk. The captives had been rounded into a group and made to sit in an opening as the Romanicans set up camp. Crowley had collapsed a few moments later. Kevin held his head in his lap as the man convulsed uncontrollably. Duke and a few of the Slants looked on in fear. His face had gone chalky, his skin ashen. Black circles rimmed his eyes, and his breathing was shallow.

Doc was busy checking his extremities. His arms were okay, but there on his left calf she spotted his problem—the tell-tale punctures.

"It's a viper bite," she said. "The poison is attacking his central nervous system. It will paralyze him and stop his breathing."

"What do we do?" asked Kevin. It looked to him that Crowley was fading fast. Whatever they could do had better happen quickly.

Doc's face was blank. "I can't do anything. But maybe they can."

She looked at her captors. Maybe they could help Crowley. Maybe this snakebite was common to them; maybe they carried an antidote. She walked to one of the guards. He gave her a look of contempt.

Using hand gestures, she motioned for the guard to come with her, but the language chasm was tough to bridge. Slowly, though, the man began to catch her drift. He drew his sword and, pointing at her, motioned for her to lead on. He followed a few paces behind.

When they reached Crowley, she pointed to the bite on his leg and made questioning gestures, as if to say, "What do we do?"

With his sword, he signaled everyone to back away from Crowley. Doc and the others moved back as the guard knelt and inspected the recumbent officer. His breathing was so shallow that his chest barely moved. The Romanican guard examined the slave carefully and looked at Doc.

In a language she did not understand, he said, "He suffers from the bite of the yellow serpent. He will die." He shook his head sideways. Doc and the others grasped his meaning.

They could not comprehend what happened next. The guard stood and pointed his sword at Crowley. In his language, he said, "Better to die without suffering," and in the next instant plunged his short sword into Crowley's exposed throat. Everyone gasped in shock. Crowley did not move as blood spurted like a small oil gusher from the mortal blow. Death was sickeningly quick. The *Broadsword* people reacted in stunned horror. Kevin reached for the guard and was brutally punched in the stomach with the end of the sword. He dropped to his knees, doubled up in pain.

Crowley's body continued to pump blackish blood, which was pooling around his head. The confused guard grunted and walked off, his favor unappreciated. Doc went to Kevin, who signaled he was okay.

"Fucking bastards," Duke said.

A moment later, four Slant prisoners were led over to remove Crowley's cooling body. He would be dragged off so scavengers could feast away from camp. No words would be spoken, no grave dug, no marker planted. Crowley's body would simply be given back to nature via its instruments of retrieval, the flying and roaming creatures that made up the disposal crew. It savage but effective.

The three *Broadsword* wanderers sat numb. They never got to know the man they had gone to such lengths to rescue. Irony, it seemed, could have a ruthless sense of humor.

Marcus and his six scouts had journeyed an hour and had come across nothing unusual. As much as he did not like it, he would have to accept the lack of evidence. No one or no thing was following them.

What he could not know was that for the last four hours JD and Arabella had tracked them on a parallel course.

The Romanicans decided to return to camp. The sun was falling fast in the western sky, and it was important to be safe and settled before darkness brought the hungry jungle to life. They tracked back, content that all was right.

The jungle fell into shadows of gray as dusk edged over the land. Angled silhouettes of twilight tumbled and danced among the trees and vines. The sounds of waking nocturnal predators echoed in the gloaming. Raptors stirred, and mammals sought burrows of safety for the coming night hours.

In half-light, JD and Arabella moved with graceful confidence. They could smell the Romanican campfires. It would be dark in less than an hour. Time to get to it. Time to dance into the fire.

Marcus was seething and could not believe it. He had been gone only three hours. Three short hours. "Where is that son of a whore?" he shouted at the man he had left in charge. The man pointed to his left. "He went off into the jungle. He was crazy. None of us could stop him. He injured two of our men as they tried to restrain him." The man was obviously shaken. Marcus took a deep breath.

"Tell me again. How bad is it?"

"One slave died from a snake bite. The giant went crazy. He injured the other two strange slaves. And the female slave, well, I . . . It's bad, sir. He tried to have his way with her, but she fought like an animal. She's hurt, but I don't know how bad."

That was enough for Marcus. The whole point of the expedition had been to capture slaves, and that idiot giant had injured three, the three strange ones the emperor would want to interrogate and be most amused by.

When the giant returned, if he returned, Marcus decided to kill him. He would have his body drawn and quartered and fed to the crocodiles and be done with the monster. Cursing, he walked off to check on the slave woman.

Duke sat like a large bear, holding Doc in his huge arms. His eyes welled with tears as he rocked her back and forth. He blamed himself. When the giant came for her, he had fought the best he could, but even his large body was no match for the giant. He had been clubbed and thrown aside like a rag doll.

Through swollen, half-closed eyes, he saw Kevin take on the mammoth freak only to be beaten down and discarded like so much garbage. It was sickening. Doc had fought like a demon as the giant tore at her clothes, his eyes locked on her like some unholy deviant. Kevin lay unconscious while Doc struggled.

Duke crawled and grabbed one of the giant's legs with his one good hand, but it had not been enough. The giant kicked him into unawareness with vicious strikes to the head. Duke had no idea how long he had been out when he finally came to. Kevin lay unmoving, his body a heap on the ground.

Through the fog of glassy eyes, he spotted Doc, sprawled facedown, her clothes in complete disarray. He crawled to her and raised her in his arms. She moaned and hung limp as he cradled her. Matted hair framed a battered face, and blood trickled from her mouth. She had been beaten. Even in the dark, he could see bruises on her arms and legs.

She stirred briefly, still fighting back in her mind, and then went slack again. He held her like a father holds a sick child. Her head pressed against his chest as he stroked her hair. He beat himself up with the thought he could have done more, should have done more. His face lined with tears, Duke rocked the injured Doc. Kevin groaned and tried to rise. Unsteady and shaky, he moved to a sitting position. His hand touched his head as if checking to make sure it was still there. He turned to Duke. Duke thought he was about to say something, but Kevin rolled forward onto the ground. He stayed down. Duke continued to rock Doc. Like Kevin, she did not move.

Arabella and JD moved like specters through the moonlight. Black lines etched JD's face, the result of ebony shoe polish. White eyes probed from a raven visage spawned from a lower world. He crept through the darkness, a reaper of death with a sword instead of a scythe. Arabella was at his side, wondering what macabre nightmare was about to play out.

Like snakes, they scaled a tree about fifty feet from the Romanican camp. From this vantage point, they could see the rhythmic flames of the roaring campfires. Romanicans squatted or sat around the blazes with blank expressions, seemingly transfixed by the hypnotic conflagration.

JD twisted to Arabella in the treetop twilight. "Stay here quietly. I'm going to scout the guard positions. Thirty minutes, maybe less."

"And if you don't come back?"

"I'm dead."

"Great, just great!"

"I'll be back. Just stay quiet."

JD slipped out of the tree and vanished into the murky forest. Arabella sat nervously, clinging to her M16 like a lifeline. She looked at her watch. Thirty minutes was going to be an eternity. She sat back quietly while the night sounds of the jungle came to life. JD, like the passing breeze, was gone.

The Romanicans were well schooled in how to make camp. Fires blazed inside a circular compound in which the men bedded down. The camp had been set up in a cleared area so predators could be seen if they approached. Guards were posted at regular intervals and circled the camp. The prisoners were bound and made to sleep at the north end of the bivouac. They were watched by six guards.

It took JD twenty minutes to recon the camp. The Romanicans had left Molly caged at the south end. She, however, did not have any guards. Under a friendly moon, JD crept to her cage in silence. The imprisoned cat sensed him immediately but made no sound. He took a water bottle from his shirt and reaching through the picketed wooden bars and poured the contents into the cat's eager mouth. In a hushed voice, he said, "Nice to see you, Moose. We're leaving."

He cut the rope binding the cage door and eased it up. In a heartbeat, Molly bounded out in silence. She turned and crouched alongside JD. He patted her huge head and whispered in her ear. She, in turn, licked his face and sprang off into the dark woods. JD went in search of a sentry.

Marcus sat around a small fire with three men. The giant had not returned, and he was concerned not for the idiot giant but for two of the captives. Both were clinging to life. The giant's stupidity only added to their burden. Injured slaves had to be cared for and transported. He did not need the aggravation or the complications. In the morning, he would have to decide if the slaves were worth the trouble or just kill them and go on with the others.

Their lives were nothing to him, but he hated losing such good property. That god-cursed giant was more trouble than the slaves. Tthe slaves' fate would be decided in the morning, but the giant's fate had already been sealed. He was a dead giant. Marcus would kill him and there would be no reprieve.

Arabella glanced at her watch for the thousandth time. JD was late. Thirty minutes late. She was scared and pissed. "Where is that son of a bitch?"

"Right here," answered JD from the limb next to her. It startled her so much that she nearly fell from the tree.

"Christ, you scared the shit out of me! What's the idea of creeping up on me like that? You trying to give me a heart attack?"

"You done?" he asked. "Come on, let's go rescue some people."

Molly met them on the ground. She rubbed against Arabella and sat.

"The captives are at the north end of the camp. Follow me," JD said.

Under the sparkling vault of heaven, they stole through the night. When they reached the camp perimeter, JD motioned for Molly to stay. He and Arabella crawled the rest of the way to the captives' area. JD spoke to a Slant prisoner, who looked at him in disbelief. The man pointed to the middle of the prisoner expanse, and he and Arabella crawled in that direction.

They came upon Duke and Kevin, sitting, holding Doc between them. Her chest expanded with breath, but she was limp as a beach towel. JD's eyes caught Duke's. He minced no words. "Tell me," he demanded in a quiet but frosty voice. His eyes hid what his heart felt, anguish and rage.

Even in the darkness, JD could see Duke's eyes water. "The giant attacked her. Kevin and I tried, but he was too much for us. He almost killed Kev." Duke's normally stout voice quivered and broke. "She's alive, but she's had a severe concussion. I . . . I just don't know, JD. Goddamn, I tried. The big bastard is a nasty son of a bitch, I just . . . I just . . ."

JD cut him off. He took Doc's chin in his hand. "You did fine, Dukie. Can you travel?"

"Fucking A."

"Kev, what about you?" Arabella was locked in a bear hug with Kevin.

"My brain's a little foggy, JD, but I'll move when I need to. We did our best for Doc." He too was filled with guilt.

JD handed Kevin his Anchluss pistol and his backpack. He turned to Duke. "Can you carry Doc?"

"Damned straight. I'll carry her all the way to the *Broadsword* if I have to."

"Good," said JD. "Arabella, you lead them back to Molly. She'll take you back to the trail we came on. Stay on it. I'll catch up to you later."

Duke took JD's arm. "JD, there are eight sentries posted around the camp and six more at the end of the captive area."

JD looked at him with the devil's own eyes. "Not anymore. That leaves twenty-five plus the giant. I slit the sentries throats earlier."

The others just stared. *That's why he was late*, Arabella thought. *He was busy killing the sentries.* "Take care of her, Duke. Get going. I'll be along."

They all moved out, JD in the opposite direction.

The Slant men had looked on with rampant curiosity. Four of the strange prisoners had just left, and now a tall, black-faced warrior stood before them. And he spoke their language.

"You men are free. The sentries are gone, so you can slip out that way." He pointed north. "I'll deal with your captors. Go. These men will bother you no more."

One Slant moved forward and extended his hand. "My name is Huang Anlun," he said. "We are grateful to you, sir. The great khan himself in the jeweled city of Banton shall hear of this. You shall be rewarded by our benevolent khan. Your name, sir. May I know it?"

JD shook the man's firm hand. "I am called Nomad. I protect the people of the steel ship. You may encounter them on the trail back."

"If we do, we shall assist them in every possible way. Be careful, friend. These Romanicans are brutal men. They know only conquest and slavery. And the giant is a demon from some northern hell."

"Go," said JD. "At some point in the future, I hope we meet again. I will give you five minutes, and then I will unleash a terrible hell of my own."

They exchanged glances. The Slant men sprinted into the void of the stygian jungle. JD drew his sword and went to find Marcus.

Molly led the way.

"Keep moving," cried Arabella.

"What about raptors and other beasts?" asked Kevin. "A lot of them are nocturnal hunters." Kevin's head pounded like a sledgehammer on concrete. Arabella prodded him on.

"Molly will let us know if anything's stalking us," she whispered. "Please keep quiet and move." She turned to Duke. "You okay?"

"Just lead on, missy. I'm right behind you."

Duke labored under the strain of Doc's dead weight but made no complaint and showed no signs of slowing. He had given JD his word. Doc hung slack over his right shoulder, his good hand cradling her legs. She moaned occasionally in a state of semi consciousness.

They pressed on, not knowing that every raptor and scavenger for miles was converging on the Romanican camp. The scent of the dead sentries filled the warm air and caught the attention of the night's carrion eaters. Even the flickering fires of the encampment would not deter them. Nothing would now.

Suddenly, Marcus stood. The others around the fire looked up in puzzlement. The night had become eerily quiet. Something was wrong. He looked at the man on his left. "Check the perimeter.

And the slave compound. Be quick!" he barked. The man ran off. "It's too quiet. I don't like it. It could be that damned giant tramping about in the jungle. I swear I'll slit his big throat!"

An eternity passed as they waited. His man strode from the darkness. He was winded. "Sir," he puffed. "All the sentries are dead. Their throats cut. The slaves are gone, and their guards are dead. Fourteen men dead, and no sign of anything. Except that the bows are missing from the weapons dump. It's strange. What do we do?"

Marcus was about to answer when from out of the darkness the whirring noise of a thrown pike was heard. A pike landed in the center of the fire. They looked to each other for explanations. A tall figure then moved out of the shadows, the gleam of a sword reflecting from his right hand. His face was striped black, and his white eyes shone with a malignant spirit. He came to within twenty feet of the men.

Around them, they heard chortles and bleeps. Raptors had found the sentries' corpses. The other Romanican were up and moving to Marcus. The stranger stood amid the confusion like a statue carved from some unholy stone. His eyes blazed with fire, yet he made no movement. Marcus challenged his silence. "Who are you? What do you want? Speak, damn you!"

"I am Nomad," the stranger said in a voice that sent ice down their spines.

"Nomad? That means nothing to me," spat Marcus. "Drop your weapon and live."

"Come and get it," came the simple reply.

Marcus eyed him closely. "Those were my men you killed and my slaves you released."

"And that was my woman and friends you beat up and enslaved."

Some of the Romanicans swallowed hard and gripped their weapons. They could sense a battle brewing. "The giant disobeyed my orders," said Marcus. "I've sworn his death as a result. I can do no more. But the emperor will have his slaves. That, I also swear." He was bold to the point of contemptuousness, arrogant to the end.

"The slaves are free men. To track them, you'll have to kill me."

Marcus laughed. "My archers could kill you now."

"Not without their bows." A sly smile stretched over JD's face. "I removed them. What will you do now? Hurt my feelings?"

The Romanican leader grew angry and motioned for three of his men to take JD. They advanced slowly, trying to flank him. The others, including Marcus, watched with fascination.

JD stood, unmoving, only his eyes followed the encroaching men. They could not believe he remained still, a statue of flesh and blood. The Romanican in the middle charged first. In true Roman form, he lunged with his short sword toward JD's chest. JD parried the blow, spun completely around, and with a deadly backhand lopped the warrior's head off. The skull toppled, hat and all, and rolled on the ground. Blood gushed, and the bone of the spine was grayish white and ghastly in the firelight. The head rolled to within feet of Marcus, its dead eyes open in disbelief.

A second warrior attacked, swinging furiously. The clang of metal rang loud as JD blocked his blows. Once inside the man's defenses, JD punched him across the left eye with the handle and lowest part of the blade. He screamed and stumbled back, his left eye gone, sliced through, leaving a ghoulish socket of tissue and gore. His hands grasped for the lost eye as he wailed in agony.

The third warrior launched forward, his sword low, in a crouch. JD drew his sword down and with a blinding move, slashed upward and sheared off half the man's face. Blood gushed in sheets from his cheek. He reeled back into the dark jungle, howling in distress.

JD stood silently, his blade dripping with the blood and gore of combat. Marcus stared at him with the coal-black pools of a fighter's eyes. The rest of Marcus's men, some twenty strong, had begun circling JD. Weapons were readied, waiting only for the order to attack.

The attack came, but not like the Romanicans had anticipated. From beyond the light of the dying campfires, dozens of emboldened raptors threw themselves into the fray. They caught everyone by surprise, and deadly fighting ensued.

The voracious raptors sprung at the unsuspecting Romanicans from behind. The engagements were fierce. The Romanican short swords were effective only at close range and to get that close to a raptor was suicide. Each of their back legs held switchblade-type retractable claws that were razor sharp. They too were excellent close-in fighters.

The battle raged, man against raptor. Raptor against man. JD against both. Severed limbs flew, and blood splattered all. The ground, the dance floor of battle, became heaped with bodies, dead and dying, of men and beasts. The din of fighting was abrasive. Men screamed, and raptors cawed and chortled. Blades clanged, and the horrible thump of steel on bone and the swish of claw through flesh resounded through the night. Rivers of blood and gore crisscrossed the ground. The sounds of slaughter were deafening. A stalemate lingered. Neither man nor beast had gained an advantage yet both were weary to the point of exhaustion. Both sides had had enough.

The raptors retreated to the sanctuary of the jungle, leaving carnage and death in their wake. JD stood among the manslaughter, covered in blood and tissue. The bodies of the dead were strewn about like litter in a schoolyard. He saw three men standing, zombies of the bloodshed. He recognized Marcus, who stood over the bodies of many dead raptors, wiping blood from his face.

JD's lungs wanted to burst. His chest heaved like a foundry bellows. Marcus, shattered with exhaustion, spied JD and shook his head. His raiding party had been destroyed, butchered by raptors and a lone stranger. He laughed to himself. Fate and the gods were fickle bastards.

"You would do well in the arena, friend. Your skill has few equals. Shall we finish what we started before the beasts interrupted us again?" He pointed to his men. "They will not interfere. Just you and I."

JD marshaled his strength and strode to meet his challenger.

"I'm going to send you back to the demon mother that spawned you in hell," said Marcus with cocky bravado. "I hope you enjoyed your dinner because you'll be having breakfast with the devil."

"The devil has never frightened me," replied JD

Marcus smiled, crooked teeth in a crooked mouth. They began to circle each other. Time collapsed. Everything blurred and merged as the two apex warriors squared off. The dance floor had been set; only the dance remained.

"JD remained," said Arabella. She was delivering the news to the *Broadsword*. "We got everyone out, including Molly. But Doc's hurt bad. She's alive but hurt. And we're at least five days out. Tell everyone we'll be home soon. I'll make contact every eight hours to conserve the radio. And I'll call when JD returns."

"Take care of the Doc," the admiral replied. "Go slow and easy, no hurry. We'll he waiting on the beach for you. Keiko is fine and adjusting well. Be careful and good luck. *Broadsword* out."

"Thank God everyone's safe," said Chief Hightower.

"But they're not, Chief," said Mr. Henry. "Doc's hurt, and JD's unaccounted for. They're in the middle of a raptor-infested jungle. Not to mention all the other monsters out there."

"Point well taken, sir," said the admiral. "I think the chief meant everyone is alive. We all know they still face difficulties. Lads, you continue to monitor the radio. Everyone else can go back to their business. We'll all meet here every eight hours for Arabella's transmission."

The group broke up. The admiral and chief remained with the twins.

"What do you make of JD staying behind?" asked the admiral.

"Some kind of unfinished business that only he could do," the chief replied.

The twins looked at each other. *Uh oh*, they thought. Something fatal was happening. The admiral could see their concern. "Not to worry, lads. Captain Stoner is extremely capable. He's probably already caught up to the others. Let me know when you hear something." He and Chief Hightower moved off.

Adam turned to Tim. "I wish JD was with the others," he said.

"It's a small thing," said Tim. "He'll be along."

The three surviving Romanican raiders were witnessing what could only be called an epic clash of masters, a master of the Roman short sword and a master of the oriental long sword. Such skill and courage had never been displayed even in the hallowed arena in Romanica.

Back and forth the battle waged, the shorter Romanican dancing in and out of his opponent's guard with the grace of a mongoose, and JD blocking and parrying every thrust and advance with the precision of a watchmaker. Both warriors were strong and in the prime of life. Both were vital and deadly. Sweat streamed from both men as muscle and reflex engaged in a quest for advantage. One was faster, the other was quicker. One was smarter, the other more clever. One was stronger, the other more durable. The sound of clashing steel echoed through the night breeze. Maybe it was the natural antagonism of a born villain toward a born hero, but Marcus sensed a flaw in JD's defense. He made a bold move.

As JD parried Marcus's blade to the right, Marcus used a head fake left but suddenly came right with the blade toward JD's unprotected neck. It was a mistake. JD ducked and swiped his sword across and up at Marcus's exposed midsection, ripping a gaping twenty-inch wound from his right hip to his left shoulder.

Marcus staggered back in horrified disbelief. Blood spilled over his legs and feet and in an inhuman voice, he howled and charged JD. With equally inhuman strength he raised his sword a final time. But death had already gripped the once mighty Romanican and would not let go. JD sidestepped the charging corpse and struck him from behind, a decisive deathblow to the back of the head. The bone of his skull made a sickening crunching sound as JD's blade struck it. The man sprawled, dead before his body hit the rugged ground.

JD dropped to his knees, bone weary. His arms were weary, his legs afire. He looked at the three remaining Romanicans. Between huffing breaths, he asked, "Want to live?"

It was unanimous. They all nodded yes.

On leaden legs, he walked over to the bedazzled warriors. "Sit down. I want to know everything about your people, the Slants, and the giant. Take your time. I want to know it all."

The three men sat with baffled expressions. The killer of so many of their comrades and their champion Marcus was asking for their history. It was bewildering amid the manslaughter around them. But they were not about to argue with the one called Nomad. Like pupils explaining their summer vacations, the Romanicans told JD what he wanted to know. Compared to fighting and the real possibility of death, talking was easy and much preferred. Nomad listened. Around them, in the dark, the night sounds of the forest grew bolder.

Dawn broke with an ice-blue sky and the promise of more heat. Slowly, like an egg on a griddle, the day began to sizzle. The exhausted rescued party of the *Broadsword* stopped at a small pond in a clearing. Duke showed obvious signs of fatigue and dehydration. He lay at the water's edge and drank freely. Arabella and Kevin attended Doc. She slumped next to a tree. They managed to get half a bottle of water down her before letting her rest. At least she looked comfortable. Duke rested next to Doc.

Kevin and Arabella walked to the water, drank, and refilled their bottles. Arabella took Kevin's hand. "I was worried I'd never see you again, old man." The "old" was lovers' silliness they both enjoyed. It brought a smile to his face, the desired effect.

"I worried about that too, kid. It's not often a class babe like you falls for an old beggar like me. I'm lucky. Thanks for the rescue."

"Just don't do it again, gramps." They embraced and kissed. The kiss led to another and another. They were kissing like juveniles at a drive-in.

"Hey, break it up or get a fucking room!" boomed Duke. "Look around. This ain't no lovers' lane. Christ, at least wait till it gets dark."

Duke was an old softie at heart. He just hated that anybody else knew it. "What the hell, go ahead. You two were made for each other. An old dipshit and a young she-devil. You'll probably have a dozen little terrorists and live happily ever fucking after. I'll just close my eyes. Then you can hump each other silly. Just keep the moaning down. Doc needs her sleep!" Duke lay back, good hand behind his head, and closed his eyes.

Kevin and Arabella looked at each other and began to laugh. "Thanks, Duke," yelled a giggling Arabella.

"I'm asleep. Fuck off!"

For five hours, the Romanicans told JD everything they knew about everything he asked about. At last, as dawn approached, JD announced his satisfaction at their answers. He told them the only reason he had let them live was so they could deliver a message to the emperor. He made them memorize the message and gave them a strange object as a gift for the emperor. And he gave them explicit instructions on how to operate the gift. "Do not deliver the message, and I will kill you. Come back this way, and I will kill you. Go."

The three hustled off. It would be nearly two weeks before they reached the mesa of Romanica.

Duke woke to find Molly nuzzled between Doc and himself. She looked up, growled, and went back to sleep. He could never feel comfortable around something that outweighed him by four hundred pounds.

"She secretly likes you, you know."

Duke looked. The weak voice came from Doc. She tried to smile, but her puffy, bruised lips would not allow it. Black eyes stared up at him.

"You're alive," was all Duke could say.

Despite the discoloration, her faced beamed. "Fucking A," she sputtered, making him laugh. "But to use Kevin's line, 'I have a headache that would kill a mere mortal.' Thanks for carrying me, Duke."

He blushed a deep crimson.

"Where's JD?" she asked.

Kevin and Arabella had joined them. They were glad to see Doc lucid and talkative.

"He hasn't caught up to us yet," said Kevin. "He's alive, Doc. Don't worry. Look at Molly." The big feline lounged like a house cat. "She'd know if he wasn't alive. So how are you, Doc? What can we do for you?"

She appreciated the subtle way he had changed the subject. "A concussion and a million bumps and bruises. No broken bones, but my brain's in a fog, and I'm seeing in triplicate. Another day, and I'll be halfway human again."

She realized they all looked at her with the same question. "No, the giant didn't rape me. He tried, but I finally got my size nines on his giant balls. I kicked the immortal shit out of them. He ran off into the jungle bellowing. I'm sure he's a eunuch by now."

They all laughed at the giant's expense.

"So what's the plan?"

"We keep moving," said Arabella. "Five days to the *Broadsword*. We sleep in the trees at night and follow Molly during the day, at least until JD catches up. We'll rest here another hour. Can you walk?"

Doc bobbed her head yes. Molly yipped in her sleep and rolled against Duke, placing a giant paw on his belly.

"I hope J Douche hurries," he mumbled. "This cat is driving me crazy."

"Not that far to go, eh Duke?" said Kevin, laughing.

"Cute, Kev. Why don't you two loveknobs go back to your groping?"

Doc tried not to laugh; it made her head hurt. But it was sure good to be back to the lunacy of normality with her *Broadsword* family. Soon, JD would make her life complete again. Soon.

JD lingered at the Romanican campsite for over an hour. Though he wanted to head out, knowing he was half a day behind the others, the nights' fighting had worn him down, and his body ached from numerous minor injuries. He gathered food and water from dead raiders and decided to take Marcus's sword. A worthy opponent although completely mad, thought JD.

He hoped to catch the others sometime on the second day. Fatigue and sleep deprivation were formidable adversaries, so he decided the first day on the trail he would take it easy, moving at a moderate pace and letting his body heal and recuperate.

That was the plan as he made his way back onto the trail. He picked up Molly's footprints right away and fell in along the same path. The muggy jungle pressed on him every step. He hoped the heat would limit the predators to resting in some cool shady place. The idea of fighting off raptors or even compys at this point was too much. The peace and quiet of the lazy forest was all he wanted. What he got was Egnid Troose.

Fifty feet ahead stood the mighty giant, blocking the trail like a small building. A five-foot sword hung in one hand; the other hand grasped a battle ax weighing at least thirty pounds. Coarse, black hair covered his body. Long, shaggy, black hair covered his considerable head. He appeared to be waiting for JD. Bulging muscles twitched in anticipation. JD dropped his pack and drew his sword. God, he wished he had had his Anchluss so he could just shot the bastard from twenty feet. He took a deep breath, rolled his shoulders, and craned neck. He heard his vertebrae crack and pop as he advanced on the giant.

At twenty feet, JD stopped. The giant spoke, his Romanican Latin good for a barbarian, "You are good, little man. You killed the bastard Marcus and many of his men. I should thank you."

"I hoped I'd run into you," said JD evenly. "It saves me the trouble of hunting you down."

This drew laughter from the giant. "I am glad to oblige. When I've killed you, I will track down the others and kill them too. I should have killed you that day in the forest. I am amazed you survived. I've killed puny men with lesser blows. But today, your blood will dry in the hot sun on the jungle floor."

JD moved two steps to his right. "You should know the woman you attacked in the Romanican camp was my friend."

"That bitch!" spat the giant. "She kicked me before I could split her open. But I will in a day or two. And I will whisper in her ear that I killed her lover and left his bones for the raptors."

"I don't think so. Today you die, giant!"

JD started to inch forward when suddenly the air was filled with spears. Dozens blotted out the sky. All had been thrown at the giant. He was a large target and too slow to react. Five spears found their marks. Two struck his chest, two his right leg, and one lance drove deep into his throat.

Then a second volley of spears showered on him, ten more striking the falling monster. And then a third deadly wave pelted him. One shattered his cheekbone and drove high into his brain.

It was over very fast. The mighty giant lay dead. Fifteen or more pikes angled from his massive body. JD stood transfixed but ready. He peered into the bush for enemies.

A lone figure emerged from the quiet jungle. It was the Slant, Huang Anlun. He strode to the giant and with a delicate foot kicked him hard in the head. He turned to JD as he yanked a lance from the giant's face. It tore loose with an awful sound. "We thought you could use our help." He smiled roundly, showing all of his teeth.

"Thank you," replied JD. "I am in your debt."

"No, sir," said the Slant elder. "We are in your debt. Go in peace, friend." He held up his right hand in a universal sign of friendship. JD did the same.

Then, like a mist that fades with the sun, the Slant was gone leaving JD to contemplate his good fortune. He retrieved his pack and headed west on the trail. Vultures had already descended on the giant's corpse. Soon, other scavengers would follow their grisly lead. The enormous body would be picked apart and stripped clean. Even the bones would be consumed. No human would care.

The third day on the journey back to the *Broadsword*, Doc had improved remarkably. The bruising on her face had retreated, but her body was still stiff and sore. The walking helped her recover. The group took breaks frequently for Doc's sake as well as to give JD time to catch up. Everyone was anxious to see him and to hear what had happened with Marcus and the Romanicans.

As dusk began to paint the jungle in shades of gray, the group began looking for suitable nighttime accommodations. A couple of redwoods close together would do fine. They had been lucky for days. No raptors or any unfriendly encounters, just a scenic hike through a forest primeval with incessant insects, oppressive heat, and lack of fresh water. It was the original Club Med package without all the bothersome extras such as clean sheets, running water, toilets, and room service.

They were seated on some small boulders, chewing pemmican and slurping water when a solitary figure emerged from the forest into the open. It was JD, sword and pack slung across his back, walking like a man who was glad to see his friends. Molly went leaping off to him, knocking him over as she reached him and lapping his face with her huge tongue. They rolled on the ground in playful exuberance, wrestling like brothers.

The others had run to meet him as well.

"You look good, J Douche," said a wildly happy Duke. He slapped his shoulder with his good hand.

"Nice to see you, son," added Kevin. "Everything went well?"

"Fine, Kev."

Arabella said, "We did good, huh?" Her face lit up.

"We did good," he said.

Doc stepped forward. Her face was still blue and purple with deep bruises.

"I'm glad to see you, Doc. I'm happy you're okay." He took her chin in his hand and gently kissed her cracked lips. She threw her arms around him and put her head to his chest.

"I love you," she said in a broken voice. "I missed you so much." He put his arms around her and pressed her close.

"I said I'd find you no matter what or how long. I love you, Doctor Matilda Moran. I will always be there for you. Always."

The romantic reunion was finally interrupted by Duke, who suggested they get up a tree before darkness descended in earnest. The familiar chortles and bleeps of roving raptors could be heard from the bowels of the forest. Soon, the night would come alive with the denizens of darkness. The sub-rosa prowlers and nightly gangsters had waited patiently all day for the cover of eventide to exploit those foolish enough to be without shelter or defense.

In the trees, they spoke for hours. JD related everything he had learned from the Romanicans. To the others, it was both intriguing and frightful to learn about so many others on the planet, all wayfarers in a hardhearted world who held no compassion for fellow humans.

A joyous reunion was then held on the beach on the fifth day of their journey home. The *Broadsword* crew was a family again, a family that through tragedy had adopted a four-year-old Slant orphan.

It was decided by popular vote to continue to sail north in search of a suitable island retreat. JD had explained to all what he knew about the Slants, the Romanicans, the giants, and the roving bands of marauding pirates. There were even rumors of an Oz-like city near the north pole. But exploration would have to wait. For the moment, all the *Broadsword* crew wanted to do was rest and reenergize. They were safe on the water in their armored, floating metropolis. For a while, at least, they would enjoy that sanctuary, island hopping their only recreation.

The second night onboard, JD slipped from Doc's sleeping arms and walked to cargo hold #2 and sat with Molly. He leaned against her shoulder and watched the ancient stars pass by the open hold. After a few moments, a small shadow moved through the doorway, dragging a blanket behind her tiny frame. It was a tousle-haired Keiko. Her sleepy eyes looked to JD.

"Is it okay if I sleep with you and the striped beast, Mister JD? Sometimes, the bad men who hurt my mom come to my dreams and scare me. I'll be real quiet, I promise."

A child of four had done what no adult male could have ever done. He took her small hand.

"Sit here next to me," he said. "This is Molly. She's a cat. You can also call her Moose. She likes that."

Molly yawned loudly as Keiko nestled in against the soft fur of her belly. JD leaned over and whispered in Molly's ear as Keiko looked on with a child's curiosity, part wonder and part interest.

JD said, "I talked to Molly. From now on, she'll be your big sister. She has no mom either. She promises to take care of you, and I told her you would promise to take care of her. Is that okay with you?"

Keiko's eyes were wide open. "I promise. She's really soft and warm. And I never had a sister before. I'll be really good for her." She kneaded the fur on Molly's shoulder. "I love you, Molmoose," she said, stroking the great cat.

JD laughed. He noticed Doc at the doorway. She walked over and snuggled next to the unlikely trio. "Molmoose?"

"Close enough," said JD. "She and Molly are now sisters. They've promised to take care of each other. Keiko couldn't sleep and wandered down here."

Doc put her head on JD's shoulder. "You're a good man, JD Stoner. This little girl has no idea how lucky she is."

They looked at Keiko, tucked against Molly's rear leg, fast asleep.

"You're like her father now because you speak her language. You okay with that?"

JD nodded. "She has nothing to worry about, Doc. As long as she needs me, I'll be there for her. I saw her mom and her village. How could I do any less?"

She smiled, and she shivered against the breeze. "I think I'll sleep out here with you guys."

Soon, only the rhythmic snoring of these four star-crossed voyagers could be heard. The night drifted on, a lazy, flickering stream.

The great coliseum of Romanica has a number of private courtyards. Wealthy patrons could purchase death matches and view them in a more intimate atmosphere, away from the screaming mob.

The most opulent of these was the emperor's private exhibition area. He sat on a cushioned marble couch and watched his favorite female gladiatrixes practice in the bright sunshine. Their naked bodies glistened with sweat as they fought with each other using wooden swords and shields. The emperor looked on like a teenager in a porn shop.

Abruptly, everything stopped. Three haggard figures walked in under praetorian guard. They were exhausted and had the look of men bearing grave news. The tallest, Correus, had been chosen as the speaker by the others long before they arrived. The emperor recognized him and smiled.

"Correus," he said. "I trust you bring good news about Marcus. We are in dire need of new entertainment in the arena. How soon until he returns?"

Correus stepped forward and bowed. He looked up with scared eyes and began. "The news is dire. Marcus and the others are dead. We had captured fifty slaves, but they escaped. We three are the lone survivors of this calamity." He paused as the news penetrated the emperor's mind.

"But how?" asked the stunned monarch. "There were fifty men and a giant in your party. How could such a thing happen? Raptors?"

"No, sire. A man called Nomad."

The emperor sat back, perplexed.

"Nomad? Nomad and his men killed all of them?"

"No, sire. Just the man Nomad. He attacked us during the night. Then raptors attacked, and it was chaos. When the raptors withdrew, we three, Marcus, and Nomad remained. Nomad killed Marcus."

The emperor stood. "You're telling me one man did this? And killed Marcus?"

"Yes, sire. Their sword fight was remarkable. But Nomad killed him. He spared us so we could give you a message."

The emperor was enraged. "What? A mere man dares deliver a message to me? To me?"

Correus bowed under the verbal onslaught, but he remembered Nomad's warning. "He also sent you a gift, sire."

"The message. I want to hear this message from the bastard Nomad."

Correus rose and stood tall, as Nomad had instructed. "The message, sire, is this. If you are a god, you do not harm those who have never injured you. If you are a man, and advance, you will be met by a man equal to yourself."

Correus paused and then continued. "He says he protects the people of the steel ship, and any Romanican who goes beyond the great wooded wall on the coast will suffer the fate of Marcus. This he swears. And he travels with a great orange—and black-striped beast covered in thick fur."

Emperor Anthonius stood in a daze. For a long moment, he did not speak. Correus had dropped to his knees in supplication.

"This Nomad dares speak to me as if I were some puny mortal! I will have a legion bring me his head on a pike! The arena sands will soak up the blood of his people. This I swear!"

He practically spit the venom-laced words. His face was red with anger. His eyes were black as death. "So what is this gift he sent me? Probably something to make amends for his blasphemy. For he knows I will surely destroy him for his insolence. Show me the gift."

Correus bowed and reached into his shirt. He withdrew an odd-looking object and set it on the marble floor. It was a kidney-shaped disk of green plastic. What the pompous emperor had no way of knowing was the object before him was an antipersonnel mine chock-full of metal splinters coated in Teflon and propelled by a charge twenty times that of a regular hand grenade. To the mystified emperor, however, it appeared nothing more than a trinket, a worthless bauble. "This is the gift he sends? What is it, a paperweight?"

"No, sire," said Correus. "Nomad said it was magic. I am to stand on the small button on top, count to five, and release my foot."

"And then?" asked a mocking Anthony.

"And then he said we would all see paradise."

The emperor scoffed. "What lunacy is this? Go ahead, Correus. I can't wait to see this pitiful magic. Step on the thing and show us paradise."

Correus obeyed. His sandaled foot trod down lightly on the object. He counted to five slowly and raised his foot. The world exploded in all directions. Before descending to hell, Correus thought he had indeed glimpsed paradise.

EPILOGUE

"Sir? Sir?" He gently jostled the snoozing old man. It was the fourth time in the last hour the old bird had faded off. He woke, seemingly confused.

"What?"

"Sir, you fell asleep again."

"Yes, well . . . What was your name again, sonny?"

The younger man grinned. "My name if Brett Tyler. I'm an investigative reporter for the *USA Today* online newspaper, remember?"

"Of course I remember. I'm old, not fucking stupid. I get tired. What the fuck. So will you when you're my age."

"And you're how old again, sir?"

"Seventy-nine last August. I was forty-four when the *Broadsword* disappeared."

"That's what you said earlier. But the *Broadsword* went down in 2002, and today is May 6, 2004. How do you explain that you aged thirty-five years in two years?"

"I told you already, douchebag. The *Broadsword* didn't go down. It went back in time ninety-two million years. And we lived in that time, traveling the seas and oceans for thirty-five years. Then, mysteriously, the ship hit another continuum window—that's what we started calling it—and it brought me back here. But I've aged the time we were gone, get it?"

"I think so, yes. So you and all the other characters you describe were on the *Broadsword* for thirty-five years?"

"More or less, yes. I'm the only one to travel back because I was the only one onboard when it hit that window. Most of the others are still there."

"You mean JD, Doc, the twins, Kevin, the admiral, and others?"

"Correct. They finally gave up trying to find the window and settled on an island. Molly passed away, of course."

"Of course." The reporter was scribbling notes on a pad in addition to recording every word. "On the phone, you said you had proof. You'll admit your story is somewhat fantastic, impossible to prove without direct evidence. What is this proof you spoke of?"

The old man leaned forward and smiled. "Many things, young dickweed." He handed the reporter an object. "Know what that is?"

The reporter eyed it closely, turning it every which way. "A bear's claw? Maybe? I don't know. What is it?"

"I'll tell you what it isn't, young skeptic. It's not fossilized."

"So?"

"So that's a switchblade toe claw from a raptor's hind leg, ninety-two million years old."

The reporter's eyes widened. Impossible, it had to be something else. "How do I know that? It could be anything."

"You're a college boy, right? What school?"

"Providence. BA in English and journalism. Why?"

"'Cause for somebody educated, you're dumb as a sack of shit! Take the claw and have it analyzed. My suggestion would be the university in Calgary or Wyoming. They'll tell you it's real. And then they will hammer you about where you got it."

"But if it's real, why not go to the government and tell your story? I'm sure they'd be interested."

The old man shrugged. "There you go again, being a fucking imbecile. The government already knows, sonny. They debriefed me four months ago. I told them the same story. And they have the *Broadsword*, the whole fucking ship. They just don't want anyone else to know it!

"And Christ, I can't give those assholes a real raptor claw. That thing has DNA in it. Some government yahoo could clone a goddamn raptor. Then we'd really be in the shit! Those are the most savage, ruthless, killing machines this planet has ever produced. They hate everything. They eat everything. And they kill for sport. No. You keep the claw. Have it analyzed and authenticated. Then come back here and I'll give you more proof."

Brett Tyler was curious and amazed, qualities of a good reporter. "What other proof?"

The old bird smiled slyly. "I know where the *Broadsword* is now, sonny." His eyebrows flicked in delight.

"Where?" Storylines began forming in the reporter's head. It was then he noticed that the small room was filled with paintings of jungle scenes. Raptors, a muscled man with a samurai sword, a beautiful woman with a doctor's bag, and two young men with devilish grins. The entire room was filled with paintings from the story he had just related.

"I'm tired now, young man. When you come back, I'll tell you more stories about the *Broadsword* and its crew. Maybe about the Romanicans or the land of the giants. Maybe about the Slants or the Shadow Eaters. And I'll give you more proof. We can talk about J Douche and those pissant twins, whatever you want. And, of course, if you still don't believe me, well then you can just double up and fuck yourself. I don't give a flying douche. Fair enough?"

The interview was over for the day. The young reporter knew it. He gathered up his things. "It will take a few weeks to check out the claw, maybe more," he said.

"Sure."

He extended his hand. "It's been a pleasure, Mister, uh, mister . . ."

"Duke," said the older man. "The Wizard of Art. I'll look forward to seeing you again. As I used to tell my friend, 'Douche, you're the fucking greatest.'"

Brett Tyler smiled. He would return soon. The story would continue.

The next *Broadsword* adventure is entitled *Moon's Cradle.*